A Spring of Magic

Ashuan Greed 3

Janna Ruth

First published in New Zealand in 2023

Copyright © 2023 by Janna Ruth

www.janna-ruth.com

ISBN-13: 978-1-99-117293-8

also available as ebook: 978-1-99-117294-5

ASHUAN GREED BOOK 3

A SPRING OF MAGIC

JANNA RUTH

For Brienchen
Without whom Ashuan never would have seen the light of day.
Thanks for 20 years of friendship!

A note about sensitive topics

There is a lot of magic and fantastical creatures in this book, but the teenagers at the core of this story are just that: they are teenagers. And as such they deal with a number of very real issues on top of the magical ones.

If you don't like spoilers and you're cool with anything, skip this note and start the book. If you like to be prepared, keep reading. I'm writing this because reading should be fun, not a bad surprise.

While this series starts out as a YA fantasy, there are mentions of sex, drugs and sadly no rock'n'roll. There will be no graphic sex scenes, but you will encounter teenagers and adults drinking alcohol, including an alcoholic mother who is neglectful to her children. As for the underage characters: the age of drinking beer and wine without adult supervision in Germany is 16. For drinking spirits and cocktails, it is 18.

As fun as it sounds, hunting monsters and wielding magic is dangerous. People will be hurt in this series and some will die. That includes characters who you got to know well. Their deaths will not be meaningless, though it might feel like that to the surviving characters. Because I'm a big fan of consequences, that means you will see depictions of grief in various stages.

In this book in particular, you will encounter a murder, and several very severe injuries. It's the finale. It'll get bloody.

Last but not least, there are instances of bullying, mostly verbal, by other teenagers. These scenes are few in between and our affected characters will rise above that.

The characters live in a dangerous world, but it's also beautiful. For every dark spot, there will be light and humour. And of course magic. Lots and lots of magic.

Enjoy!

Love, Janna

Part 1

Parties & Illusions

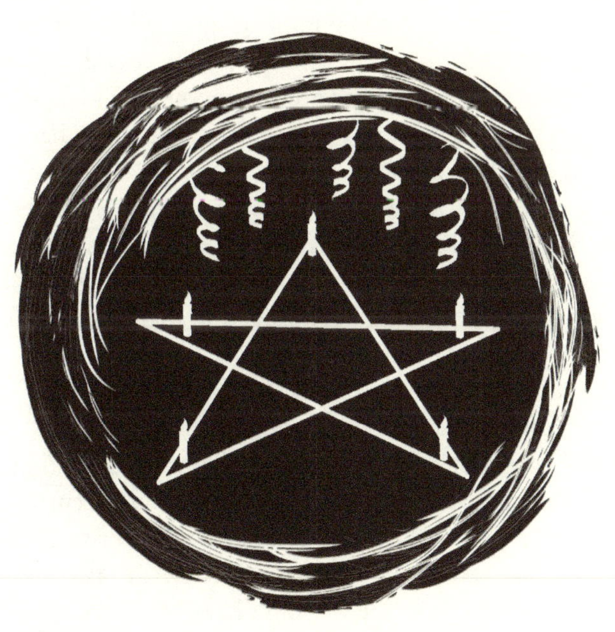

Lucille

Lucille shuffled her feet as she stood with the other students from the two Greenvalley High French classes at the train station, nervously awaiting the train's arrival. Signing up for the student exchange had seemed like a good idea a few months ago. What better way to practice her favourite language and make new friends? Now, with frequent monster attacks in her hometown, her own magic, and an ominous prophecy involving a ruthless archdemon on her mind, it seemed like a disaster in the making.

Among her friends, only Matt shared her fate. He'd only started learning French at the beginning of the year and usually dreaded class. "Please tell me you're just as nervous as I am." Lucille only had to worry about exposing her magic. If Matt's partner found out he was sharing a room with a half-demon, he'd be running back to Marseille.

But Matt only frowned. "Why would I be nervous?"

"What if something goes wrong?" She immediately thought of the Blood Night. Matt had said it was a one-time occurrence, but who knew what other demon traditions would surprise them in the future? Not that Lucille would mention it. Their team was slowly getting back together, and she wouldn't hamper that progress with a bout of ill-placed curiosity. "For example, what if your mother turns up suddenly while you're eating dinner with your exchange student?"

Matt gave her a doubtful squint. "Then, I guess he's got something to look at." He sighed. "Lucille, she's not going to turn up. New Year's was a one-off occurrence. All of it."

Lucille winced as he casually called out her real concern. "I'm sorry. I just... I *am* nervous. Amélie is going to think I'm awfully snobby."

"Your parents *are* awfully snobby."

That only added to her worries. While the other students would share rooms with their exchange partners, Lucille's partner would have her own room, including an en-suite bathroom. And she'd see more of Albert and the maids than Lucille's father and Linda. The only bright spot about her spacious living quarters was that she would be hosting the party of the year by the end of the week.

They were approaching the end of April. On the thirtieth, the Harz region would be flooded with tourists who came to celebrate Walpurgis Night, a heathen relic entrenched in witchcraft. It was believed that the witches flew to dance on the Brocken, Northern Germany's highest peak. Nowadays, only tourists would climb the Brocken, while the real witches met somewhere quieter, and the teenagers of Greenvalley came to her big witch bash.

A low whistling sound whirred in the distance, and white clouds of steam rose above the trees. "They're coming!"

Lucille could see Cheryl quickly touching up her make-up, while Cian and Shayna stretched their necks to catch a glimpse of the steam train. That was the other problem. She'd be spending time with Cheryl and her friends this week, a punishment she surely hadn't deserved.

The small, black steam train finally arrived and came to a stop with a loud screech. The doors opened, and a group of French students exited, curiously taking in their new surroundings. Mrs Lindenberger, the French teacher, greeted her counterpart from the school in Marseille and introduced Adrian, the Head Boy, who was overseeing the exchange today.

Lucille's nervousness was replaced by sudden excitement at seeing the other students and hearing their lightning-fast French, while Matt was the one who looked a little green now. "Matt... how much French do you actually know?" She doubted Chay had provided him with a French teacher in Hell.

"Not nearly enough."

Mrs Lindenberger clapped her hands, and the excited chatter died down as the students gave her their attention. "Listen up. First off, bienvenue à Greenvalley. We are happy to welcome you here and hope you'll have a wonderful experience. This is Monsieur Charpentier from our Marseille partner school, and this here is Adrian, our Head Boy, who is responsible for this week's program."

"Me and the rest of the student council," Adrian said with a smile. "C'est un plaisir de vous revoir."

"Well, Adrian will now tell you who you're going to stay with. Please find your partner as soon as your name is called." Mrs Lindenberger nodded at Adrian, while Monsieur Charpentier repeated the instructions in French for his students' benefit.

Adrian looked at his phone and began to read aloud. "Amélie, you're with Lucille."

Lucille raised her hand and waved to a pretty girl with a long brown braid. Amélie grabbed her luggage and came over. She leaned in to greet Lucille with two kisses on the cheeks.

"Salut, Amélie." Lucille introduced herself in fluent French and asked how her trip was.

"Long and exhausting," Amélie answered likewise. "This little train is so slow, but the view was breathtaking. Everything is so green."

Lucille laughed. "That's where we got our name from. It's finally spring again." In fact, Greenvalley's trees had been sprouting since late February thanks to the magic hidden in the woods.

"Could you guys talk a little slower?" Matt asked, sticking to German. "I'm getting a headache."

"So sorry," Lucille said, amused. "C'est Matt."

It only took one glance for Amélie to truly appreciate Matt's presence. "Hello, Matt." She leaned in to kiss him on the cheeks as well, causing his mood to improve spontaneously. "It's nice to meet you," she said with a heavy accent.

Lucille grinned at his predictable reaction. A loud hiss in front of her distracted her, though. Quickly, she discerned the source. Cheryl was throwing a tantrum about her partner, an unassuming girl with glasses and a clothing style that could best be described as eclectic.

"I'll complain to Adrian. This is not what I asked for. I bet Samantha did this to spite me," Cheryl mused loudly, with no regard for the girl next to her.

"Why would Samantha do that?" Cian scrunched his nose. "You must have similar interests to be matched with each other. I mean, I don't even get what the problem is."

"The problem is that she doesn't meet Cheryl's beauty standards," Shayna explained helpfully. Luckily, she was called up to meet her partner just then, narrowly escaping a bitch fight.

Cheryl huffed indignantly. "I will not be seen with this eyesore all week. Much less stay at her place in Marseille."

"Eyesore?" the poor girl repeated. "I don't understand." Compared to Amélie, her German was much cleaner. She'd obviously understood most of what Cheryl had said.

"Matt," Adrian called, distracting Lucille from Cheryl's drama. "Your partner is Dion."

Matt raised his hand halfway. His lacklustre gesture was reciprocated by a beautiful black boy with striking green eyes, who pulled his luggage towards them as if he'd much rather jump back onto the train. Judging by how Amélie immediately clung to his arm and pulled him closer, she was friends with him. If not more.

"Dion, looks like we're going to spend a lot of time together," Amélie chatted excitedly in French. "This is Lucille, and this is your partner, Matt. Be nice," she hissed almost inaudibly.

"I'm always nice." His eyes trailed over to where Cheryl was laying down some ground rules for her poor exchange student. "Stupid cow," he muttered.

Lucille was about to say something when she noticed a bird settling on the sign above Cheryl's head. A second later, it shat on her nose. Instantly, she started screaming, while the people around her burst out laughing. Even Shayna couldn't hold back.

"Did you—?" Lucille was about to ask Dion, but he turned away from her abruptly and faced Matt.

"Is it far to your home?" he asked rather rudely. "I'm tired. And hungry."

Matt stared at him, unable to make sense of the French. His eyes widened as panic set in.

"Oh, we won't be going home straight away," Lucille explained in place of Matt. "We'll take the bus to school and have lunch there."

Dion sighed, losing interest in Matt and turning to Amélie. "T'as encore de ces fameuses noix? Je suis affamé."

"Bien sûr." The two of them started chatting in French, making fun of Cheryl's misfortune and commiserating with Michèlle, which seemed to be the name of Cheryl's exchange student. Neither of them cared much about the exchange students they'd been paired with.

After everyone had been paired up, the teachers herded them towards the bus. Once again, the French students chose to stick together, and Lucille felt her excitement ebbing. Amélie had seemed nice enough, but with Dion around, she was completely ignoring her.

"Can I switch with Cheryl?" Matt muttered, staring daggers at Dion's back. "She gets her arm candy, and I get someone who speaks German."

Lucille didn't share his communication problem. Her French was impeccable after the boarding school's education. "Arm candy?" Dion was certainly that. Forbiddingly handsome, with broad shoulders and striking green eyes. "He *does* look good, doesn't he?"

Matt just snorted.

Later that day, after a tour around the school, Lucille was finally able to take Amélie home. Her exchange student had been excited when the chauffeur had relieved her of her luggage. And her eyes grew big as soon as the Villa de Cerque came into view.

"You live in a castle?" While Amélie knew a bit of German, she was much more comfortable in French. Something she had in common with almost all the other students in her class.

Lucille chuckled. "It's just a mansion, not a castle."

"*Just* a mansion." Amélie giggled. "You could host the entire class in here."

"Well..." Lucille regarded the only home she'd ever known besides the boarding school. For the first time, she felt a bit embarrassed. "I *will* host a huge party on Friday!"

Amélie clapped her hands excitedly. "Oh, that sounds fabulous." Her face fell. "But I don't have anything to wear. Please tell me that there are some nice boutiques in town."

Lucille grinned. Now, here was finally someone who enjoyed shopping as much as she did. "We can go tomorrow in our free time. I know a couple you might like."

The car parked in front of the main entrance, and Lucille and Amélie got out. The chauffeur took care of the luggage, while Albert greeted them in his usual formal manner. Amélie just kept walking through the doors with her mouth and eyes wide open.

"Do you want the small tour or the long one?" Lucille asked, amused.

"How many hours does the long one take?" Amélie shot back.

"At least five!" Lucille pointed up the stairs. "I'll show you to your room."

Amélie had been given one of the guest rooms near Lucille, with her own bathroom. A bouquet of fresh flowers decorated the side table, and the kitchen had sent up refreshments. Excited, Amélie ran her fingers over the wooden headboard before letting herself fall on the bed, squealing at the springiness. "This is like a luxury holiday. I'm *so* grateful they assigned us. You're like the coolest girl." She sat up. "This room, a mega party, and you can speak French fluently. This is just perfect."

"I'm glad to hear I pass," Lucille laughed and curtsied for fun.

Just then, Amélie's phone rang. She took one look and rolled her eyes. "Dion." She accepted the call and began twirling a strand of her hair around one finger. "Do you miss me already?"

Lucille left her to her call, trying not to read too much into what she'd heard. After seeing Amélie and Dion at the train station and later at school, she'd already guessed the two were very close. They made an extraordinarily pretty couple, in Lucille's opinion, but she couldn't help feeling a little disappointed.

Dion had piqued her curiosity. He was a handsome young man with a startling gaze. But there had been a moment outside, where she'd been under the impression that he was a lot more than he pretended to be. As if he was only playing the disinterested jerk to keep anyone from looking too closely.

She sighed. Or perhaps she was making this up, because she couldn't get those green eyes out of her mind.

"Gosh, he's such a drama queen about this trip," Amélie suddenly explained. "Turns out that while I get a room big enough to invite the whole class over for a sleepover, he only gets a mattress on the floor. And there's a dog."

"Does he not like dogs?" Lucille thought about Matt's accommodation and wondered how the Traidous men would cope with an extra person in their tiny flat. Those green eyes in her mind, she wondered if she should invite Matt and Dion to stay at her place for the duration of the exchange. It could be fun.

"He didn't grow up around animals, and they make him a bit skittish," Amélie explained. "To be honest, I think he doesn't appreciate how they see right through his act."

"So, it *is* an act!" Embarrassed, Lucille covered her mouth. "Sorry. That..." She needed a distraction fast. "Are you two dating?"

Amélie's eyes widened. "What? No! Dion doesn't date."

"Not at all?"

"He says love is an illusion. Which doesn't keep him from making pretty eyes at girls."

Lucille sat down next to Amélie and sighed. "He really does have pretty eyes."

Amélie burst out giggling. "Oh no, he's already put his spell on you. Don't worry, you're not the first."

"I wouldn't say he's got me under his spell." Spells, after all, were her speciality. The thrill of flirting washed through her, though. "I'm just saying that he has pretty eyes. Please don't tell him."

Amélie was still grinning. "Oh, believe me, Dion knows he's got pretty eyes. He also knows how to gaze at you with them until you want to rip the clothes from his body *and* yours." She rolled her eyes and sighed.

"Oh, so sex is not an illusion?" When Amélie nodded and blushed, Lucille snorted. "Well, in that case, he should get along with Matt splendidly. He's the same."

Amélie sat up straight, her eyes wide. "Oh, please tell me more about Matt. You two are friends, right? I mean, Dion has pretty eyes, but god, Matt's a beautiful man."

The tour was quickly forgotten as the two girls chatted about boys and giggled through the afternoon hours.

Matt

"Here we are." Matt gave the door a little push, making it bump into the wall. In front of him was the narrow corridor with the coat stand and shoe rack that led straight into the living room. From where he stood, he saw the door to his father's room, and not much more. Crumbs came running, slunk around his legs, and barked excitedly.

Next to him, Dion raised an eyebrow, as if to say he wasn't very impressed. He never uttered a word, though. Just as he hadn't spoken all the way home. They'd been together for four hours now, and Matt had the feeling that this week was going to last forever. He could barely string a simple sentence together in French, and Dion never even tried to speak German.

Meanwhile, the over-excited puppy was starting to take in the new arrival, sniffing his legs, before putting his paws on Dion's thighs. While Crumbs was just a baby—a six-month-old baby—he'd grown quite a bit. Dion flinched and almost stumbled back out of the flat.

Matt sighed and got a hold of Crumbs, gently leading him away from the French boy and showering him with attention to make up for the lack of enthusiasm on Dion's behalf. "He's just curious who the new guy in our home is. Who's a good boy? Yes, yes, you are." Crumbs rewarded him with a wet kiss on his nose, then trailed off into the flat, circling his feeding bowl.

As before, there was no reply. Dion just looked as though he was regretting every life choice that had led him here.

"Not a dog fan, I take it," Matt muttered to himself. He stood up and straightened his shoulders before leading the way in. Once they were in the living room, he quickly pointed out the facilities. "Kitchen. Bath. My father's room. My room."

He opened the door so Dion could stow away his luggage. The room wasn't big enough for a second bed, so all Matt had to offer was an air mattress. It was either that or having Dion sleep on the couch in the living room. If their communication continued to be as painstaking as it was, Matt might consider moving himself.

As if he had evoked it, Dion turned to him and said, "Ce n'est pas très grand."

"Uh..." He had no idea what Dion had just said. Probably a complaint. Or maybe it was a question. "You can put your things over there." He pointed to the little space behind the air mattress.

Dion raised his arm and let his bag fall onto the air mattress, displeasure oozing out of him like the air did from the mattress. As the bed slowly deflated, he continued to stare at Matt.

"I'll get it pumped up correctly next time." He'd only figured out how to do it this morning. Surely Dion could cut him some slack. If they could find a way to communicate.

Matt reminded himself that he was the host and had agreed to ensure Dion's well-being. As irritating as the French boy was, he didn't hold a candle to Samantha. "Es tu... uhm... hungry?" Matt asked, feebly looking for the proper word in his head. He knew that much, didn't he? Manger. Manger was eating. "Es tu mangé?"

Dion's impassive mask broke as he snorted.

Obviously, he'd made the wrong choice. Annoyed, Matt turned around and walked off. "Just come along."

He didn't really care whether Dion followed him or not. He was going into the kitchen to grab a bite, and then he would take Crumbs for a nice long walk until he no longer wanted to wring his guest's neck.

As he got closer to the kitchen, he heard some clattering. Hope flushed his veins. His father was home and could help him. Matt had no idea whether René spoke any French, but he knew how to deal with this. He dealt with moody children all day long—himself not included.

But the person in the kitchen wasn't his father. It was his sister. His *demon* sister. "Menuha."

Menuha whirled around, a wide smile on her lips. "Hello, Matt. You've got impeccable timing. I was going to cook something, but I have no idea what buttons to press on this machine. Last time I tried to cook in Ashuan, humans were still using a wood-powered stove, but I didn't see any wood, and I think the food goes into the hole now."

Curiously, Matt leaned to the side to catch a glimpse of what was going on behind her. She had managed to put the roast in the right spot, but the oven was cold. "You're cooking?" He'd never seen her cook in Hescaryn.

Meanwhile, Menuha had discovered Dion and greeted him just as enthusiastically. "Hi. I'm Menuha, Matt's sister. Half-sister, actually, but nobody cares about that."

Dion stared at her as if she'd come from another world—which technically, she had. "C'est trop petit. Où vas-tu dormir?"

Just like Matt, Menuha had no idea what he was talking about. Matt turned on the oven, then shrugged. "I don't understand him either. He probably thinks you're too small." It was the only word he'd picked up from the flurry.

Menuha chuckled at the idea she had to be taller. If anything was too high to reach for her, she could easily fly up. Which was absolutely not allowed to happen while Dion was staying. The last thing he needed was his guest running back home and telling all of France about the monsters in Greenvalley.

"Come with me." He pulled Menuha out of the kitchen and onto the little balcony next to René's room, leaving Dion to fend for himself.

"Why am I too small for him?" Menuha asked, still confused. "I'm as tall as he is."

"Perhaps he's into taller women." As if that mattered. His guest would *not* be having sex with his sister! "What the hell are you doing here?"

"I'm visiting you."

Matt sputtered. "Why?" Internally, he wanted to throw up. The last time his siblings had spontaneously arrived, it hadn't ended well for him. "Is Caspar coming too?"

"Absolutely not!" Menuha shook her head. "I'm here because I was worried about you. After your Blood Night, you acted all weird, and then you left Hescaryn again."

"I was *not* acting weird."

"You didn't have sex at all while you stayed at the residence," Menuha explained drily.

Matt shrugged the notion off. "I wasn't in the mood."

"As I said. You're acting weird." When Matt groaned, she regarded him with pity. "How are you?"

He had no idea where to even start. "Perfect. I even had sex," he added spitefully. The memory of Cheryl still clung to him. It had been alright while they were going at it, but afterwards, he'd felt no more relaxed than before.

Menuha studied his face. "Are you sure?"

"Half my friends can't stand being in the same room as me, and I'm supposed to play babysitter for a French guy who refuses to communicate with me. I'm perfect, really." Especially now that his demon sister had decided to drop in, because *she* was worried.

"If you want to talk—"

"No! I want to know why you're really here. And stop pretending to care about me."

Menuha sighed. "I *do* care. Fine. It's the humans. Spending New Year's with your friends was more fun than I'd had in a century."

"Speak for yourself." There wasn't a single fun moment he remembered from his birthday.

Menuha smiled generously. "Your friends are amazing. The way they stood up for you, how you interact with them... Usually, when you tell a bunch of humans you're a demon, they run away screaming or try to kill you, but your friends did neither. Instead, they were curious to hear more."

Matt began massaging the bridge of his nose. Samantha had been carrying around a dagger designed to kill demons ever since that night. And Fabian still didn't trust him not to murder any of his friends. "I think you're wrong."

"Please, Matt. Let me stay with you. Just for a couple of weeks. I want to get to know them more. I want to get to know *you* more."

Out of all of his siblings, Menuha was the one person he would actually trust to mean what she said. She loved humans, always had, and there was not a single grudge he held against her. All his life, she'd been kind and supportive. Apart from the fact that she was incredibly close to Caspar, his tormentor. And as much as Matt tried, it was impossible for him to fully separate the two. "What about Caspar?"

"He won't miss me." Menuha scrunched up her nose as if the notion was outright ridiculous. "Matt, I know you think we're inseparable, and it's true to an extent, but that's in demon terms. We've gone years without seeing each other. He won't come looking for me if I stay away from Hescaryn for a little bit. I promise."

Matt sighed. "I suppose there's no reason to say no to you." There had been a lot, but Menuha had outmanoeuvred him on all of them.

"You won't regret it!" Menuha cried and threw herself around his neck. "Thanks, Matt! You're the best."

"Okay, okay. Just... don't burn the house down while you're cooking." Her eyes grew big, as if wondering how she could possibly burn the house down with a human stove that didn't even run on a fire. "And stay away from Dion. He's not supposed to know what I am. Or what you are."

A little more serious, Menuha nodded. "Pretend to be a human. Got it. I can totally do that."

Matt wasn't quite as sure, considering she hadn't even known how to turn the oven on. But if Menuha showed his friends that not *all* demons were bad, perhaps they'd be able to trust him again. It was worth a shot.

"I'm regretting ever signing up for French class. This exchange is the worst," Matt complained to Lucille as he and the rest of the group set out to hike the Witches' Trail, a mountain walkway stretching almost a hundred kilometres. They wouldn't walk all of that in a day, just the part between Greenvalley and the Witches' Dance Floor near Thale, but it would take them a few hours at least.

"You have to be open-minded. Amélie and I get along great." Despite her usual preferences, Lucille was wearing some sensible hiking boots for the day.

Matt snorted. "Because you can speak her language. I can't wait until this week is over."

Dion was still refusing to talk to him. He was outright chatty today as he hung around his friends. He'd even joked with Amélie, the pretty girl Lucille had got as a partner. Their French chatter was far too complex and fast for Matt to grasp, but Lucille seemed to understand every word—and *hated* it.

Her forehead creased, and all the good mood drained out of her. "You're right. They are the worst."

"What did they say?" Matt despised how he couldn't understand a thing.

Lucille lowered her voice and muttered under her breath, "Amélie just told him how he could have sex with me in a hundred different rooms." Her mouth twisted bitterly. "And she made fun of how much I gushed about his eyes."

"You want to have sex with him?" Matt shrugged and regarded Dion anew. He hadn't even noticed his eyes on that sour-puss face. "There are better guys. He doesn't speak a word of German, though I'm starting to think he's just pretending. And he hates Crumbs."

"He *hates* Crumbs?"

Matt rolled his eyes. "You know how he is. He's a puppy. Wants to play, begs for snacks. Dion ignores him completely. He doesn't even want to be in the same room as him. Like, I now have to keep Crumbs out of my bedroom for the week. And taking him on our walk was apparently a big offence. Scowled the whole way through and kept repeating some question in French that I didn't understand."

He kicked a pebble off the path and watched it roll down the hillside into the valley below them. It was a beautiful day. Not too warm and not too cold, with little wind. Perfect for a long hike, if it weren't for the company.

"Have you tried talking to him in French? In my experience, speaking their language goes a long way," Lucille said carefully.

"Unless you butcher it. Like me." Matt sighed. "Look, I only picked French because my mum said it was the language of love. Honestly, I think she's never met anyone from France." He stared daggers into Dion's broad back.

"Well..." Lucille started to sound amused. "I personally think it's a beautiful language."

"Because *you* can speak it."

Behind them, Shayna and Cian caught up, joining them on the narrow path. "You also having problems with your partners?" Shayna asked. "Natalie babbles non-stop, never slowing down. And as soon as one of her friends comes, she lets me fall like a hot potato."

"Bernard is quite nice. At least, without the others," Cian said with a shrug. "And he can speak a decent amount of German."

Matt stretched his neck to check out the group of French students. "Which one is Bernard?" If there was a nice German-speaking French student, he wanted to make his acquaintance.

"The one giving you longing glances from time to time," Cian admitted. "He asked me last night if you were... you know, into boys, by chance."

Now *that* was interesting. "I'm into anyone... who's willing to communicate." There! His eyes met those of a curly-haired blond guy with glasses. Matt wriggled his eyebrows and flashed him a quick grin to see him redden instantly. "He's cute."

"Is that so?" Cian asked, strangely thoughtful.

In the meantime, Lucille asked Shayna, "Where's your Queen Bee?" Now that she'd said it, Matt noticed that Cheryl was nowhere to be seen. She would've been complaining about how the hike had ruined her stilettos, or something stupid like that.

"Off sick," Shayna replied. "Developed new allergies overnight."

"Her request for changing partners was denied," Cian added helpfully.

"Poor Cheryl." Matt's own partner woes were suddenly forgotten as he exchanged another glance with Bernard. "Excuse me, while I go practise my French."

Behind him, Lucille snorted. Matt left her in Shayna and Cian's care and caught up with the boy who, as he saw Matt approaching, fell behind his own group. "Salut."

"Salut," Bernard said shyly.

"Je n'ais..." This time Matt intentionally stumbled over the unfamiliar vocabulary, then laughed charmingly about himself. "Sorry, I..."

"It's okay." As expected, the boy came through for him. "I can speak German a little bit. I try."

"I'm Matt." He reached out his hand. "Cian said you were curious about me." As the other boy took his hand, ready to introduce himself, Matt leaned in and whispered, "The answer is yes."

Bernard's face blushed heavily. A smile broke through his embarrassment, and he laughed. "That's superb. I mean... uhm..."

Matt grinned at him. Now *this* he could work with. The next two hours passed easily now that he had someone willing to communicate—and more than that. Bernard marvelled at the beautiful mountains they walked across, soaking up the folktales of feisty princesses, sneaky dwarves, and the devil himself, while Matt amused himself by teaching him naughty words until he was convinced Bernard couldn't wait for the trip to be over and free time to commence. Folktales be damned.

After three hours, they finally reached the Witches' Dance Floor on the hills above Thale. Even though it was the beginning of the week, the mountain top was packed with tourists. A gondola brought visitors up from the town below, but more were hiking up. Tourist shops and food trucks surrounded the main attraction, which was crowded with people. It was a bunch of naked bronze statues of the devil lording over the witches that worshipped him. A pretend witch home invited people to take a spooky tour, and across the plaza, a mini-golf course beckoned with statues of wooden mountain spirits. In a few days, on Walpurgis Night, this place would be even more packed with the biggest party of the year.

Before Mrs Lindenberger had finished her speech about the forty-five-minute lunch break, Matt pulled Bernard behind the witch house and started kissing him. At first, the boy seemed overwhelmed, but then he quickly leaned into it and enjoyed Matt's offering.

Behind them, people squealed as they toured the house. Bernard broke off the kiss. "You're impossible," Bernard sputtered as he came up for breath.

"Just your local devil," Matt answered with a grin.

It highly amused him how the whole area had once worshipped the devil. He wondered what demon had had their fun with the locals. Definitely someone from the House of Lust, if the stories of orgies were to be believed. Back in the day, the 'devil' had invited witches to him, and they'd worshipped him with their bodies in exchange for their powers.

The last part was most definitely a lie. The witches he knew drew their power from the magic flowing through the mountains. And they were more into protecting the region from demons than dancing and fornicating with them. Matt sighed. It would be much more fun if the stories were real.

While he continued kissing Bernard and feeling him up, his imagination kept getting away from him. He imagined himself on Walpurgis Night, a fire burning in the clearing that was Greenvalley's spring of magic. And he wasn't alone, but dancing around the flames with his own little witch: Samantha. A naked Samantha.

"Damn it!" He punched the wall next to Bernard's head, biting his own tongue. Why was he thinking of Samantha while making out with another man? She *hated* him. And he hated her. Or at least, he tried to be indifferent about her. Whatever they'd once almost had was long lost, buried under blood and snow.

"Is everything okay?" Bernard asked slightly intimidated. He awkwardly readjusted his glasses with flushed cheeks.

Matt stroked his face, drinking in the beauty of arousal in Bernard's face. "Yes, I'm good. Better even." He was better without Samantha. She'd never dance around naked with him, or sneak away from a school function to make out in a semi-public space. Bernard, however...

He leaned forward to whisper a devious plan into the other boy's ear, while letting his hands wander across his body. It would keep him occupied enough to forget all about Samantha and her stupid vendetta against him.

Rachel

Rachel watched Samantha and Fabian goof around between the aisles of the second-hand shop they were visiting together after school. On Friday, Lucille was throwing her big Walpurgis Night party, and the three of them were shopping for cheap outfits that could be turned into some proper witch rags.

With Jan off doing his own thing, and Lucille and Matt busy with their exchange students, it was just the three of them. Almost like before all the horrible events of last year. Samantha was clearly enjoying her Matt-free time, putting Fabian through a series of silly outfit changes, of which only half were suited for a witchy costume.

"You should totally dress up as a witch." Samantha held a plaited skirt to Fabian's hips that would have been out of fashion even for her grandmother. "Shake things up a little bit."

"With the whole school watching? No thank you!" Fabian turned the skirt around and checked how it looked on Samantha. "Too boring. You wore that look two years ago."

Samantha put the skirt back on the rack. "Which is why I offered it to you." She went back to browsing the racks.

"Hey, can you help me with the Physics homework after this?" Fabian asked.

Rachel opened her mouth and shut it again. They'd been planning to go to her house after this. And she hadn't exactly planned for Samantha to join them there.

"I don't have Physics tomorrow," Samantha said in a sing-song voice. Then she rolled her eyes. "Adrian asked me to take over the museum tour tomorrow, since he has an important meeting ahead of his big exams. *And* because it's the Witch Museum."

"That's not fair!" Fabian complained predictably. "Look, I make an awesome guide. We've been there so much I know all about it. Please tell the school you need my help," he begged with big eyes.

Samantha laughed, but then her eyes met Rachel's, and she looked a little embarrassed. With a vague smile, she turned back to Fabian. "And leave Rachel all alone with Herbert? I can't do that." She nudged Fabian.

It was that physical touch that seemed to make Fabian remember his girlfriend was standing right there with them. Rachel sighed. "I wouldn't mind." She knew how torturous each Physics class was for Fabian. And if he'd rather spend the day with Samantha, she wouldn't like it, but she'd understand it.

"Nonsense!" Samantha shot back immediately. "Besides, school would never agree. You suffer through Physics, and I will suffer through a morning with Matt *and* Cheryl."

"Stick to Lucille," Fabian advised, not taking the refusal personally. "Maybe you can have some witchy fun with the Elite Clique while you're in Kessler's home." The Witch Museum was the former house of a famous local witch, Margarete Kessler.

"Anyway..." Samantha let the word drag on. "What do *you* think about this skirt, Rachel?"

The new skirt she'd found fell straight to the ground on Rachel's short legs. Not the most flattering choice. Rachel couldn't really feign the same excitement as her friends about Walpurgis Night. While the history of it was interesting enough, in the end, it was a loud party with grotesque faces and costumes, crackling fires and, in some places, celebratory witch burnings. They only burned straw puppets, but their symbolism was easy enough to understand.

"What do the real witches do for Walpurgis?" she asked Samantha. "Like, what does your grandmother do?"

Samantha looked through the clothes rack, trying to find something better after deciding that the length didn't fit. "Oh, she meets up with the other witches in Harzgerode. They switch places every time, but basically, they go to a place in the forest where magic runs and perform a ritual, before sitting down and exchanging news. It's like an AGM for witches."

"Have you ever been?" Surely, a witch meeting would be more interesting than a party at Lucille's house.

"No. Until recently, I didn't meet the requirements of being a witch. And now... Well, I'm getting better, but my grandmother said that I—and I guess Lucille—are still considered apprentices. We'll be invited once the time is right." She sighed, letting go of the garments. "It's not going to be this year."

"Which is great news," Fabian interjected. He put his hands on Samantha's shoulders and grinned at Rachel. "Because this year, Lucille is making up for all the times she missed out on Walpurgis Night. She's going all in, and it's going to be epic. And you can't miss it. Both of you!"

Samantha turned into him, laughing. "Why do you think we're here, looking for costumes, doofus?" She bopped his nose, then pushed past him to examine another rack.

Fabian looked after her, then held out his hands for Rachel. "What do you want to go for? Full witchy or sexy witch?" With any other boy, it would've been clear what he preferred, but Fabian's question seemed genuine. He cared about her wishes, not what he hoped for. If he even hoped for anything.

Rachel tried to imagine herself dressing up like some of the other girls, but it only made her uncomfortable. "Samantha would kill me if I didn't go full witchy." She grabbed the plain skirt rejected by Samantha and Fabian earlier. "I'll make something out of this."

"Alright. I'll be your devil for the night either way." Fabian grinned. "I've got some great theatrical make-up and prosthetics ready to go."

"Tell me more." Rachel hooked her arm with his as they followed Samantha down the aisle.

After their shopping trip, Rachel and Fabian returned to her home without Samantha. Her friend had wisely feigned some plans of her own when Fabian had invited her. One part of Rachel was glad about it, thinking that she deserved some time alone with Fabian. The other was ironically worried about being alone with him. They'd never had their big talk. Fabian made it too easy to keep going as they were, and so the weeks had passed without them changing anything about their relationship.

"What shall we do tonight?" Fabian asked expectantly.

Rachel opened the door and fumbled for an answer. "What about a movie?" She saw her mother in the living room. "Or perhaps not."

"Oh, hey, you two!" Her mother got up from the couch and smiled vaguely. "Did you want to use the living room? I can go upstairs. Or leave the house altogether, if you've got other plans."

"Mum, please..." Rachel didn't need her mum making thinly veiled sexual allusions as well. Though eighteen years old, Rachel didn't feel ready for sex. She'd thought she would be by now, but the idea of it still held no appeal. Not even if it meant making Fabian happy. Like with big, loud parties, Rachel just wasn't into it. And slowly, she was beginning to doubt she ever would be.

"I'll go. It's such nice weather. A walk, and maybe a coffee, would do me good." Her mother grabbed her jacket, then winked at them. "Don't do anything I wouldn't do."

The door shut behind her, and Rachel begged for the ground to open up and swallow her whole. "I don't think there's anything my mother wouldn't do or hasn't done." She smiled at Fabian. "Movie?"

"As long as it's not a horror movie," Fabian quipped.

"Learnt my lesson."

They settled on the couch, and Rachel let Fabian pick some silly comedy while she prepared some snacks and drinks. With everything set up, she sat down next to him, and he started the movie.

About ten minutes in, Fabian's arm fell on her shoulders, and he pulled her a little closer. Rachel instantly tensed and hated herself for it. What was she so scared of? She wanted Fabian! He wasn't even doing anything, just holding her with his eyes glued to the screen. And yet, there was an inexplicable knot in Rachel's tummy, as she dreaded something that wasn't happening, anyway.

"You know, we should do our Physics homework," Rachel said, before quickly adding, "after the movie, I mean."

Fabian turned his head and frowned at her. "How do you get from drunken party antics"—he pointed at the screen—"to our Physics homework?"

"Well, those people are still going to school, right?" Rachel hadn't truly paid attention to the movie. "I was just thinking, because you asked Samantha earlier."

"Oh, she said, she'd send me her notes on the experiment. That's almost as good as a report. I can make the rest up." Fabian's attention was drawn back to the screen, and he laughed.

It wasn't the first time Fabian had copied his homework from Samantha, and it likely wouldn't be the last, but Rachel couldn't ignore the sting when he passed her over for Samantha's scraps. She wasn't truly jealous, she told herself. The relationship between her two best friends was over. Samantha had long since moved on, and Fabian seemed happy and content with his lot. But the emotional connection between them was as strong as ever. And despite being Fabian's girlfriend, Rachel had the feeling she was no closer to him than she'd been before.

He was no longer trying to become intimate anymore—something Rachel should've been happy about. And yet, she wasn't.

Confused and annoyed, Rachel snuggled into his arms and concentrated on the movie. There really was no reason she couldn't enjoy being with Fabian if she shut her brain off. That was the most important thing. Shutting off the part that kept over-thinking and over-analysing every little detail until it no longer held any appeal.

Fabian was her boyfriend. Just as she'd always wanted. They were good. And any doubts were all in her imagination.

Samantha

Samantha loved Greenvalley's Witch Museum. In her opinion, it was even better than the big one in Thale, because the house had once belonged to a witch. Margarete Kessler was one of Greenvalley's most famous inhabitants—or rather infamous, since she'd been tried for witchcraft and had died in the fire. Samantha had no idea if the poor woman had held any real powers, but either way, she'd been the victim of mass hysteria and foul play. And something about that had always spoken to her. So much so, she'd even dressed up as Margarete on Walpurgis Night before.

Today, she was accompanying the French course and their exchange students. None of them were expecting her to give a tour, so all she really did was tag along with Lucille, who'd never visited the museum before.

"Is that..." Lucille pointed at a hairy pair of trousers with obvious appendages on the *outside*.

Samantha giggled. "The penis of a devil. Yes. Those pants are supposed to make you rich. And they curse you at the same time."

"There's no way in hell I would put these on," Lucille declared, still pulling a face. "They're not exactly a fashion statement."

"No. Not really." They were truly bizarre. And even after all these visits, Samantha hadn't found out why the pants were fashioned the way they were, or whether they were supposed to imitate the actual skin of a devil. "Either way, they got demons dead wrong."

"True. Speaking of..."

Just then, Matt joined them, tucking his shirt back into his pants. "What did I miss?"

"Well, I guess it *does* symbolise how demons never keep it in their pants," Samantha mused.

Matt's eyes narrowed. "You got a problem with that?"

Lucille put a hand on Matt's arm, but Samantha rolled her eyes. "Excuse me. I've got work to do."

She slipped into a neighbouring room before Lucille could stop her and took a deep breath. It had been nice not to deal with Matt for a few days. He could run around with some French girl or boy and leave her alone for once.

But her relief was only short-lived. "Hi, Sammy," the dreaded voice of Cheryl trilled. A second later, she'd hooked her arm with Samantha's and was dragging her along. "You must feel right at home here. I bet old Kessler was your ancestor. Have you inherited her broomstick for the flight on Friday?"

It wasn't the first time Cheryl had brought up that particular joke. "What do you want?"

"Oh, you're our guide today, aren't you? I need you to show me something."

There was no escaping Cheryl's iron grip without making a scene. Samantha let herself be dragged into the room that was dedicated to Margarete Kessler's trial. Along the walls, several items of her possession were exhibited, between them information signposted in three languages. The room was dominated by a huge contraption, though, one that looked like an oversized scale with two cages instead of scale pans. One of them was weighted down by a huge rock, while the second hung in the air.

As they approached it, Samantha figured out what Cheryl was trying to do. "Oh no."

"It says here that witches were tested on these scales," Cheryl announced, sounding awfully chirpy. "If they weigh less than the counterweight, they're obviously witches. I just don't get why? Why do witches not weigh anything?"

The answer shot to the tip of Samantha's tongue. *Because people believed they had to weigh next to nothing to be able to fly on broomsticks.* Instead of saying so, she tried to wriggle her arm out of Cheryl's grip. To no avail.

Cheryl kept pushing her until she faced the open door of the second cage. "Come on, Sammy, let's settle this once and for all. You must be dying to know whether you're a real witch after all these years."

While the exhibition piece invited people to try out the ridiculousness of the biased trial, Samantha had no interest in testing it in front of all people. But the grip around her arm was starting to hurt, and Cheryl kept pushing her against the iron bars. A small crowd of students was already gathering, drawn in by Cheryl's show.

If I do this, it'll be over sooner, and she'll move on to someone else, Samantha thought, and gave in. She climbed into the cage with a huge sigh and closed her eyes. Naturally, the upper cage didn't move a bit.

The door clanged shut. Samantha's eyes flew open.

"What are you doing?" She grappled for the door, but Cheryl was holding it shut.

She grinned at Samantha before getting out a pen to jam it into the primitive lock. Then she turned to the others. "Would you believe it? She doesn't weigh a thing. You really *are* a witch. Just like Kessler." Cheryl pointed at the portrait of the old woman.

Margarete Kessler had been a middle-aged woman with an unfortunately long nose and big teeth. Her eyes were like two dark beetles, which gave her a creepy stare that may have scared children—and enough people to accuse her of witchcraft.

"Be careful you don't start looking like her!" Cheryl warned, then laughed. Several of the students around them, even some of the foreign exchange students, laughed along with her.

Samantha's eyes were burning. Her throat felt tight as she stuck her fingers through the bars and tried to grab the pen. She would not cry in front of everyone. And certainly not in front of Cheryl. But her eyesight was compromised by a shimmering curtain, and she only managed to touch her fingertips to the pen, lacking any grip.

Just then, a hand touched hers and gently moved her fingers aside. Samantha blinked to see Cian trying to remove the pen. It was a bit jammed, but he got it out within a few seconds and swung the door open.

"Thank you," Samantha whispered, too ashamed to hold his gaze.

Cian offered her his hand to climb out. He smiled good-naturedly. "Come on, you featherweight."

"Cian!" Cheryl said, offended. "What are you doing?"

"You lost something," he said matter-of-factly, and threw the pen to her.

Samantha used the distraction to climb out and swiftly walk away before the unshed tears fell after all.

"Sam!" Lucille called. She and Matt must've only just arrived in the room.

"What was that?" Matt asked, looking disgusted with whatever he'd seen.

Samantha fled into Lucille's arms and pulled her out of the room. "Nothing." The last person she needed to detail her ordeal at Cheryl's hands to was the guy who'd put her through much worse.

While Lucille put an arm around her, she explained to Matt, "A witch trial. People back then were convinced that witches weighed nothing. Otherwise, they wouldn't be able to fly. Another test was to tie them up and throw them into a lake. If they swim, witch. If not, not a witch. Still dead."

"Man, seems like those people knew even less about humans than demons," Matt mused.

"Why don't you educate them?" Samantha shot back. He didn't truly deserve it this time, but it helped her rid herself of the negative energy Cheryl had instilled in her. "Gosh, I hate her so much," she whispered.

Lucille gave her a pitiful smile. "You and me both. Come on, let's check out ghosts for a change."

They had now reached a room dedicated to modern occultism. It was filled with stories about ghost sightings, such as the Brocken Spectre, and objects used in séances. Lucille was checking out a Ouija board. "Do you think we should get one for Friday?"

"I don't think that's a good idea." Even though they were most likely fake, Ouija boards creeped Samantha out. The last thing they needed was a ghost infestation at the party.

"Why not? What's the deal with these?" Matt asked, confused.

Lucille rolled her eyes. "Apparently, you can use them to summon ghosts and ask them questions. The ghosts then move the planchette from letter to letter to answer. But, as it says here, it's all due to the Carpenter Effect, which is an ideomotor phenomenon. So practically, people are so tense with expectation that their muscles twitch towards an answer. Or people are faking it to give each other a fright. We did it once at Rosemary and nothing happened."

"I still wouldn't risk it. We know ghosts exist." The one time Samantha had tried it all by herself—since Fabian wouldn't touch it with a ten-foot pole—she had given herself a massive fright.

"I won't use it. I was only thinking of getting one for decoration," Lucille assured her. "I can't wait for Friday! I've never been in Greenvalley during Walpurgis Night."

Slowly, Samantha was recovering from her earlier embarrassment. "You've missed a lot. It's my favourite day of the year." The one time pretending to be a witch was not weird or something to laugh at. Though she was sure Cheryl would find something else to torment her with. "Please tell me you didn't invite the Elite Clique."

"I didn't invite them," Lucille said, but then her face fell. "They RSVP'd, nonetheless. But look, there will be about eighty people. We'll stick together and shield you from them." A wicked glint entered her eye. "And if they won't leave you alone, we'll show them what real witches do with those that laugh at them."

Samantha shuddered. "Sometimes you scare me." But it comforted her. Cheryl may have made fun of her for pretending to be a witch for years, but this year, there was no pretending.

This year, she truly *was* a witch.

Jan

In Jan's opinion, the best thing about school was a free period. Thanks to a lack of relief teachers, there was no one to cover Zobel's classes while he was too sick to work, which meant they had five extra free periods this week. As usual, Jan and his friends spent them in the school hall, seated around their standard table. While he, Rachel, and Fabian were playing a round of Skat, Samantha was folding flyers.

"A donation drive?" Jan asked, showing some interest in her activity when the current round ended.

"The cafeteria is asking for a rebuild."

Fabian snorted. "Another excuse for raising prices, I'm sure. Is anyone still able to afford food here?"

"Lu is," Jan mused. "Though she brings in her own five-star lunch."

"Guys?" Rachel whispered. "What's Matt's sister doing here?"

Jan stretched his neck to check the entrance. Sure enough, Menuha was walking into the cafeteria, her eyes wide with wonder. "What the hell?" he whispered.

Under the table, Fabian was forming a delta with his fingers, while Samantha slipped one hand into her backpack, watching each of Menuha's steps with trepidation. Jan stretched out on his chair, raising his chin to meet the challenge.

"Matt's not here," he said.

"Oh, I'm aware." Disconcertingly, Menuha was smiling at all of them. "He's on a trip with Dion. I just wanted to check out his school while I was here."

"Visitors need to report to the office," Samantha muttered, unable to bend her rule-abiding backbone.

Menuha looked confused for a moment. "I didn't know that." She cast around, searching. "Where is the office?"

"Forget the office!" Jan leaned forward, slapping his palm on the table. "Why are you really here?" He already had trouble understanding why a half-demon would attend school.

"As I said, I wanted to check out the school," Menuha repeated.

Baffled, Jan took a moment to consider the possibility she truly could be here for that reason. It just didn't make any sense! Anger was churning in his stomach. Demons were strolling around Greenvalley, attacking people at parties, selling drugs, and stealing the town's magic. Now they were taking over the school. He was tired of the supernatural messing with them. "Bullshit! Nobody's interested in school. Samantha excluded."

Menuha ignored his outburst and turned to Samantha, her eyes wide with excitement. "You're also interested in the human world?"

"I *am* a human." Samantha's hand was still in her backpack. Jan wondered what she was hiding in there that could harm a demon. Some potion, perhaps.

"Right. Silly me." Menuha laughed. "Sorry, this is all new to me. I've been to Ashuan before, but things change so fast here. It feels like a whole other world compared to last time."

Slowly, Fabian raised his hands again, relaxing his fingers. "Why do you have an interest in the human world?"

"Probably wants to take over," Jan suggested. That was something demons did, wasn't it?

"No, that would be unnecessary," Menuha assured them. "I find Ashuan fascinating. You have such a short life, and yet you fill it with purpose."

Jan exchanged an uneasy look with Fabian. He didn't feel especially purposeful outside of the occasional monster hunt.

"Matt grew up so fast!" Menuha continued, ignorant to how the mood around the table had changed at the drop of his name. "You know, demons take a much longer time to grow up. *If* they ever come of age. An eighteen-year-old demon is still running around with blood steeds." Her entire face lit up. She seemed to have great memories of what sounded like some dangerous creatures. "Within a demon's childhood, you humans come of age, build families, have whole careers, and change the world profoundly. I admire that."

Even Samantha had been worn down by Menuha's unashamed friendliness and pulled her hand out of her bag. "Why do *you* call him Matt and not Melchior? Isn't that his demon name?"

"Does he prefer that? I thought he liked Matt more whenever he's here."

"I have no idea what he prefers," Samantha said decidedly, as if she hadn't just asked about him herself.

Menuha sighed and began to observe Samantha closely, leaving Jan wondering how much she'd understood of what had happened that fateful January night. "He is going through a lot at the moment, rethinking many things. The Blood Night confused him, I think."

If she'd hoped to have an empathetic discussion about Matt's woes, she'd picked the wrong conversation partner. Samantha packed up her flyers and got up. "I need to bring these to the office. I'll see you guys later." Then to Menuha, she said, "Have fun looking around school."

"Sam..." Fabian called, but Samantha was already rushing off. "You need to excuse her," he explained to Menuha. "She doesn't like talking about the Blood Night."

Menuha wasn't quite as ignorant as she'd pretended to be. The over-excitement abated, and a serious expression took over her face. "That day must have been so scary for you all."

"Scary?" Rachel asked drily. "Matt killed Daniel. He was Samantha's boyfriend."

"The young man Melaney was so interested in?" Menuha asked, then explained, "She noticed right away that Matt couldn't stand him. Apparently, Samantha was the reason."

Jan exchanged another look with Fabian, who swallowed. "Well, he was quite obviously jealous," he confirmed. "But that's irrelevant, isn't it?"

"Jealousy?" Menuha frowned, as if the very thought Matt could be jealous of a human boy was too foreign. "It shouldn't have mattered, but half-demons are different. Chay once told me that he'd *wanted* to kill the people he killed, but—"

"Woah!" Jan almost fell off his chair. "Chay's Blood Night?" The seer had alluded to it, saying he regretted what had happened back then. Had that been a lie, then? If he'd *wanted* to kill them?

"Yes, Chay's Blood Night is the stuff of legends in Hescaryn. He killed hundreds over two or three days, left hardly anyone alive," Menuha explained, as if discussing someone weeding their garden.

Jan felt the blood drain from his face. Fabian looked like a ghost, and Rachel swallowed. None of them said a word. And here Jan had thought it had been some legendary party. Not a gory blood bath.

"He doesn't like to talk about it," Menuha mused thoughtfully. "I have no idea what happened exactly. I only met him about one-and-a-half centuries later."

Jan's feeble mind latched onto this unnecessary detail like a lifeline out of the blood-filled visions. "150 years? How old is he really?"

Menuha blew off some air, as if he'd asked her to solve some complex maths formula. "About 260 or 270 years? I'm not quite sure."

"And you are?" Fabian asked, just as eager for an answer that involved no blood.

"Turned half-a-millennium twenty years ago," Menuha declared proudly.

Jan was starting to feel a little dizzy. "Cool, cool. And you've been to Ashuan before?" No wonder Menuha thought things had changed so much. When she'd been young, there'd still been kings and queens around Germany.

"Yes. I like to visit from time to time." The excitement was back in her eyes. "Every time I get here, it's like a completely new world. Like these things!" Menuha grabbed Fabian's cellphone from the table. "Everyone has one of these in their hands at all times. They must bring you great satisfaction."

"Uhm, sure," Fabian said, looking around awkwardly, as if he was afraid Menuha was going to break his phone.

Before Jan could generously explain the marvel of smartphones to Menuha, someone bumped into his chair and put their arms around his shoulders. Meg.

"Hey," she said cheerfully, and kissed his temple. "We got out five minutes early."

Jan twisted in his chair to get a real kiss. From the corner of his eye, he saw Anne approaching as well. As usual, his little sister was annoyed about having to spend time at their table, but she sat down nonetheless. Right next to a demon.

"Uhm…" He was frantically trying to find a reason to send the two of them away again.

But Meg immediately latched onto Menuha. "Who are you? I haven't seen you before, have I?" As if to make it clear Jan belonged to her, she climbed onto his lap, one arm still around his neck.

"I'm Matt's sister, Menuha," Menuha said with the same kindness she'd shown before.

"Oh, hi!" Meg leaned forward again, wriggling her bum on Jan's lap. "I'm Meg. Samantha's little sister. Hi."

"Anne," Anne said shyly, not adding her claim to sisterhood.

Jan found it hard to concentrate with Meg so close to his nether regions. He was sure she knew exactly what she was doing to him.

Menuha seemed delighted to make their acquaintances. "So nice to meet you. You're Samantha's little sister. May I ask you something, then?"

"Uhm, I don't think it's a good idea," Fabian said at the same time Meg assured Menuha with a resounding, "Sure!"

"I'm trying to figure something out," Menuha started. "Did Matt sleep with your sister last year?"

Anne's eyes bulged, Fabian sputtered, and Rachel started remixing the cards she'd already distributed.

Jan burst out laughing. "He wishes."

"No, he doesn't," Meg declared. "Why would Matt be interested in my sister? She's so boring."

Jan rubbed her back, and despite being of a completely different opinion, he said, "Exactly."

"They haven't," Rachel announced quietly. Her eyes fixed to the table, she said a little too fast, "It's not fair to talk about something like this without the relevant parties present, but they haven't. Sam said she had no interest in becoming one of his conquests."

Fabian jumped straight on to the declaration. "That sounds like Sam. She's looking for love. Nothing Matt could give her. And apart from that, the two hate each other now."

"And I still don't know why," Meg mused.

That was a good thing, in Jan's opinion.

Meanwhile, Menuha had taken in all their opinions, nodding thoughtfully. Her gaze landed on Fabian at last. "Love?" she asked.

Fabian reddened promptly. He checked with Meg and Anne, then proceeded to stumble over his words, "You know the... the one true love. Mr Right. The one that sweeps her off her feet. Gosh... Rachel's right. It's not fair to talk about her when she's not here."

"Huh." Menuha thought about it a little more, then smiled. "I'll ask her myself, then." She immediately got up, then looked around. "Which way is the office?"

"Next to the gate?" Anne answered, a little confused but helpful.

"You really shouldn't..." Fabian started before trailing off as Menuha jumped up anyway.

"Thanks so much for the chat. I'll see you around!" she announced and made her way through the students leaving their classrooms. A second later, the bell rang.

Jan blew up his cheeks and puffed some air. "Now that was fun."

"Talking about sex..." Meg put both her arms around his neck and leaned in until she could whisper into his ear, "You're going to bring condoms to the party, aren't you?"

The whole seating arrangement, combined with the talk of sex, had already excited Jan far beyond what was proper at school. Now this not very innocent question had him grinning like a fool. He put his hands on her hips. "It'll be the most exciting Walpurgis Night of your life."

Lucille

One positive aspect of the student exchange was that Lucille got to visit all the historical places in the area. It was embarrassing how little she knew about Greenvalley and the Harz region as a whole, but she had received a crash course in it at the town history museum, hiking the Witch's Trail, visiting Wernigerode Castle, the Witch Museum, and now as they descended into one of the marvellous flowstone caves under the mountains.

The first part was an introduction to the mining in the area, which made Lucille a little uneasy as she remembered the wyrm they'd encountered in the Greenvalley Coal Mine. But the further they went in, the more natural the caves became, and when they entered one of the larger caverns, she wasn't the only one who marvelled at the natural wonder.

Water glistened on the stalactites and stalagmites, making their surfaces shimmer like milk. Rust and cream-coloured bands mixed in a beautiful display of colours that were impossible to capture with her phone camera.

"It's so beautiful," Amélie said, for once walking with her.

"It is." Over the last few days, Amélie had stuck with her group of friends. Even at home, she was mostly on her phone. "I hope you're enjoying your stay?" Lucille hadn't forgotten how she'd ratted her out to Dion.

Amélie smiled. "Yes. It has been a lot of fun. I thought Greenvalley would be boring because it's so small and there's no beach, but I love all the fairytale stories. Witches and devils. It must be so much fun living here."

"You have no idea." Fairy tales were a lot more exciting when they turned out to be real.

"Are you alright?" Amélie asked suddenly. "You're standing here all alone."

"That's because Matt..." Lucille looked around to see if she could spot him anywhere, but he had successfully separated himself and Bernard from the group without either of the teachers noticing. "Matt is busy."

Next to her, Amélie sighed. "Yes, I noticed. I wish he was busy with me, but I guess Bernard is more exciting."

The conversation began to grate on Lucille. When the week had started, she'd been delighted to talk boys with Amélie, but after the betrayal, she couldn't keep up the pretence anymore. "Or Bernard has been a bit more open to making new connections."

Amélie gave her a long glance. "A little too open, if you ask me. But I guess you meant that as a dig at me."

Lucille sighed. She would've much rather appreciated the beauty of the cave rather than fight with Amélie, but she also knew she had to stand up for herself. "Am I wrong? As soon as one of your friends arrives, I only see the back of you. Even at home, you're constantly on your phone. And what you said... I'm fluent in French, so I've heard what you said about me to Dion."

"I..." Amélie opened her mouth and closed it again. "Listen, I've seen dozens of girls fall for his tricks."

"His trick is to be an all-around jerk?" Lucille asked unimpressed. Everything she'd heard from Matt didn't speak well of the pretty French guy.

Amélie opened her mouth wide in outrage. "He's not a... You've got him all wrong." To Lucille's horror, Amélie waved Dion closer. "He doesn't let many people in for reasons you don't understand. I was only protecting you, but fine, go get your heart broken on a meaningless exchange." She walked over to Dion and whispered something to him before leaving Lucille alone with him.

Dion sighed deeply, his act already putting Lucille off. "Look," he said, "I am not interested."

"You don't even know me," Lucille said, then remembered she was mad at him. "And just because I think you're not bad looking doesn't mean I'm interested in *you*." Her self-respect was wavering, though, as she looked into his green eyes. Even down here in the cave, they were startling, as if they were made from moss.

Wonderful, soft moss that clad the cave like an underground forest. And from the moss, long furry legs rose until the massive body of a spider appeared. Lucille let out a little scream, drawing the attention of the whole group.

"Lucille? Is everything alright?"

Lucille blinked. There was no moss and no spiders, only shimmering cold flowstones. Mrs Lindenberger had a hand on her shoulder and looked concerned. Embarrassment crept up Lucille's cheeks. "I-I just had a drop hit me in the neck. It surprised me."

"Right. Well, let's move on, shall we?"

After Lucille nodded, the teacher went back to the front. Meanwhile, Lucille searched for Dion. He had been standing right in front of her, but now he was nowhere to be seen. Amélie stood with her friends, chatting and laughing. Then she turned to her empty right and nodded as if someone had said something to her. And there Lucille saw him.

She rubbed her eyes in confusion. She could've sworn he hadn't been there before. He even seemed to flicker, as if she wasn't supposed to see him. That settled it. Something was off about him, had been since the first day. And Lucille was going to find out what it was.

Especially after he'd left her alone with a spider.

She strode forwards and grabbed him by the arm, drawing him away from his group. "What do you think you're doing?" she hissed in German, momentarily forgetting that he never spoke the language.

"Je n'ai sais pas..."

"Oh, drop the act!" Lucille whispered furiously. "You did something to me, and I want to know what."

Surprisingly, Dion glanced over his shoulder as if to make sure they had enough distance between them and the others. Then he turned to her. "What do you mean *I* did something?"

"You can speak German," Lucille asked surprised. And almost free of any accent.

"I've been learning it for ten years," Dion said, slightly annoyed. "Not that I enjoy speaking it."

Lucille narrowed her eyes. "But you've pretended not to understand a word Matt said."

"What's up with him? He speaks French as if he's never attended a single class in his life."

"That's about right," Lucille said, considering how Matt had only started French lessons in the last six months. He... She noticed how she was getting distracted. Again. "You pretend things. Like you pretend not to speak German. You pretend to be a jerk. And you pretend to leave me in a forest with spiders."

Dion's eyes widened. "Is that what you saw?" he asked, more curious than surprised.

"What do you mean what I saw? You... you created that!" Lucille was pretty sure of it now. What she wasn't sure of was the expression of wonder that suddenly seemed to light up Dion's face.

"You're like me." Even his voice was struck with awe. "You saw through my illusion."

"Illusion?" She was dumbstruck for a moment.

Dion's face fell again, and he shook his head. "Forget it. I thought because you... never mind."

He was about to turn away when Lucille grabbed his hand. "I know magic exists if you're worried about that," she whispered, while the group slowly overtook them.

Both of them waited patiently until they'd passed. Then Dion squinted at her. "Do you, now?"

"I'm a witch," Lucille declared.

"Prove it."

Lucille was of the opinion she didn't need to prove anything to him, but her curiosity got the better of her. He knew illusion magic, and he wouldn't tell her more if she didn't build a little trust between them. "Fine."

She stepped closer to shield herself from the rest of the group who had stopped not too far from them. In the gap between them, she turned her palms upwards before whispering, "Scintilla."

Sparks flew up between them. Dion hastily put his hands on top of hers, his fingertips touching her wrists slightly. Then he smiled for the first time, his eyes glinting with surprise. "Wow, they're even warm."

Lucille delighted in his joy. "What about you?"

"I can't do that. I only know about illusions. Images, smells, touch..." He twirled his finger and a line of sparks flew up between them.

They looked just like hers, but when Lucille reached for them, her hand passed right through the illusion. "Since when can you—"

"All my life," Dion said, and his lips curled with bitterness. "I've never met anyone like me outside of my family. And they... It's all an illusion." He snorted softly.

Lucille thought of her own family and all the pretending going on in her home. This was the real Dion, she thought. A tiny piece of what was hiding behind that aloofness. No pretence. "I get it. I may have a hundred rooms to have sex in, but they're all empty," she quipped, pushing the old pain down.

His eyes widened a little, and his cheeks darkened. "I—"

Hasty steps sounded behind them. Dion and Lucille stepped away from each other without a word. A moment later, Bernard and Matt appeared, both stopping short when they saw the other two.

"Hey," Matt said with a lazy smile before turning to Bernard. "Told you we'd find them."

Bernard muttered something in French about not wanting to be lost underground, never to be found, and hurried further along. It looked to Lucille as if Matt had taken it a little too far by sneaking away in an endless cave system.

"I hope we didn't interrupt anything," Matt said cheerfully, as usual not minding other people's feelings.

"Tú—" Dion started, but when Lucille glared at him, he switched to German. "You're impossible. You might only be fooling around with Bernard, but he's got a boyfriend back home. I guess you care little about that."

Struck by surprise, Matt stared at him. "He never mentioned him." Then he looked Dion up and down. "You really were doing it on purpose. Jerk."

"Matt," Lucille said with a warning.

"Whatever." Matt clicked his tongue and followed Bernard.

Just then, Mrs Lindenberger called out to them to hurry.

"I don't like him. He's cocky," Dion muttered.

"Well, you should be careful you don't come across as too cocky yourself," Lucille said, slightly amused. "And besides, you're in Greenvalley now, where there are quite a few like me." She lowered her voice. "Perhaps you shouldn't provoke someone with demon blood."

She left a gaping Dion, feeling suitably avenged for the spider illusion he'd thrown at her. Now that they were even and dropping all the pretences, things were looking up again. Perhaps this student exchange wasn't so bad after all.

Matt

Four days. For four days, Matt had attempted to strike a connection and made a fool out of himself. And all this time, his exchange partner had stood there and pretended to be just as ignorant as him. Of course, he was an illusionist! Matt wasn't sure why he hadn't seen that before. He'd met some of his demon kin, and they'd always left him with a headache.

"Why are you even here?" he asked as soon as the two of them had returned to the flat. "Is it all a big joke to you?"

"Why are *you* here?" Dion dropped the pretence, answering in near-flawless German. "Do you think I'm going to bring you home to my family so you can murder or seduce them as you see fit?"

"I don't care about your family!" There was that, though. In a couple of weeks, their class would travel to Marseille, and what had sounded like a chance to see some more of Ashuan—the *sea!*—was beginning to show some serious flaws. "Look, I don't know what Lucille told you, but I'm not going to murder your family. That only happened once."

Dion took a sudden step back. "It happened once?"

Matt rolled his eyes. So, Lucille *hadn't* told him about the Blood Night. No, he'd done that to himself. "Forget it. Look at it this way: if I were interested in murdering people, you would be at the top of my list."

That came out completely wrong. He couldn't even fault Dion for slowly backing away.

"I meant that you're still alive, even though you've been a real jerk. You've got nothing to worry about." Surely, Dion could see his point.

"I'm not helpless," he whispered.

Matt snorted. "You mean your illusions? They wouldn't stop me. They're not real."

Somehow, his words made Dion set his jaw and straighten his shoulders. "They *feel* real." When Matt didn't look too impressed, he hissed, "I can craft illusions out of your own mind. You'd be your own tormentor."

"Sorry, Dion, but that trick might work on humans, what with all their little self-doubts and regrets, but it's pretty useless against a demon. We don't torment ourselves." Matt had himself almost convinced. Demons didn't waste time on past failures. And neither would he.

Dion twisted his mouth. "You really are a cocky bastard. As you wish. I'm going to meet the others. I'll see you at the party once you've gotten over yourself. Or... actually, don't bother."

And with that, he grabbed his jacket and fled the apartment. Matt glowered at the door. Who did this upstart illusionist think he was? Get over himself? Dion had been the one who had been acting all haughty this week, dissatisfaction oozing out of every pore but never voiced aloud. Matt certainly wouldn't run after him and beg for his forgiveness.

He turned away and walked into the kitchen to fill up Crumbs' food bowl. The puppy was excitedly wagging his tail, knowing exactly what was about to happen. Matt smiled. "We're going to have a nice—"

He froze. "Daniel?"

There in front of him, casually leaning against the kitchen counter, stood Daniel, idly playing with a knife, while fresh blood ran down his face, soaking into his hair. His stomach was a ruin where Matt's sword had stabbed him. Despite all his gruesome injuries, he exuded much more confidence than he'd had in life. Superiority was written across his face.

"You're finally here. Let's get started," Daniel announced, as if he'd been waiting for Matt to join him for dinner all afternoon.

Matt could only stare at him. Words formed themselves sluggishly in his mind as he tried to make sense of what he was seeing. An illusion. Dion had practically warned him what he was going to do. An illusion crafted from his own mind. "You're not real."

Daniel didn't seem to care about that. He grinned and gripped the knife tighter. "Not real." Then he drove the knife into his own wound, making Matt wince. "Dead."

Matt's breathing came harder. He still wasn't able to move. Crumbs was slinking around his legs, begging for food, but his soft fur was like a distant memory. "I..."

Bored with stabbing himself, Daniel pulled the knife from the ruin of his wound. "Let's play."

The words echoed in Matt's mind. He vaguely remembered having said something similar to Daniel on the night he'd killed him. But before he could form an appropriate response, Daniel threw the knife at him. Unable to move, the blade hit Matt in the shoulder.

The sudden pain jump-started his brain at last. He reached for the knife, feebly grabbing the hilt, and pulled. Blood glistened on the blade. It reminded him of how it'd glistened on the edge of his sword under the lanterns.

Only an illusion. Daniel wasn't here. He was a figment of his imagination. Dion hadn't even known about him. Matt waited until his pulse had calmed again before turning around with all the intent of marching away.

Daniel stood before him, a cruel smile twisting his mouth.

"You're dead," Matt told him. "What do you want from me?"

He shouldn't have asked. Don't engage the illusion. Ignore it.

"Justice," Daniel hissed, though there was a wicked gleam in his eyes.

Ignoring him just didn't work. There had to be another way. Matt's eyes locked on the gaping wound in Daniel's middle. He hated this, but Daniel didn't leave him any choice. He wasn't real, anyway.

Matt drew his sword. "If you're so intent on dying again, I'm happy to help."

He dashed forward, and with one big swipe, drove his sword into Daniel's shoulder until it got stuck in his chest. And in the kitchen table.

Crumbs was barking, but it was only a sound at the edge of Matt's awareness. He'd be able to deal with the dog once he'd got rid of Daniel. Unfortunately, his adversary appeared behind him, unharmed.

"Impressive swordsmanship," he said, sounding bored. "But that won't work this time. I'm no longer weak or pathetic like you." And with that, he kicked Matt's back.

The force threw Matt into the dishwasher. Unwashed dishes rattled and broke as they toppled out of the racks, while the edge pressed into Matt's stomach. Grunting with pain, he whirled around and shot black magic at Daniel. Wood splintered and Daniel went down. Crumbs shot out of the kitchen with a high-pitched yelp.

This time, Daniel didn't move. He was lying there, blood pooling beneath him, eyes staring empty at the ceiling. Like he'd had on New Year's Day.

Matt took a few deep breaths, slowly assuming control over his racing heart. The moment he'd calmed sufficiently to start thinking about what to make of this mess, Daniel's corpse sat up and grinned. "Just a joke."

Matt's face muscles went slack. Daniel was unkillable. He was impervious to all his attacks, sword or magic. And he simply wouldn't go away.

"Oh, come on, Matt," Daniel said with a particularly condescending brand of pity. "I thought you liked these kinds of sick games. Don't you want to impress your brothers? Show your mummy who's a good demon boy?"

It was too close to the nightmare Matt had experienced two months ago. His mother didn't care about him. Not this way. But *he* cared. He cared so much that he screamed at Daniel and launched into a flurry of attacks.

Sword, magic, fists. They all became one as he threw Daniel into the living room and battered his body with everything he got. Blood splashed everywhere. It coated the walls and soaked into the carpet. And the whole time, Daniel was laughing. Laughing!

Then the dead boy turned things around, and suddenly Matt found himself on his back, shielding himself from Daniel's much stronger—and more effective—blows. It was his own blood that decorated the living room, seeping from so many wounds he couldn't heal them all.

A few minutes later, Daniel was above him, Matt's sword in his hands. A smile played around the corners of his lips as he put the tip of the sword against Matt's chest. "Are you sick of the game yet? Dying for it to end?"

Matt gasped for air. He was in so much pain he couldn't even move. And he wondered if *that* was how Daniel had felt by the end. Had he yearned for that final strike that would kill him and relieve him from his torment?

"You're not real!" Matt cried.

He couldn't be. Matt *knew* he wasn't. And yet Daniel only shrugged. "Does it matter? The pain is real." He lowered his weight onto the sword, and Matt saw it slip beneath his ribs. "You wanted to kill me."

"No!" Everyone said that, but it wasn't true. The Blood Night had been outside of his control. He'd been powerless against the instincts that had grabbed hold of him. "It wasn't on purpose."

The tip of the sword sunk deeper, and Matt gritted his teeth in pain. "Matt!" Daniel sounded disappointed. "I thought we were friends now. Friends don't lie to each other. Or do they?"

"No," Matt gasped.

"So?"

The pressure kept increasing until he was about to lose his mind. "Yes!" Deep in his heart, Matt had known it to be true. He'd wanted Daniel gone. And on that night, he'd wanted him dead.

Daniel smiled happily. "Because of Samantha."

"Yes." She'd gone off and dated this random guy, after all. And then she'd paraded him around at his birthday party.

"That must have been so hard for you," Daniel mused, still leaning on the sword. "There you are, practically throwing yourself at her. You're a born charmer, good-looking, strong... and she introduces you to me. A simple human." He spoke almost the exact thoughts that were running through Matt's head. "Not an easy thing for someone so used to getting what he wants."

Blood was flowing from around the tip. Matt groaned in pain. "What do *you* want?"

"I already told you. Justice."

Matt gasped for breath. The pain was excruciating. "But you're dead. There is no justice. It's just…" He was breathing harder. "It's just another human construct. The only thing that matters is strength." It was what he'd been taught day in and day out. Caspar had never suffered from justice, no matter how much Matt had cried for it. Either you were strong enough or you were dead.

"Not for Samantha, it doesn't," Daniel said, unimpressed.

"Samantha doesn't understand." Desperation was creeping into Matt's voice. He'd tried to explain it to her, but she wouldn't even listen to him.

Daniel had stopped smiling, his face darkening. "She'll never forgive you."

"I can live with that." Sure, it bothered him at the moment, but he'd get over it.

A snort, and the sword slipped even deeper. "I thought we were beyond lying to each other." Daniel no longer held back. He pushed the sword forward until Matt was screaming below him. "You like her."

"Go away!"

"Not until you tell me the truth," Daniel hissed.

There wouldn't be much time left to tell the truth. "What else do you want to know?" The pain drove Matt insane, and something burst inside out of him. "Yes! Yes, I wanted to kill you that night. I wanted to make you suffer, to make you bleed, to make you go away. You had no right to barge in there and steal Samantha away from me. Just because—"

"Matt?" The voice didn't belong to Daniel. It was familiar. Gentle. Female.

"Menu?" Matt blinked at his sister, then back at Daniel. But the dead boy was gone, and with him the rest of the illusion vanished. There was no sword, no blood. The only damage to the flat was that which Matt had caused in his insanity.

He slowly got up to a sitting position and looked down at his chest. No blood there, either. He was completely unharmed. But he was shaking. Sweat was running down his face, plastering his hair to his forehead and his shirt to his chest. His pulse was racing, and breathing hurt. "It was only an illusion."

"What did you see?" Menuha asked, kneeling down next to him.

Matt waved her off. "Nothing... I... Forget about it." It wasn't real. None of it was real. Apart from the pain. The pain deep inside of him was still there.

"Matt, I heard you!" Menuha said firmly. "Was it him? David?"

"Daniel," Matt corrected automatically.

Behind her, the door opened as his father returned. René stood in the hallway and stared. "What happened in here?"

Shame flooded Matt. In his frenzy, he'd been throwing around black magic and punching the floor. A vase was broken, and a chair was lying on the carpet. He knew it would be worse in the kitchen where he'd driven his sword into the countertop. "I'm sorry."

"He was in the throes of a powerful illusion," Menuha explained in his stead. "Though who cast it, I don't know."

"It doesn't matter," Matt whispered. Dion was irrelevant. As he'd explained, the illusion had been crafted from his own mind. Matt had been his own tormentor, and he'd managed to surpass all of Caspar's previous attempts.

Shuddering, he let his forehead sink against his knees, taking one shaky breath after another. All this time, he'd pushed what had happened away, had refused to acknowledge it, but deep inside, he hated it. Hated what had happened. Hated what *he'd* done. And hated himself more than anything.

"Hey," Menuha was stroking his back, uncharacteristically caring. "It's over. You're alive."

"Yeah..." Alive was good, right? Then why did he feel so bad about it?

The hand on his back fell away as his father came closer and put his arms around him. Matt didn't want his comfort—he didn't deserve it—but his resistance weakened, and he sank into the embrace, feeling weaker than he'd ever had before, yet somehow safe.

"Matt," René said softly. "You'll get through this. *We'll* get through this."

But who would he be when he finally came out the other side?

René held him tight while stroking his head. Matt's throat tightened, and his eyes burned with an unfamiliar sensation. Then Crumbs returned and pushed his wet nose under René's arm and against Matt's cheek. Instantly, Matt reached out to him, wrapping his arms around the puppy in a way he couldn't with his father. Fingers sinking into Crumbs' golden fur, Matt took one painful breath after the other.

Slowly, he pushed his feelings back until they were safe and out of reach.

The past couldn't be changed, but that didn't mean his future was lost. He just had to fight a little harder for it.

Fabian

On Friday afternoon, Fabian went straight to Samantha's home from school. "If Lucille wants us to arrive before six, we need to get started right away," he announced as soon as they'd slipped off their shoes and gone upstairs to Samantha's room. Fortunately, all the utensils were already deposited here.

"Can I get us something to drink first?" Samantha asked, slightly amused.

"Why didn't you get it before we came up here?" Fabian sat down at the desk and took a deep breath. They had less than three hours until the start of the party, and he had to do at least three sets of make-up and prosthetics, starting with Samantha. "Sorry. It all sounded much better before I considered the actual time we would need."

Samantha giggled, then gave his shoulders a quick massage. "Relax. It doesn't have to be perfect. Now get your craft supplies ready while I get some drinks. If I'm going to be body painted, I'll *need* something to drink."

"Don't forget straws!" Fabian called after her. Better be safe with the face colour.

Alone in the room, he bent down to the bags of make-up and costumes to get everything ready. For Samantha, that meant green body paint, lipstick, a prosthetic nose, plus grotesquely twisted fingernails. For himself, he put aside some red and black paint and a set of horns. He'd thought about going topless to make the costume more effective, but the amount of work on his whole body put him off that idea. That and the fact that it was a school party.

A robe would have to do, though that would make him look more like a Sith lord than some sort of demon. Considering that demons were almost indistinguishable from humans, it was probably a good thing.

Samantha was taking her sweet time. When she finally returned, she'd brought apple juice and a bag of chips. "When's Rachel coming over?"

"Once she's gotten dressed, I think." At least, that was what Rachel had said at school. She probably didn't want to hang out the full three hours before the party, watching Fabian paint until his hands were sore. And since her make-up would only consist of a fake nose and a few warts, she'd take relatively little time.

"If you want the paint to be seamless, you need to take off your top." Fabian hoped that didn't sound too weird. He truly was only interested in the art side of it. Why go to all the trouble of painting her green if one could see strips of white skin peeking out from underneath?

Samantha seemed to think the same and shrugged out of her top, leaving only her bra on. Then she dutifully sat down on a chair opposite to him and pinned up her hair. "Do you need to see the neckline of the dress? It's not very deep." She used her hands to show him where she thought it would fall on her breasts.

Despite the ship having long sailed, Fabian felt the heat creep up his neck. Art. Art, he told himself, trying his best not to think about how in a few minutes, he would run his paintbrush across the top of her breasts. At last, he decided it must be the memory. That and the fact that he hadn't had sex in a year, despite having had a girlfriend for half as long.

Somehow, Fabian managed a perfectly nonchalant, "We'll fix it later if there are any pale spots left afterwards."

The next half an hour was spent with painting Samantha's neckline, arms, and back green, while trying not to think too hard about where his paintbrush went. He was proud of himself when he stood up to give his work a good look. No spots, even colour distribution. Only the face was still bare. But before he would tackle her face, he would have to attach the prosthetic nose.

"This feels weird." Samantha was doing her best to keep perfectly still, but her nose twitched on its own accord from time to time.

"Just while the glue dries," Fabian promised.

Both their smartphones buzzed, and Fabian slapped Samantha's hand away as she reached for hers. "Not while you're drying."

Samantha snorted, annoyed. "What does it say, maestro?"

Fabian glanced at the message. "It's from Matt. He's bringing Menuha to the party."

"Great." Samantha let out a giant sigh. "All in the spirit of Walpurgis, I guess."

With her nose dry, Fabian started the more careful process of painting her face. "Speaking of Menuha. Did she ever catch up with you?"

"No?" Samantha sounded confused. "Was she looking for me?"

For a moment, Fabian contemplated whether he should tell her about the weird conversation they'd had in her absence. He decided it was only fair. "She was interested in whether you and Matt—"

"Hate each other?"

"Have slept with each other."

Instantly, Samantha lowered her face, forcing him to hold his paintbrush away from her. "What? If he dropped off the earth tonight, I wouldn't care. I certainly wouldn't sleep with him. And if he thinks there's a chance in Hell that'll happen, he's more deluded than I thought." The green vein on her neck pulsed angrily.

"He didn't ask," Fabian hurried to say. "And his sister meant before all of that. Before Daniel." He bit his lip. "You didn't, did you?"

"Of course not!" Taking a deep breath, she forced herself to relax again. "We almost kissed one time. Hardly something to write home about for a lust demon." She closed her eyes, but the muscles in her cheeks kept twitching as she fought whatever memories haunted her.

Fabian dipped the paintbrush back into the pot. "Why would his sister be interested in that?"

"I don't know," Samantha whispered.

"I know she's a demon, but she seems... nice." Disconcertingly nice. Like a fluffy cat inviting you to stroke it only to scratch you bloody if you got too close.

For a long time, Samantha didn't say anything, working her jaw while Fabian carefully applied paint to her face. Then, after a little while, he barely caught the whisper, "He also seemed nice."

Before Fabian could say something, they heard the bell ring downstairs. "I'll go." He put down the pot and carefully lowered his paintbrush before going downstairs to open the door, only to get a fright.

"Rachel!"

His girlfriend had put on a check-patterned, sack-like skirt and a blouse of the colour of washed-out pink. A triangular scarf covered her hair, but the thing that had scared him was the huge hump on her back that made her body look grotesquely off-balance.

"Great job!" he exclaimed. "You even gave me a scare. Come upstairs, I'm almost done with Samantha's paint job. Then I can put the finishing touches on you."

"Spoken like a true artist," Rachel joked.

"What can I say? I have the best muse."

They returned to the room, where Samantha had used the time to put on her dress and the green lipstick. The dress was a black corset style top with an equally black skirt that had been torn until the fabric hung down in tatters around her hips, while she'd left the simple bustier alone. Fabian was pleased to see that there would be no glimpses of her real skin colour under all that green, but his gaze caught a little too long on her neckline.

"Hello, Rachel. That hump looks amazing!"

Reminded of his girlfriend's presence, Fabian coughed and grabbed the paint pot. "Shall I finish your face? Your eyes are still untouched." While he dipped the paintbrush back inside, he checked his watch. "And then I really need to get my stuff done. You can do your nails by yourself, right?"

"Or with Rachel's help." Samantha smiled.

He proceeded to finish off the job with the green, then accented her eyes with black. "That's as much as I can do with a brush. You might want to touch up with make-up yourself."

"Thanks." Samantha regarded herself in a little handheld mirror. "You outdid yourself. Great job."

She freed the chair for Rachel, who'd been sitting on the bed, and grabbed her hairbrush to comb her locks the wrong way. Fabian winced as he watched the black mass puff up into a storm cloud. He did *not* want to be in charge of untangling it after the party.

An hour later, Rachel sported a hideous nose, several warts, and deep lines that aged her face as much as the hump aged her body, while Fabian's face was bright red, clashing devilishly with his ginger hair. Black lightning stripes accented his jawline and cheekbones, while two horns protruded from his hairline. In the meantime, Samantha's parents had come home from work, while music and giggles from next door told them Jan and Meg were also getting ready.

Samantha's hair was one big black cloud, spreading out from underneath the black witch hat she'd been using for several years. "Quarter past five. We should get going," she announced.

"Is Jan driving?" Fabian asked, packing up his stuff. He'd got his driver's license in the Easter holidays and occasionally borrowed the old family car. It would be a tight fit with five people, but easier than taking the bikes.

"Yeah, though I'm not sure I'm ready to trust my life with him," Samantha joked, then knocked on her sister's bedroom door.

As per house rules, the door had to be opened while Jan visited, much to Meg's dismay. That apparently didn't stop the two from passionately making out on the bed and flying apart at Samantha's knock.

Jan straightened up and grinned sheepishly. He was wearing a cheap set of horns and had put yellow contact lenses in. The uninspired costume was completed by a plastic trident. Meanwhile, Meg was definitely going for sexy witch, with a black mini dress, two different coloured striped stockings, and pointy, black nails. "Is it time?" she asked, a little too excited.

"Are you driving?" Samantha asked Jan.

"Yes! Though one of you better drive back, because I will definitely drink." He grinned wildly.

Meg clapped his chest. "Shh, not so loud. My parents are downstairs."

"Actually, I'm right here," Ben announced, having just come up the stairs. He took all of them in. "Wow. Great job, Beanstalk." He clapped Fabian on the shoulder. Then he leaned towards Samantha. "I want you to keep an eye on your sister at all times."

"Dad!" Meg groaned.

Ben raised a finger. "Hey, we allowed you to go. That doesn't mean the rules don't apply. No alcohol, no sex."

Meg grimaced. "Ew." Then she crossed her arms while Jan wisely kept quiet. "What's the point of going to a party if you can't party?"

"You're welcome to stay with us and go to the bonfire in the city square instead," Ben offered innocently.

Meg threw her arms up dramatically and stomped out of her room with a defiant, "Fine, I won't have fun then."

Ben sighed, once more turning to Samantha. "I trust you'll keep her out of trouble. And call me about the driving. We'll pick you up."

"We're going to sleep over," Samantha said instead. When her father's brow twitched, she added hastily, "And I'm sharing a room with Meg. I promise to do my very best to keep her out of trouble."

Fabian thought that even her very best would not be enough to keep Meg from throwing some teenage tantrum, but between them, they might stand a chance. If Jan didn't take her side.

He sighed. With Meg hell-bent on letting out her wild side and real demons prowling the dance floor, this Walpurgis Night would be one for the ages.

Lucille

"Part of me wants to kill him," Matt told Lucille when he arrived with Menuha an hour before the official start of the party.

Lucille had been warned that Menuha was in Greenvalley and going to attend her party, but she was actually delighted. It might have been a bit premature, but she liked Matt's sister and saw no reason to mistrust her. Matt, however... "Which part of you *exactly* wants to kill him?"

Matt rolled his eyes. "It was a figure of speech."

"Don't pretend that's obvious." She looked around to see whether she could spot Dion anywhere, but the illusionist hadn't joined Matt. "Where is he?"

"In town with Amélie, I assume." Matt had lost interest and picked up a pastry from the buffet. Between bites, he eventually admitted, "We got in a bit of a fight. I called him out for playing me all week."

Lucille felt a little sorry that the two of them had wasted their entire week on pettiness, but the mention of a fight made her wary. "What did you do to him?"

"What did *I* do to him? He caught me in an illusion." Matt swallowed, belatedly concerned about his pride. "I mean, he barely did anything, but... he almost got me killed. While he walked off in a huff, I... Never mind." He devoured the pastry and went for a second to avoid talking about it.

"If I understand it correctly—" Menuha chimed in.

"Don't!" Matt glared at her.

Menuha's shoulders deflated. "Don't you think it is something your friends should know?"

"Absolutely not! Lucille will just read something into it that isn't there and bother me for the rest of the evening."

Lucille promptly crossed her arms, her curiosity piqued. "If you didn't want to be bothered all evening, you shouldn't have phrased it that way. Now I'm going to be pestering you until you tell me what I—your *friend*—should know."

"You've got a party to throw. You don't have time for me."

She smiled sweetly. "Too bad you came an hour early."

"Shouldn't the others be here by now, too?" Matt tried to deflect.

"Oh, I get it now," Menuha exclaimed. "You don't want to tell Lucille because you need to tell Samantha first."

Instantly, Matt started to choke on his pastry, spitting flakes all over the floor and across his lips. Once he'd recovered, he wiped his mouth and took a deep breath. "She's literally the last person I want to talk to about this."

Lucille couldn't help herself. This was getting more intriguing by the minute. "Matt, just tell me. What kind of illusion did Dion confront you with?"

"I need a drink," Matt announced and walked right past the buffet table laden with drinks. On second thoughts, he returned, grabbed Menuha by the arm, and stalked off again.

"Running away won't help you," Lucille called after him. All thoughts of pursuit came to a standstill, though, when she saw Dion and Amélie enter the room.

Amélie had a shopping bag under her arm and was looking around in wonder. When she spotted Lucille, she leaned over to Dion and left again, presumably to go to her room.

Meanwhile, Dion had been staring at her the second he'd crossed the doorstep. A soft smile played around his lips the longer he stood there. Lucille felt her heart flutter and the corners of her mouth stretch. All thoughts of Matt fled as she bounced towards him. "Hey."

"Nice set-up," he nodded towards the witch-inspired decorations all over the ballroom. "Appropriate, not just for today."

Lucille laughed. "You got me. I do enjoy a good broomstick ride from time to time." The minute she thought about his illusions, the altercation with Matt returned to her mind. "Uhm... Matt just arrived a few minutes ago. He says you trapped him in an illusion?"

"He got himself free?" Dion asked. "I kind of hoped he'd stay trapped for the rest of today. He threatened me. Said I was first on his list of people to murder."

Lucille began to massage the bridge of her nose. It sounded to her as if Matt had put his foot in his mouth once again. Or perhaps the whole leg. "I'm sure he didn't mean it that way."

"He said it happened once." Dion grimaced and made air quotes. "Only once."

Matt had told him about the Blood Night? "Uhm, I don't know what to say..." She shook her head. "Dion, you *are* safe with him. I promise. He's just... all over the place at the moment. What kind of illusion did you trap him in?"

"I have no idea. It's a mind-based illusion where the magic feeds off the victim's own fears and doubts. He said, being a demon, it wouldn't work on him—"

"But he's half human," Lucille surmised. She was simultaneously impressed by the potential illusions seemed to bear and worried about Matt. If he'd been confronted with his darkest parts... Well, there was only one thing Lucille could think of that would torment him. And it absolutely had to do with Samantha. "Dion, I know you and he don't get along very well, but he's my friend, so please don't do it to him again. Unless, of course, he actually threatens your life."

Dion looked up to the ceiling as if to ask for heaven's mercy. "After what you said, I *was* scared. How can you be friends with a demon? Aren't they some kind of monster?" He pointed at the devil masks hanging from the ceiling. "Sinister seducers on their best day, horrifying creatures the rest of the time?"

"Those are just stories." Though sinister seducer was pretty much Matt's go-to coping mechanism. "He's going through something." She knew she couldn't leave Dion hanging with that, so she quickly came up with a simpler version of what was going on. "He doesn't act like it, but he's in love with a friend of mine. They were sort of going out, but he blew it, because he's still learning what it means to be human.

So now she hates him. And he doesn't cope well with it. Going back and forth between denial and—"

"Torment." Dion sighed. "Fine, I won't bother him anymore. If he stays away from me."

"I'll have a word with him." Lucille smiled sadly at him. She took a deep breath to clear her mind. "So, an illusion of the mind. How does that work?"

Dion laughed, seemingly glad she'd changed topics. "I could tell you, but it would sound like gibberish. Basically, all illusions are based in the target's mind. The more a target believes in what they see, the stronger it becomes. Logic is an illusion's enemy. And your biggest asset if you ever find yourself locked in an illusion battle."

He picked up her hand and stretched out her arm, his gaze trailing a vein. "Some of them are subtle," his finger brushed over her wrist softly as a feather, "just small things that lead to disorientation, while others are full-on. In your face." Dion's lips curled slightly as he intertwined his fingers with hers. "To make them believable requires some strength."

Lucille had held her breath the moment he'd taken her hand. Now she let it out with a shudder. "Fascinating." She shook her head, laughing about her own enthralment. "You said only an illusionist could see through illusions."

"Yeah, that's the gist of it. Some people's minds reject them. Their sense of logic makes it hard for them to accept an illusion, but they don't register something is off. You, however, noticed." He beamed, and Lucille marvelled at the whiteness of his teeth. "It might just be because you're familiar with magic. But I would bet my left arm you're a budding illusionist as well. And I'm left-handed."

She burst out laughing and used the motion to lean into him, her arm touching the length of his. "Show me."

Dion's eyes got stuck on her lips a little too long. "Right," he said, his voice unsteady. "An illusionist's biggest tool is their mind. For a simple one, you need to envision whatever object you want to create perfectly in your mind. Not like a picture, but like a 3D image. And more than that. You also need to consider smell and feel, perhaps even sound." He laughed softly. "But let's not make it too complicated." Then he pointed at the buffet. "Can you replicate that grape?"

Lucille turned to focus on the fruit collection. There were slices of apples, fresh strawberries, dragon fruit, and a bunch of grapes. She narrowed her eyes and concentrated on the egg-like shape of it.

Dion laughed. "What kind of grape is that?"

A single grape had appeared on the plate next to it, but it was the colour of eggshell, not the rich purple of the real grapes. "I'm sorry, I only concentrated on the shape of it."

"You managed that easily enough." Dion took a step forward, pulling her with him to pick up the grape she had created.

Lucille tried her best to uphold the shape and change the colour while she was at it, but Dion was much faster. Despite it being only an illusion, he held the grape between his thumb and index finger and watched its colour changing to a delicious purple. Then he brought it up to her mouth and squeezed.

Once again, Lucille forgot how to breathe. She trailed the grape with her eyes and gasped when the juice hit her lips. It was as sweet as a real one. Sweeter even. It formed beads on her lips, then ran down her chin.

Panicking about making a mess out of herself, she quickly wiped her chin, but her fingers came away dry. The grape was gone again.

Instead, Dion was looking at her, his own breath shallow and intermittent. "You look very beautiful today."

"You look—"

"Wasn't there supposed to be a fire?" Matt had returned, but stopped short. "Oh, it's you."

Even Lucille couldn't deny the dangerous undercurrent in his voice. She let go of Dion and stepped in between him and Matt. "Are you done sulking?" she asked.

The tension eased. "I wasn't sulking. I... Looks like I've interrupted something." Matt was quickly becoming a master of deflection. "I'll take myself elsewhere."

"Don't," Dion begged. He sighed deeply. "Matt, I... I owe you an apology. Two, I guess." Matt raised an eyebrow, and Dion continued, "I'm sorry I left you alone with my illusion. That was irresponsible. And my grandfather would have my hide for it if he knew." He took a deep breath. "And I'm sorry about pretending I didn't understand a word you were saying. It was silly of me."

Impressed, Lucille turned to Matt. "Do *you* have anything to say to Dion?"

"That illusion was messed up," Matt retorted, completely missing her cues. "You almost got me killed."

"Illusions don't kill anyone," Dion protested, confused.

"They do if your victim truly believes they should be dead," Matt informed him icily.

It took a moment for Lucille to fully understand what he was saying. "Matt, you don't—"

"It's okay," he said, a little too quickly. "I survived. And I'm not planning to get myself killed by any means." He nodded at Dion. "You didn't know, and I... I probably deserved that after telling you it wouldn't affect me. I honestly thought it wouldn't."

The two boys stared at each other in silence. Although Matt hadn't apologised for his own behaviour, Dion relaxed. "I trust you did." Then he said to Lucille, "You're right, he's much more human than he pretends to be."

"What?" Matt piped up instantly, looking outraged.

Dion only grinned. "You might be the biggest illusionist of us all. You've even got yourself fooled." Then he rubbed Lucille's back. "I'll go and find a bathroom. Can't wait for the party to start. It'll be the only one with real witches and demons."

Lucille could only sigh about that. "Let's hope they all play nicely. Especially you!" she said to Matt. The last thing she needed was for Matt and Samantha to get into an epic fight on Walpurgis Night.

"I'll do my best not to step on her toes. But I can't promise anything."

It had to suffice.

Samantha

Lucille had gone all out for her first Walpurgis Night party. The driveway put every American Halloween display to shame, while the entranceway looked as if Lucille had bought every wooden witch doll souvenir in the region. The party itself was in a ballroom big enough to hold at least a hundred people. Fake spiderwebs hung from the ceiling, and between them, frightening devil masks. The lights were dim, and a smoke machine set up for a mystical atmosphere. Several brooms hung at mid-height, as if invisible witches were flying through the air.

On one end, a buffet table was overflowing with food, though the centrepiece was a huge bowl of May wine, an aromatised wine punch with the distinct fragrance of sweet woodruff and strawberries. On the other end, a DJ was preparing his setlist for the night. This early in the night, there were only a few guests, with the personnel still making last-minute arrangements.

The sight was so overwhelming, Samantha even forgot to be annoyed at Meg, whose bad mood had brought them all down during the drive here. Her momentary awe was quickly dampened when she saw Matt and Menuha standing with Lucille. Neither had got the memo about dressing up as witches or devils. Matt was being his usual handsome self, and Menuha was wearing oddly fashioned pants and a nearly see-through tunic.

Lucille noticed them and waved excitedly. She was wearing a beautiful skirt that was shorter in the front, like a dress straight out of a Western. With it, she'd combined a corsage that pushed her breasts up enticingly, the rubies of her necklace shimmering above them.

Samantha couldn't say it was a particularly witchy outfit, but she looked gorgeous.

Next to her, Matt was almost subdued. Though, considering the alternative could've been him coming in his demon form, complete with leathery wings, Samantha much preferred this lacklustre version.

"Wow!" Lucille greeted them before proceeding to stalk around them and regard their costumes from all sides. "I'm starting to realise I completely underestimated the witch factor of Walpurgis Night. That make-up is *brilliant*!"

Samantha pointed at Fabian. "It pays to have an artist best friend."

Revelling in the praise, Fabian bowed dramatically. "Thank you, thank you. I aim to please."

"I am impressed," Lucille said, and clearly meant it.

"You texted about the bonfire?" Jan asked.

Lucille sighed. "Yes! It was supposed to be built up during the day, but the guy we hired to do it never showed."

"You got the wood?" When Lucille nodded, he leaned over to Meg to kiss her before clapping Fabian's shoulder. "Come on, junior scout. We're going to make fire!"

"You mean I build a bonfire while you stand around and give me stupid tips?" Fabian joked.

Jan grabbed two bottles of beer from the table. "Helpful tips. And I'll hold your beer."

Fabian seemed content with that arrangement, and the two of them went outside on the patio.

Next to Samantha, Meg had crossed her arms and pulled a face, as if the entire party was disgustingly lame. "Can I go now, or do I have to spend the entire evening with you, dying from boredom?"

While Lucille frowned, Samantha said, "You know what Dad said." It's not like she enjoyed the arrangement any better.

Meg rolled her eyes spectacularly. "Yeah, yeah. Can I at least get a drink, or do you have to hold my hand for that as well?"

Samantha sighed, resigning herself to failure. Meg took that as a "yes" and stalked off towards the May wine.

"Uhm, I had actually planned this as an eighteen-plus party," Lucille said, sceptically watching Meg pour herself some punch.

"I know, I'm sorry, but you can thank Jan for that. He put it in her head to come along." And Samantha was sure it wasn't the only thing he had put in her head.

Lucille was still frowning. "She doesn't look like she wants to be here."

Samantha winced. "Well, my parents aren't stupid. They let Meg go, but with the caveat that I look after her. She doesn't like it. I don't like it either, but I'm now the bad guy."

"Meg is in one of her Megzilla moods," Rachel added helpfully. She'd never got along with Meg.

"What's up with your skin?" Matt asked, frowning deeply. "I get that you're dressing up as witches and demons, but shouldn't you guys know better what they look like?"

For a moment, Samantha had almost managed to tune him out. Now she noticed how excited Menuha seemed as she took in their costumes, while Matt glowered at her. "Are you telling me *that* is your costume? It's not very convincing, even if you are a demon. Perhaps I can get you a sword? A little bloodbath livens up every party."

Matt gasped for air. He looked as if he'd been about to say something else, but now his eyes narrowed. "And does that idea make you so sick you've already turned green?"

Samantha glared at him. Before she could answer, though, Lucille got between them. "Hey, guys, can't we please just enjoy the party?" She turned to Matt and Menuha. "It is customary for this night to dress up. Pointy hats and long noses are how people have always visualised witches."

"And the green colour?" Matt asked, still confused.

"Gosh, when are you finally going to get a pop culture tutor?" Samantha shot at him. After dealing with Meg's moodiness all the way here, she had zero patience for his ignorance.

Matt breathed in through his nose, nostrils flaring. Then he turned on his heel. "Let's check out the food, Menu." As he and his sister stalked away, Samantha heard him mutter, "Looks to me like both Kollmer sisters are in a bad mood."

Samantha almost threw something at his head, but lacking an object, she let it go. Meanwhile, Menuha looked over her shoulder and mouthed, "I'm loving all of it" at her. Samantha massaged her temples in an attempt to avoid a massive headache.

When she turned back to the others, she found Lucille smiling pitifully at her. "Come on, I'll introduce you to someone. That'll make you feel better." She looped her arm into Samantha's and waved Rachel along as she guided them over to the French students.

Despite her involvement in the program, Samantha had spent next-to-no time with the actual exchange students, but she saw how Dion's eyes glinted as soon as he caught Lucille's gaze. Samantha subtly checked her friend, and sure enough, there was a smile dancing on her lips.

"This is Matt's partner, Dion." The handsome student had peeled away from the French group to meet them. "He's an illusionist. Proper magic."

"For real?" Samantha had heard of witches weaving powerful illusions, but she hadn't met any.

As if to confirm Lucille's announcement, Dion spread his hands like a street magician. Suddenly, there was a bat in his hand, its tiny claws holding on to his fingers. Once he stroked its back with one finger, the little creature took flight, only to vanish the moment it entered a shadowy place.

Samantha was deeply impressed. She could've sworn the cute bat had been real.

Lucille nodded excitedly. "You see? And he says I could be one too. I don't know about that, but wouldn't it be cool?" Belatedly, she introduced them to him. "These are Samantha and Rachel. Samantha is a witch like me, though her speciality is weaving spells, and Rachel wanders the dreamworld. She even glimpses the future from time to time."

"Not that it's particularly helpful," Rachel muttered.

"Wow. C'est magnifique." Dion laughed. "So many witches in one place. I thought it was all make-believe, but there truly must be something magical about these mountains."

"Yes, it's magic," Samantha said, amused. As promised, her bad mood was blown away by this exciting revelation. "There's a spring of magic not too far from town. Rivers of magic flow through the entire region," she explained, much to Dion's excitement.

In a few moments, they were excitedly comparing notes. Weaving a proper illusion was completely different from her own magic, and yet similar enough to find parallels. Over the last two months, she'd gotten better and better at it, but she was no match for Dion's perfect illusions. While she amused herself, the guests started to arrive.

Forty minutes later, the party was packed. Music was playing, and people were dancing or chatting. As usual, Samantha didn't know what to do with herself at a party—especially because her friends seemed to be busy elsewhere—so she'd resorted to taking her responsibility of watching Meg seriously. Standing near a wall, she'd observed her dancing with some friends or acquaintances she'd found and making far too much use of the May wine for the short amount of time that had passed.

And now she'd gotten herself ensnared by the Elite Clique.

All four girls had surrounded Meg, as if she was their new best friend, and Meg was lapping it up. Samantha, meanwhile, felt her skin crawling. Sure, eight years ago Ani had been a good friend to Meg, back when she'd also been best friends with Samantha, but ever since Cheryl had entered the stage, Ani hadn't spared so much as a single glance for her younger sister. Her sudden interest now didn't bode well at all.

Samantha was just about to brace herself and draw both Cheryl's and Meg's ire, when someone bumped into her shoulder. Laughing, the guy with a wood-cut devil's mask turned around to apologise, but then stopped.

"Sam?" The voice was hollow under the mask and unrecognisable. He pushed his mask up to his forehead, revealing himself as Cian. His eyes ran her up and down. What he saw seemed to delight him greatly. "Wicked costume."

"Thanks," Samantha muttered. She couldn't help but smile because he immediately got the reference. Still, anxiety won out. She reminded herself that she couldn't be sure of his kindness. While they got along splendidly in Chemistry, he was a friend of Cheryl's. One could never be too cautious around the Elite Clique. No matter how charming they appeared.

Cian grinned wildly. "I love it when girls really go for it. All these sexy vamps, sexy witches, sexy Little Red Riding Hood... it gets so lame. While this," he pointed at all of her, "is awesome. Hey, do you want a drink?" He waved at one of the servers who was walking through the crowd in addition to the buffet. "It's so hot under this mask."

"It looks hot," Samantha commiserated.

"Thanks." Cian gave her a cheeky grin, which made Samantha curse her unfortunate choice of words, and grabbed two glasses of Coke from the tray. He handed one to Samantha. "Well, it's only once a year, right?" After drinking hastily from his glass, he belatedly clinked it against hers. "I was hoping to see you tonight."

"Is that so?" Samantha sipped from her own glass, still waiting for the other shoe to drop.

"Yes! I was going to ask you something about redox reactions." And there it was. He was asking her about school, the only topic she was worth conversing with.

Cian waited for three seconds before he burst out laughing. "That was a joke. As if I was only thinking of redox reactions during Walpurgis Night."

Samantha breathed in, somewhat relieved. Maybe she was judging Cian prematurely. "You wouldn't have been the first to ask." People found all sorts of occasions appropriate to ask her questions about schoolwork.

"Ouch." Cian winced. "I guess you have a reputation."

She raised her eyebrows. "Like what?" Samantha was one-hundred-percent sure that she was at the bottom of any popularity lists, so whatever reputation she had couldn't be good. Not after Cheryl had carefully curated her image for the last eight years.

"As being kind and helpful. And smart," Cian explained to her complete surprise. "Plus, you don't make people feel dumb when they ask. Like in Chemistry. God knows I would've already thrown my Bunsen burner at Robert after one of his dumb questions. But you stay patient and never once snap at him. Or anyone."

Which practically meant she was a pushover, Samantha thought, but bit her tongue. Cian *was* being nice to her. So, instead of refuting him, she leaned into it. "Robert definitely tests my limits. If we don't stay vigilant, he'll blow us all up one day."

"Is that why you always put him on the menial tasks?" Cian asked, amused.

Samantha felt her cheeks grow hot. "You noticed that?"

"Well, duh! Not that I'm complaining. I'd much rather take over the tricky bits than wash out glasses or measure something. So, by all means, keep Robert busy. And from blowing us up."

Slowly, Samantha was warming to him. "I just really like staying alive."

"Me too!" Cian finished off his glass. "Hey, do you want to go outside and see whether the bonfire is burning?"

Even at her most self-conscious, Samantha couldn't think of any boring reason why he'd be interested in that. Which meant that the only explanation was that Cian *wanted* to spend more time with her. "Sure. I'd like that."

They were about to go when Shayna suddenly caught up to them. Her eyes were wide, as if she'd seen a ghost. She grabbed Samantha's arm, digging her fingers in painfully. "Sam! You need to come. Your sister. She's sick or something. Please..."

Instantly, Samantha started running. Shayna led her out of the ballroom and into a smaller room further down the corridor. It wasn't a bathroom as Samantha had feared, but some sort of sitting room. All the furniture had been moved to the side, so there was enough space for a group of people to sit around a Ouija board. Only there was no one. Just the ominous board and a half-burnt candle.

Samantha's heart grew cold. This looked like a trap. The Elite Clique had successfully lured her here to have their fun with her. And they'd brought a Ouija board because she was a witch.

She turned to Shayna and crossed her arms. "This isn't funny."

"I never said it was!" Shayna cried. "We..." She swallowed several times. "We were summoning a ghost, and Meg... It was supposed to be just for fun. Cheryl was planning to move the planchette and give Meg a fright, but then your sister started convulsing. Like she was shaking and went completely unresponsive." Tears stood in her eyes as she looked around the empty room. "I have no idea where she is now."

And, of course, the other three Elite girls were nowhere to be seen. They'd fled at the first sight of trouble brewing. That was *if* there truly had been a medical emergency.

"Man, Shayna, do you have to pull this shit all the time?" Cian complained. He had followed them here and wasn't pleased at all.

"We didn't do anything!" Shayna cried. She shook her head, while a few tears ran down her face. "What if she was feeling better and returned to the party?"

Frothing on the floor, before getting up and walking away. Samantha rolled her eyes. That line of events was very unlikely. Which meant this really was just a big joke at her expense.

The question was just whether the joke was on Meg, or whether she was in on it.

"I need to search for my sister." She left Shayna with Cian, who instantly started to berate her, and went to look for Meg.

Jan

When Lu had said the person responsible for the bonfire hadn't shown, Jan had expected this to take ten minutes max. But the moment they'd found the wood neatly piled up around the corner, it was clear it was going to take a very long time. The fire pit hadn't even been built. For half an hour, he and Fabian had laboured away, carrying the provided logs to the stone area where it could burn down safely. By the time they were finished, sweat was ruining Fabian's magnificent paint job, and they well and truly deserved their beer.

As they sat near the pile of wood, taking a break, Jan decided to breach the important topic of the night. "Hey, uhm... could you keep Sam busy for the rest of the night so I can slip away with Meg?" Annoyingly, Meg's father had guessed their original plan and convinced Samantha to watch her sister's every step. As annoyed as Samantha had seemed, Jan knew better than to hope she'd do anything but heed her father's wishes.

Fabian raised an eyebrow. "You really want to have sex with Meg here?"

"Well, if there is a quiet room for us to do it in without the chance of someone barging in, it's in this mansion."

"I don't know." Fabian put his beer down and knelt by the pile of wood to get the fire started.

Jan groaned. "Hey, come on, don't pull the big brother card just because you've known Meg since she was a baby. She's not a child anymore. She wants this as much as I do."

"I don't care about Meg," Fabian claimed with a shoulder shrug. "She's annoying. I never know what to do with her."

"*You* don't need to do anything. I'm the one doing her." Jan grinned, insanely proud of his clever play on words. Especially when Fabian made a face. "At least, I want to. Please, help a man out." A thought crossed his mind. "Unless, of course, you've got plans for tonight." Jan wriggled his eyebrows for extra emphasis.

Fabian turned to him and frowned. "Like what?"

Jan boxed his shoulder, annoyed over his friend playing dumb. "You and Rachel. I suppose with her mother being so neglectful, you've got much fewer problems getting into her pants."

"We haven't gone there," Fabian said quickly, as if to shut him up.

"You haven't?" Jan counted backwards in his head and was shocked to realise that his friends had been together for half a year. Almost as long as he and Meg had been a couple. "What are you waiting for? An invitation?"

Fabian was concentrating on the fire a little too hard. Jan saw his shoulders bunching and twisting, as if he had to cut the words from his muscle strands. "It hasn't happened yet."

"Then make it happen!" Jan groaned and shook his head. "Plan a romantic date or whisk her away to a room here."

"Sure."

If that wasn't a lacklustre response, Jan was prepared to swallow a log. "What's the matter?"

"Nothing." At last, Fabian looked back up. "Nothing is happening, Jan. Not when I'm around Rachel. I don't even think about it."

That was odd. Not a single day passed for Jan without thinking about sex. "What do you mean nothing's happening? Is it... not working?" He tried for subtlety, glancing at Fabian's pants.

"I don't want to," Fabian said instead.

"What?" Jan had completely lost the plot now. "But aren't you..."

Fabian sighed. "I like Rachel, and I like being with her. It's uncomplicated and easy-going. I'm not interested in taking it any further. It... it doesn't even cross my mind when we're alone. Not anymore."

Jan still didn't get it. "Man, that's the only thing on my mind when I make out with Meg."

"Well, perhaps we don't make out enough," Fabian said, and turned back around to light the fire.

For a few moments, Jan tried to digest what Fabian had truly been saying. When he arrived at the conclusion that his friends weren't just not having sex but practically refrained from *any* kind of make-out session, he started to have concerns. "You're still a couple, though, aren't you?"

"Yes, still going strong," Fabian said a little too fast.

If that wasn't the problem, perhaps the two were taking their time—a very long time—before committing to anything. "But you're not..." Jan had no idea how to ask this. "I mean, with Samantha, you—"

"Yep." Fabian had managed to coax a flame to life. "I'm not a virgin, if that's what you're asking. My relationship with Rachel is just different. But good."

Jan didn't believe a word. No man went from a healthy sex life to complete abstinence. He figured it wasn't really his problem, though. "If you're happy that way."

Fabian stepped away from the fire, which was now licking at the bottom logs, slowly spreading. "I think so." He picked up his bottle and took a long sip. "This should do it. I'll keep watch if you want to go inside to... well, to do whatever you need to do."

"Sam?" Jan had no issue instantly switching topics to what mattered.

"Send her out to me." It wasn't quite as good as he'd hoped, but it would have to suffice.

As it turned out, Jan found Samantha easily enough, but before he could even put his ploy into motion, she had a go at him. "Where's Meg?"

"Where...?" Jan cast around the room. "You've lost track of her?" He had to give it to Meg. Slipping out of her sister's sight was a commendable feat.

But then he noticed how worried Samantha was. She shook her head in annoyance. "I saw her with Cheryl. Then Shayna came to get me with some horror tale of Meg convulsing on the ground, and since then, she's been gone."

Jan's jaw fell open as he tried to follow the hectic summary. When he'd finally grasped it, a cold fist closed around his heart. "If those girls have broken so much as a fake fingernail of hers, they're in trouble."

He took a deep breath, trying to calm himself. Once more, he glanced around the room. Cheryl wasn't hard to find, as usual, attracting a crowd of admirers. Her best friend Ani was flirting with some upperclassman, while Jennifer had found her boyfriend and was making out with him on the dance floor. The only one who looked a little worried was Shayna, who entered the room with Cian. But those worries were quickly forgotten when she was invited to a game of pool with Alan and his current girlfriend.

"Have you asked Lu?"

Samantha shook her head, exhausted. "Not yet. You were the first one I ran into. I hoped she was with you—and also hoped she wasn't with you."

Jan raised an eyebrow. "Okay. You go ask the others for help. I'll go check the bathrooms."

She nodded and hastened away. Jan took a moment to orient himself, then headed for the door Shayna had come from. Mentally, he was checking off the places Meg could be. In the bathroom, throwing up, locked in some dusty cupboard by the Elite Clique, or simply lost in the Villa de Cerque. The one place he didn't expect her to be was right in front of him as soon as he entered the corridor.

"Meg!"

So much for all that drama. Meg looked fine to him, if a little confused. Jan glanced over his shoulder and saw Samantha with Lucille and Matt, wildly gesticulating and probably getting into some unnecessary fight along the way. Perfect!

He put an arm around Meg and turned her back the way she'd come. "Quick, before your sister sees us." Let Samantha get distracted by some wild goose chase, while he and Meg turned up the heat.

Meg narrowed her eyes, but she came along willingly, if not exactly eagerly. Together, they entered the next-best room. The wallpaper was a bit tacky, and someone, probably Linda de Cerque, had a questionable taste for art, but there were two comfortable armchairs and an equally comfy sofa.

"Perfect." Jan announced as he closed the door. "This should do, right?"

Pulling Meg close, he kissed her gently on the lips. She groaned, but then she grabbed his neck, her pointy fake nails digging painfully into the sensitive skin, and kissed him back with a vigour that surprised him. Jan shuddered, instantly aroused, until her nails dug a little too deep and a fiery trace burnt across his neck.

"Ouch!"

Meg let go of him, her mouth at a sensual half-open. She took one long glance at him before pushing him towards the armchair. "Take those clothes off." Her voice was a lot huskier than usually.

Amused, Jan straightened himself. "Is that how we're going to do it?" The dominant act turned him on more than he wanted to admit.

While she regarded him with a haughty look, he undressed slowly. Or as slowly as he could manage with the powerful urge inside of him to just rip the clothes off his body. When he was done, she regarded him once more. She smiled, and his breath hitched in his throat as he fantasised about all the things that smile promised. "Sit down."

Jan didn't even consider not following her command. He sat down and waited expectantly for Meg's next step.

Her smile deepened, and she came closer to kiss him once more. Jan moved his hands towards her so he could undress her, but she slapped them away. It was all pretty hot. And surprising.

Meg straightened again. Suddenly, there was a rope in her hand. While Jan tried to figure out when she'd got it from, Meg bent over him once more to tie his arms to the armrests. Jan gasped as the rope cut into his skin.

As arousing as all of this was, it was also a little overwhelming for their first time. Meg was a virgin. He should be taking the lead, gently guiding her. Instead, he was tied up in some sort of kinky foreplay. "Shouldn't we—"

She put a finger to his lips, and he shut up again. Maybe he should just enjoy what Meg was doing to him.

Her finger pulled down his bottom lip, then ran over his chin and down his naked chest. He forgot how to breathe as the finger neared his nether regions. Meg put her hand on his thigh and locked eyes with him. Jan was begging for her fingers to move, but instead she only smiled that wicked smile of hers.

"As much as I enjoy your offer, there are things I need to do," she said in that new deep, sultry voice of hers. "I'll come back to you later."

Jan stared at her, dumbfounded, as she retreated to the door. Once there, she gave him a cheeky little wave before slipping out, leaving him alone in the dark, naked and tied up.

"Meg! Hey..." The door shut. "Shit!"

This certainly wasn't what he had planned. In fact, it confused the hell out of him. Though he had to admit it was also damn hot.

Fabian

The fire was burning well and slowly drawing in a crowd. Fabian was losing himself in the play of the flames as they licked and consumed the wood. The crackle was drowning out everything else. He didn't even register his own thoughts as he stared into the flames.

Darkness had already settled when he was suddenly woken from his trance by Rachel slipping her hand into his. "Found you."

Fabian pulled his gaze away from the fire and put his arm around her shoulders, made difficult by the awkward hump. "Hey. How's the mood inside?"

She rolled her eyes. "Typical party. The longer it runs, the dumber people act. Meg has managed to slip away. Samantha's pretty upset."

"She'll be with Jan," Fabian said with a sigh. While he didn't really care all that much for Meg, she *was* like a little sister to him. A little sister who did what she wanted, anyway. "It's quite nice out here," he said instead, and kissed Rachel's head. "Especially at the fire."

The flames reflected in Rachel's dark eyes as she looked up at him. "You did a beautiful job. It's burning a little too high now, but that'll change soon enough, I guess."

"Too high?" Fabian checked with the pyre, which was about the height of his chest. Not really the biggest fire he'd ever seen at Walpurgis Night.

"To jump over it," Rachel explained. "Don't you remember? The couple that jumps over the fire together, stays together."

He hadn't been to many Walpurgis Night fires that were low enough for that tradition. Usually because the risk was deemed too high. And somehow the risk was all he concentrated on, rather than the romantic notion Rachel had voiced out loud. "I'd be too scared of catching fire."

She frowned and took a moment to sort her thoughts before she replied, "If something *did* happen, you'd be able to put it out fairly easily."

"Truuue..." Fabian drew out the word. He supposed there was no harm in a silly tradition. It wouldn't *really* mean they'd stay together forever. And besides, wasn't that something he wanted? He thought of Jan and his utter confusion when Fabian confessed his lack of sexual interest in Rachel.

Sex didn't matter. He liked Rachel. Liked being together with her. But *forever?*

He was about to say something else when a black cloud exited the ballroom behind them, followed by a multitude of screams. It covered the sky, then broke into hundreds of small bats that quickly dispersed, leaving the Villa de Cerque behind.

The screams stopped; instead, people were cheering and whooping now. Fabian overheard one of the guys nearby praising the spooky factor of the party. Meanwhile, he exchanged a glance with Rachel.

"Either Lucille cast a spell, or we're in deep trouble."

Rachel nodded, and they both hurried back inside. An uneasy feeling settled in Fabian's stomach. The last time a spell had gone wrong, Lucille had set her mansion on fire. He didn't want to find out what spooky spells she would test to make sure her party was a success.

They didn't get far down the corridor when Ani hurried past them, wiping blood from her face.

Blood.

"Ani, are you okay?" They were no longer friends, but that didn't mean Fabian was heartless enough to ignore when she clearly was in pain.

"I'm going to the toilet, you dumbass!" Ani shouted, her usual abrasive self.

But in the moment she'd looked over her shoulder, he'd seen blood flowing from her nose, ears, and eyes. Shocked, Fabian stumbled backwards. "You're bleeding," he said, as if that wasn't obvious. *Ani was bleeding from the eyes.* That meant... that meant she needed immediate medical attention. "Do you want me to—"

Ani reached the bathroom marked for the girls' use tonight, anger distorting her face. "Are you hard of hearing? This is a toilet! So, piss off!" She opened the door, then slammed it shut in front of him.

Fabian returned to Rachel, unable to shake his worry despite Ani's bitchiness. "I've no idea what's going on there, but it didn't look good."

"Do you want me to check on her?" Rachel didn't sound particularly excited about the prospect.

"If you don't mind." Ani might not want any help, but she shouldn't be alone while blood was pouring from all her facial orifices. "You're the best."

Rachel squared her shoulders and followed Ani into the toilet. When she didn't come out again within the first two minutes, Fabian decided she was handling whatever Ani was throwing at her just fine. Time for him to find out what was suddenly going on here.

Matt

"Is that an illusion?" Matt asked as he watched the last bat leave the ballroom.

Next to him, Dion shook his head. "If it is, it's not one of mine."

Matt checked with Lucille, who was leaning on Dion after having made moon eyes at him all night long. He certainly wouldn't put it past *her* to go all out on a witch party by putting some real spells on display.

She huffed with indignation. "I did not order a colony of bats! Or summon one!"

The lights went out, and the music broke off. Muttering rose all around them. Surprisingly, the students weren't frightened, but full of excitement. "Great effect show!" he heard someone shout.

"Erit lux," Lucille whispered, and instantly, bright light flashed through the entire room.

Matt blinked until his eyes watered. If anyone had been planning to attack them in the darkness, he hoped they'd be just as blinded. But when his sight returned, nothing had changed. There was no monster, and the students were cheering for what looked like a spontaneous illusion show.

While Dion kept the masses entertained, Lucille, Menuha, and Matt turned to each other in a huddle. "What's the meaning of this?" Matt asked.

"I have no idea." Lucille looked around worriedly. Her fingers were twitching around her open palm, as if tempted to turn the light off again. "There was no magic on the plan, I promise."

"So, it's another witch?" Menuha asked.

"Sam wouldn't do that," Matt said reflexively. Why was he defending her? She certainly wouldn't do the same for him.

Something crackled in the air, and in the next moment, the real light and music returned. Lucille closed her hand to a fist and sighed with relief. "What if it was just a power outage? You know, just an ordinary blackout?"

"What's a blackout?" Menuha asked, confused, but Matt waved her off. They didn't have time to explain the whole concept of electricity to Menuha. "What about the bats? How do you explain them?"

Lucille shrugged, clearly overwhelmed. "I don't know."

Meanwhile, Dion had finished his show and turned to them. "I can keep people distracted if something happens. But this was either the work of an illusionist who far surpasses my skill level or dark magic."

Matt shuddered just thinking about what kind of illusions someone stronger than Dion could craft. His had already almost succeeded in killing him. "Okay. Let's split and do a quick survey of the room. We know most of the people here, so if we see anyone who's not familiar, they might be our mystery witch."

"A powerful illusionist can also render themselves invisible," Dion noted.

"Great." Just what they needed. "Let's take a look first."

They split up and walked through the crowd. Everywhere Matt went, he heard people buzzing about the special effect show they believed Lucille had paid for. It wasn't the first time Matt had wondered about how wilfully ignorant most people in Greenvalley were. Despite being surrounded by magic and several supernatural deaths per year—including the ones he'd been responsible for—they latched onto any explanation, no matter how feeble. Of course, the de Cerques would procure an entire colony of protected, trained bats to perform at their party.

While he was searching for the culprit, his eyes were looking for a particular, currently green-skinned, person. Samantha shouldn't be difficult to find with that ridiculous—though surprisingly enticing—outfit. And if there truly was a witch behind the attack, Samantha was their best chance to unmask them and undo their spells. Matt told himself that was the only reason he needed to find her.

Last time he'd seen Samantha, she'd been in conversation with Cian. Matt had watched them with clenched fists, remembering only too well how the Elite Idiot had treated her at Alan's party. She'd been reduced to tears by the end of it, running from the party, and Matt couldn't shake the feeling that today wouldn't be any different. Cian was bad news. Especially when he made Samantha laugh and fall for his tricks again.

But Cian was with Alan and Shayna in some faraway corner, and there was no sign of Samantha's signature black curls.

With his attention elsewhere, Matt almost stumbled into Jennifer and Boyd, who'd retreated to a corner to make out. Matt may have wished he could make out with someone—anyone would do—but he had no interest in these two idiots going at it.

Just then, Jennifer screamed and pushed Boyd away from her, catching Matt's attention in the process.

"Jenny?" Boyd seemed so confused by her sudden reaction Matt assumed he wasn't responsible for his girlfriend's sudden distress.

Jennifer didn't answer, too busy gathering air for another scream. Then she turned around and ran towards the buffet table to pour herself a drink. Matt watched her raise the glass to her quivering lips. The moment it touched her mouth, her eyes bulged, and she let the glass fall.

Glass splintered, and the drink sprayed her feet. Instead of stepping out of the danger zone, Jennifer stomped around the spot, screaming. "Squash them. Squash them!" she cried.

No one came to her help. The people who noticed were either laughing or getting out their smartphones to film Jennifer's meltdown.

Her behaviour was too erratic to be a coincidence. Jennifer was seeing something no one else was, and it freaked her out. She stomped around the glass with no regard for her feet, screaming her heart out. *Squash them.* Was she seeing worms?

He only had to imagine raising a glass of worms to his lips for his body to shudder involuntarily. For once, Jennifer had his full sympathy.

"Matt." Suddenly, Fabian was at his side, baffled by Jennifer's odd behaviour. "What's Jenny doing?"

Right now, she was turning back to the buffet, only to scream louder than ever before. Unable to take whatever the vision was throwing at her, Jennifer ran from the room.

"Someone's targeting her with an illusion, I think," Matt surmised. He glanced in the direction where Dion was standing, seemingly in conversation with another exchange student. Could Dion have been lying? He hadn't exactly been shy about expressing his distaste over spending time in this town.

"Well, whatever's going on with Ani isn't an illusion," Fabian said, still bewildered. "The blood running out of her eyes and ears was real. We just saw her in the corridor."

Matt frowned. Jennifer *and* Ani? "She had blood running out of her eyes and ears?"

"It looked horrible." Fabian shuddered. "I wanted to help her, but of course, she wouldn't let me near her. Rachel's with her now, and hopefully, she can convince her to get checked out by a doctor. This better not be anything bad."

"Oh, it is." Matt discarded the idea that Dion was behind it. He had no connection to Jennifer and Ani, but the two girls were connected to each other. Them, plus Shayna and Cheryl. He couldn't see Cheryl anywhere, but he thought he saw Shayna leaving the party hastily as well. Four girls. All of them from the Elite Clique. And they'd been stupid enough to anger a witch.

"Don't take this the wrong way," Matt said carefully, "but I think Samantha might be the one behind this. She's quite big on revenge lately. And she believes Cheryl did something to her sister." She'd been distraught when she'd asked them earlier whether they'd seen Meg. Apparently, the little Kollmer girl had got herself tangled up with the Elite Clique and been burnt.

Unexpectedly, Fabian frowned. "And so she's doing what, exactly?"

He had a point there. While Samantha was supposedly getting better at weaving spells, she was still only starting out. Even so, Matt wouldn't put it past her to improve by leaps and bounds once she'd got the hang of it. "Someone's put a curse on the Elite Clique girls. It's either Sam or some powerful unknown witch who, for some reason, bears a grudge against them."

"There are, like, a million people with reason enough to target those four," Fabian said promptly. "Where *is* Sam?"

"I don't know," Matt admitted.

But he knew he needed to find her more urgently now than before.

Rachel

When Lucille had invited them to her party, the last place Rachel had imagined herself to end up was to locked in with Cheryl's bestie, Ani, while she bled all over the frothy bathroom throw carpet.

"What do you want?" Ani whined, her usual viciousness considerably mellowed by bloody tears. "Want to watch me die?"

"Are you?" She wasn't usually that confronting, but the ridiculousness of the statement had brought out Rachel's callous side.

Ani whimpered, bopping up and down on the closed toilet seat like some little child. She grabbed handfuls of toilet paper to dab at her eyes, achieving nothing but further smearing blood all over her face. "It won't stop. I bet I have cancer—"

"You do not have cancer," Rachel replied promptly. She was pretty sure Ani would've known she was sick *before* starting to bleed from literally every orifice.

"How would you know?" When Rachel only stared at her, Ani grabbed more toilet paper to press against her nose. "My clothes are a mess!" Her clothes were nothing compared to her blood-smeared face. "What if I die here? On the toilet. At some party?"

Rachel could think of worse ways to die. While Ani was bleeding, the blood wasn't gushing from an open wound as it had with Nico. Still, the memory of him made her queasy, and she decided to make a better effort with Ani. This time, she wouldn't just stand around and stare. First, she needed to get Ani to stop panicking about dying. "Well, that would be one giant mess, wouldn't it?"

Ani stared at her, shocked. Then she burst out laughing. "That would be the last thing I'd worry about."

While Rachel secretly agreed, she picked up a towel, put some water on it, and started wiping Ani's face. "Do you want me to call 112?"

"No! That would be so embarrassing."

If Ani was still worried about embarrassing herself, it couldn't be too bad. "So, what happened? Did you eat something bad?" There was no cause Rachel could think of which would make one bleed from the eyes and ears. Apart from what she'd seen in horror movies.

"Nothing. I was flirting with Chris. We wanted to get a room, but then, suddenly, I started bleeding on him. Not in the room!" Ani explained pointedly.

"Could Chris have put something in your drink?" She had no idea which Chris Ani was talking about. There were at least three in their year.

Ani grimaced, bewildered. "Why would he do that?"

"To get into your pants?" Why else would men put something in women's drinks?

Once again, Ani laughed. "Oh, Rachel, he doesn't need to spike my drink for that. I enjoy fooling around. Not like you, I suppose. You're still a virgin, aren't you?"

Rachel backed away. She'd completely lost control of the conversation. How did they get from dying in Lucille's bathroom to her sex life? "How is that relevant?"

Ani took a moment to watch her thoughtfully. "Are you asexual?"

The question took Rachel by surprise. Her initial reply was, "No! I've got a boyfriend. Fabian." But did that matter? Asexual people were in romantic relationships all the time. They simply had no interest in sex. Just like she didn't.

"Oh, please," Ani continued, clicking her tongue. "That whole relationship is so fake. I would say you're his fill-in, but to qualify for that he'd need to show *some* interest."

Rachel stared at her in shock. There was nothing in Ani's off-hand comment that Rachel hadn't come up with herself before, but to be confronted with it by someone who barely even knew her?

"Don't look at me as if you're Bambi and I shot your Mum. There's a reason Fabian doesn't want to sleep with you despite your... '*relationship*'." Ani put air quotes around the word for unnecessary emphasis.

Immediately, Rachel began to defend Fabian. "You don't even know him. Fabian's not like other guys." He was kind and sensitive, not in a constant horndog state like so many of her classmates.

"Oh, trust me, Fabian is just like other guys. I bet if you check under his bed, you'll find just as many porn magazines as in other boy's bedrooms." Ani rolled her eyes with disgust. "And I don't need to be friends with him to say that. I only have to remember those horrible years when he practically undressed Samantha with his eyes and wanted to jump her at school." She spat, blood mingling in her saliva. "Fortunately, they broke up. But. If you want my honest opinion—"

There was nothing Rachel wanted less from her.

"—if you and Sammy were naked in a room with him, Fabian would beg Sammy to let him screw her," Ani finished, looking altogether pleased with herself. "Just saying."

Just saying. Rachel almost spat as well; there was such a bitter taste in her mouth. "So, you think I'm ugly? Is that what you're saying?"

"No!" Still, Ani took a moment to quickly assess her. "In that outfit, for sure. What were you thinking? Definitely not sex." She laughed at her clever joke, blood coating her lips. "But you're not ugly. You're plain, normal. What I'm saying is that I have no idea what Fabian sees in you, but it's not someone he wants to get into bed with."

Rachel wished it was easy to refute her. She'd become keenly aware of the fact that they'd been together for six months and hadn't done more than kiss. And even that was only occasionally, lately. There had been a time when Fabian had indicated he was interested in more, but he hadn't made a proper attempt in ages. And he'd rejected her suggestion to jump over the fire together.

Anger simmered in her stomach. Why was she letting Ani play her this easily? As usual, the girl was spewing nothing but poison. Rachel should know better than to let it get to her.

Instead, she pointed out the more immediate thing. "You're bleeding from the mouth." Whatever was wrong with Ani was getting worse.

As her eyes widened in horror, Rachel continued, pretending not to be invested in her health at all, "I don't know if you're going to die from this, but I would definitely want to see a doctor if I were you." Drily, she added for maximum effect, "While you still can."

As predicted, Ani went straight back into panic mode. She jumped off the toilet to look at herself in the mirror. Blood was definitely dripping from her mouth now. Rachel was about to turn away, but Ani grabbed her wrist, almost crushing her bones. "Don't leave me alone! I don't want to die."

Rachel sighed. "Let's get you to the hospital."

While Ani grabbed another towel to hide her face behind, Rachel opened the door. This party was already a bust. Accompanying Ani to the hospital could be no worse than watching other people jump over the fire, while Fabian feigned some flame phobia. At least, this way, she wouldn't have to think too much about whether Ani's analysis hadn't been spot on.

Fabian

"Have you seen Samantha?" Fabian asked Robert, growing more and more desperate. But like all the others he'd been asking, the answer was no.

"This party's lit!" an excited Robert exclaimed. "Did you hear Jenny had a mental breakdown over spiders and bugs in her drink? I wonder if she got her hand into one of those mushrooms. Lucille smuggled some in, right?"

"I highly doubt that." While Fabian wouldn't put it completely behind Lucille to try a psychedelic mushroom, he couldn't see her offering them up for grabs at her house party. "Listen, I need to find Sam, so if you see her, tell her to call me."

He'd been trying to call her, but the phone just kept ringing and ringing.

"Sure, I'll tell her," Robert promised before running off to bother the next person.

Fabian kept hurrying down the corridor, leaving the noise of the party behind. There were an endless number of rooms, most locked or dark and empty. He was just about to turn back when he heard a soft sniffling noise.

Ice trickled down his spine. "Sam?" How many times had he found her exactly like that, hiding in some corner, crying her heart out?

He pulled back the curtains, ready to fulfil his best friend duties. But instead of puffed-up black curls, he was looking down at Shayna's fashionable pixie cut. "Shayna?"

She jerked her head up and stared at him with reddened eyes. "Fabian. What are you doing here?"

"I..." He pointed at the bench she'd been sitting on. "May I?"

Shayna nodded, apparently still stunned by his presence. Fabian lowered himself, keeping as much distance between them as he could. He probably should've turned away and left her alone, but he was unable to walk past someone crying, even if that someone was Shayna.

"What happened?" he asked instead.

She barked a short laugh. "You'd never believe it."

Thinking back on Ani's bloody disaster and Jennifer's invisible nightmare, he shrugged. "Why don't you try me? You know I'm best friends with Samantha."

"True." Fresh tears formed in her eyes. Shayna blinked rapidly and took a deep breath before she said, "I think I got cursed because of Meg."

"Because of Meg?" Fabian was still piecing together that particular drama.

Shayna almost burst into tears again. "We just wanted to squeeze her for info about Sam. Have some fun with her." She sighed and shuddered. "You should've seen how she practically threw herself at Cheryl's feet. Pure hero worship. As if Cheryl was the Goddess of Fashion or something silly like that. Ani took one of the Ouija boards lying around for decoration, and we pretended to summon a ghost. But then... Meg started shaking. She was completely unresponsive. And when I finally got Sam, she was gone!"

So that was what had gone down. "And now you think Meg cursed you?" Fabian found his pity was quite limited tonight.

"Who else would it be?"

"You mean because there couldn't possibly be someone else with a grudge?" Unfortunately, Matt's theory about Samantha being behind the targeted curses was becoming more and more likely. At least she knew how to put a curse on people, unlike Meg.

Shayna didn't get his meaning immediately. When she did, she rolled her eyes. "You mean all the haters?" After Fabian stared pointedly at her, she raised her hands. "Sorry. I know Cheryl isn't the easiest person..."

Fabian raised an eyebrow. "Fine, I'm not either. Happy? Or do you want me to say that on video?"

"Wow! That must be some hardcore curse." He couldn't see what was wrong with Shayna, but it must've been something horrible if she was that desperate.

"I ate a finger. My finger!"

He had not expected *that*.

"Here!" Shayna held out her hand for him but was hiding the fingertips in her fist. All he could see was her thumb glistening with saliva, its nail chewed.

Fabian had to push past the nausea that was rising in his stomach to take her hand. Shayna clenched her fingers tighter, swallowing a whimper. Gently, he brushed her knuckles to coax her into opening the hand. When she finally did, her entire body collapsed, and she burst into tears.

"I chew fingernails when I'm nervous!" she cried.

She hadn't just chewed her fingernails. All four of her fingertips were bloody messes. Half a nail was missing from the middle finger.

The urge to throw up became almost overwhelming. Bile rose in his throat, leaving behind a sour taste, but somehow, Fabian managed to keep the contents of his stomach down for Shayna's benefit. "That's horrifying." In his opinion, it beat Ani's and Jennifer's curses by a long shot.

"Do you know how hard it is *not* to continue eating?" Shayna said, her voice choked in tears. "Oh gosh, I'm going to eat myself!"

Fabian had never spent more than five minutes with one of the Elite Clique girls alone, but when Shayna broke down in tears, he couldn't hold back. He scooted closer and pulled her into his embrace. Shayna wrapped her arms around his neck and hung on for dear life, her tears quickly wetting his shirt.

"It'll be alright." He desperately hoped he wasn't lying.

Even more so, he hoped this wasn't Samantha's work.

Samantha

It took Samantha almost an hour to find her sister. In that time, she'd grown more and more frantic. At first, she'd been convinced it was all just a big joke, but Meg's continuous absence worried her. What if she really had been writhing on the floor? What if Cheryl had panicked and hidden her in some broom closet while Meg was still unconscious? The frequent bursts of magic around Samantha didn't help settle her frazzled nerves in the slightest.

Just when she was about to give up and call her parents to tell them what had happened, she saw Meg standing by the buffet, smiling to herself.

"There you are!" Samantha rushed to her side, fussing over her.

"Here I am," Meg announced, clearly unimpressed. "Could you please stop that?"

Samantha let her hands sink. "Shayna said you collapsed on the ground." It came out more accusingly than she'd planned.

"Shayna?" Meg looked slightly confused. "Is she one of those stupid girls who tried to take me on?"

Meg was well aware who Shayna was, as well as any of the other "stupid" girls. "Are you okay?"

Her sister didn't hold herself as she usually did. There was an air of mature confidence around her. No slouching, no looseness in the limbs, instead a straight back and haughty glance Samantha had first mistaken for Meg's usual cockiness.

"I've rarely been better." She smiled cruelly. "Right now, I'm having the time of my life, showing those silly geese what it means to take on a witch." Meg's eyes were glowing with arousal. "Don't you think, sister?"

Meg might've said sister, but Samantha was convinced she didn't mean it the way one usually did. There was something deeper, a connection on a base level. "You're not my sister." Samantha was sure of it now. "Meg wouldn't touch magic with a ten-foot pole."

"That stupid thing." Meg snorted. "She's just as ignorant as the rest of them. Just look at them, impressed by a show of meagre illusions." She spread her arms and laughed, but then her glowing eyes settled again on Samantha. "But you're different. You're a true witch. And I'm not saying that because that biased witch trial proved it. I can smell it." Her nostrils flared slightly.

Samantha almost took a step back. The witch trial? Slowly, the memories of Cheryl's cruel joke earlier this week came back to her. And suddenly, she realised who she was talking to. "Margarethe Kessler?" Meg smiled proudly. "I *recognised* you as a real witch." For a moment, the confirmation of her long-made-up theory excited her. But then she saw into Meg's blue eyes and found not a trace of her little sister. Margarethe Kessler might have been a real witch, but she wasn't above using her magic against others. "What did you do with my sister?"

"Just a simple possession. I only want to have a bit of fun," Margarethe announced. "Girls like your sister have all sorts of fun in my home. I hear them ridiculing my face, as if their youthful beauty was to last. And they pretend to burn on the pyre like me, as if it was nothing but a grand joke. It was more painful than any of them can imagine." She eyed Samantha, and Samantha found herself unable to resist feeling the connection she'd always felt between them. Margarethe had died in the fire over people's superstitions, and centuries later, the descendants of the same people thought it funny and used the display of her death to make silly videos for their social media outlets. While safe from witch burnings, Samantha had experienced her own share of ostracisation and torment for daring to be different.

"So, what about you, sister?" Margarethe asked. "It's the night of witches. Will you dance with me and teach these mortals to fear our power?"

And the connection sizzled out again. "I'm a good witch."

Margarethe laughed, a sharp and cutting sound. "Oh, you stupid, stupid girl. Whether you're good or not is not your decision, but the devil's only."

Samantha thought of Matt deciding her worth and shuddered. "The devil can stay in Hell where he belongs."

That didn't please Margarethe, and she snorted. "Today's generation is useless. Weak simpletons, all of you." She gave her another of her haughty looks. "Fine, then. Stay here and out of my way!"

She moved her fingers to weave a quick spell. Samantha didn't even have time to see the individual threads before the spell hit her. Margarethe walked away, but when Samantha tried to follow her, she could no longer move her limbs. Even her lips wouldn't open. All she could do was see what was in front of her eyes and try not to panic at having found herself caught inside her body's prison.

Dozens of students walked right past Samantha over the course of the next ten or fifteen minutes, not a single one so much as glancing at her. She couldn't use magic. She couldn't run away. And she couldn't cry for help.

Samantha had never noticed how small her body was until she was stuck inside of it. Her mind wanted to expand, break through the barriers that confined her, while every inch of her skin was itching as if ten thousand ants were crawling over her. She would've screamed, but that would've required some movement, however small it was.

To make matters worse, when somebody finally took notice of her, it was in the shape of Matt's demon sister, Menuha. She, of all people, walked straight up to her, her eyes glistening with delight.

"There you are! I was hoping to catch you alone." Menuha quickened her steps, and Samantha could've sworn she'd space-jumped that last metre.

The itching on her skin became even worse as Menuha continued chatting happily. "I've been dying to ask you something. About Matt," she clarified, to Samantha's dismay. She paused. "Are you okay?"

Samantha almost cried. She was so far from being okay it was almost laughable. But she could do neither. Her face muscles were just as paralysed as the rest of her. It was a small wonder she was able to breathe.

Menuha had finally caught on that something was wrong. She leaned forward and snapped her fingers in front of Samantha's eyes. Samantha didn't blink, though she really wished Menuha would keep her black-magic-hurtling hands further away from her face.

"I assume you aren't wilfully ignoring me. I realise you're not a big fan of demons at the moment, but I never offended you, so that wouldn't make sense."

In Samantha's opinion that would make a lot of sense. While Menuha had attacked no one that night, she hadn't exactly been upset about the deaths. And Samantha could've sworn the demon knew how to kill and did it far more often than her kindness towards humans might suggest.

Menuha reached into a pocket of her tunic and pulled out what looked like kindergarten craft. It was a bundle of twigs bound in a shape that had no familiarity to Samantha, though it vaguely looked like a letter. "My brother Caspar is a healer and a magician. He studied magic during his first century and learned how to bind and break runes. Since I'm his favourite sister—" She broke off and thought a little longer about what she was about to say. "Well, I'm probably the only person he can stand, really. In any case, he made me this anti-magic rune. Easy to use, very helpful. Watch this."

Without hesitation, she pressed the rune between Samantha's breasts. Samantha felt the heat rise in her cheeks—so blood circulation was still working—then the rune broke and dissolved in decades-old sawdust.

Samantha's entire body eased up. The itching subsided slowly, but it was replaced by odd muscle pains from standing in one position for too long. Reflexively, she moved a hand to her chest to swipe away the dust, only to realise as she did so that her limbs moved again.

"Thanks," she muttered, and wondered what the payment for Menuha's help would be.

Menuha simply smiled. "No worries. Now, tell me how you got yourself into such an unfortunate situation."

"My sister is being possessed by the ghost of a witch who lived here more than three hundred years ago: Margarethe Kessler. She's... an evil witch. She's cursing people. I don't like those people, but they don't deserve to be cursed. And I need to free my sister from Margarethe's grasp."

"Do you know where she is now?"

"Not right now." Though there was a dark note in the magic rivers around them. Something big was about to happen.

"Then let's search for her," Menuha said cheerfully, as if the threat of an evil witch was nothing to her. She hooked her arm into Samantha's and dragged her along. "While we do that, you can answer some questions I have about Matt."

Samantha closed her eyes and breathed through her nose. With her sister possessed by a powerful witch on the loose and a bunch of nasty curses flying around, Matt was really at the bottom of her priorities. Not that he was ever likely to assume a higher position. "Menuha... I understand the human world is fascinating and interesting to you, but this is my *life*. I don't want to talk about Matt. I don't like him." She freed her arm from the demon. "What I want to do is find Meg and free her from Margarethe Kessler's evil presence. Don't you understand that?"

Menuha stopped to think about it, her eyes narrowing. "Your sister is important to you."

"Of course she is! She's my little sister. I promised to take care of her." And she was failing spectacularly tonight.

"How peculiar," Menuha said, and started walking again.

Samantha sighed. Having her human emotions dissected as if she was some kind of exotic animal made her itch all over again. She pushed the thought away to concentrate on what was really important: finding Meg.

Now that the spell was broken, people no longer completely ignored her. It wasn't long until she ran into someone she knew. Cian.

He took one glance at her and asked, "You still haven't found Meg?" Samantha shook her head. "Shit. Listen, there is some weird stuff going on. Shayna—"

A sudden scream echoed through the room. At the same time, several people pointed at the ceiling in terror. Samantha and Cian looked up to see the lifeless body of a girl with blonde corkscrew locks hanging from the ceiling, almost completely covered in spiderwebs.

"Is that Cheryl?" Cian asked.

It most definitely was, and it fit with what had been happening all evening long. Margarethe Kessler was targeting the Elite Clique and anyone else who got in her way. To Cian, though, Samantha feigned ignorance. "Hard to say."

Cian hadn't even heard her. He was taking a few steps closer to check out the body and try to identify it.

Samantha had to think on her feet. The situation was quickly getting out of control. The witch was picking off the Elite Clique one by one. If she found Cian, who knew what she'd do to him? And he certainly didn't deserve to be cursed tonight. She turned to Menuha and decided to take a chance. "I'll try to unravel the spell. Can you keep Cian safe and distracted for me?" Despite his continued friendship, she didn't want him to see her *doing* magic. The Elite Clique would immediately latch onto it, feeling justified for their years of bullying. They might even claim *Samantha* had cursed them. And the last thing she needed this year was a witch hunt. "Unless you have another one of those runes?" Menuha could easily fly up there and free Cheryl from her predicament. And all Samantha would have to do was explain how Matt's sister had grown wings and flew.

"No, the last time I needed one was 120 years ago. I never carry more than one with me." Menuha smiled reassuringly. "But don't worry. I'll take care of the boy. He'll be well-entertained."

Instantly, Samantha cursed herself for suggesting it. Entrusting Cian into the care of a demon of the House of Lust was the opposite of what she'd planned for him. But at least he'd be alive. "Thank you."

While Menuha went off to flirt with Cian, Samantha turned her attention towards Cheryl. Even this far away, she could see the green strings of magic that held her in place, presenting as spiderwebs. Sweat soon covered Samantha's forehead as she hooked her own magic into the spell, using it to cut some strings while loosening up others.

Slowly, Cheryl's body began to lower. The crowd, who had been so scared a minute ago, hushed, as if collectively holding their breath. They were watching Cheryl's every move. Half-way down, Cheryl's body got stuck. Samantha pulled more forcefully, but Cheryl was moving neither up nor down.

"Have you decided to play with the dark powers after all?" Margarethe's scathing voice rang through the ballroom like a whip crack.

People shuffled around, and slowly, a corridor formed between Samantha and the girl who appeared to be her little sister. Margarethe had one hand on her hip, every inch of her small body a challenge. "Very well, little witch. Let's see how strong you are. And whether you have the guts for it." The last sentence came out with a dismissive hiss.

Samantha almost fainted. Now she was caught in a witch duel in front of everyone she knew. And the price was her bully's life.

Lucille

Lucille and Matt had finished searching the ballroom and were now heading down the hallway, when a scream echoed through the corridor.

"Where did that come from?" Lucille asked, alarmed. Screams were never good. Especially not at her party. "Was it Meg?"

"Didn't sound like her," Matt muttered before trying the next door. "Anyone in here?" The room was dark, like all the others had been.

After trying countless rooms so far, she really didn't expect a resounding, "Yep. Me."

She knew that voice. "Jan?" Lucille walked into the room and turned on the light, then quickly covered her eyes and turned her back to him. "Gosh, Jan. I certainly didn't need to see *that* today." What was he thinking, sitting stark naked in a dark room?

"Only today?" Matt asked, sounding rather amused. He didn't seem to have a problem with what he saw.

"Could you untie me instead of staring at the best part of me?" Jan sounded disgruntled.

Lucille had turned so fast at the sight of his naked body she hadn't even seen the ropes that tied him to the chair. Again. What was he thinking? Knowing Jan, he hadn't used his brain at all.

Matt snickered. "You're sure that's the best part of you?"

"I'm cold!" Jan bellowed, though he eased up quickly. "Please."

Lucille left it to Matt to help Jan out of his precarious situation while she tried her best not to lose her mind. Everything was going wrong today. Why couldn't they have *one* party that didn't end in blood and tears? Or included naked friends.

From the sounds of it, Jan was getting dressed as fast as possible. "Lu, you can turn around again, and you—" he was talking to Matt "—could have stared a little less."

Matt didn't let the complaint bother him. Highly amused, he asked, "Who put you in this position?"

"What do you mean, who? Meg did, of course," Jan barked.

"Meg did?" Lucille was well aware Samantha's little sister could be a bit feisty, but to believe she had tied her boyfriend to a chair naked was asking a bit much.

Next to her, Matt was still fighting his amusement, though his efforts weren't particularly good. "So, was the waiting worth it, then?" he sputtered.

Jan regarded him darkly. "We didn't have sex." For some reason, Matt burst into laughter. Annoyed, Jan tapped his foot. "Someone must have bewitched her or something. I mean... that wasn't Meg. I think."

"You think because she tricked you into this compromising position, she must be cursed?" Lucille asked. It was such a typical male reaction. Jan got duped, so it must have been some imposter.

"It wasn't a trick." Jan groaned and raised his hands, giving in. "Yes, fine, it was one, and I fell for it, but since she left, I've had a lot of time to think, and Meg didn't move the way she normally does. And her voice was different. She... I got carried away, I admit, but she was *not* her normal self."

The amusement was wiped from Matt's face, and he was suddenly serious again. "That sounds more like possession than a spell."

"Do I have to order a priest now?" Lucille half-joked. Everything was turning to custard. At Matt's blank expression, she explained, "To perform an exorcism, I mean." That was what one did with a possessed person, wasn't it?

Matt only frowned deeper. "You're a witch. Why would you need to bring in someone else?"

"Perhaps because I have no idea about exorcisms," Lucille suggested. There had been no mention of them in her grandmother's notes. "But hey, Rachel can talk to ghosts."

"I was perfectly able to talk to her as well," Jan said drily. "Didn't exactly help."

That ruled out that particular solution.

Matt shook his head, taking charge of the situation. "What we need is a lot of salt for the banishing circle and a litany for you to recite. Your magic will do the rest."

He made it sound so easy, yet Lucille didn't even know where to start.

"I bet we can Google a litany," Jan mused and got out his phone.

Lucille stared at him blankly. "Google will tell me how to perform an actual exorcism and banish this ghost?"

Jan turned his phone screen to her, grinning proudly. "18,000 hits. They've even got YouTube videos showing you how to do it."

"And they work?"

"We could try them one by one," Jan suggested with a shrug of his shoulders.

Testing 18,000 litanies. It sounded like a recipe for disaster. "Let's get some salt from the kitchen." After that, she would swing by her room and check her spellbooks again.

The three of them agreed on that much and left the room, only to run into Robert in the corridor. The boy's grin was so wide it was a small wonder his cheeks hadn't split. "Lucille! Your party is the best!"

"Thank you, Robert." At least someone was enjoying themselves. "But I have to—"

He wouldn't even let her speak. "It's almost like there's real magic in the air. They're going to talk about that floating corpse under the ceiling for years to come."

Lucille felt her face muscles go slack. "Floating corpse?"

"In the ballroom, yes. It almost looks like Cheryl. Nice touch." He grinned even wider.

Lucille shared a quick look with Matt and Jan. Neither of them shared Robert's enthusiasm. Quite the opposite. They looked as concerned as she felt. Matt nodded. "I'll go get as much salt as I can carry from the kitchen. And candles."

"I'll take care of Robert here," Jan announced, then grabbed Robert's arm to pull him along. "Show me that corpse." Matt vanished as soon as Robert's back was turned to him.

Lucille took a deep breath, before she ran to the ballroom as fast as she could.

It was almost impossible to push through the crowd of people in the room. Everyone's attention was up in the air. There truly was a floating corpse—or something like it. *Cheryl's* floating corpse, wrapped in spiderwebs. She moved up and down like a strange tug-of-war marker. For a moment, Lucille thought Dion was behind a spectacular illusion, but he was looking up at the body as bewildered as everyone else.

By the time Lucille had managed to forge a way to him, she'd found out who was behind the invisible forces at play. On one side of a corridor stood Meg, a wild grin on her face, while opposite, Samantha had taken position, her fingers weaving furiously, sweat leaving pale traces on her green skin. The students around them were completely enthralled and excited.

Just then, Cheryl's body fell to the ground with adrenaline-spiking velocity, only to stop mere centimetres away from the ground. Lucille checked with Samantha and, sure enough, her friend was breathing hard, fingers cramping up.

"I thought I should help you out a bit, seeing as you struggle so much to keep up," Meg mocked. Whoever possessed her had more magical power than any of them. She snapped her fingers, and Cheryl shot up again, this time hitting the ceiling with a smack.

"Dion," Lucille tried to get his attention while the crowd winced at Cheryl's impact.

He seemed surprised to see her, horror in his beautiful eyes. "What is going on here?"

"Welcome to the real Greenvalley," Lucille said bitterly. She pointed at Meg. "That is Samantha's little sister. She is likely possessed by the ghost of some powerful witch who seems hell-bent on raising some ruckus. Can you distract people with an illusion while we get this sorted?"

"Possessed?" Dion's face muscles were still slack with terror. "Lucille, I can do illusions, but not of this size. Everyone is already too engrossed to be distracted, and... I believe she's going to kill that girl."

Lucille took a deep breath. It certainly looked like that. "Let's hope not. Samantha is already fighting her. Now, I need to exorcise this ghost while Meg's distracted. And somehow, we need to make it all look like some giant show. In which nobody dies tonight." She nodded shakily to herself. Not a single part of this plan sounded doable. "You don't happen to know a working exorcism?"

Dion shook his head. Lucille sighed. *18,000 hits?* One of them had to work. She got her phone out and browsed the litanies.

The overwhelming majority of them were in Latin and easily translatable for her. Surprisingly, Lucille was able to feel the power in the words. Not every combination was filled with magic—most of them were gibberish that didn't even follow basic grammar—but at last she found it. A litany full of words thrumming with power, even as she read them from the bright screen of her phone.

"Got it."

"Good." Matt arrived suddenly at their side, carrying with him enough salt to cover half the floor and a bunch of candles. "Banishing circles always work best with salt and fire to contain them. Shall we?" He looked up at the floating body.

Just then, the crowd backed away as one. A myriad of small spiders was crawling towards Cheryl, almost covering half the ceiling. Lucille raised her hand to her mouth, while next to her, Matt was squeezing his eyes shut and breathing shallowly.

"That's only an illusion," Dion said a second before Lucille saw it, too.

"The spiders aren't real," she whispered, wondering why the witch bothered with such an illusion when she had already proven she was stronger than Samantha. "Unless, of course, she isn't."

Matt shuddered, mumbling the word illusion over and over. His eyes flew open. "She isn't what?"

"Stronger than Samantha." Lucille latched onto the idea instantly. "She's a ghost, isn't she? How much of her magic is real and how much of it is an illusion?"

"I don't follow," Matt said, but at least he was no longer stunned by the sight of spiders.

Behind him, Dion nodded. "But I do. She uses illusions to bolster her power, convincing Samantha she can never compete. And to distract her. Look."

He pointed at Samantha, who was weaving even more frantically. One by one the spiders fell from the ceiling and vanished into thin air, only to be replaced by new ones.

"She's draining Samantha with illusions while keeping the only spell she can perform right now alive." Dion's grin was a bit loopy. "Well, we can use the same trick. Be prepared to be wowed by Samantha's 'real' power. Go on, do your thing. I'll keep that witch on her toes."

With a flick of his wrist, small green flames danced around the ceiling quickly consuming the spiders. Then the flames bunched together and flew towards Meg. Gasping, Meg changed her weave into a shield, but Samantha's illusionary flames kept crawling along the invisible line. Meg's eyes widened with horror.

Matt and Lucille nodded to each other and jumped forward to spread the salt neatly around Meg. Some students noticed them and pointed, whispering excitedly. Lucille decided not to worry about them. They'd assume it was all part of the grand show they'd enjoyed so far. But then she had a different idea. "You, you, and you, come here."

Confused, the students she'd pointed at came closer. Quickly, Lucille brought them into position and put a candle into each of their hands. "Meg has been possessed by an evil witch. Together, we can free her." Now they all looked excited to help. "You need to stand in the circle. Don't move."

Meanwhile, Jan and Robert had joined them as well, also taking up positions in the circle. "This is awesome. So cool," Robert babbled, while Jan rolling his eyes. Lucille began her second round to light the candles.

Matt had only just finished the circle when Meg noticed him. "Salt?" she asked, then laughed. Raising her hands, she mumbled an old spell.

Lucille knew there was no time. She quickly reopened the browser on her phone and looked up the litany. "Exorciza mos te, omnis immunde spiritus..."

She never got any further, because in that moment, a terrible whirlwind rose around Meg. Salt flew everywhere, and the candles blew out one by one.

Matt

Salt was pelting his skin and burning in his eyes. Then Matt heard a blood-curdling scream, and without thinking, he jumped through space in front of everyone.

He reappeared behind Samantha a second before they both crashed into the buffet table. The finger food was sent flying, and the table cracked in two. Samantha landed on him, still screaming, while Matt caught the brunt of the impact. Food slid towards them from both sides, including the large bowl of May wine. Matt's arm shot up, smashing the bowl out of the way, while at the same time pushing Samantha back to her feet with inhuman strength. Then he was buried under food and soaked in drink.

"Seriously?" Samantha huffed, but she dug through the mess to offer him a hand. "Someone could have seen you."

"A thanks would be nice," Matt grumbled as he grabbed her hand and let her pull him back on his feet. "And I reckon they're a tad distracted by everything else that's happening."

Yet another scream tore through the room. The strings that had held Cheryl up for so long were unravelling, quickly unwrapping the queen bee. She came to a sudden stop when the strings around her legs tangled, dangling her head two metres from the ground.

"Don't you dare let me fall!" Cheryl screamed, suddenly awake.

"Listen," Matt said, wiping his face clean of sauces and condiments, "the only real spell Meg is using is the one that's holding Cheryl... and the wind, I guess. Everything else is an illusion. You can beat her."

Samantha scoffed, looking as if she was about to cry. "I'm not so sure about that. I don't think I have much more in me."

He stopped cleaning himself to stare straight into her eyes and held her gaze. "Lucille is ready to exorcise her. She just needs a moment of peace to do so. You can do this. I believe in you."

Something strange was passing between them. Samantha held his gaze, gulping heavily. Then she gave him a sharp nod and turned away, ending whatever weird thing had happened. "Alright."

Matt shook his head in confusion, sending pretzel sticks flying. *Concentrate on the situation ahead,* he told himself. "Where do you need me?"

He half expected her to say, "as far away from me as possible," but Samantha took a deep breath, assessing the situation. "Ready to catch Cheryl. I'll take the witch."

Not his favourite task, but if that was what she needed to fully concentrate her efforts on Meg, Matt would do it. He and Samantha moved closer until they stood directly under Cheryl. Samantha faced Meg, her hands already weaving again, while Matt stared up at Cheryl. She looked taken aback, but the expansive white in her eyes told him how scared she was. "Don't worry. I'll catch you."

Meg was summoning another storm, and he could feel the wind pushing against him. Cheryl was starting to sway and scream again, forcing him to move with her.

Then, suddenly, the wind turned on itself, and Cheryl was swinging the other way. Matt threw a quick glance at Meg and Samantha. Samantha was in deep concentration, sweat running streaks through her green paint. She had her arms raised, fingers still moving. Meg, however, was distracted by invisible attacks and the very real wind that was battering her from all directions.

It wasn't only the wind that had turned on Meg. Everything had inverted. The salt rippled back in waves until she wasn't so much surrounded by a line of salt as standing in a field of white.

Jan shot into motion, quickly lighting all the candles once more with his lighter, while Lucille took position again.

"Exorciza mos te, omnis immunde spiritus..." Matt heard her raise her voice, and he turned his attention back to Cheryl who would fall the moment the spell released her.

"I will not leave!" Meg shouted, her words distorting into a scream.

"Yes, you will." Samantha's voice was like steel, and Matt couldn't help an exciting shudder running down his backbone.

Lucille became louder and louder until she was yelling at Meg, "Sicut deficit fumus deficiant. Sicut fluit cera a facie ignis, sic pereant peccatores a facie Dei." The storm inside the salt circle roared. "Vade, satana! Vade!"

As if someone had snuffed out a flame, magic left the hall. The wind died down in an instant, the candles went out, and Meg sank to the floor. A second later, Cheryl fell from the ceiling, straight into his arms.

Silence.

For a moment, no one moved. Nobody did as much as breathe. Then one person started to clap, and within seconds, there was a roaring thunder of applause as people clapped, stomped, and cheered.

Matt paid little attention to Cheryl as he put her on her feet, his eyes glued to Samantha, who smiled cautiously and made an awkward curtsy. Behind her, Lucille took full advantage of the attention and soaked up the celebration with a big smile on her face. "I hope you enjoyed our show."

"Don't you *ever* do this again!" Cheryl pushed off him and stalked over to Samantha.

Samantha looked as if she'd completely forgotten Cheryl was there. "What do you mean?" she asked, playing dumb. "I didn't do anything to you."

Cheryl's face was red, and spittle flew from her mouth. "You pulled off this sick show. This was a trick, right? A witch? You?" She was struggling to find appropriate words in her shell-shocked state. "Just leave me out of it! Out of everything! Otherwise... otherwise—" She grunted wordlessly and stalked off on shaky legs, much to the amusement of the people around them.

Matt rolled his eyes, and his gaze met Samantha's. Shock was setting in, and her lips quivered. Sure enough, her hands were shaking as well. Remembering the strange little moment they'd shared before, Matt started walking towards her, but Samantha broke his gaze and muttered, "I have to look after my sister."

She hurried off, and Matt felt as if someone had punched him in the stomach. Stunned, he watched as Samantha joined Jan, who'd picked up Meg, and started fussing over her. The three of them soon vanished in the crowd, while Lucille and Dion continued to play the show angle with some bonus illusions.

After a while, the applause quieted, and the crowd mingled again, and Matt felt more alone than he ever had before.

"You look a little messy." Menuha slipped to his side, wearing a wistful smile. "What happened?"

Matt simply nodded to the broken buffet table, which was being cleaned up by the hired staff. "Tried to catch Samantha before she fell into it." It had been a necessity. Samantha didn't have his healing powers. She would've been hurt if he hadn't been there. And if she'd been hurt, she no longer would've been able to keep the witch who'd possessed Meg in check. There was nothing else to it. He'd done it for the sake of all of them.

"Where have you been?" he asked curiously.

"Oh, I had an interesting chat with Cian," Menuha said, pointing to the blonde guy meeting up with Alan, who seemed to fill him in on what he'd missed. "Samantha asked me to distract him."

It reminded Matt he'd seen Cian and Samantha chatting before. Chatting and laughing. "And? I'm sure he took full advantage of it, didn't he?" No wonder Cian had missed all the action; he'd enjoyed some action of his own in a corner of the ballroom. "Those Elite Idiot brains drop their pants as soon as they see a pretty girl." And his sister was more than pretty.

"Oh, we didn't have sex," Menuha said in the most curious voice before immediately launching into her human fangirl mode. "I was planning to, because frankly how else do you keep someone distracted from a witch duel? But he wasn't into it. And he was nice enough to explain it to me. So, apparently, he's got a crush on someone else, and that prevents him from having fun with me, even though he's not dating the girl he likes or anything. It was fascinating. It's not like he's pining over this other girl—or boy. He didn't really say who it was—but he's just not interested in anybody else at the moment."

She nudged his elbow. "It helped me understand *you* a bit better."

"How so? I have fun whenever I want." Though, if Matt was completely honest with himself, it wasn't really that fun anymore. Just a habit he couldn't shake. "I'm not like Cian."

"Did you know a lot of humans use denial in situations that—"

Matt groaned and strode away quickly. "I need to clean up." And then he needed to find himself a date—maybe that Amélie girl of Lucille's—someone to wipe away the strange thoughts he was beginning to have around Samantha again. The girl who hated him. For a very good reason.

What was even the point in thinking about her?

Rachel

Within two minutes of convincing Ani to get medical assistance, the bleeding stopped. Ani dabbed her face with toilet paper, but no more red bloomed on the white. Her eyes widened. "I'm going to live!" Excited, Ani grabbed Rachel by the hands and jumped up and down, squealing with delight.

Awkwardly, Rachel endured the strange interaction until Ani had calmed down again. "I would still suggest seeing a doctor."

Ani waved her off. "I feel good. If I start bleeding again, I might, but first, I need to clean up. And..." She paused, suddenly filled with unfamiliar uncertainty. "Uhm... thank you for... well, for being there for me, I guess."

Rachel was surprised Ani even remembered to thank her, but she was as bad at accepting thanks as Ani was giving them. "Fabian asked me to."

"About that." Ani grimaced, and Rachel instinctively braced herself. "I know you're not going to believe me, but I... well, I would be very surprised if you two are going to get intimate after all." Then she shrugged, turning back to normal. "But who knows? He's obviously into losers, so good luck!"

She stalked off, and Rachel resisted the urge to massage her temples. *What a wasted hour*, she thought. She hadn't been able to help Ani, and only barely managed to keep her panic at bay. And all that for the price of unsolicited relationship advice throwing a party for the demons in her head. Not that Rachel believed she was a loser, but in the relationship department... Ani might just have a point. She and

Fabian had been together for six months, and any time he'd tried to be intimate, she'd shut him out. Even Samantha and Lucille had told her she wasn't sending the right signals. And now she didn't even know anymore whether she wanted to send any signals.

"Rachel!" There he was. With long strides, Fabian came down the corridor and closed the distance between them. "Did you get anywhere with Ani?"

Ani. Talking about Ani was a safe topic. One they were clear about. "Not really, but she's alive and well. The curse was broken in time, I suppose."

"Yeah, it must've targeted the Elite Clique girls, because I ran into Shayna, and you wouldn't believe what she experienced." He shuddered, the memory affecting him as well, obviously. "Not that I'm allowed to tell you. She had me swear on all my chickens and Merle."

"And you'll keep that oath?" Rachel asked, wondering whether Shayna would otherwise sneak onto the Bendtfeld property and wring all the chickens' necks, before moving on to the kitten.

Fabian shrugged and put an arm around her shoulder. "Let's just say I'm really glad we weren't the target of those curses for once. Shall we see whether the bonfire has burnt down yet?"

He steered her in the direction of the outdoor terrace, and her heart started racing. "What if it has?"

"Then I'll owe you a jump, won't I? I might have to drink another beer to build up enough courage, but let's dare the fire."

His grin under all those freckles made her heart ache. She wanted this fantasy so much for them both. Him eager to jump the fire with her to prove his love to her. And her jumping with him because she believed in them. It would consolidate their love and turn their future bright and hopeful. But was it love? Did Fabian really love her, or would she always be no more than the consolation prize? The achievable girlfriend. And more importantly, did she love him, or was it the fantasy of love she wanted? The one she'd harboured in her dreams for such a long time?

"Only if others are jumping," Rachel said at last. "I had more than enough attention from Ani today, don't count on me starting the ritual." She shrugged. "It's not like it means anything, anyway." As if a jump over the fire would change the way she felt about Fabian. As if it would keep their bond unbreakable, no matter how brittle it was. Did she really need the pressure of some silly tradition on top of everything else?

Fabian looked at her sideways. As usual, though, he accepted what she'd said only too readily. "Yeah, you're probably right."

It still hurt he wasn't fighting her for it.

Lucille

"This room is far enough away from the party so she can have some peace and quiet," Lucille said, opening the door to one of the guest rooms on her floor.

Behind her, Jan was carrying Meg, who was still unconscious, and laid her on the bed. Samantha took off her sister's shoes with all the care of handling a fragile egg, while Dion watched from the door.

"Will she be alright?" Dion asked.

Samantha looked up at him, her beautiful make-up completely ruined by the exertion of the fight. She'd already lost the fake nose and was tearing off her fake fingernails. "Possessions are quite demanding. She's sleeping now, but she should be fine in the morning." Her gaze wandered to Lucille. "Thanks for letting her stay here. I already failed at the whole supervision thing, but I won't fail now. I'll stay with her."

"Rubbish. You'll go back to the party and soak in the applause. I'll stay with her," Jan said gently. "You've already done enough for her."

"But don't you want to go to the party?" Samantha said, slightly confused.

Lucille was equally surprised. Normally, Jan wouldn't give up on the chance of free booze and parties. Especially since he'd seen little action so far. A decisive lack of it, if she considered how he'd spent the last two hours.

Jan scoffed at her. "Are you really expecting me to party while my girlfriend recovers from a ghost possession? By the way, I'm never going into that museum ever again." He shuddered, likely thinking about the fact it was Margarethe Kessler who'd tied him up naked. "Look,

Sam, it's not the night together I aimed and hoped for, but I'll take it." Surprisingly gentle, he brushed Meg's hair with his hand. "I'll take care of your little sister. You've got nothing to worry about. I won't take advantage of this."

With a sigh, Samantha got back up to her feet. "I don't think that little of you." Then she smiled. "Thank you."

"Go and drink a beer for me." Jan shooed them out of the room.

Samantha made a face. "Perhaps some May wine. If there's any left."

The three of them left the room, and Lucille closed the door. "You didn't fail your sister. You saved her. I mean, I wouldn't tell your parents about it, but you're a good big sister. Now come here." She opened her bag and gave Samantha a quick clean-up. "There, that's better. Not as good as Fabian's work, but pretty enough."

"That battle was quite something," Dion chimed in as they started moving again. "I've been surrounded by illusions all my life, but real magic is... wow. The way you turned her spell onto her was magnificent." He gesticulated wildly, and a swath of illusionary salt swirled around his fingers. "Amazing."

Samantha only gave him a tired smile, but Lucille hooked her arm into his and grinned. "Now, don't sell yourself short. We couldn't have done this without you making Margarethe believe Samantha was completely dominating her."

Dion smiled lazily, accepting her praise with languid ease. "I've had a lot of practice. It feels good to have used it for a good cause for once."

Together, they found their way out onto the terrace where the bonfire was burning. Music was playing, and a few brave souls—or some drunk ones—jumped over the flames. It seemed to be another one of Greenvalley's small-town charms. A year ago, Lucille would've laughed at the cheesiness of such rituals, but now it made her sigh happily.

They'd been out on the terrace for less than a minute when Cian joined them. "There you are," he said, singularly focused on Samantha, which Lucille found quite peculiar. "I wanted to find you after that show you delivered, but you were suddenly gone."

"I had to take care of Meg," Samantha said, sounding overly cautious.

Cian grinned. "Not breaking character. I like it! No, but for real, this was the best Walpurgis Night anyone has ever seen." He gave Lucille a quick nod. "Kudos, de Cerque."

Lucille didn't even bother to reply, since Cian's attention was already back on Samantha. She leaned into Dion and enjoyed the spectacle in front of her. Perhaps she should suggest the two of them jumped over the fire.

"Well, I guess I had no choice but to lean into my reputation." Awkwardness was oozing out of Samantha, and Lucille remembered her misguided love spell only too well. Cian had always been a little too intimidating for the shy girl, so used to being on the outside. But that girl didn't exist anymore. That girl had just duelled an evil witch in front of all her classmates and defeated her.

"True, your reputation precedes you." Cian nodded, then offered Samantha his hand. "In that case, my Good Witch of the Green Valley, may I ask you to the Witches' Dance?"

Samantha hesitated and Lucille gave her a little push. "Go!" she whispered a little too loudly.

Samantha reddened while Cian laughed. He leaned in and said, "Come on. The real witch has left the building." The comment confused both Lucille and Samantha. Had he noticed what was going on? But then, he added, "I mean Cheryl."

If that wasn't fitting, Lucille didn't know what else was. It was almost a shame they'd had to save Cheryl from Margarethe Kessler's ire today. She didn't know anyone else who would benefit from a little curse.

This time, Samantha laughed. "True. Alright. Let me get my broomstick so we can ride to the dance. I hope you're not afraid of heights."

Cian grinned and pulled her towards the fire where other people were dancing wildly. Maybe they wouldn't jump over the fire tonight, but it looked like they were going to have some fun together.

Lucille sighed and leaned into Dion again. "You won't believe this, but I once accidentally put a love spell on Cian. Turns out that even without my spell, he has a little crush on Samantha."

"Just shows that you've got a gift." Dion put his free hand on her arm and slowly trailed down to her fingers. "A keen observation is paramount for illusion work. The closer the illusion is to reality, the more convincing it is."

Lucille turned her hand slightly so his fingers landed between hers. "So, hairy spiders in a forest while we're in a cave was close to reality?"

"It wasn't very convincing, was it?" A cheeky grin appeared on his face. "Though honestly, it wouldn't surprise me if you've seen hairy spiders in a forest around here."

She grimaced, able to imagine it only too well. "Gosh, I hope not. I had enough of spiders when they attacked us en masse at the zoo." His eyebrow crawled up. "Yes, let's not talk about the very real things we have here in Greenvalley." She intertwined her fingers with his. "You said I've got a talent for illusions. I want to give it another try."

"Then do it. I don't think there's anything you can't do." His eyes spoke with such pure admiration, Lucille found herself lost in their green once more.

It felt like an eternity ago when they'd been all alone at her party while he taught her about illusions by crafting a grape. Even now, she could taste the sweetness of that imaginary grape on her lips. And by the looks of it, he could too.

Dion laughed softly. "Not bad."

Lucille was insanely proud that she had grasped the basics. Illusions didn't have to be visual. They could be anything. A taste. A smell. A touch.

She shuddered at the feeling of his lips on hers, while he still looked her in the eyes, a hand's width away from her. The illusion was so good she could even taste the grape she herself had put on his lips. And it aroused her more than it should have, standing in the middle of her party.

"I love this," she admitted, heat burning in her cheeks as she focused her eyes on his chest, "but perhaps we shouldn't do this in front of everyone."

"In front of who?" Dion asked softly.

No one seemed to notice them, and one by one, the people around them winked out as if they were nothing more than holograms, until she and Dion were all alone outside, bright stars above them, and the heat of the fire crawling over her arms.

"Impressive," Lucille breathed. Her mind could barely grasp the enormity of his illusion. "But now it's time for something real."

And with that, Lucille snaked her hand around the back of his neck and drew him closer. His real lips were even more intense than the illusion of them, though there was no grape juice left. Instead, what she tasted was him. No illusions, just Dion.

"I thought you didn't believe in love." Lucille laughed softly, slightly out of breath as she came up for air.

"I don't," Dion admitted, looking a little pained. "But you're on your best way to convincing me otherwise."

She kissed him again, pushing away the doubts that tried to tell her this was reckless. That she couldn't lose her heart to someone who'd grown up with illusions, receiving and crafting them, without ever holding on to anything real. Someone who didn't even live here. "You're going to leave in two days."

Dion held her face between his hands, cradling her cheeks with endless gentleness. "But you'll come visit me soon."

In two weeks, they'd be leaving for France. She'd have one more week with him. One more week of illusions.

"Let's make the most of it, then."

Part 2

Memories & Sunshine

Lucille

The student exchange in Greenvalley had been filled with long hikes in the forest and stuffy museums. Marseille welcomed them with blue skies, sunshine, and a glistening ocean.

"Now that's what I call a cultural program." Lucille closed her eyes and breathed in the salty, slightly fishy air while the wind caressed her shoulders. But there was also a feeling that was more than just the wind. No wind could find the hard spot between her shoulder blades and massage it out of her.

She opened her eyes and found Dion standing not too far from her with some of his classmates. He gave her one of those cheeky smiles of his she'd come to fall for, and she laughed.

"What's so funny?" Matt asked next to her.

Like all the other students, they were in their swimming clothes, and nearly every female's gaze—and some males'—were on them. Or rather on Matt. Lucille couldn't blame them—he looked like an underwear model in his shorts: chiselled abs, bronze skin, sun-bright hair, and all. With his towel flung over his shoulder, he had the cool guy style perfected to a T.

A year ago, Lucille would've been all over him. Today, she only had eyes for Dion.

"Nothing," she answered, her gaze never even leaving Dion's face. "Absolutely nothing."

Steps sloshed through the sand as someone ran up behind them. "Gee, thanks for waiting," Jan announced. He grasped their shoulders. "Shall we go brave the waves?"

Lucille sighed and turned into him. "I still can't believe they chose you to replace Henk. You don't even speak French."

"I suffered through it for four years. Just got rid of it as soon as I could." Jan shrugged with his left shoulder and grinned. "Tu veux nager avec moi?"

"Look at that." She probably shouldn't have been surprised every time Jan chose to exhibit a piece of information he had retained from his twelve years of schooling, but she couldn't help it. "You might be better than Matt at it."

"Hey!" the blonde protested.

Jan grinned widely, clearly enjoying this rare triumph. "Say that again."

The wind caressed her cheek again, while the impression of fingertips ran down her spine. Lucille shuddered. "I… uhm, I actually need a refreshment." She started walking towards the group of French students, eyes locked once more with Dion.

"Yeah, me too," Matt announced, breaking off to the side, apparently having decided on his newest conquest.

"You know swimming is also very refreshing!" Jan called out, but his voice was quickly drowned out by the murmur of waves and the squawking of seagulls.

Then she was in Dion's real arms, and the world fell away. It was just the two of them, alone on some tropical beach, where the sun glistened on azure water and the sand was golden. A lonely crab walked sideways to the water. "I thought you wanted to show me Marseille and not some faraway dreamland." Amused, she kissed his lips.

Dion held her, his fingers following the trail of his earlier illusion. "But I'd much rather be somewhere faraway with you. Besides, you always make me feel like I'm dreaming."

Lucille buried her fingers in his soft hair and pulled him closer. "Then keep dreaming."

She was about to kiss him again when a scream tore through the edge of their illusion. In a blink of the eye, the real world returned, and they found themselves in a tight embrace between the others. Not that anyone cared, as their attention was on the water where Ani—who had taken Cheryl's place after the queen bee's refusal to live a week at her French exchange partner's house—was screaming.

Alan was sloshing through the water towards her. Ani stopped screaming long enough to tell him about some creature in the water. For a moment, Alan ducked down. When he came up again, he angrily threw some seaweed at Ani. While Ani started screaming as soon as it hit her chest, the rest of the students turned away with bored mutters.

"Are all mountain girls like her?" Dion muttered. "I mean, apart from you?"

"Screaming bloody murder because of some seaweed? Not the ones I know, but it's pretty on-brand for Ani."

Dion snorted. "Just like sneaking off for a quickie is on-brand for Matt, I suppose."

Lucille followed his line of sight. A little further down the beach, Matt was flirting with a girl around their age, clearly making up for his lack of French with his abundance of charm. Just as he was about to put his arm around her and lead her away, Mr Zobel, who was accompanying their trip as a male chaperone, caught up with them.

They couldn't hear what was being said, but judging by Matt's annoyed expression and the fact the girl made a quick escape, it wasn't going well for the quickie. Matt's face was all thunder and storm as he drudged back through the sand, kicking the grains ahead of him.

"...still a school excursion," Zobel was saying as they passed Lucille and Dion on their way back.

"I don't need anyone to protect my innocence," Matt muttered.

Dion chuckled into her shoulder, the soft vibration reminding Lucille of what they'd been up to before their interruption. "Monsieur Zobel doesn't seem to know Matt very well if he thinks there's any innocence left to protect."

"Or maybe he knows him too well." She wrapped his arms around her, and the world fell away once more. Lucille sunk into his chest, breathing in the salty air. Then she turned around, snaking one of her arms back to his neck. "Where were we?"

Somewhere, Ani was screaming again, but Lucille tuned her out as she fell into a deep, sensual kiss with Dion. Her other hand ran over the smooth skin of his sizeable biceps. Dion held her tight, his fingers slowly trailing her back, leaving behind a line of goosebumps. Behind them, the waves of their illusion rushed in, a soft murmur that was the perfect backdrop to their tropical make-out session.

Until it wasn't.

The crashing of the waves became more real and tangible, seagulls screeched, and the murmur of people mixed with the sounds of paradise. Dion paused, turning his head to the side as if listening to something Lucille couldn't hear.

The illusion broke away, and the murmurs became agitated shouts and whispers. People pointed at the sea, while some were pulling their phones out. Ani was nowhere to be found at first, but then Lucille noticed her arm frantically hitting the waves before it submerged again. Alan was nearby, but instead of diving after her, he backed away. And suddenly, Lucille saw it.

A big dark shadow lurked under the waves. It was a bulbous shape with long, curly extremities, one of which broke through the surface and hit Alan in the chest, sending him crashing into the shallow water.

"Was that a tentacle?" Lucille asked before checking with Dion. "Is this one of yours?"

"No." Dion shook his head, his eyes fixed on the water.

Meanwhile, Matt and Jan were sloshing through the sea. They ran past Alan and dived underwater. Anxiously, Lucille watched as they came up for air, had a quick discussion, and went back down again. Not to be outdone, Alan followed their lead and dived back in.

More tentacles whipped through the air, spraying water everywhere. Alan's head popped back up, sputtering. A tentacle wrapped around his mid-section and pulled him underwater. People were screaming, and Lucille saw a lifeguard running towards them. Then Alan came up again, and a second later, Jan appeared, dragging an unconscious Ani with him. Together, he and Alan brought her to the beach, where the lifeguard took immediate action to resuscitate her.

Shocked silence reigned as everybody's attention focused on them. Only Lucille was still staring out at the sea. The water had calmed, and the dark shadow seemed to retreat into deeper waters. Something wasn't right. Something was missing.

"Matt!" Lucille realised with a start.

Less than a second later, her missing friend broke through the surface, gasping for air. Lines of red circles crisscrossed his upper body, but the tentacles no longer reached out to him. The monster was dead, dissolving into flecks of darkness as they watched.

Fabian

Ever since spring had come to Greenvalley, Samantha had dragged Fabian from flower shop to park to garden show in search of her Emblem of Power. They'd even combed the forest. Without luck. If the divine flowers were growing in Greenvalley, they hadn't yet bloomed. Which apparently meant it was time for drastic measures.

On a sunny afternoon that could've been spent outside, they were instead holed up in the back of the Magic Circle with a bubbling cauldron.

Fabian peered at the wine-red liquid. "Do you really think this is going to work?"

"I've got no idea," Samantha admitted, while chopping some dried herbs into the mix. "But it's worth a shot. It's called the Potion of Finding Lost Things, after all."

"Don't you need to have something first before you can lose it?" It wasn't like he wanted to discourage Samantha. He just couldn't imagine how a potion would help them find the elusive flowers.

Samantha halted, quietly counting down time with the help of her fingers, while she spoke. "I'm working on the assumption that my previous soul owner lost it. The flowers are mine. These fingers just haven't held them yet. Thirty." She sprinkled a powder into the potion in a spiral motion. "The worst that can happen is nothing."

"Nothing isn't a bad thing," Fabian said gently. "You know, maybe the emblems can't be forced. Mine practically fell into my lap. On the risk of sounding really old, I think they'll come to you when the time is right."

"That *did* sound really old." Samantha laughed and reached for the ladle to perform a series of complex motions. "There's no harm in trying, though."

"With a recipe covered with a patina of dust between the floorboards of our attic." They'd found the page last weekend when helping his parents shift some furniture up there.

Samantha shrugged and paused to watch the potion. "Recipes don't go bad. And hey, look at it this way: perhaps the recipe needed to fall into my lap."

Fabian winced, once again succumbing to Samantha's superior logic. "Fine. Just don't blow us up."

For a few moments, Samantha busied herself with preparing the next ingredients for her potion, measuring everything as exactly as if she were in a chemistry lab. Fabian settled on a chair and pulled out his lunchbox to eat the rest of a sandwich.

"Hey, Fabi," Samantha asked after a while, "can I ask you something?" Fabian made a non-committal sound, busy chewing. "We've been spending a lot of time together lately. Is everything okay with you and Rachel?"

"Yeah, sure," he said automatically, when in fact nothing was okay. He just didn't really understand what the source of it all was. And he was too afraid to ask. With a sigh, he ran his hand through his hair, noting that he'd need a haircut soon. "Look, I... she's pulling away, I think. To be honest, I don't even know if we still have a relationship."

They hadn't spent any time alone since Lucille's party. Perhaps even since before that.

"What do you mean, you're not sure?" The potion needed time to cook, so Samantha's green eyes focused on him.

Fabian put his lunchbox down with a sigh. "You know, when we first got together, I thought why not? What's the difference between a romantic relationship and the relationship I had with Rachel? The kissing, sure, but take that away and what do you have left? It's still the same thing, Sam. I like her. She's important to me, and I enjoy spending time with her. But it's just more of the same. There's never more than that. And now it's even less."

Samantha took a deep breath. "Sounds to me like you'd be better as friends. I'm not telling you to break her heart or anything, but as much as I would love this for the two of you, I think you're right. You don't seem like you're in love. Neither of you." She straightened her back, ready to return to her potion. "Which is surprising, because she was so in love with you last year."

"Well, a lot of things happened last year." Perhaps they shouldn't have got together so soon after Nico's death. Rachel had still been grieving. *He'd* still been grieving. They'd both lost him, and perhaps being together had been Fabian's way of holding on a little longer. "I feel horrible."

Bent over the recipe, Samantha gave him a quick smile. "Don't. These things happen. Take it from someone who's been there." She picked up a handful of cut roots and carried them over to the cauldron. "I love you very much, Fabian, but it wasn't that kind of love."

The familiar ache reared its geriatric head. It was really more a memory of the love he'd borne for her. "Is that what this is?" He'd been so hurt when Samantha had broken up with him, and all this time, her reasons had made no sense. How could someone love a person, yet not *love* them?

"Could be. Or it's something else." Samantha threw her root pieces into the cauldron and stirred a couple of times clockwise before changing direction. "We're still young, after all. We're not supposed to have it all figured out. Or stay together forever." She turned away to grab a glass bottle filled with a purple liquid. "Hey, perhaps this potion could help you find what you've lost. It's almost done."

"What I've lost?" Fabian got up to peer into the cauldron once more. The potion was now a foamy green. How was he supposed to find something he didn't even know he was looking for?

Samantha simply smiled, reminding him of one thing he *had* lost somehow. Then she placed exactly three drops into the foam. Fabian watched them sink, slowly forming big purple circles. The foam began to swell, then rise.

"Is it work—?" The foam was rising too fast. In a split-second, it had reached the rim of the cauldron, and still, it bubbled on. Potion dripped over the sides onto his shoes. Fabian jumped back. "Sam!"

She shrieked, invisible behind a mountain of foam. "Fabian!" The entire room filled with foam as liquid sloshed over the ground. "Fabi!" It even distorted her voice, making it sound lighter, almost child-like.

Fabian slipped on the liquid and hit the ground. The pain made him want to cry with an overwhelming intensity, but he managed to bite down on his tongue and keep the tears in. Like a big boy.

The foam receded as quickly as it had come, leaving behind nothing but a few bubbles and a slightly damp floor. Fabian wiped the bubbles from his shirt and shook his head. "What the hell, Sam?" So much for not blowing them up.

"You're not allowed to use bad words."

Was she being serious? A plethora of "bad words" came to his mind, all of them appropriate. "Uhm, you just flooded the entire room and brought foamageddon on us. You know how my mum will freak out, right?" A weird sound stopped him. "Are you crying?"

He got back to his feet, holding on to the rim of the big cauldron, and made his way around it. There, in the middle of the last remaining soap bubbles, sat Samantha. And not Samantha. At least not the Samantha he'd seen a minute ago. Her hair in two puffy pigtails, his five-year-old best friend sat in a puddle, crying her eyes out.

"Holy shit!"

"You're not supposed to curse all the time, Fabi!"

Fabian whirled around at the sound of his mother, feeling instant guilt rising in his chest. Caroline entered the room and shocked him almost as much as Samantha had. She was still his mother, though there were fewer lines in her face, and no grey streaks in her hair. But most importantly, she was bigger than him. Much bigger than him.

Panicked, he checked his own body, frantically touching his face and chest. He was most definitely no longer eighteen. "This can't be happening."

"Hey, darling." His mother bent down to Samantha and pulled her up to her feet. "What happened?"

Samantha was still crying, slinging her little arms around Caroline. "Fabian was mean to me, and then he said it was all my fault."

Fabian shuddered when his mother glared at him, a perfect mix of outrage and disappointment. "Fabian Frederick Bendtfeld—what did you do now?"

His head was still reeling from everything that was going on. "Me? Nothing!" That excuse had never flown high with his mother. "Samantha brewed the potion. Suddenly, there was foam everywhere, and now Sam and I look like this." He pointed at himself.

"Like what?"

"Like children!" Couldn't she see how this was a problem?

Apparently, his mum found it amusing. "You *are* children. Come on. You two know you're not supposed to be in here. Let's go play outside." She let Samantha down, who had already forgotten all about her tears, and was happily skipping through the door.

Fabian looked around frantically. He was suddenly five years old again. Thirteen years had gone, yet he seemed to be the only one who remembered. Samantha—the *one* who'd come up with this potion, the genius he always turned to—was some happy-go-lucky preschooler. Entirely useless. And to top things off, he was no longer in the Magic Circle, but in his parents' kitchen at home. What was happening?

His gaze fell on the cauldron, which was lying on its side. Purplish liquid was still swirling in the bottom. Fabian made a quick decision. While his mum's back was turned, he grabbed his lunchbox and scooped up as much of the potion as he could without touching it.

"Come on now," Caroline said with a sigh.

He barely got the lid on before she put her hands on his shoulders and gently steered him out of the kitchen.

Jan

To Jan's chagrin, not every day of the exchange was to be spent at the beach. Today's excursion was to some famous museum about European and Mediterranean history in particular. Jan was almost falling asleep standing, but Lu was exalted. She kept dragging them from one exhibition piece to the next, excitedly reciting the labels and telling them some supposedly cool facts. The actual cool thing was a bridge that led to a 17th-century fortress in the harbour, practically untouched by time.

It was there, in some breezy corner, that Jan, Matt, Lu, and Dion huddled together to finally discuss what they'd seen the day before.

"But if it really was a giant octopus, shouldn't it have stayed in the deep sea?" Lu asked after Matt had described what they'd seen underwater.

Jan shuddered at the memory. He'd seen an octopus at some aquarium before. They were fascinating and a little bit weird, but what he'd seen in the shallows of the sea had been the stuff of nightmares. The creature that had pulled Ani under had been at least three metres long, with a multitude of tentacles that were almost as thick as his thighs. Freeing Ani from their grasp had been almost impossible. "Perhaps this octopus was on holiday."

Predictably, Lu punched him in the arm for that. "I remember reading that they fall apart if they come up too high. That's why it's nearly impossible to preserve one."

"This one was definitely not falling apart until after I shot enough energy into it," Matt said. He stretched his neck to lock eyes with Amélie and raised his hand to smile and wave at her.

Zobel stepped in between the two, and Jan watched Matt's face fall. "Keep moving, please. We're going to return to the bus in five minutes," he called out.

The four of them left their corner with Matt muttering, "Can somebody please explain to me what his problem is? He doesn't care what I do in Greenvalley, so why here?"

"Because *here* you are under his supervision." Jan slapped his shoulder and grinned. "He's taking his job very seriously, you know?"

"Listen," Dion said softly, "I did some research last night, and it appears that this wasn't the first time something like this has happened in the area. There have been other animal attacks. Sea creatures of all sizes."

Matt narrowed his eyes and looked at him sideways. "I gather this is not normal for this region?"

"I wasn't previously aware of giant kraken attacks, no. Though I wonder if my grandfather knows more about it. He's been living in the area his entire life, so I'd be surprised if he was oblivious." Dion paused and sighed. "Actually, I wouldn't be surprised if he was the one to cover it all up. Make people think it *is* normal that, occasionally, a tourist drowns off the coast because he's being dragged into the deep."

"Your grandfather is the type of person who'd cover that up?" Jan asked.

Dion shrugged. "'If it can't be fixed, make it disappear' has always been somewhat of a family motto." Lu took his hand and squeezed it.

It could've been the Kerscher motto as well. Jan left it to Lu to comfort Dion over whatever family trauma he was suffering from. His own parents were masters of ignoring the obvious, and they would totally prefer some illusion of reality over an occult explanation. "So, animal attacks? Are we—?"

"What do you want to do?" Matt asked before Jan had even finished asking. "Patrol the waters? One underwater fight was enough for me but be my guest."

He had a point there. Jan didn't particularly relish the idea of facing off against another sea creature while trying not to drown. "Maybe they have a nest somewhere."

"They might, but I'm not going to search for it," Matt announced somewhat upbeat. Smoothly, he sidestepped Amélie and slid his arm around her waist. "Hey, beautiful."

"Hands to yourself, Matt!" Zobel called from far behind them.

Matt rolled his eyes heavily and let go of Amélie. "Will I see you tomorrow night?" They had one evening off, at least.

Amélie was obviously just as keen on spending more time with Matt. "Bien sûr."

"About that," Jan said, making sure to enjoy every syllable of what he was about to say, "Zobel asked me earlier to make sure we stick together as a group. And he specifically assigned our group."

Matt narrowed his eyes suspiciously. This was gold.

"He's no monster, so the three of us plus our partners get to stick together, but we're also being accompanied by Alan, Shayna, Cian, and their partners." And now it was time to enjoy the show.

Matt didn't disappoint. His face fell, and a furious glint filled his eyes. "Who does he think he is?" he hissed, almost frothing at the mouth.

"Our chaperone." Jan laughed and clapped Matt's shoulders. "Just be glad he didn't insist on accompanying us as well. It's the small things."

"I would've wrung his neck if he did."

"Matt, relax." Lu nudged his side. "With such a big group, it'll be impossible to keep track of everyone." She wriggled her eyebrows, then shrugged. "And if Alan and his troupe are making trouble, Dion and I will practise our illusion magic."

To prove a point, Dion wrapped his arms around Lu and kissed her passionately. Some of the other students whooped, while Matt turned around for Zobel, desperate to get his attention on this brazen flaunting of the rules. Zobel, however, was busy misguidedly helping a statue on a tour of the fort. Jan started laughing.

"Very funny," Matt said when the two lovebirds broke off their kiss. "You'd better come through on that offer."

Jan enjoyed watching him stalk off. Half-demon or not, Matt needed to be pushed off his high horse from time to time. It kept him human.

Jan put a hand on Lu's shoulder. "Please don't let him get away with Amélie, or whoever he's into tomorrow night, too soon."

Lu only rolled her eyes, but she didn't say no. They were all going to have some good old-fashioned fun.

131

A SPRING OF MAGIC

Jan put a hand on Lu's shoulder. "Please don't let him get away with Amélie, or whoever he's into tomorrow night, too soon."

Lu only rolled her eyes, but she didn't say no. They were all going to have some good old-fashioned fun.

Matt

Matt couldn't believe he was forced to spend the evening with the Elite Idiots. Not once in his life had any grown-up cared how he spent his time. Not his mother, not his father, not anyone. And now, Mr Zobel, of all people, felt responsible for his proper conduct. For a moment, Matt toyed with the idea of simply seducing his teacher to make a point, but he still had a whole year of Politics and German classes ahead of him, and besides, he wasn't that desperate.

Instead, he trailed behind the group, separated from Amélie by the two blokes from the Elite Clique, or as he liked to call them, The Soccer Heads. There was no love lost between them, despite the three of them—make that four with Jan—being on the same school team. Alan had made it instantly clear that he saw Matt as a threat to his pseudo-star power, and his best friend had followed along, like the idiot he was.

This particular idiot was now glancing at him before making the terrible decision to pause walking until Matt had caught up. "Hey." Cian grinned at him, as if they were the best of friends. "Can I ask you a question?"

Matt grunted, hoping that would be enough to shoo the boy away again.

Cian took it as consent. "I've kind of been wondering this for a while, but is there something going on between you and Samantha?"

"Absolutely not." How did he get that ridiculous idea in his head?

"Really?" Cian's eyes lit up, and Matt suddenly felt his stomach churning. "Because I heard rumours..."

What rumours? Matt almost wanted to ask, but instead he said the truth. "She hates me. I can't deal with her. We fight every time we get together, so no, there's absolutely nothing going on between me and Samantha." He wanted there to be something, though, and the pain in his stomach deepened.

"You see?" Now Alan barged in. "I told you he wouldn't be interested in someone as plain or weird as Witchy Sam. You can plough ahead."

Matt clenched his fists, but he forced himself to react to the meaning behind the words, not the insulting words themselves. "Plough ahead?"

Cian dragged his feet a little and grimaced. "Don't listen to him."

"Little Cian here is head-over-heels for Samantha," Shayna explained, enjoying her friend's discomfort a little too much. "But he's too scared Cheryl will scratch his eyes out if he makes a move on her."

"I'm not scared!" Cian bellowed back, drawing the attention of the others now. He took a deep breath to calm himself. "Yes, I've got a crush on Samantha. So what?" He faced Matt again. "I wanted to make sure I'm not stepping on your toes or anything, but if I'm not, I think I'm going to ask her out on a date when we get back. And Cheryl can go to Hell."

Matt doubted Cheryl wanted to visit Hell after what she'd experienced on Walpurgis Night, but he saw no problem with sending Cian there, all of a sudden. "You're stepping on my toes." He hadn't forgotten Samantha's tears after Cian had kissed and humiliated her in front of everybody.

Cian stopped short, frowning. "Didn't you just say there's nothing going on between the two of you?"

"There is." A lot was going on between the two of them. All those accusations, thinly veiled insults, and threats. Samantha hated him, and Matt would be damned if he let this idiot anywhere close to her. "I forgot."

"You forgot?" Cian's confusion increased. He looked like a proper idiot now.

Before he could ask again, though, a stranger put his arms around Matt and Cian's shoulders from behind. "Hey, hey," he said with a thick

French accent. "You are tourists here? Looking for a party? Club over there, free drinks in the next hour."

If he hadn't been so annoyed, Matt might have considered flirting with the stranger. He was a good-looking man in his early twenties, tanned from the southern sun, with deep, dark eyes. Instead, Matt freed himself from the arm, accidentally mirroring Cian as he did so. "No, thanks."

"What are you talking about?" Shayna stepped forward. "Free drinks sound lovely."

"Yeah," Alan chimed in.

The stranger laughed. "Good, good. Come along."

Matt narrowed his eyes suspiciously. But the group was already in motion, lured in by the promise of free drinks and a good party. He was about to protest and tell them to take caution, but it was only Cian and him left.

"Well, then," Cian said and made to follow the others.

Matt wrapped his hand around his wrist and squeezed until Cian gasped in pain. "Listen closely, okay? Sam and I might not be together, but you keep your fingers off her or I swear to you, this won't end well for you." As soon as he'd spoken the words, Matt knew he shouldn't have said them. They were wrong in a way that left a very bitter taste in his mouth.

Cian tore his arm free from his grasp. "You're such a weirdo, you know?" And with that, he stalked off, leaving Matt alone with his conflicting feelings.

"I don't like this," Matt muttered to Jan as they took seats at the bar.

There actually was a club and it was well-visited, considering how hidden it was in the backstreets. True to the promise, they'd been offered vouchers for free drinks upon entry, something Jan was taking full advantage of. But something still felt off. Or perhaps Matt was just in a foul mood after the whole fiasco with Mr Zobel and the annoying announcement of Cian's intention to date Samantha.

"You don't like that this French guy is flirting with your Amélie," Jan said with a laugh.

Matt watched the two in question without even flinching. Somehow, he found himself utterly unfazed about the fact the girl he had planned to have fun with tonight was currently enamoured with someone else. He realised he wouldn't even mind if Amélie went off with the other guy.

"Lighten up, Matt. There's plenty of fish in the water. And some sea creatures." Jan clapped his shoulder, then turned around to grab his beer and walk onto the dance floor. He wasn't much of a dancer, but that didn't stop him from grooving to the music.

His seat wasn't empty for long. Instead of dancing with his friends, Cian slipped into it, coming annoyingly close again. "Hey, I wanted to apologise for outside. I think we had a bit of a misunderstanding."

"You can't be serious," Matt muttered, wondering what divine being he had angered to be put through the wringer like this.

"Look, I don't have a problem with you," Cian continued, painstakingly oblivious.

"That may be so. But I've got a problem with you."

That wiped the friendly smile off Cian's face. He scowled at Matt. "And why's that?"

Matt took a deep breath. He had absolutely no patience for this conversation. "Let me phrase it like this: you and your Elite Clique friends are dumbasses who think they're so super cool, and everyone wants to be like you or be your friend, when in fact, you're just a bunch of bullies who can't back it up."

The fold between Cian's eyebrows deepened. "Not that I care much, but if there's someone who thinks he's super cool and everybody wants him, it's you. We're just having fun."

"Yeah, with other people's feelings."

Cian shook his head and scoffed. "You know, why don't you tell me what you really think? I've never done anything to you, have I?"

Matt had to stop and think—or rather stop himself from lashing out again. It was true. Cian had never bothered him directly. Perhaps glared at him from time to time, but that could've easily been his own fault. The reason he liked Cian least of the Elite Clique was frighteningly simple. "Not to me, but you've hurt Samantha."

Cian's eyes widened. "What are you talking about? I like Samantha. I've never made fun of her."

"Really? Then how do you explain last year?" And all the times before he'd known her, when Cian had hung around with Cheryl. "You took her to that party, getting her hopes up, and once there, you humiliated her in front of everybody. I bet Cheryl loved that." Matt slipped from his bar stool, hot blood racing through his veins.

"That's not what happened." Cian refused to meet his challenge, staying seated in his chair. "I agree that the kiss was a bit premature—I hardly knew her then—but it was genuine."

As genuine as a kiss due to a love spell could be, Matt thought smugly. And perhaps that thought should have given him pause. Cian couldn't completely be held accountable for his actions that day. Love spell aside, there was one thing Matt could blame him for. "You know she ran from that party in tears? I didn't see you following her outside."

Cian glared at him, but he didn't protest. Before Matt could double down, his attention was suddenly caught by a breathtakingly beautiful woman with bright violet hair who had just entered the club.

She gazed around as if she owned the place, smiling at Dion and Lucille slow dancing and Shayna flirting with a stranger. Then her eyes locked with Matt's, and her face brightened. "Beau."

The girl said something in French to her friend, and it was as if the entire club listened. When the last word was said, she smiled at Matt again.

His stomach unclenched, and he forgot all about Cian and his stupid confession. He even forgot about Samantha. What did it really matter to him who broke her heart? It wasn't his to protect.

Matt was halfway through the room when he noticed a motion to his side, where Amélie was leaning into her flirting partner. The tanned man lowered his head to kiss her neck, white glinting in the lights. White. Glinting. In the lights.

"Vampires."

A violet-coloured tentacle wrapped around his chest and pulled him closer. The girl's face was still beautiful, but tentacles moved under the dress, and sharp fangs flashed as she smiled. "It's merpires, beautiful."

Then she opened her jaw and bit him.

Fabian

One thing Fabian had completely forgotten was how beautiful the Kollmers' garden had been thirteen years ago. While staying home with first one and then two kids, Samantha's mother had put a lot of work into their backyard. Colourful flowerbeds surrounded a terrace, while a multitude of fruit trees and bushes lined the rest of the garden. It was too early in the year to steal a snack, but Fabian could see lots and lots of green strawberries. In front of the terrace was a meadow large enough to play badminton and have a paddling pool in the summer. A sandpit in the corner rounded out the little paradise. But Fabian's favourite thing was the herbal snail garden with its spiralling stone borders. He wasn't allowed to step on any of the plants, so it was a real challenge to balance.

Samantha was busy taking care of a small flowerbed that belonged to her, and currently sprouted a selection of forget-me-nots and weeds, while their mothers enjoyed a coffee on the terrace, and baby Meg was getting her hands dirty in the sandpit. It was a beautiful spring day, and Fabian couldn't be more content with his lot. Except...

Balancing on stones wasn't going to get him back to his old life. Or his new life. Future life!

Annoyed with himself, he jumped off the snail and took a deep breath. With every minute that passed, his concentration was getting worse. There were moments when he was completely engrossed in his childish needs—he would play with a toy car for half an hour and forget all about the magic potion that had caused his state. And Samantha was worse.

Despite this being all her fault, she had no recollection of her future self. Which was quite a big problem, since he had no idea how to get them back.

"Hey, Sam." Fabian sat down next to her and watched her taking great care replanting a dandelion. "That's a weed."

She glared at him. "It's pretty."

"Yes, but technically..." Fabian waved it off. It didn't matter how they classified weeds. "Listen, I need you to focus. Do you remember whether the potion you made had a reverse spell or something?"

"I didn't make a potion." Samantha turned her attention back to the flowerbed.

Fabian stayed around for a while before he remembered the urgency of their situation. "Listen. I've got the potion." He ran to the terrace, grabbed his lunchbox, and returned to her. "Do you remember this?"

Samantha leaned over and peered inside. The liquid was still as purple as before, though there was no foam on top. "Is that painting water?"

"What?"

"You know the water for the paint brushes. You were painting this morning, weren't you?"

Fabian snapped the lid shut again. "No, it's not painting water. It's a powerful potion. A witch's potion. You *made* it."

"I don't understand." Her bottom lip quivered, and he was reminded of how she'd thought he'd been telling her off yesterday.

"Don't you remember anything? We're not five. We're supposed to be eighteen." His own eyes filled with tears of frustration. He couldn't make a potion. He had no idea how to fix this.

Samantha's face brightened, and she laughed. "Silly Fabi. If we were eighteen, we would be at work, and we would be married and have kids."

Her utter conviction shocked him speechless. Married at eighteen? It was utter nonsense, of course, but back then they'd both believed in it. Heck, he'd believed it until last year. Though, naturally, the actual act of marriage would have been a few more years in the future.

While Fabian pondered what he'd lost, Meg toddled over, a flower upside down in her clenched fist.

"Hey, Meggie." Samantha stretched her arms out and helped her little sister sit. "What do you have there?"

"For you!" Meg pushed the flower into Samantha's lap.

Samantha's eyes grew big. "Is that for me? Oh, thank you, Meggie. That's lovely." She bent over and gave her sister a kiss. Then she held the flower out to Fabian. "Isn't it pretty?"

It was indeed quite pretty. The shape suggested they were part of the lily family, but the blossoms showed lush purple and blue tones, with a hint of fiery red in the middle. Bright yellow pistils rose between the petals, while black dots covered the outer leaves. As Samantha moved it around, the colours seemed to change in the sunlight.

There was something important about the flower. Something Fabian needed to remember, but all he could think of was how pretty it would be in Samantha's hair. He reached out to take the flower from her and put the stem into one of her pigtails. Samantha winced a little when he pulled her hair too tightly, but she held still. "Now *you're* pretty."

"Aww." Apparently, Julienne had overheard them, as she was on her way to Meg. She patted Fabian's head. "You're such a nice boy today, Fabi. Now come on, Meg. I can smell you're due for a nappy change from here."

Fabian watched her pick up the little girl and sniff her bum, despite her previous claim, before grimacing. His eyes followed her as she carried Meg to the terrace and quickly stopped to tell Caroline about the cute interaction she'd witnessed. Then something else caught his attention. A group of young students walked past the fence, chatting and laughing. And he recognised the guy in the back.

The memories hit him like a truck again. That's right, he wasn't here to play with Samantha. He needed to find a way out of here. Back to his own time and adult body. "Mr Traidous!"

As he ran to the gate, the young guy in the back stopped. When Fabian had entered first grade a year later, Mr Traidous had seemed like a full-blown adult, but now, with his eighteen-year-old mind, Fabian noticed how young he'd really been. He wasn't as flawless as Matt, but he was a good-looking guy. A human version of Matt in a few years.

"Do I know you?" René asked, sounding amused. His friends had stopped as well, curiously peering down at Fabian.

"Yes! No! Not yet," Fabian said and shook his head, trying his best to focus. "You need to help me. Samantha has brewed a magic potion and now we're five-year-olds again. And you are... what? Twenty-four?"

René frowned a little. "That was a really good guess. So, I'm assuming you weren't five years old before?" His tone made it clear that he was only playing along.

Somehow, Fabian had to make him understand that this wasn't some silly game, but real. "No, I was eighteen yesterday."

"Are you sure?" He was still frowning, but then he cocked his head sideways. "Where do you know my name from?"

Fabian's chest was flooded with relief. His head felt suddenly airy. They were on the right track. He had knowledge his five-year-old self shouldn't have. "You're Matt's daddy. He's my friend and—"

"Oh, dear, I'm so sorry!" His mother was running up to them. Her hands wrapped around Fabian's shoulders like two vices while she pulled him away from the gate. "Don't mind him. He's got a very imaginative phase right now. Come on," she said to Fabian. "You're not supposed to talk to strangers."

"But we're not strangers!" Fabian cried out. This couldn't be happening. Not when he was so close.

Behind him, René had paled and gone all rigid. His good mood was gone, and he needed a friend of his to pull him away to start moving again. A slew of emotions passed on his face, all too complex for Fabian's shrinking brain to understand. And then he walked away, fast and determined.

"What were you thinking?" Caroline asked, crouching down so she could look him in the eye. "You're acting weird, Fabi. Are you getting sick?" She put her hand against his forehead to check his temperature.

Fabian shook his head. He felt fine—if one ignored the dreadful weight of disappointment. "Mummy, can we visit Samantha's grandma?" Elda would listen to him. She would know what to do.

"We can't. Elda's still at the conference in Fulda. She won't be back until the weekend."

"That's too long!" Fabian noticed he had no idea when the weekend would be. He couldn't even remember which day they'd attempted the potion. But deep inside, he feared that any hour longer would be too long.

"Don't be silly. Now go and play with Samantha. Perhaps in an hour, we can all go and get some ice cream."

His brain short-circuited, and he screamed, "Ice cream!" before the thought had even fully registered in his mind. Arms wide, Fabian zoomed to Samantha to tell her all about the exciting news, his meeting with René already forgotten. "We're going to get ice cream."

"Awesome!" Samantha's eyes glistened likewise. She was patting a big mound of soil and poured the colourful water from his lunch box over it.

"What did you do with your flower?" Fabian asked, noting that her hair was empty again.

"I planted it." Samantha pointed at the small mound of soil in front of her. "So new ones can grow. My granny told me it's important to give back to nature. It's all a circle," she said wisely. "Magic flows in circles."

Fabian swallowed her explanation without a doubt in his mind. "Okay. Do you want to play hide-and-seek?"

Samantha nodded exuberantly. "You hide first." She covered her eyes. "One, two..."

Later that day, after a trek out to the playground and two scoops of ice cream, Fabian was sitting at dinner with his parents, figuring out how high he could swirl his spaghetti into a tower.

"Fabi, don't play with your food," his mother gently reminded him.

Fabian snapped out of it with a jolt. "I know that!" he said more to himself than to his parents.

His father laughed, though. "Then why are you doing it?"

That was a really good question. He knew he wasn't a five-year-old, and yet he kept behaving like one more and more often. He had no autonomy over his own time, instead being transported by his mother from one place to the other. Nobody listened to him or took him seriously, and sometimes Fabian couldn't even take himself seriously. Being eighteen seemed like a fever dream. Especially when one added water magic and fighting monsters, and all that.

"I don't know," he mumbled. "I think it's some sort of reflex."

"Wow, that's a big word. Did Sammy teach you that?" his mother asked as she leaned over to cut his spaghetti into pieces.

Even as a five-year-old, Samantha had always been ahead of him. "No." Petulantly, he crossed his arms. "Sam is incapable of helping me at the moment."

That made his mother pause. "What do you mean, darling? Help you with what?"

"With the potion." He pointed at his plate. "I don't need you to cut my spaghetti, for example. I'm supposed to be eighteen years old!"

She retreated with the cutlery. "Excuse me. I didn't realise you were such a big boy all of a sudden."

"No, the problem is that I'm such a little boy all of a sudden."

His parents exchanged a confused glance. Then his father put a hand on his arm, completely dwarfing Fabian's hand. "You're pretending to be an adult, right? Ben and I always played that when we were young."

Fabian pulled his hand away, his little face turning red with anger. "I *am* an adult." Tears were stinging in his eyes, and he furiously rubbed his face to keep them in. "Look. Sam brewed a magic potion yesterday. The Potion of Lost Things or something like that. Suddenly, it developed an enormous amount of foam that filled the entire room, and once it was gone, we were back in our childhood bodies."

"That sounds like a very complicated game," Caroline said carefully.

His father sighed and leaned back in his chair, a disgruntled fold forming between his eyebrows. "I told you not to let him play with that magic stuff. It's confusing him and filling his head with things he can't understand."

"I can understand it perfectly fine. Better than you because I can actually *do* magic," Fabian replied, heated.

"Sure you can." Joachim patted his head absently while giving his wife a pointed look.

Caroline took a deep breath, then the warm smile was back, and she addressed Fabian. "You seem very upset—"

"Because you're not listening to me!"

Taken aback, she shared another glance with his father. "I'm sorry, Fabi. That is very bad of us. What were you trying to tell us?"

He didn't know. All his reasons were gone. Tears were running down his cheeks, and his stomach felt too hot and tight, but he couldn't remember why he was so angry. Only that it was important. Something was very important, and he needed to figure it out. But it was too hard. It was too hard, and he was too little. And that made him cry even harder.

When his mother got off her chair to take him into her arms, he clung on to her and cried his heart out, unable to articulate what it actually was that had made him so upset.

Lucille

"Merpires?" Lucille asked no one in particular.

One moment, she'd been dancing with Dion, thinking about ways they could slip away and spend the night alone. The next, the atmosphere had shifted, giving her the impression she'd fallen into a lion enclosure. Their friends were still dancing, but the other guests were staring at them with hungry eyes. Very hungry eyes. And a girl who was half-vampire, half-deep-sea-creature was biting Matt's neck.

"Maritime vampires," a huge guy to her right explained in a friendly tone. "During the day, we hide from the sun in the sea. At night, we drink the blood of tourists." He let her see his fangs, which looked more like shark than vampire teeth.

"This is so weird," she heard Shayna say. The Elite Clique girl had stopped dancing and was frowning heavily. "Is that woman trying to eat Matt?"

Lucille shot a quick look at Dion. They couldn't possibly fight these vampires in front of the Elite Clique. Not if it couldn't be helped. "Can you distract everyone?"

Dion didn't question her. His forehead creased with concentration, and a second later, Shayna shrugged and resumed her dancing as if nothing was out of the ordinary. Her friends and their French exchange partners were similarly distracted, and the vampires, or whatever they called themselves were no longer eyeing them. Instead, all their attention had shifted to Lucille, Matt, and Jan.

"Thanks, beau. Guess I'll take care of these vampires. Globus igneus." Green flames burst from her hand.

"Merpires," the shark-man corrected her with a hiss. Then he lunged at her.

Lucille threw her fireball into his face. Shark-man screamed and stumbled backwards, but the two merpires next to him burst into seawater, and her flames fizzled out before they managed to do proper damage. The water from their shift splashed her top, making the fabric stick to her chest. "Very classy!"

It might not have been a good idea to anger the merpires. The one she'd hit was still on the ground, pressing fins into his eyes. But the other two had shifted into walking sea creatures. Both of them were also inspired by sharks, with rows of teeth in a too-wide mouth, grey fishy skin, and signature back fins.

"Lu!"

Her head whipped around just in time for her to see a piece of wood flying at her. Jan had broken a chair over some merpire's head and broken off the legs. She caught hers and whirled around to sink it into the fishy underbelly of the nearest two-legged shark. The other snapped at her, taking off a piece of her skirt. Lucille stumbled back and threw a lightning bolt, frying him right there and then. The merpire she'd staked didn't turn into dust like normal vampires would. Instead, he burst into seawater, drenching Lucille from head to toe, making her gasp.

In the short reprieve that followed, Lucille saw Matt slicing off two of the purple tentacles that had held him with his sword. He looked angry, but otherwise alright. The merpire lady was not so happy.

Searing fire wrapped around Lucille's neck. Instinctively, she raised her hands, only to jerk away when they, too, were stung. Whatever held her pulled her closer, and Lucille crashed into the bar, her fingers unclenching around the makeshift stake. Fine white strings were wrapping around her legs and arms. Stinging jellyfish tentacles! In front of her, a woman with tentacle hair smiled cruelly at her.

Lucille screamed in pain as fire erupted across her skin. The woman was suddenly in her face. She opened her jaw and made to clamp down on Lucille's neck, when a sword sliced through her, separating the jellyfish head from its female body. The tentacles around Lucille's limbs vanished as seawater washed over her, taking some of the sting away.

Matt stood behind the dead merpire, his face covered in bright red, angry circles. "Are you okay?"

"Watch out!"

A sea serpent struck him, sinking its teeth into his shoulder. Matt grunted in pain, but before he had even turned, Jan stabbed the snake with a pool cue. Matt repaid him by blasting a white shark into oblivion, who'd been hot on Jan's feet.

"I hate these vampires," Matt said, massaging his shoulder.

"Merpires," Lucille corrected him, unable to stop herself from chuckling.

The amusement was short-lived, though, when a group of six merpires drew closer around them. Behind Lucille, the bartender grinned at her with too many rows of teeth.

"Plan?" Jan asked, wheezing from another asthma attack.

"You take the left. I take the right," Matt announced, and tightened the grip around his sword. "Lucille covers our backs."

Which meant she had to deal with the shark behind her. He was still grinning, and then he began to morph. His face widened, while his nose and mouth combined into a pointy snout. His mouth ripped open, making space for all those extra teeth, and he grew until his head smashed into the glasses above the bar. Unfazed by the rain of glass shards, he snapped at her and chomped through the bar in one big bite.

Wood splintered, and Lucille jumped backwards. A thick tentacle wrapped around her knee and jerked her across the floor. Jan made a grab for her, but he only succeeded in breaking her fall before he had to whirl around and block the shark's teeth with his cue. One bite from the massive jaw, and the two ends were flying across the room.

Slimy tendrils covered her lower body, and Lucille shuddered. An icy trail shot up her back and something wrapped around her neck again. With Jan fleeing from the massive shark merpire, and Matt fighting off four merpires by himself, there was no one to help her. Dion was too busy keeping himself and the others safe, and Lucille couldn't gather enough air to speak a spell.

Her mind raced. A million spells came to her. If only she could weave like Samantha. And then it hit her. Samantha had likened the spell weaving to illusion work.

It needs to be close to reality to make it easier to believe.

Lucille began by imagining their roles were reversed. She was on top, strangling some poor merpire with magical vines. It didn't take long for one of the merpires to notice her. He shot over, fast as an arrow, and ripped off her head. Or rather that of his fellow merpire.

There was something disconcerting about seeing her own head rolling across the floor, but the pressure around her neck subsided and the slimy weight on top of her was replaced by wetness. She could breathe again, while the merpire stomped off to join the fray around Matt.

Lucille checked quickly and decided that Matt could hold out a little longer. Instead, she switched Jan with one of the merpires running after him, just as he slipped and slid over the floor, crashing into the pool table. The shark chomped down on his friend, and Lucille quickly changed targets until he had killed all the merpires around him. Just as she started to worry about what to do with him next, Jan ran him through with the second cue.

Whirling around, she saw Matt in danger of being torn in two by a couple of krakens who had wrapped their tentacles around his sword arm and other hand. Once more, Lucille did her magic, prompting a deep pain in her stomach that made her head swim for a moment. The krakens let go of Matt to wrap themselves around their colleagues, and Matt raised his free hands to shoot energy at both groups.

Nothing but seawater remained.

"My shoes are ruined." Lucille's mind was wiped clear, and the pain in her stomach was almost all-consuming. She was also wet to the bone and shivering.

"They say salt water is good for asthma," Jan said behind her, "but I respectfully disagree." He took out his inhaler and took a few puffs. "I've always preferred mountain therapy, anyway."

Matt stared at the both of them and started laughing. "So much for leaving these monsters to themselves."

"They insisted on it." Lucille rubbed her belly, slowly realising the pain she felt was hunger. Somehow, using so many illusions had made her hungry. "I could go for a nice bouillabaisse right now. Like, a whole pot of it. Dion?"

He looked as famished as she was. "You're done?"

"One more illusion?"

The sprinkler started spraying and screaming ensued as the others woke from their illusion. Shayna tried to cover her hair, not noticing how it never actually got wet, and ran out the door, followed by the others. Only Cian remained seated at the bar, a forgotten drink in his hand, covered in a fine mist of glass and wood. "What happened?"

Matt took the drink from his hand and pulled him to his feet, casually wiping the debris off him. "You, my friend, had a little too much to drink."

Lucille and Jan watched them leave the club. She was sharply reminded of Cian's declaration of love earlier in the evening, but found herself too exhausted to care. Jan shrugged likewise. "A little bit of gaslighting is better than cutting him into pieces, I suppose."

"It was a onetime occurrence, remember?"

"We'll see." With another shrug, he went behind the bar and salvaged some drinks.

Lucille left him to it and wrapped her arms around Dion. "I meant that about the bouillabaisse. I'm famished."

He put his arm around her shoulder and smiled. "Me too, but maybe a burger instead. I'm not really in the mood for seafood, you know?"

Rachel

Rachel hadn't been back in Fabian's dreams since the Walpurgis Night party. Instead, she'd focused on exploring what she wanted in her own dreams. In those, Fabian was the most attentive, most supportive boyfriend she could wish for, who worshipped the very ground she walked on.

No, that wasn't right either. Love wasn't worship. Rachel wiped that version of Fabian away.

Unfortunately, her life experiences hadn't given her enough examples of what love was. Her parents had always seemed to despise each other, and what she remembered of her paternal grandparents had been nothing more than a tolerated companionship. The only thing she had to compare was the romantic love in books and Fabian's unwavering obsession with Samantha.

With a sigh, Rachel pulled up a dream where she met Fabian the same way Samantha had. As children. If the three of them had been best friends from early childhood, surely, he'd love her like he loved Samantha.

Together, they built a treehouse in the park. Without a single protest, Rachel got to be the princess, while Samantha pretended to be the wicked witch that held her captive, and Fabian was the prince come to rescue her. Soon, Fabian and Rachel had teamed up against Samantha, tickling her to a witchy death.

A time jump, and they all met at the pool, splashing and fooling around. When Samantha was momentarily distracted, Rachel and Fabian decided to prank her by diving underwater. The light shone through the water, painting a wave pattern onto Fabian's pale, freckled skin. His eyes gleamed, and he smiled. In this dream, they could hold their breath forever.

"What are you doing there?" Nico stepped into the dream, calling Rachel up to the surface. He stared at the pool with a disconcerted look. "What about me?"

The dream broke into a million pieces.

Rachel stood in her meadow, shell-shocked. In her desire to be Fabian's childhood love, she'd forgotten to include Nico in her dreams. She'd forgotten her twin brother.

"It's just a dream," her fellow dreamer reminded her. He bent down and picked up a piece of water on the ground. "You can be anything you want to be in dreams. Even an only child with two best friends, one of whom will be the love of your life."

"That's horrible." She almost choked on the words.

But Nico shook his head. "It's freedom. Every mind needs to be allowed to dream. As long as it doesn't mistake it for reality."

Pouting, Rachel hugged herself. "I know what's real. He doesn't love me. There. How is that better?"

"It's not. Reality isn't better or worse. It just is. While dreams..." He waved his hand about, and a wind picked up all the pieces and brought them together until they made up a three-dimensional mosaic of the boy she loved. "They can be whatever you imagine. An adoring boyfriend."

Dream-Fabian bent forward, cradling Rachel's face tenderly.

"But there's one thing they'll never be."

Rachel braced herself for what was to come.

"Real."

The vision burst again, its pieces becoming the very stars shining above them.

Nico gave her a sympathetic smile. "Talk to him." He set off walking, fading away with every step.

In her heart, Rachel knew he was right. What was ailing her couldn't be solved in the dreamworld. But what if facing it in the real world destroyed what little she had? Made her hold on to it until it dwindled down to nothing, while there was still some chance for it to grow?

She straightened her shoulders and woke herself up.

Beep—Beep—Beep—Beep...

Once again, Rachel only heard the busy signal when calling Fabian's number. She'd been trying for over an hour, but the line was always busy. He hadn't responded to her texts either. Nor had Samantha.

So far, Rachel had resisted calling her. Even though deep inside she *knew* the two were talking to each other—who else would Fabian have hour-long conversations with?—she didn't want it confirmed. She didn't believe something was going on between them. Fabian was too sweet to cheat on her, and Samantha wouldn't change her mind. But other than that, the two of them had slipped back into their incredibly close relationship.

And Fabian spent far more time, both in and out of school, with his best friend than with his girlfriend.

Not all of that was his fault. Or so Rachel tried to tell herself. She still struggled with the signalling, partly because she didn't know what signals she wanted to send. She hadn't exactly thrown herself at him. But they'd been together for six months, and instead of feeling closer to him and secure in their relationship, she saw him slipping back into old behaviours. Like talking to Samantha on the phone for hours instead of her.

Ani's words came circling back, each time wounding her more than before: *If you and Sammy were naked in a room with him, Fabian would beg Sammy to let him screw her.*

By now, Rachel realised it wasn't sex she wanted from Fabian. For some reason, the thought of them getting hot and sweaty under the sheets did nothing for her. She liked his kisses, but she didn't miss them during the day. No, Rachel craved something far more basic—his companionship.

From the first time she'd met Fabian and Samantha, she'd wanted what they had. Sure, Rachel had had her brother, and she and Nico had been close, due to being the only ones in their family who cared for each other, but there had never been that kind of ease; the jokes, and the teasing. The random hugs. Too much pain had always laced their relationship.

She'd fallen in love with Fabian because of his carefreeness. At times, he'd felt like the polar opposite of her, with his loving family who'd always be there for each other. He'd never really known worry or loss, but it hadn't made him conceited like some of the other kids. No, Fabian was kind and sensitive, and while Samantha often complained about his thoughtless behaviour whenever they were at odds, Rachel thought he wasn't like any of the other guys. Not brutish like Jan, and not cocky like Matt.

Fabian was the man of her dreams. But dreams were not reality. No one knew this more than Rachel did. And as kind as the real Fabian was, he wasn't drawn to her.

Beep—Beep—Beep—Beep...

Tears fell on Rachel's knees, leaving behind dark spots on the jersey. When had it all gone wrong? If he'd never loved her, then why was he with her? Why had he kissed her? Wanted even more... back then, when it was still early days? Did he think he was doing her a kindness? Had she disappointed him? Had he *hoped* for more?

Despite promising him to think about it and let him know where she stood, Rachel had never done so. It had been too scary to face the complicated feelings inside her, this simultaneous wanting him and *not* wanting him. It was so much easier to believe in the dream. To believe that Fabian didn't mind, they never did more than kiss—and not even that lately—because he was understanding and not like other guys. And why wouldn't he be? He'd never pressured her, had barely even voiced his desire. What if he was like her, not that interested in sex like everybody else? Or asexual, as Ani had called it.

But then she remembered the other things Ani had said. How much he'd been into Samantha, how hungry, how... *completely in love.*

Rachel swallowed heavily. Why did she give Ani so much power over her relationship? Why trust a girl who'd been nothing but superficial and cruel—who barely even knew Fabian anymore—over her boyfriend? Or her best friend? Samantha and Fabian would never hurt her. Rachel was *sure* of that. Fabian was over Samantha. Samantha was definitely over him. But their friendship, that warm, beating heart of their relationship, was as strong as ever. Rachel shouldn't envy that. She was Fabian's girlfriend, after all. But what was being his girlfriend worth if he spent all his time with someone else? What part of him belonged to her if she didn't have his desire, his heart, or his companionship?

She shook her head, blinking away more tears. These thoughts were tearing pieces from her flesh, leaving her to bleed out. *Nico would say I'm spending too much time in my head.* And the Nico from her dreams would tell her to live, not lose herself in dreams. It was time to find out which Fabian was reality. The love of her dreams? The bane of her doubts? Or something in between?

Once more, Rachel took the phone into her hands. She could do this. It was time to stop chasing a dream and face reality. Because if Rachel wanted to get anywhere, she needed facts. Not doubts, not fears, not vicious whispers from a snake. It was like maths—with known facts, only one solution was possible.

Instead of Fabian, she called Samantha.

Beep—Beep—Beep—Beep...

Fabian

Fabian had never liked the dark. Or the attic. And especially not the attic in the middle of the night. Something was whistling up there. A ghost, perhaps.

"There are no ghosts," he told himself, repeating what his father always said. But something about voicing those words triggered a memory. Ghosts totally existed. His friend—no, girlfriend—Rachel even talked to them. He had nothing to fear from a ghost. Unless it wanted him to avenge some long-dead relative and fight a mountain wyrm.

He shook his head. "Stop being silly. And focus!"

But focusing was becoming increasingly harder, and his childish fears almost overwhelmed him as he climbed up the stairs to the attic and opened the door. It was quite heavy, but he managed to lean it against the side and climb through.

Some of the roof tiles were a bit worn, so it wasn't completely dark. With his eyes accustomed to the darkness, Fabian looked around. Huge cupboards loomed over him, like the giants from the stories he liked so much. Or not so much if monsters were real.

The whistling was louder here, but he couldn't see a ghost. Instead, he tried to remember where Samantha had found the recipe. It had been halfway to the tiny window after they'd shifted a cupboard out of the way. And the cupboard was still standing there.

Fabian almost cried again. There was no way he could shift the cupboard on his own. Not when he was barely a meter tall.

Still, he continued forward and looked around the cupboard. Under one edge, he could see the corner of a sheet of paper. The recipe! Carefully, he pulled. It moved a little, but then he heard the faint sound of ripping paper.

"Careful, Fabi. Careful." Destroying the page wouldn't do him any good.

He looked around, searching desperately for a solution, when a sudden bang as loud as a thunderclap over his head froze him to the spot. The heavy door to the attic had fallen shut, sending tremors through the wooden boards. Fabian fell on his bum and started crying.

It didn't take long for steps to come up the stairs. The door was opened again—and secured with a metal bar this time. His father was first, looking around wildly, until he found Fabian sitting in the dust and crying. "What the hell were you thinking?"

"Language, Joachim!" His mother had slung a bathrobe around herself and turned on the little light for the attic that was out of reach for him. "Fabi, what are you doing up here?"

"Yes, explain yourself!"

Fabian looked up at his towering father and cried even harder.

Caroline rushed to his side and pulled him into her embrace. "It's alright. Hush now. Mummy's here."

"It's not alright." His father shook his head, still looking angry. "I want to know what he's doing here in the middle of the night."

"Perhaps he's sleepwalking."

"Oh, he's awake!"

Fabian didn't like his parents fighting, and he definitely didn't like his father being mad at him. He slung his arms around his mother's neck and buried his face in her shoulder. "I only wanted to find the recipe for the anti-potion, so I can be big again," he cried, swallowing half the syllables.

His mother sighed greatly. "Fabi..." She sounded so tired.

"Okay, I've had enough of this," Joachim declared. "The lad is completely out of control. He'll be grounded tomorrow. Some quiet time in his room will do him good."

"You really think that'll help?" Caroline asked, but she shook her head and sighed. "Very well." She nudged Fabian and kissed his tear-stained cheek. "Did you hear Daddy? Tomorrow, you'll need to stay in your room."

How was he supposed to find a way back to his old body when he was confined to his room? "You can't do that to me. That's deprivation of personal liberty."

"Maybe he's getting that from the shows you always let him watch," his mum said to his father as she carried him towards the stairs.

This couldn't be happening. He was already losing the plot. A whole day in his room would kill any chances of Fabian returning to his normal life. "You don't understand!" he cried and strained against his mother's grip. "I need to find a way home. I'm the only one who remembers. Please!"

His mother struggled to hold him, and they both almost fell down the stairs. "Give him to me," Joachim said, and a moment later, Fabian found himself in the stronger arms of his father, unable to move as much as he had before. "Hey, Fabi, listen. If you behave tomorrow, we're going to play some board games when I come home from work, okay? Your choice."

Fabian didn't care about board games. Not really. He wanted to wake up from this terrible, terrible nightmare. But there was no waking. And there was no way back.

Hot tears burned in his eyes as he cried into his father's pyjamas.

The next day was just as frustrating as Fabian had imagined. He tried to leave himself visual cues by drawing pictures of what had happened, but his art skills were considerably inferior to those thirteen years in the future, and he barely recognised his own drawings.

After what seemed like endless hours of boredom, the door opened, and his mum entered with Samantha. "Hey, Fabi. Look who's here to visit."

"Yes!" Samantha was exactly what he needed. A wild plan formed in his head. She might only be a five-year-old, but she *was* a genius. If he gently led her to the right place, she'd figure it out. She had to. "Do you want to play?"

His mum left them alone, smiling serenely, and closed the door again. Samantha rolled her eyes and grinned. "That's what I'm here for."

"Awesome." Fabian had to focus now if he wanted to get this right. "Listen. I found out that there's a treasure in the attic. We have to get up there, but we can't let anyone see us."

Samantha listened closely. "Anyone?"

"Yeah, there are evil guardians. Gargoyles." He listened for his mother and heard her in the kitchen, where she ran her little potion business that would later evolve into the Magic Circle. "They're in the kitchen. You need to guard the door while I climb up and open the attic. Then you follow me. I'll explain the rest upstairs."

Samantha's eyes sparkled with excitement. She loved a good role-play. The more magic, the better. And she was a fabulous snitch.

Caroline never saw her as she kept guard, while Fabian snuck out of his room and up the stairs to the attic. He avoided the stair that always creaked and pointed to it for Samantha. Then he carefully opened the door again. This time, he secured it. "You can come," he whispered for Samantha.

She followed him quickly, avoiding the same step, and joined him upstairs. Together, they walked over to the cupboard, and Fabian pointed to the yellowish paper corner. "You see that. That's our map. We have to get it out of there without alerting the gargoyles."

"It's too heavy." Samantha said, after attempting to push the cupboard away. Then she peered inside. "What if we empty it first?"

"You *are* a genius!" Fabian felt elated at their progress. After carefully emptying out the cupboard—and making quite a mess around them—he could lift the cupboard just long enough for Samantha to pull the recipe out.

She looked at it and frowned. "That's not a map."

Fabian snatched it out of her hand. "It's a magical map. You need to brew a potion—like a witch—to reveal the treasure's location." It was the same recipe. He was sure of it. But no matter how much he tried he couldn't decipher the words. A terrible realisation hit him. "Sammy? Can you read?"

"Of course I can read."

Fabian let out a big sigh of relief. "Good. Let's return to my room. It's safer there."

Together, they climbed down again. While Samantha guarded the other set of stairs, Fabian quickly returned to his room. Once there, they sat down at the little play table and looked at the paper together. Fabian stared at the words, but they made no sense. He found a couple of Fs, but that was all. "I can't read," he realised with shock.

Samantha snatched the recipe from him. "I can." Slowly, she began deciphering the recipe.

Fabian found it incredibly hard to listen to her laborious and often wrong attempts, but at point eighteen, he jolted upright. "Read that again."

Samantha's enthusiasm was waning, but she did his bidding. "Eighteen. Keep some of the crystal tear liquid, step one, separate. This will be your anti-po... potion. Now put three drops—"

"Step one. We need to brew the antipo... anti-potion. You just put the drops in without putting some aside. Or perhaps you did, but I have no access to it."

"What are you talking about? I didn't do anything." Frustrated, Samantha pushed the recipe away.

Fabian reminded himself that she was just a child—like him. "The big you. Anyway, we need to brew this little potion. Can you gather the ingredients from my mum's kitchen? Bring a pot as well."

Samantha bit her bottom lip. "Fabi, I'm not allowed to take things from your mum's kitchen."

"Of course you are. The kitchen is also *my* kitchen. And I say you can take whatever you need."

Surprisingly, it worked. Samantha snatched up the recipe and left the room. Fabian leaned back in his little chair and let the relief flush his nerves. They were going to do it. In a few hours, he'd be back in his body again. Until then... He looked around and regarded the mess in his room. Paintbrushes were strewn around, and his pencils were all over the floor. "I could clean up in the meantime, I guess."

It didn't take too long, and by the time he was finished, his father knocked on the door. "Wow. Did you clean up in here?" When Fabian nodded, he smiled. "So, you *can* be well-behaved."

"Daddy!"

Joachim grinned and ruffled his hair. "I know you're almost always well-behaved, right?" He went down on one knee and took something out of his back pocket. "Look what I got you."

It was a bright red toy car. "A car," Fabian commented, not quite feeling it. "Wish that worked when I was bigger. I would clean up my room for a real car."

His father laughed. "Still playing an adult, aren't you?" He put the car in Fabian's hands. "Go on, play a little. And then you can come down and pick a board game."

As soon as the car touched Fabian's fingers, all his grown-up pretentiousness was wiped away. He loved this car. It was new and shiny and so very red. Forgotten were the board games and forgotten was the magic potion. All Fabian cared about was zooming through his room with his brand-new toy.

Lucille

It didn't take any illusions to make Matt's date possible. With both Lucille and Matt drenched, the others believed their excuse of calling the night quits and returning home. They didn't care that, soon after, they went home with the wrong partners.

"Do I have to worry about him breaking Amélie's heart?" Dion asked as he led Lucille down a food street. His jacket hung over her shoulders, shielding her damp see-through dress.

"I think she's well aware that it's nothing but a sexy fling. Aware and keen," Lucille added. Then she regarded Dion with a long look. "What about me? Is this more than a fling?"

Dion sighed. "How could it not be? You live how many kilometres away? I can't teleport like Matt, and even my illusions have a limit."

"Because they'd otherwise eat you alive," Lucille said quickly to direct the conversation into less murky waters. She was well aware her romance with Dion had been doomed from the start. "Which reminds me... Food. Now."

He laughed and pulled her to the side. In front of them was a charming little eatery that promised gorgeous burgers and fries. "Sit. I'll be back in a second."

Lucille took a seat outside. Though her dress had been wet, the late spring night was warm enough for her to be comfortable. It wasn't too late, so there were still many people on the streets, most of them locals who spoke her favourite language. Lucille felt right at home. She could easily imagine living here, tag-teaming with Dion to keep the streets safe from maritime monsters, then finishing with a candlelight dinner to close off the night.

"There you go." Dion returned with a breadbasket and sat down opposite her. "I've ordered two of their burger meals and got this to tide us over until they arrive. Oh, and wine." He nodded at a server who leaned in to pour them two glasses of red.

"Merci beaucoup." To her delight, he even lit the candle between them. "I've never had such a romantic burger."

"You've never dated me."

Lucille clinked her glass with his. "Touché." For a moment, she allowed herself to sink deeper into the illusion. Wouldn't she and Dion make the perfect couple? She'd fit right in with Marseille, and he could teach her so much. This night would never have to end. "I wish I could stay."

"I wish you could, as well," he answered without fail. "I've never had something real like this." Dion laughed softly. "Which is ironic, because it isn't truly real. We've only got tonight and a couple of hours tomorrow morning." The joy around his lips dissipated and was replaced by bitterness. "It might as well be another illusion."

She reached over the table to grab his hand and shook her head. "That's not true. What we had was as real as it gets. It's just the wrong time, wrong place. That kind of situation. I'm needed in Greenvalley." There was a whole prophecy about it. Lucille couldn't really imagine leaving her friends to themselves. Not with an archdemon waiting to strike. She stroked his fingers. "But perhaps you could inject some realness into your life?"

"What do you mean?" He turned his hand to hold her fingers.

"Amélie said you don't believe in love, and you said that all you've ever known have been illusions. But the world is real. There are real people out there. Amélie, for example. She sees you as her friend."

"I do have friends," Dion protested.

Lucille tightened her grip. "But they don't know anything about you. Look, I've had my share of superficial relationships. Until last year, I spent all my time at boarding schools. I was raised to please. And I was good at it. I even believed that I was happy. Well, almost. But I always felt like there was something missing, something more real, and when I switched schools to Greenvalley, I found it. My magic, and with it, friends who really cared, who knew all about me: my fears, my insecurities, all the things I used to hide from everybody." She let go of his hand as the burgers arrived. "Try it."

"You mean I should tell Amélie about the illusions?"

She picked up a fry. "Why not? She's your friend. I doubt she'd run the other way if you confided in her." The potato was wonderfully crisp on the outside, silken heaven on the inside. The salt prickled on her lips. "I'm not saying you should shout it from the rooftops, but you need to get out of that house. You need a good dose of reality."

Dion laughed again. "I'll still miss you."

Coquettishly, she winked at him. "I'm not gone yet."

"Very true." And as he grabbed his burger to eat, his eyes practically devoured her.

Lucille allowed herself to return the gaze likewise. There was a hunger left inside of her food alone couldn't fill. And she would make the most of this magical night. She could always sleep on the way home.

Samantha

"Fabi? I think I've got everything." Samantha heaved the bucket with the ingredients onto the low kids' table. Her arms were hurting from carrying everything for such a long time, and she was starting to get tired. As exciting as the game had sounded, it wasn't really fair that she had to do everything, while Fabian...

Fabian played on his carpet with a shiny red car, not paying her the least attention. "Fabi!"

He looked up, confused. "What?"

"I've got the things for the treasure potion." Samantha pointed at her bucket. It had been incredibly hard to not only read the recipe but also the different labels and match them up.

"What potion?" Fabian asked innocently.

Samantha stared at him, incredulous. "The potion that will reveal the location of the treasure." Blank face. "Fabi!"

"What?"

"Forget it!" Frustrated, Samantha stared into the bucket. It was just like her mummy always said. The boys went to play with their cars, while the women had to wash, and clean, and cook. "I'm taking this down to the kitchen." It wasn't like she could cook anything on a table. Not even a magic potion.

Samantha was well aware she was allowed to stop playing Fabian's game now, but it had evolved into something else. Fabian clearly wasn't interested in treasure hunting anymore, so instead, she pretended to be a witch, just like her grandmother. This potion wasn't a mere treasure finding potion. It was something much bigger. It would defeat tatzelworms.

Her grandmother had once read to her about this terrible mountain monster, which would stand up to its full size—half a metre—when threatened. Most tatzelworms were cowards and ran, but if they managed to sneak up on you, they would screech so loudly it could burst your eardrums—like diving too deep in the pool.

She was convinced she'd seen a tatzelworm on a weekend hike with her daddy and Fabian. Then, the tatzelworm had fled—even the bravest one wouldn't go up against three people—but she'd been afraid to meet one on her own ever since. This potion would help. With it, she would be safe and hunt the monster, just like her grandmother.

"I'm going down to the kitchen. Do you want to come?" Samantha said loudly, not really expecting Fabian to listen.

While he didn't look up, he did follow her down, driving his car along the handrail. Caroline was in the kitchen, making some of her own potions, but paused to regard them curiously. "What are you guys doing here?"

"I am making a potion against the tatzelworm," Samantha declared, and raised her bucket in an attempt to put it on the stove before it all came tumbling down.

Caroline stopped her. "Here, let me help you. You get the step stool, and I'll put this here. Do you want a proper pot?"

Excitement bubbled in Samantha's tummy when she heard the question. "Will you turn the stove on?" She loved helping with the cooking, but she rarely was allowed at the stove.

"Of course." Caroline twisted the knob to number one and put a pot on the stove. "Has the tatzelworm been bothering you a lot?"

Samantha put the step stool in front of the stove and climbed on top. Behind her, Fabian was exploring the kitchen with his toy car. "It has. I think it wants to break into our garden." She took out the recipe Fabian had given her. It was a complicated recipe with a lot of steps, but Fabian had only wanted her to do step one, and she was already convinced that step one was the potion against tatzelworms. "Have you ever seen one, Caro?"

"No, thank god." Caroline sounded very glad. "If that potion works, I might carry a bottle too, though."

"That would be very wise." Samantha poured her ingredients into the pot and reached for a wooden spoon to stir it.

Caroline was soon distracted by her own potions, so Samantha worked quietly and concentrated. In the pot, the liquid had taken on a delightful shade of purple. "Does this look good?" she asked. "I think it needs mustard seeds." They were big magic enhancers her grandmother had once said.

"Of course. Here you go." Caroline put a small number of yellow seeds into her hand, and Samantha took great care not to let a single one roll through her fingers. "What recipe are you using?"

Samantha let the mustard seeds fall into the pot before giving Caroline the recipe page. "This one."

"Wait a minute. Is this out of one of my books?" Caroline turned around. "Fabian!"

Fabi looked up from his play, confused by the sudden sternness in his mother's voice. Samantha was about to explain that they'd found the recipe under a cupboard and not in a book when the water in her pot bubbled up. Foam rose and spilled over the edges of the pot and onto her dress. Frightened, she let out a scream and stumbled backwards.

Caroline whirled around to catch her, but foam engulfed her, Samantha, and the entire kitchen. Samantha cried out in fear. Suddenly, there was only air. Everyone was gone, and then she hit the floor, and a sharp pain exploded from her bottom. "Ow."

"Is it over?" Fabian asked from somewhere inside the foam. He no longer sounded like a five-year-old, though she instinctively knew it was him.

Of course she did. She talked to him at least once a day. Slowly, the memories returned to Samantha, and suddenly, shame crept up her tear-streaked cheeks. "I am so, *so* sorry."

The foam dissipated slowly, revealing the back room of the Magic Circle and Fabian with a red toy car between his big hands. "You better be." He didn't truly sound angry, though. Instead, he looked at the toy and chuckled. "So, the Potion of Lost and Found—or whatever it's called—returned my favourite toy car to me. I'd wondered where it had gone."

"I'm glad you got something out of it." The embarrassment still tormented Samantha. Had she really just turned Fabian and herself into five-year-olds? What had happened? Had they been in an alternate reality? Or had they travelled in time? If so, where was Caroline? Slowly, she began to realise how dangerous her course of action had been. And all for... "The garden!"

The garden was a mess. Half the fruit trees had died at some point, and the rest were hardly producing any fruit. Only the wild blackberry was flourishing and desperately crying out for a trim. The once carefully manicured lawn had become a paradise for insects that had encroached on the flowerbeds. Sometimes, a flower or herb would break through, but it all happened without rhyme or reason. The chaos made it almost impossible for Samantha to orient herself, even though the memories of being five were as fresh in her mind as if it'd happened yesterday.

Fabian was helping her, but he stopped the moment Rachel arrived at the gate. After they'd recovered from their weird trip, they'd discovered several missed calls and unanswered texts on his phone. Wherever the potion had taken them, they'd been gone from here.

Rachel's face was perfectly impassive, which told Samantha she was angry. She left it to Fabian to explain what had happened and continued her search. With all the overgrowth, she spent most of her time stomping down brambles and pushing aside weeds.

"You texted?" a cheerful voice called from the gate.

"Lucille!" Samantha waved at her from the overgrown meadow, a little too enthusiastically. "You're back!" With Lucille, there would be no awkward silences. Especially since it looked like Jan and Matt were accompanying her.

The three of them entered the garden through the screechy gate. "Arrived this morning," Lucille said as she stalked over to the terrace.

She clearly regarded the meadow with the unique disdain of someone who'd had a gardener at her disposal all her life. "Don't tell me you want us to mow the lawn."

"Might be a good use for the divine sword, don't you think?" Jan asked, eliciting an eye roll from both Matt and Samantha. "Guys, Marseille was amazing. We met merpires. Half-sea-creature, half-vampire. It was epic."

"Yes, awesome." Samantha was happy to hear all about merpires any other time, but right now she needed to find something. "If anyone sees a small mound, shout out."

Matt raised his eyebrows. "A small mound?" There were dozens of small mounds everywhere. "What are you even looking for?"

Samantha wouldn't let him curb her enthusiasm. Not today. "Something very important." She was almost sure she was at the right place. The distance and angle to the terrace were just as she remembered. She bent down to dig when Fabian knelt next to her.

"It was a little more to the right." He pointed at a grassy knob, then handed her a shovel. "Do you want to do the honours?"

Samantha laughed as she took the shovel from him. "I can't believe I buried Freya's Flowers."

"I can't believe Meg gave them to you. That girl is an emblem magnet." Fabian used his fingers to help her pull out the grass. There was a light in his eyes whenever he regarded her, and she couldn't help but feel the same excitement.

Though Samantha was extremely glad to be back in her eighteen-year-old body and mortified that she'd almost lost it, it had been nice to spend a day or two carefree with Fabian. It reminded her of how lucky she was to have him as a friend.

"Why would you bury your emblem?" Rachel asked, confused. When Fabian had explained the situation, he'd been deliberately vague. Neither of them cared to admit to their friends that they'd spent the last few days as preschoolers. *That* would stay between the two of them.

"Doesn't matter. The important thing is they're still there." Samantha felt her heart flutter. If she'd buried the flowers thirteen years ago—or in an alternate reality—then they must have rotted away, or they'd never existed in the first place.

But they were there. Samantha could sense the magic growing in them. Her fingers carefully removed clumps of soil until she saw vibrant colours in the earth. They were exactly as they'd been in her memory. And yet there was more to the flowers than she'd seen as a child. They were grown from magic and fertilised with magic, like a miniature spring. One nudge from her, and the magic would reweave itself, offering a different configuration. They were a perfect fit for her.

"You're crying," Fabian said softly. He reached over and wiped his soil-stained thumb over her cheek.

"They're just so beautiful." The Power of Change. Samantha had read all about it. A weaver like her could manipulate the inherent magic in Freya's Flowers to access different kinds of magic: fiery red for death, soft pink for a peaceful sleep, vibrant purple for healing.

Fabian took the flowers from her hand and grinned at her. She knew exactly what he was going to do. This time, he didn't pull her hair and simply put the flowers behind her ears. With a wink, he whispered, "And now you're beautiful."

Samantha laughed. She couldn't help herself. The waiting was finally over. She had her own Emblem of Power and the best friend she may as well have wished for. Everything was wonderful.

"Well, there you go," Matt muttered, always reliable when it came to raining on her parade. "You can stop fretting, and we can turn to more important things."

"More important than a prophecy about the end of the world?" Samantha asked dubiously.

"Like what? Harassing Cian?" Jan asked, sounding weirdly upbeat. He glanced at Samantha and grinned wildly. "It turns out, Cian—"

"—is *such* an idiot," Matt said, a little too hastily.

Samantha shook her head and glowered at him. "No, he's not. He's very kind. And smart." While they didn't spend any time outside of Chemistry class per her own wishes, she counted him as a friend. They had a lot of fun together.

Matt narrowed his eyes, not saying anything. For at least a minute, no one spoke. Then he spun around and walked off. "Not my problem."

"What?" Samantha was confused. What did he even mean? She checked with the others. "What's not his problem?"

Jan opened his mouth, but Lucille was quicker. "Don't mind him. He's sore that Mr Zobel wouldn't let him out of his sight to... well, do his usual things."

His usual things. Samantha tasted bitterness on her tongue. Matt would never change. "I might have a new favourite teacher."

"You and me both," Jan laughed. "You should have seen them. Matt was *this* close to losing it." He quickly changed tunes when he noticed what he'd just said. "Hey, is Meg home?"

Samantha nodded at the house and watched him go. Meanwhile, Lucille had braved the meadow and regarded the flowers with glee in her eyes. "You finally found them. That means the emblems are complete. We truly *are* the Six."

"Does that mean we have to fight that demon now?" Fabian asked, sounding just the slightest bit whiny.

Rachel snorted. "It'll be time for the prophecy soon, I bet."

As ominous as she'd made it sound, Samantha couldn't truly worry now. Not today. Not when she was finally reunited with what she'd lost. The part of her she'd always craved. "My magic," she whispered.

Tomorrow, the world could go to Hell. Today, she would bask in the sun of her childhood memories and the magic she'd found.

Part 3

Vengeance & Shakespeare

Matt

While Matt enjoyed human school and all the interesting subjects it had to offer, there was one he wasn't particularly keen on. His father had said it was an easy way to make up for the missing points on his schedule, and more importantly, it had required no previous knowledge, not like French did. Even so, he dreaded Friday afternoons, especially now that their end-of-year performance was getting close.

"I never should've signed up for Drama," he moaned as he took a seat onstage with the rest of the class.

"You say that every week, but look who's nabbed the male leading role," Lucille teased. She pursed her lips soon after. "While I have to fight Cheryl to get a shot at playing Hero." She glanced over to where Cheryl and Jennifer were excitedly talking about the play. For once, the queen bee had to be content with playing the second fiddle as Jennifer far surpassed anyone in acting. But that second fiddle was contested by Lucille, and neither girl would give in.

Matt rubbed his hands over his face. He was tempted to give his role to one of the girls, but the teacher wouldn't have that. "I was *voted* into it." How that was a fair process, he had no idea.

"Not without reason."

"And that reason being my acting skills or my good looks?"

The fact that Lucille didn't reply was answer enough for Matt. He looked up as the familiar pat-pat of Mrs Wertstein's high heels came down the atrium. The teacher was a head smaller than nearly every student present, but what she didn't have in size, she made up for with personality. And garish styling. As usual, she wore her faux leopard print coat over a neon-coloured top. Her lipstick today was a deep mauve, while her eyelashes were painted electric purple. The look was complemented by tightly curled blond locks that rivalled Cheryl's signature corkscrew locks. In fact, if Matt hadn't known any better, he would've guessed Mrs Wertstein was Cheryl's mother.

She certainly had the same shrill voice when she welcomed them all. "Hey, lovelies. Are you all excited for next week? We only have six more days left to rehearse until it's show time."

Matt's stomach turned at the announcement. To prepare them better, Mrs Wertstein had emptied their schedule next week, so there was still plenty of rehearsal time left, but still... it was only one week until he'd embarrass himself in front of both students and teachers.

"Have you decided who gets to play Hero, yet?" Cheryl asked, as predictable as clockwork.

Mrs Wertstein seemingly enjoyed the eagerness mixed with anxiety from her two contenders before she shook her head. "Not yet, my dear. Monday, I'll pick the most reliable, most convincing Hero. Today, Lucille will start with act one."

Next to Matt, Lucille smiled smugly.

"Now!" Mrs Wertstein clapped her hands. "Everyone! Places for scene one."

With a big sigh, Matt heaved himself onto the stage and took his place behind the curtain with Alan and a few of the others who'd enter the scene later. Onstage, Jennifer, Lucille, Robert, and Chris set the scene. Cheryl stood at the bottom with Mrs Wertstein, arms crossed and glowering. Just the audience they all needed.

Matt knew all his lines, but that was the easy part. Every one could say a few lines. Only few could say them as naturally as Jennifer, who managed to transform her usual haughty self into the witty charm of Beatrice.

"Don Pedro approaches!" Robert called out, giving the boys behind the curtain their cue.

Matt wasn't the only one who dragged his feet, instead of confidently striding onstage like the soldiers they were.

"Boys!" Mrs Wertstein mouthed loudly, and they all straightened up a bit.

The dialogue started anew with the banter the piece was known for. "This must be your daughter," Raoul who played Don Pedro said.

Chris as Leonato answered, "That's what her mother told me."

"Were you in doubt? That you had to ask her?" Matt was glad he hadn't missed his cue.

"No, Signor Benedict, since you were only a child then."

Matt barely stopped himself from wincing. Perhaps it wasn't just his good looks that had scored him the role of Benedict, but his well-known reputation. It was because of that thought he almost missed his response to Raoul and stumbled over his words. "Signor Leonato might be her father, but he wouldn't... *she* wouldn't want to walk around with his head on her shoulders for all Messina to see. As alike as they are."

Jennifer hardly missed a beat as her character inserted herself in the conversation. "I'm surprised you're still talking, Signor Benedict. Nobody cares for you."

"What, my dear Lady Disdain? Are you still alive?"

"Matt!" Mrs Wertstein's shrill voice cut through Jennifer's reply. "Where is the tease? The joy Benedict feels when he spars with Beatrice? The sharpness of his wit? You're still saying these lines as if you're reading them from the script."

He tried his best for the rest of the play, but by the end, he knew it wasn't nearly enough.

"I'm disappointed, Matt," Mrs Wertstein said to him as they packed up. "You know your lines. I give you that, but you're not playing with Jennifer. Take some time at home and practice with a mirror, will you? The replies need to be sharp like a whip crack and yet convey tenderness." She turned around as she saw Lucille coming their way. "You did really well, Lucille. Keep it up and on Monday you'll get the premiere spot."

Lucille beamed at her and hooked her hand into the crook of Matt's arms. "I'm *so* going to get the role," she whispered excitedly as she pulled him along. "Cheryl stumbled three times in her act."

"Lucky you. Apparently, my wit isn't sharp enough," Matt grumbled.

"Well, it isn't," Lucille said without mercy. "But I had an idea. This will heighten your performance significantly. Mrs Wertstein won't know what hit her on Monday."

Matt knew he should've been hopeful, but Lucille's words only served to fill him with dread.

Dread was a word too mild for Lucille's sinister plan. To prepare for the big play, she had invited everyone into her home for the weekend and enrolled their friends to read the other roles while she and Matt practised. And naturally, she'd given Beatrice's role to Samantha.

"What, my dear Lady Disdain? Are you still alive?"

"How could disdain die while she has such food to feed on as Signor Benedict? Courtesy itself turns into disdain in your presence." While Samantha was only reading from the script, her words carried more than enough sharpness to slice him in half.

Just being in her disdainful presence enraged Matt enough to counter her wit word for word. "Then courtesy is a turncoat. All the ladies love me, except you." How true that was. "I wish my heart was not as hard as it is, because I love none." Also true.

Samantha grimaced before ducking her head to read the next line. "A dear happiness to women: they'd otherwise would have been troubled with such an obnoxious suitor. Fortunately, I'm of a similar mind. I rather hear my dog bark at a crow than a man swear he loves me."

"I hope you'll never change your mind. It might save the gentleman who could love you from a scratched face."

"Scratching couldn't make your face any worse. No disfigurement could make you uglier than your soul already is." And she went off script again.

"Do I hear Lady Disdain approaching once more?" Matt answered likewise.

Samantha narrowed her eyes. "She's not approaching; she's charging you."

"Uhm, guys?" The two of them had completely disregarded Fabian who was supposed to oversee their recital. "This isn't part of the script."

Matt rolled his eyes. Of course, it wasn't part of the script. They'd been practising since the morning, and sooner or later, the charged energy between them always made Samantha interpret the lines as she saw fit. She couldn't be in a room with him without getting another dig in.

"I'm just saying," Fabian trailed off.

"I'm with you," Matt said sweetly. "I would love to practise my lines, but someone always sabotages me."

Samantha managed to make herself look entirely innocent. "If I read the text, it's not right. If I play Beatrice, it's also wrong."

Scoffing, Matt shook his head. "Beatrice isn't half as hateful as you are."

"Hateful?" Fabian piped up. "I thought the two were in love with each other." He flicked through his manuscript. "I'm sure I saw a kissing scene later on. Perhaps—"

Samantha cut him down before he even made his suggestion. "There's also a scene in which Benedict beats up Claudio. Perhaps you two want to practise that one? Though I'm sure Matt has this one down to a T."

"If you don't want to help me, just say it."

"I don't want to," Samantha said without missing a beat.

Matt ignored her. "This was Lucille's idea. I'll get there without any help."

She snorted. "As if." Upon his glare, Samantha raised her chin. "We all know why you got the lead role, don't we? Spoiler, it's not your acting expertise. Though you did make a convincing human."

"Did I now?" Matt knew full well why he'd been chosen, but it grated on him that Samantha was aware as well.

He crossed his arms while she glowered at him. A minute of charged silence stretched between them, only broken by the screeching of Fabian's chair as he got up hastily. "I'll tell Lucille to do another scene." And with that, he ran from the room.

"Wait! I'll come with you." Samantha jumped up and made for the door, but Matt was faster. He grabbed her wrist and slammed the door shut in front of her. "Take your dirty hands off me!"

Matt had no idea what had got into him, but he couldn't let her go. Not like this. "Why do *you* think I got the part?"

Despite him having her jammed in between his body and the door, Samantha groaned. "You're such a cocky bastard."

Cocky? Now he wanted to hear her answer even more. "Tell me."

Samantha sighed heavily. "Because of your good looks, of course." Then she smiled mistakenly sweet. "Not everybody knows how ugly your soul is, right?"

He should've been outraged, yet Matt felt only amusement. Was this how he was supposed to play Benedict? Matching her sharp tongue for sharp tongue, while secretly yearning for more? "So, you think I'm good looking?"

Her eyes were ready to murder him. "I think that you're a disgusting bastard through and through. And now let me go."

Instead, Matt came even closer and looked her in the eyes. His voice was smooth silk. "And if I don't?"

"Then..." But she lost her train of thought as their eyes locked. He was now so close that he could feel her chest rise with every breath. They'd never been this close before. Her lips trembled...

All of a sudden, Samantha pulled up her knee and hit him right where it hurt the most. Demon healing powers or not, Matt fell to his knees and doubled over as he gasped in pain.

"Then I'll put impotent on the list of your many, many flaws," Samantha quipped, opened the door, and vanished down the corridor.

Lucille

"... I'm telling you, Benedict is sick with love for Beatrice," Lucille said, her voice rising dramatically as she pretended to peer out the window. "Cupid's crafty arrow is made of this. It can wound just by hearsay. Now begin. Look how Beatrice is approaching, close to the ground to listen in."

She turned around to Rachel and Jan, who were sitting on the ground with their copies. None of them spoke, not even after a pointed stare from Lucille.

"Jan!"

"Oh, shit! Is it my turn?" He only now flicked through the pages. "Where are we?"

Lucille sighed. "Ursula says—"

"Ursula?" Jan made a face. "I'm not playing Ursula!"

Only years of practised countenance prevented Lucille from rolling her eyes. "Please, Jan. There are only female roles in this scene. I won't think any less manly of you."

Jan crossed his arms and glowered at her. "What's in it for me?"

"Seriously?" It was a testament to her own desperation that she even considered rewarding him. "What do you want?"

His answer came too prompt to be spontaneous. "The keys to your winter garden."

Rachel coughed but kept wisely out of it. Lucille had to be stupid not to get why he asked. "Fine. You're gonna get the winter garden. For one night only." She took her position. "From the top: I'm telling you—"

The door opened, and Fabian came in, hastily closing the door behind him. He sat down next to Rachel and blew out some air.

"Wow, that's a record!" Jan announced, way too excited.

Fabian shook his head. "They'll never get through the first scene. Or any other. Sooner or later, Samantha has a go at him."

Lucille gave up any pretence and let herself glide into her chair. "Perhaps it was a bogus idea. I thought it would help Matt's acting if Sam played opposite to him. You know, with all the vitriol the characters sling at each other—"

"Oh, there's vitriol. And Matt's acting is fine. A little too fine. It almost seems like he's enjoying it." Fabian shook his head, clearly exhausted. "But listening to them is pure torture."

"And you left them alone?" Rachel asked. Lucille couldn't help but notice that she had made no motion to get close to Fabian. "Won't that end in bloodshed?"

Hope rose in Lucille's chest against all odds. "What if they finally talk? Hash it all—"

The door was opened yet again, and Samantha stomped in, a storm in her eyes. "Gosh! I hate that guy."

"Or not," Lucille whispered, her hope squashed under Samantha's heavy footfalls.

"He just tried to seduce me!" Samantha was beside herself. "Or perhaps he tried to trick me into believing he would seduce me, so I look stupid. He's got such a sick mind!"

Matt appeared next to her, his own face distorted by rage. "I'd like to know what you were thinking! You didn't need to get physical."

None of the others managed to get a word in. They'd long since given up trying.

"Why?" Samantha whirled around, crossing her arms. "You seem fine. Mr Half-Demon knows how to take a beating."

"As if you remembered that," Matt hissed back.

Samantha's hands flew to her hips, and she leaned forward better than Jennifer had ever played Beatrice. "Next time, you might want to consider that before you try to assault me."

"*I* was assaulting *you*? You were the one who—"

"Shut up!"

The sudden shout made Lucille jump. Jan had shot to his feet, fists clenched. "We all get that you can't stand each other—"

"It's a bit one-sided," Rachel muttered, and Lucille quietly agreed with her.

"—but your constant fighting is seriously getting on my nerves." Jan grabbed Samantha by the shoulder and exerted just enough pressure that her legs folded under her. "You're going to play Ursula." Then he grabbed Matt's arm. "And we're going for a drink."

Matt stared at him, bewildered, but then his mask slipped back into place, and he shrugged. "Sure, whatever."

The two of them were almost at the door when Jan jerked his head at Fabian. "Are you coming?"

"What? Me?" Fabian scrambled to his feet. "Yeah sure." He brushed Rachel's shoulder. "I'll call you later, okay?"

"Sure."

Fabian rushed after the others, and the door fell shut, making Lucille jump again. So much for practising with her friends. "Awesome..."

Samantha burst into tears. "I'm sorry." For a moment, the tears came too fast and furious for her to regain control, but before Lucille could offer her some tissues, Samantha took a few deep breaths and calmed herself. "I'm trying. It's just... Every time I see him, anger fills me. This isn't me. This was never me, but... it's just... He just keeps on living. He *killed* several people, and he gets to go to school, take part in student exchanges, perform in silly plays, take the soccer team to victory..." Again, she dabbed her eyes, blinking furiously. "He killed Daniel, and it's like it doesn't matter. At all. To him or anybody else."

"That's not true," Lucille hurried to say. "Of course it matters. And he cares!" As Dion had once mused, Matt was the greatest pretender of them all. All his callousness was nothing but a mask. She was sure of it. "I believe he just doesn't know what to do."

"An apology would be a start," Samantha shot back.

Lucille winced. "I know. And I've been trying to tell him, but every time I mention it, he stops listening."

"It's supposed to come from him. His apology isn't worth shit if you're feeding him his lines." Samantha's shoulders heaved, and her face distorted in a tortured grimace. "I'm sorry, Lucille. I'm sorry I'm ruining all the good things." Wiping her cheeks one more time, she picked up Jan's discarded script from the floor. "You need this practice, right?"

Lucille shrugged uncomfortably. The play seemed so inconsequential after Samantha had just bared her soul, but it was important to her. More than she had admitted to anyone. "Mrs Wertstein will make a decision on Monday on whether I get to play Hero on opening night, or whether Cheryl nabs the role."

Samantha winced. "Cheryl doesn't hold a candle to you."

Lucille appreciated the loyalty. "I know, but... I really need this. My father won't buy a ticket to see me run around the background. And he's got other plans on the second night."

This time, Samantha managed a smile. "We got you."

"I can read Ursula," Rachel offered likewise.

Lucille's biggest nightmare came true when she arrived at school on Monday, only to find the stage empty. Irritated, she got her phone out and read Cheryl's message again.

Cheryl: Wertstein wants to meet us at the stage at 8 for the final decision. Good luck, loser.

Well, here she was. It was eight o'clock, and the stage was right in front of her. But nobody was here. Lucille was about to type a desperate reply when she noticed what she was doing. "Cheryl..."

She felt so stupid. When had Cheryl ever been helpful? Cheryl wanted the role as much as she did. If Mrs Wertstein had asked her to inform Lucille of the meeting, Cheryl would've conveniently forgotten about it. And Mrs Wertstein wouldn't have asked only Cheryl in the first place.

Lucille's fingers tightened around the phone, and she allowed herself to grunt and stomp her foot. She couldn't believe she'd fallen for such a simple trick. But there was no time to wallow in self-pity. She needed to find the drama class. And fast.

They weren't in the classroom, nor in the cafeteria, where the grumpy owner glared at her for stomping in and out without buying anything. The atrium was just as empty, and then Lucille remembered what Mrs Wertstein had said last Friday. If the weather was nice, they'd practice outside in one of the fresh air classrooms.

The fresh air classrooms weren't real classrooms, since they lacked actual walls or a roof, but a bunch of wooden benches under the trees. There, behind the buildings of the lower grades, she finally found the drama class. Naturally, they were already in the middle of a recital.

"I'm so, so sorry," Lucille said to Mrs Wertstein, whose eyes were fixed on the wedding scene. "I was under the impression we were practising on stage today."

The teacher wrinkled her nose. "And why would you think such a thing? Did you not listen to me on Friday?"

"I did. I just—" In the front, Cheryl was grinning smugly before launching herself in a theatrical monologue. "I came in late and must have forgotten."

Mrs Wertstein shook her head, clearly disappointed. "I hope you realise that I won't put you on as Hero on Friday because of that."

It couldn't possibly be true. "But I practised all weekend!" Lucille was pretty sure her friends hated her by now for making them go through it again and again.

"And still, you might be late for opening night." Mrs Wertstein shrugged. "I'm sorry, Lucille. At this point, reliability is more important to me than your passion for theatre. Cheryl will play Hero. You're the understudy. Now, excuse me while I work."

Fury made it impossible for Lucille to reply sensibly. She clenched her fists and took several deep breaths. One little trick, and Cheryl had outmanoeuvred her. She'd been practising all weekend, thinking it would be a decision on merit, but of course, Cheryl would play dirty. Glowering, Lucille watched the queen bee overplay Hero's rule in her triumph.

"You won't get away with this, Cheryl," she promised quietly. "I will have my revenge."

But for now, Lucille would keep her cool and watch her rival for weaknesses. And pretend it didn't matter to her. She sat down and grabbed Mrs Wertstein's newspaper, reading up on the "Act of jealousy ends in murder" front-page article.

Samantha

Lucille was taking the loss of her role hard. It was the only way Samantha could explain her sudden interest in following up on a case. Malcolm had been awfully quiet for months and seemed to have given up on Greenvalley's magic, and the few monsters they'd encountered were dealt with quickly. But that was no reason to check on criminal cases now.

"It's a crime of passion," Samantha said carefully over lunch break. "There's nothing supernatural about it."

"What about this?" Lucille waved the *Greenvalley View* around as if using it as a fan. "The accused claims to have had her back turned while someone stabbed her fiancé to death. But when she turned back around, there was no one to be seen. Plus," Lucille said triumphantly, "they haven't found the murder weapon yet." She finally lowered the newspaper enough for them to see.

Rachel shrugged. "I'd also claim I had no idea who killed my fiancé if I was accused of murder. Doesn't mean there's an invisible killer."

It was only the three girls, since Jan had decided to keep Matt and her separate. Samantha didn't mind the reprieve, but she couldn't shake the impression that the division was *her* fault. It had been almost half a year since Daniel's death, and she hadn't moved an inch in her stance. And why should she?

Frustrated, she started reading the article for herself. "Wait a minute. I know her!"

"Huh?" Rachel and Lucille leaned in. "Who is it?" Rachel asked.

"Saskia. She was my choir leader for a few years. My mum's friends with her." While Samantha wasn't close with her, she had fond memories of her time in the choir. And she would've never assumed the gentle woman would turn out homicidal. "I can't believe it." Then again, she would've never guessed Matt capable of murder until he went and did it.

Lucille misinterpreted her outcry as interest. "The entire thing is mysterious. The homicide happened behind closed doors. Only Saskia and her fiancé Markus were present. So, if she didn't do it, who did? Or what?"

"I thought she had a clear motive," Rachel interjected. "Jealousy?"

"Yeah, apparently, she confronted him about a bra she found. Juicy fact—it belongs to her best friend."

Samantha gave Lucille a tired look. "That's a pretty strong motive. I'm afraid she's just stalling."

"Well, I'm not the only one who thinks things don't match up." Lucille leafed through the Greenvalley View until she landed on the 'Mythological News'—a joke section the newspaper had included a few decades back on behalf of the council's branding campaign. "Philipp Vendenberg also thinks we might be dealing with an invisible killer."

'Wrongly accused: real killer might be invisible' read the headline.

"You mean he's making fun of it?" Samantha had always been on the fence about Philipp Vendenberg's articles. On one hand, they were well written and had excited her when she'd first come across them. On the other, the last year had made it abundantly clear Vendenberg was making it all up as he went.

Lucille gave her a dead stare. "Look. I've called our family attorney, and he agrees with me and Philipp. The case is strange. He has agreed to talk to Saskia, and we can accompany him."

"Really?"

"I guess money talks," Rachel muttered, then grimaced. "Sorry."

Lucille leaned back. "Do you want to come or not?"

In the end, both Samantha and Rachel decided to check it out. Samantha because it was Saskia, and Rachel because she was curious. If there was a magical reason behind the murder, Samantha swore she'd find it. She couldn't accept that all the people in her life turned out to be cold-blooded killers.

They met Mr Petersen, Lucille's family attorney, in front of the police station. He was a tall man in a sharp suit with thin-rimmed glasses and a trustworthy smile. "Ms de Cerque, how lovely to see you."

"Mr Petersen." Lucille shook his hand with a confidence Samantha envied. "This is Samantha Kollmer and Rachel Hadden. Samantha knows Ms Partnick from a few years back."

Samantha still thought this was a bad idea, but the attorney smiled at them. "Wonderful. Our appointment is in five minutes. Let me do the talking, okay?"

As he led the charge, Rachel leaned over to whisper. "How is he going to convince the police to let us in?"

Lucille wriggled her fingers. "With a little help from me."

Samantha reminded herself that she wanted to talk to Saskia, and that this unethical use of magic wouldn't really hurt anyone.

Mr Petersen had no problem getting them admitted as law interns, and not even showing their IDs blew their cover. A policewoman led them to a room. The three of them took seats at the back of the room, while Mr Petersen took the chair at the table and prepared himself.

It didn't take long for two policemen to lead Saskia in. Her eyes were red from crying, and she sniffled. But that wasn't the only thing Samantha saw. Saskia seemed to be surrounded by a cloud of red.

She sat down as Mr Petersen got up to shake her hand. "Ms Partnick. I'm Mr Petersen. We talked on the phone."

Saskia nodded, unsure despite the threatening cloud around her. "Yes, thank you so much for taking on my case. I didn't do it, you know?" Her voice was full of desperation.

Mr Petersen sat back down and raised his hands in a calming manner. "Let's start at the beginning, okay? Please tell me what happened that night with as much detail as you can remember.

"Okay." Saskia took a shaky breath before squaring her shoulders. "I was cleaning our flat when I found a bra under the couch. It belonged to my best friend, Inga. I know that because I was with her when she bought it. I didn't like the colour, but she bought two of them. Can you imagine, my best friend—?" She swallowed and shook her head. "Markus had been acting a bit weird lately. He never wanted to do anything, but I would've never thought he'd cheat on me. I was overwhelmed, so I started making dinner. Then I heard him come home, but I couldn't... I couldn't confront him. Markus knew right away that something was wrong and started with the standard excuses. I couldn't hold it back anymore and screamed at him."

Behind her, the red intensified, and for a split-second, Samantha saw something else in it: a woman with three faces, all three of them grim and unforgiving. Gasping, she jabbed Lucille with her elbow, but her friend only looked confused.

Meanwhile, Saskia was close to tears again. "He told me to stop, but I just kept going and then... then he was lying at my feet. There was blood everywhere and not a sound from Markus."

Samantha very nearly left the room then, her mind dragging up the memory of Daniel lying in a pool of frozen blood. Without even looking at her, Rachel took her hand and squeezed it tightly. That and the strange apparition behind Saskia kept her in the room.

"He told you to stop?" Mr Petersen asked. "What were you doing to him?"

"Nothing!" Saskia swallowed heavily, her arms tense as if her hands were clawing into her knees under the table. "I thought he meant my rant. I was completely steamrolling him, but it angered me that he wouldn't even let me be upset about it. As if I didn't have the right to be upset when *he* cheated."

Mr Petersen leant forward, obviously confused by her statement. "It says Markus was stabbed to death."

"I know!" Saskia shook her head. "But I was busy cutting onions for dinner. I didn't do it."

"Does that mean you had your back to him?"

She nodded hastily. "Yes. I looked at him once, but I couldn't stand his puppy eyes. I mean, they're not that bad. But they make me fall for him, and in that moment, I didn't want to fall for him. But that doesn't mean I wanted to kill him."

Brown puppy eyes. A different pair flashed in front of Samantha's eyes. Matt had been so close she'd felt the heat of his breath on her lips. And there'd been something in his eyes that made it almost impossible for her to resist. She hated herself for having these thoughts. But she hated him even more.

"Please calm yourself. I'm on your side." Mr Petersen had a steady voice that oozed of confidence. "There was a calling card on the kitchen bench." He showed her a picture. "Nemesis—Relationship Advice. When did you get a hold of them?"

"The card was in the mailbox that day. It was as if the postman read my mind, or rather knew what was going on behind my back," Saskia explained.

Mr Petersen nodded. "Did you call them?"

"I did. Normally, I talk about these things with Inga, but... well..." Saskia swallowed heavily. "I talked to them about half an hour before Markus came home."

"And what advice did they give you?"

"None! They just listened."

Mr Petersen sighed, but Samantha focused on the red-shimmering woman behind Saskia. *Nemesis.* Not exactly a name one would choose for a relationship advice service.

"Ms Partnick, you need to be honest with me. Otherwise, I can't help you." Mr Petersen started to sound a little exasperated.

"I *am* being honest! I have no idea what the stupid calling card has to do with my fiancé being dead. Yes, I ranted to them, but I would never kill him. I hate blood." Saskia's voice broke. "I would never even think of stabbing someone with a knife. Markus just fell. What if he was sick? Or someone stabbed him before he came up, and he tried to tell me, but—"

"Please!" Mr Petersen raised his hands. "Calm down. We are still waiting on the coroner's results. Unfortunately, our time for today is over, but I'll be back tomorrow. I want you to think about what exactly you've done between finding the bra and Markus' return. I have to remind you..."

Saskia listened to him with big eyes as Mr Petersen packed up and then opened the door. A policeman came in, but Saskia jumped up and grabbed Samantha's arm. "Sammy, please, you need to believe me—"

Instead of Saskia, Samantha stared at the three-faced woman in red. Her fiery eyes seemed to bore into Samantha's mind, dissecting all the complicated feelings churning inside of her.

"Ms Partnick, please step back!" the policeman commanded before nodding at Samantha. "You can go now."

Samantha didn't hesitate and rushed out to catch up with the others. Lucille was taking her leave from the family attorney, but Rachel was waiting on the other side of the road.

"And what do you think?" Rachel asked. "You look like you've seen a ghost."

"Something like that." Samantha shuddered. In her mind, she could still feel the red woman's glare, as if she'd stuck burning fishing hooks in her flesh. "There was someone with her. A woman with three faces. Saskia had no idea she was there."

Lucille joined them. "A woman with three faces?"

Samantha nodded. "She had a red aura. That's the same kind of magic Lucille uses. It's called the form-shaping magic as it forces spells and similar magic into shape. Nemesis. It's another word for archenemy, isn't it?"

"It's also the name of the Roman Goddess of Vengeance," Lucille said.

"How fitting." Rachel crossed her arms and pushed out her bottom lip. "So, what does it mean?"

"Saskia must have called upon her. Accidentally, I assume." Saskia had literally called someone, at least.

Lucille nodded thoughtfully. "Well, I guess that means I was right."

It took Rachel and Samantha a moment to understand what she meant. "Yes, congratulations?"

Lucille deflated again. "I know it's nothing to be happy about. But at least we can help Saskia. We need to find out more about Nemesis and... well, figure out how to prove her innocence."

"I don't know about that, but I'll hit the books." Samantha checked the time on her phone. "I need to meet my dad at the workshop. Call you later?"

They said their goodbyes, and Samantha hurried away. But no matter how much distance she brought between herself and the police station, the weird sensation in her mind never lessened.

Rachel

The dreamworld was her happy place, as it had been so often. But Rachel wasn't happy. Instead, her mind circled around Nemesis, the Roman Goddess of Vengeance. Once she'd arrived home, she'd read up on her. Nemesis, a daughter of Nyx, had been a goddess of justice. Though today's popular opinion turned her into some kind of avenger, she'd started out as someone who gave every person their due, good or bad. Other sources claimed she resented whenever that due balance was disturbed, and yet others saw her as divine punishment.

Rachel decided to look for herself. The goddess herself might not have walked the paths of the dreamworld, but the recent events had left their traces. After visiting her this afternoon, it wasn't hard to find Saskia's dreams. Or rather, her nightmares.

She and Markus had lived in a small apartment with one bedroom, a living area, and a small kitchen. Saskia stood in the latter surrounded by mountains of carrots, onions, and broccoli. She was chopping away at them, though the mountains of uncut vegetables only rose and never shrunk. On the fridge behind her, the bright red calling card shone like a beacon.

"Hey, darling." Markus was home. He stood behind Saskia, opening the upper button of his shirt and loosening his tie. "How was your day?" He turned to open the fridge but stopped at the sight of the calling card. "Relationship advice? Is there something you're not telling me?"

Saskia kept cutting, but now the thing she was cutting into pieces was a purple bra.

"I can explain that," Markus started.

"Inga. You cheated on me with *Inga,*" Saskia said pointedly, keeping her back to him.

Still, Markus flinched and held his left side as if in pain.

"My best friend."

Under his fingers, blood bloomed. "Saskia. It's not what you think."

Saskia threw her head back and gave a haughty laugh that quickly turned into a sob. "Do you really think I'd fall for that? How stupid do you think I am?" Her knife hit the wooden board with more and more force, leaving behind purple grooves.

Markus groaned and sank against the fridge. His face was sweaty, his breathing laborious.

"How long, Markus? You probably laugh about me, right? Silly little Saskia is pretending to be the perfect housewife while you two have fun. Damn it! I gave up my job placement for you!"

"Stop it. Please stop it!" Markus could barely hold himself upright. Blood was gushing down his face from a cut.

Saskia burst into shrill laughter, her back still turned to him. "Stop it? I'm only just getting started. You're the worst! You left me to do everything while you worked long nights. But you weren't working, were you? No." She paused for a moment to wipe her tears, then grabbed another carrot. "I hate you. I wish you were dead."

Rachel almost jumped in between them in a vain attempt to stop her words. Not that it would have helped. True to her word, Saskia never turned around, but Markus gasped. Blood dripped from his mouth, and his eyes widened. He slid down the fridge door, leaving behind a red smear. Then he was dead.

"Nothing to say now, huh?" And at last, Saskia turned. "What—"

Her scream tore the dream apart. It unravelled quickly as Saskia woke. Not thinking, Rachel jumped in and grabbed the red calling card from the fridge before the dream winked out.

She landed hard on her meadow, the impact sending petals swirling into the air. Rachel half-expected the card to be gone, but it was still there, bright red and burning hot. Only here, a string connected the card to a flower she knew only too well.

"Fabian."

"Don't go." Nico appeared behind, his forehead creased with worry. "Let go of it. Just let it go."

It only piqued her curiosity more. What was in his dreams that Nico didn't want her to see? He always thought he needed to protect her from the dreams. But the dreams were her dominion. They couldn't hurt her. Not even Saskia's nightmare had fazed her, though in reality, she would've been horrified.

"Please..."

Rachel ignored his warning, drawn to the dream she'd visited so often. Nico didn't join her. But Nemesis did.

As usual, Fabian's dream was wet. In this case, there was torrential rain. But it wasn't only water that fell from the skies. Bright green frogs fell on her head and jumped away merrily. Rachel glanced around, searching for Fabian when she heard laughter. She raised her hand to push aside the rain and stopped cold.

In front of her was a bus stop. Two people had looked for protection from the weather there, both already soaked.

"You're making it rain frogs!" Fabian pretended to be outraged, but his boyish grin gave him away. He was about fourteen or fifteen. "You *must* be a witch."

He nudged an equally young Samantha's nose and sent her giggling. "It wasn't me." She shrieked when a sudden flush of water came down, splashing them despite the shelter. "What do we do now?"

"I don't know." But Fabian's eyes had locked with hers, and suddenly, Rachel could hear both their hearts racing.

She wanted to look away, but the dream was more powerful than her. In front of her, Fabian and Samantha began to kiss each other. They aged as they did so, only growing in passion. And then they were naked, no longer in the bus stop, but in his room under the blankets.

Rachel stared dumbly at the two of them until Fabian's emotions grew too heavy for her to bear. When she left the room, she only saw red.

Fabian

"I'm going!" Fabian called out as he grabbed his backpack and swung it over his shoulder. For a moment, he eyed his jacket, but the weather outside looked sunny and warm. A T-shirt would do.

As he slipped into his shoes, Merle came and slunk around his legs, meowing for attention. Fabian gave her a few strokes and scratched her behind the ears. "I'll be back soon. It's a short day." He laughed. When most of his school days had eight or even ten units, a day with only six classes was the short one.

He opened the door and almost stumbled into Rachel, who had her hand raised towards the bell. "Hey!" he said in surprise. They hadn't walked together for ages.

"Hi."

Fabian leaned in for a good morning peck, but Rachel turned away and started walking. It was such a smooth movement, it almost seemed unintentional. "Are you okay?" he asked, hurrying to catch up.

"Not really, no."

It was one of those days. Rachel had her unreadable, impassive face on, and wouldn't speak a syllable more than needed. It grated on Fabian, because he could never tell whether she was mad at him, in her own world, or simply didn't care for his presence. "Will you tell me what's bothering you?"

He didn't truly expect an answer, but Rachel squared her shoulders. Her voice was perfectly flat when she said, "I think we should break up."

Fabian missed a beat and stumbled over his feet. "What? Why?" *What was going on?*

"Because you don't love me."

Her answer sent him reeling. Fabian felt as if the world had been put into fast-forward, skipping entire hours between two seconds. He'd just been walking out the door, and now his girlfriend was breaking up with him? Completely out of the blue?

He forced himself to concentrate on the accusation. *Because he didn't love her.* It was such a loaded statement. Sometimes Fabian didn't even know what love was. And what he felt for Rachel was... *complicated.* It was certainly some kind of love, but was it *love* love? And what had made Rachel decide it wasn't?

"And you got that from...?" Fabian asked provocatively. If there was one thing he didn't like, it was being told what he felt and didn't feel.

Rachel kept walking, forcing him to move as well. "We've been together for half a year, and you haven't shown the slightest sexual interest."

Fabian opened his mouth to protest. "That's not true!" He'd tried to make a move, and every time she'd shut him down. "You—"

She finally looked at him, but her eyes were cold and full of accusation. "Do you know how many sex dreams you have that feature Samantha or complete strangers? You even had one with Shayna. But not a single one featuring me."

Heat crawled up his neck, and he knew he was going to show his brightest tomato blush. "Th-that's n-nonsense." He didn't have sex dreams. No, of course he had sex dreams, but they were his and his alone. "They're just dreams. And you can't just watch them at your pleasure."

"Believe me, it wasn't a pleasure," Rachel said flatly. Then she sighed and her face turned a little softer. "I'm don't always do it on purpose. It's just that I'm drawn to your dreams, always have been. But it's not nonsense, as you say. Those dreams are part of your subconscious, and it's pretty obvious that I'm not a factor in your sub-conscious."

She sounded so infuriatingly sensible when none of this made sense. How could she hold him responsible for what happened in his dreams?

"You're a factor in my conscious, though?" Right now, a very irritating one.

Rachel stopped and fully turned to him. "Are you saying you're entertaining fantasies about me while you're awake?"

"Obviously not now while we're on our way to school and you're telling me what I feel and don't feel."

"Right." Rachel seemed to have come to a decision. "Then answer the question yourself. Do you love me?"

She might as well have slapped him with a cold fish. Fabian wasn't in the mood to say "I love you" and almost said so. But then he reminded himself that he *did* care for her. And that this was obviously upsetting to her. If he was completely honest with himself, he'd shied away from fully examining his feelings. Partly because he didn't want to hurt her, and partly because even after six months—or all these years they'd been friends—he still didn't know how to take her. Nico used to say that Rachel buried her feelings deep inside of her, while Fabian wore his on his sleeve.

His answer had been too long in the making. Before he even managed to open his mouth, Rachel shook her head. "That's what I thought."

As she walked away, panic gripped him. This couldn't be happening. Not like this. Not in this cold, distanced way, where he didn't even get a word in, because Rachel had already thought it through for them both.

"Love takes time!" Fabian called after her as he lengthened his strides to catch up with her once more.

"Six months, Fabian."

It had taken him almost a year to say those words to Samantha. "I know, but—"

Rachel straightened her back, her voice soft. "It's over, Fabian. You wanted to give this thing between us a try. I'm sure you did so with the best intentions, and I was stupid enough to trust you. After all these years, I should've known that I'm nothing but a friend to you."

Again with this explaining his own feelings to him. Fabian's desperation grew. He wanted a real conversation or at least a chance at it, instead of this trial-like accusation and condemnation in one fell strike. "Rachel!"

They'd reached the school. In front of the gate, Samantha was waiting for them. Rachel walked straight past her, with nothing but a, "He's yours again."

"What? Why?" Confused, Samantha looked from Rachel to Fabian.

Fabian couldn't fault her. He was still too confused by this morning's sudden attack. "Rachel, can you wait for me?"

"Just leave me alone!" And for once, there was true emotion on Rachel's face. Tears glistened in her eyes, while her mouth was a thin, angry line.

"Ra—"

Cold water rained down on him as if someone had emptied a giant bucket over his head. Next to him, Samantha shrieked, as part of it splashed her, too. Meanwhile, the other students around them laughed and pointed. Some of them even got their phones out to record them as if this was all some giant prank.

Samantha stared at him, aghast and puffing. Fabian rushed to say, "That wasn't me." Even when the water had been entirely out of his control, it had never done anything like this. There wasn't even a water feature near the gate.

"Sure." Rachel must have stopped when the water came down, but now she snorted. "Well, I guess it's a familiar situation for the two of you." And with that, she entered the school grounds.

Fabian and Samantha stared at each other in confusion. Neither of them tried to run after her.

"What does she mean?" Samantha asked before regarding her wet top with a grimace. The fabric clung to her breasts like a second skin.

A flash of a dream he'd had returned to him. Fabian sighed. Angry at himself and at Rachel, he tried to wring out his shirt. "Apparently, she saw something in my dream that she didn't like." He hardly remembered what it was, but he could imagine it only too well. Naturally, Rachel would balk at seeing something like that. "She broke up with me."

That took Samantha by surprise. "What? Rachel?" As if Rachel couldn't possibly be the one to draw the line. In Fabian's mind, she'd done a great job.

Before he could say something though, Matt walked by, his arm around some younger girl. He smirked at Samantha and wriggled his eyebrows. "Nice view!"

Samantha pulled a face, fury taking over her features. But then she shook it off and checked out her dilemma. The fabric of her top had become see-through, and every line of her bra left a visible ridge.

Exasperated, she took Fabian's hand. "Come on. Let's go to admin and ask them if we can change our clothes."

Since wringing out his T-shirt had hardly made a difference, Fabian gave in and followed her. Even his shoes were wet, making a squelching noise every time he took a step.

This hadn't been his fault, Fabian told himself. Why would he douse himself? Rachel, yes, but himself and Samantha? That made no sense. Just as Rachel's breakup made no sense. Sure, he hadn't been head-over-heels for her, but neither was she. Plus, she'd known that going in. And to blame him for things his subconscious spun together at night?

Fabian shuddered. It creeped him out.

Matt

"You're challenging me!" Matt called before turning to the non-existent audience with spread arms as if to garner their approval. He turned back, facing Alan, who had his arms crossed and shook his head.

"I think you've lost your mind."

It was only the two of them in this scene, and apart from Mrs Wertstein, no one watched them. Lucille was busy glowering at Cheryl, while Cheryl was focused on touching up her make-up with Jennifer.

Matt didn't care. In fact, he liked it much better when no one paid him any attention on stage. He took a step towards Alan and growled. "What do you mean?" Contrary to the love scenes, this scene came easily to him.

Alan turned his nose up. "That love has—"

A loud scream tore through the stage area. Cheryl had jumped up, her make-up tools scattered on the ground as she regarded herself in the mirror. Bright red pimples covered most of her face. "What is this? I look like I was attacked by bees!" Some of the pimples were oozing.

"Maybe you're allergic." Jennifer was trying to help her friend, but Cheryl almost hit her in the face in her vain panic.

In the meantime, Mrs Wertstein was practically skewering Cheryl alive with her look. "Go, wash your face! I'm sure it'll go away quickly."

Cheryl barely paid her any heed, already rushing out through a side door, Jennifer hot on her heels.

"Matt, Alan," Mrs Wertstein said in an apologetic tone. "Start again from 'What do you mean?', please."

Next to Matt, Alan shrugged, as if he couldn't care less about Cheryl's dilemma. Not that Matt did. He barely understood the whole make-up craze. They faced off again and Matt repeated, "What do you mean?"

"That love has clouded your judgement. It's Beatrice who's made up your mind."

Matt stepped closer, now almost nose to nose with Alan. "A word."

"Go on."

Instead of another line, Matt swung his arm, pretending to hit Alan. They'd rehearsed the scene well. A little scuffle to entertain the audience. Neither of them would make any impact, but they pretended to. Matt feigned another attack, and Alan ducked. Then he hit back.

And planted his fist squarely in Matt's face. Bones cracked and blood shot out of his nostrils. Sudden pain exploded in the middle of his face.

As far as relatively harmless injuries went, a broken nose was one of the most painful. It was like tenterhooks inserted into his brain and then pulled out through the nostrils. It took Matt a few seconds to gather his wits.

With the clarity came the rage. "Are you out of your mind?"

Alan looked confused. "I didn't..." He regarded his hand as if it he only now realised it belonged to him. "I swear I didn't mean to hit you."

Matt didn't believe a word he said. That hit was no accident. It took intent and force to break a nose. He pressed his arm against his nostrils in a vain attempt to stop the blood flow.

"Oh, dear!" Mrs Wertstein jumped up in horror. "Are you okay?"

"No, I'm not okay." He would be, though, and if it happened here, people would start asking questions he couldn't answer. "I guess I'll take myself to the school nurse?"

"Yes!" Mrs Wertstein sounded almost relieved, as if she was glad she didn't have to take responsibility for the accident. "You go and keep me updated. Lucille, jump in for Hero, please. We're going with act three, scene one."

Alan was still looking horrified as the others took their place. "Matt, I—"

"Spare your breath." Matt climbed off the stage, took his bag, and slung it over one shoulder. As he left the auditorium, his bones were already resetting themselves.

He still went to the school nurse, assuming Mrs Wertstein would check with admin whether the accident had been lodged. Fortunately, no one had realised that his nose was broken, so he might get away with a particularly gory nosebleed. The secretary who doubled as a school nurse was certainly horrified to see him. She gave him a bunch of tissues and told him to go down to the sickbay and wait for her there.

Matt was about to open the door when he heard a very distinctive voice.

"I can't control my dreams!" Fabian cried out agitated. "This is just so wrong. I mean... Do you know what I mean? It's one thing she can walk in them, but to use what she sees against me when I don't have control over my actions there?"

Matt paused with his hand on the handle when he heard Samantha answer. Naturally, she was with Fabian. "Why don't you tell her that? That it doesn't mean anything. That you want to be with her and only her. Fight for her."

Matt frowned. It sounded as if Fabian and Rachel had had a fight, which was a surprise to him. The two of them seemed far too mellow to ever get into a disagreement with each other.

"After this morning?" Fabian snorted. "I bet the whole school knows about it. You saw them taking out phones."

"They know you and I were suddenly very wet, nothing more. Rachel doesn't talk." Matt had wondered why Samantha's shirt had been practically plastered to her breasts.

"She hates me."

Samantha wouldn't let that stand. "No, she doesn't. She's just disappointed. Fabian. I know you two have your issues—" news to Matt "—but if she's important to you, if you want to have this relationship with her, then tell her. *Talk* to each other."

"She won't let me talk," Fabian whined, although he soon seemed to gather himself. "Thanks. I'll give it a try." There was a moment of silence, and Matt almost entered when Fabian raised his voice again. "Talking of hate. Do you think you'll ever forgive Matt?"

Matt let go of the door handle and leaned against the wall. He certainly didn't want to go in there now. Especially because he really wanted an answer to the question Fabian had posed.

"Of course not," Samantha said almost instantly. "He's a murderer."

It was exactly what Matt had expected. To his surprise, though, Fabian came to his defence. "Well, yes, but... he wasn't exactly sane in that moment."

Matt frowned. Since when had Fabian been on his side? He'd always made it very clear he was firmly on Samantha's.

"Believe me, he *wanted* to kill Daniel. And he's happy he did. Or why do you think I'm not getting an apology?" Because Matt had no idea what to apologise for. They both knew the facts, and it wouldn't change a thing. "Why are you asking?"

Just as curious, Matt leaned a little closer. "It's only that sometimes I wish things would be like before... everything, really."

There was a bit of silence, as if Samantha had to think about it for a while. Fabian wasn't the first to voice his annoyance at their prolonged fight. Lucille had beleaguered Matt before, badgering him to apologise, and Jan had even thrown a tantrum. It wasn't Matt's fault, though. He would welcome the chance to talk to Samantha, make her see that as horrible as it all was, he hadn't wanted this to happen. But Samantha shut him out. Completely and always.

Thus, it surprised him when she suddenly admitted, "You and me both." A pause. Then, "You know I feel like I didn't just lose Daniel, but Matt as well." Fabian must've given her a strange look, because she scoffed softly. "We *were* friends. I liked him. I liked spending time with him."

The pain in Matt's healed nose began pulsing again, not like a stabbing sensation, but something deeper, more profound.

"Before you met Daniel, everyone assumed you two were going to have a thing." Fabian didn't sound particularly happy about it.

Neither did Samantha, who groaned loudly. But then she said, "Yes, perhaps."

Matt almost gave himself away as he jerked away from the door. Samantha *had* been interested in him? He hadn't just imagined it? Why, oh why did Daniel have to exist, he asked himself, not for the first time. Things would've been so much easier if not for the blasted student who'd serenaded Samantha with his smooth voice.

"And I would've got my heart broken," Samantha clarified. "As lovely as he was, it was just pretend. He's half-demon and obviously doesn't know true emotions. I would've been one of his endless string of sex partners. But it still hurts. And not only because of Daniel." Her voice tightened as if she was fighting some of those true emotions. "It's silly, I know, but I practically grieve someone who never even existed in the first place. Because it was all a lie. That 'before' you're craving so much—it was just a lie."

"Why aren't you going in?"

Matt jumped when the secretary came down the corridor. She had a first-aid kit in her hand and was quickly approaching. Before Matt could stop her, she'd put her hand on the handle and pushed the door open. Inside the room, Fabian and Samantha had changed from their normal clothes into their PE uniforms.

"Oh, good, the two of you are done," the secretary announced at their sight. She put her first-aid kit down and turned back to the door. "You can leave your clothes to dry and get back to class. I'll write you an apology for your teacher." Then she put a hand on Matt's arm. "I'll be with you in a second, sweetie."

As she hurried off again, Matt faced his friends. Neither of them said something at first. Samantha stared at him, a complex swath of emotions on her face. He couldn't bear her glare. His eyes wandered down to where her short pants showcased her supple thighs.

"What happened?" Fabian asked.

But before Matt could answer, Samantha had grabbed Fabian's hand and pulled him towards the door. "Doesn't matter. We have to go to class. Leave Matt to his make-believe games." She was well aware whatever injury he'd had long healed.

"I don't have a choice," Matt protested, "everybody saw it." His words only found the door that slammed shut behind Samantha.

Frustrated, he sat on the sickbed. Why couldn't he fix this? He wanted to, but every time he stood in front of her, all his good intentions flew out the window, and he managed to offend her. Either he said the wrong thing, or he gave her the wrong look. Something always went wrong.

He recalled her admission that she missed him as well. If she'd known he'd heard it, she likely would've denounced it furiously. Samantha had developed feelings for him. They'd been laced with doubts because of his sexual activity, but she was wrong if she believed he'd have hurt her. Though he *had* hurt her, but not as she'd feared. And now she was convinced she'd dodged a bullet, because he couldn't possibly have loved her back.

But there had been something. Something unexplainable that was so different from everything Matt had ever known.

"It wasn't all a lie," he muttered.

And to his surprise, his nose began bleeding again.

Jan

Despite not keeping his end of the bargain, Lu had taken pity on Jan and given him the keys to her winter garden. They weighed heavily in the back of his jeans when he met Fabian and Matt in a café after school. He could tell both were already over the meetings, but Jan loved this "men time". And he certainly needed it today.

But for now, he was forced to listen to Matt and Fabian exchanging horror stories. "My nose wouldn't stop bleeding for ages," Matt said, while Fabian nodded and added, "and by fourth period, I had wet my PE clothes."

Jan snickered. When the two of them glared at him, he spread his hands apologetically. "You realise how that sounds?"

Fabian groaned. "I didn't pee myself. I doused myself with water, or somebody doused me, or I don't know."

"Yeah, and my body heals itself," Matt chimed in. "It doesn't suddenly start bleeding again."

"Great, okay. I'm with you," Jan hastened to say, though he had no idea what to make of their individual stories. Fabian was known to have little control over his water powers, and he didn't understand what the big deal over a nosebleed was. "That sounds like you both need a drink. While you wait for it, can I run by my plans for Meg tonight?"

Matt leaned back and crossed his arms, looking less than enthused, while Fabian made a face. "If you have to." They both knew he and Meg were planning to have sex.

"So, I've got access to the de Cerque winter garden, which is this insanely romantic setting. No risk of anyone coming in tonight, either.

Lu assured me of that. So, I made a playlist of some smooth beats, and I was thinking of putting candles everywhere."

"Do you plan to have sex with her or set her on fire?" Matt asked.

Fabian sprayed the table with coffee as he burst out laughing.

Jan narrowed his eyes. "Man, for someone with that much experience, I thought you knew what it meant to crank up the romance. Girls like this shit. Tell him that, Fabian. You didn't slam Rachel against a wall, pull out your—"

"Stop!" Fabian looked absolutely horrified. "Please. Rachel and I never had sex. And now we never will, because she broke up with me."

"She did what?" Jan checked with Matt, but the other didn't seem surprised. "Why?"

Fabian grimaced, and his face darkened. "Because she caught me having dream sex with Samantha. And apparently a whole lot of other women."

Jan noticed how Matt's hand tightened around his glass at the mention of dream sex with Samantha. He only then realised what Fabian had said. "Woah, back up. Rachel is blaming you for what's happening in your dreams?"

"It's not fair, is it?" Fabian asked, just as outraged.

"No, it's not," Jan said while Matt shrugged.

"It might be different when it happens all the time." Matt let go of the glass, trying to hide a thin fracture by turning it around. "I mean, if you're constantly dreaming of having sex with other women, something's obviously up."

Jan remembered the chat he'd had with Fabian at the Walpurgis Night. "Maybe it's for the best. Come on. I'll shout you another coffee. Or something stronger." He took care of the transaction before settling back down. "Now, I don't need to ask Matt about his first time. While I'm sure you've deflowered a great many people, you're not exactly an expert in our human needs."

Matt raised an eyebrow, his lips twisting upwards. "I'm not?"

"You just said you don't do romance. And the first time should be romantic. So, Fabian. What did you do for Samantha?"

Fabian turned bright red as if he was some prepubescent idiot, while Matt took to staring into his glass. "I think you're overthinking it. When Samantha and I were ready, it happened naturally."

Jan groaned, annoyed with himself. "Yeah, okay, stupid of me to ask. Samantha isn't that complicated. Meg, on the other hand—"

"—is a lot of work?" Fabian understood him. Meg had huge expectations for her first time and waiting this long had only served to make them even bigger.

Matt rolled his eyes. "Just do it!"

"Not an expert," Jan informed him, annoyed. Then he took another glance at Matt. "If I didn't know any better, you look like you're in need of some sex yourself."

Matt gave him a flat stare. "Contrary to you, I *am* having sex. I'm not just talking about it."

"Yeah, but contrary to me *you're* super tense and pissed." Surely, they were allowed to mention Samantha's name from time to time. "Look, I get Samantha's got it out for you, but—"

"She's not in the wrong there!" Fabian protested, only to quiet down quickly. "Sorry. I understand we all want to get along, but this has to come from you, Matt."

Matt only stared into his glass. Then suddenly, he took it and drank the rest of his Coke. "You're right," he said as he put the glass back down. "I am in need of some sex." And with that, he stood up and joined the group of giggling girls who'd been making eyes at him for a while.

Jan watched him for a moment, envious of how easily he wrapped them around the finger. "Yeah, 'just do it' doesn't work for most of us mortals."

"Don't compare yourself to Matt." Fabian moved his chair to block Jan's view. "You've done the right thing with waiting until Meg was ready. I mean I hate to imagine it, but she deserves her first time to be magical and romantic and all of that. A winter garden date sounds fancy. You've got the music, the candles. Condoms?"

Slowly, Jan relaxed. "Yeah, of course. What do you take me for?"

"Sounds like you're all set. That girl loves you. She actually wants you. Believe me, I know the difference."

"I'm really sorry about Rachel, man."

Fabian shrugged. "It's alright. I still think she's awesome. We just weren't meant to be."

Jan couldn't help but be impressed. "You sound like an adult."

"Ha ha." Fabian made a face. "In a way, I'm glad she broke up with me. I wanted this thing to work out, but I was kidding myself. I just wasn't into her that way."

"That sucks." Rachel had definitely been into him, though obviously, she'd had other ideas for what that meant in the bedroom. "Alright, so Meg..."

Lucille

While the boys were doing their thing, Lucille had invited Rachel and Samantha over for a research-heavy sleepover. They had movies, hot cocoa, and a dozen creature books to sift through. So far, there hadn't been any tangible information on Nemesis that couldn't be found on her Wikipedia page.

Lucille put yet another book away, sighing at the growing pile of discarded material. In her opinion, it was time for a break. As it turned out, there was a hot bit of gossip she desperately wanted to talk about. "Rachel?" The girl looked up from her laptop. "What's going on between you and Fabian? I heard he broke up with you?" Nemesis had to wait. If Rachel needed her, Lucille had enough ice cream to fill the night.

But Rachel only gave her a flat stare. "*I* broke up with *him.* If Fabian had any say in it, we'd be going on like this for forever."

Samantha winced but kept out of it. She'd obviously already had enough intel from the other side and didn't need any more details.

"Is that not a good thing?" Lucille asked, confused.

"You think it's a good thing to be with someone who doesn't want to be with you?" Rachel frowned slightly. "I personally think that's a bad thing."

Her answer only confused Lucille more. To her, Fabian had been the perfect, attentive boyfriend. Not terribly exciting, but steady. "I was under the impression you loved him."

"I do. Did." Rachel shrugged. "But he doesn't love me." She gave Samantha a pointed look. "Or does he?"

Samantha obviously hated being dragged into it. "I don't know. I…" Another glance from Rachel sobered her. "Not the way he loved me, no. I'm sorry."

"It's not your fault," Rachel said surprisingly kindly. "I know you two wanted this to work out between us, but Fabian never loved me the way I loved him."

"I thought you made a cute couple." The words slipped out of Lucille's mouth before she could stop herself.

Rachel's stare was withering. "We're adults who were in a real relationship, not some cute love story in a book."

Called out like that, Lucille very nearly rolled her eyes. "So, what? You wanted him to invite you into our winter garden like Jan?"

"In your winter garden?" Samantha asked, suddenly on high alert.

"Yes, he borrowed my keys and…" Lucille trailed off, since Samantha jumped up and rushed to the window that showed the garden behind the house.

Lucille joined her more slowly. Through the branches in front of her windows, she saw the glass roof of the winter garden. Exotic plants covered the walls, so they couldn't actually see anything going on inside, but the unmistakable shine of candles flickered in the darkness.

"She said she was sleeping at Anne's," Samantha said, a little helpless.

Lucille had never had a little sibling, so she viewed the whole thing in a much more relaxed way. Meg was sixteen and old enough to make her own decisions. "Let her enjoy this. It's not like Jan pushed her." Not after that first drunken incident. "He's obviously taken great care to make sure this night would be magical for your sister. Leave the worrying to your parents."

Samantha sighed heavily and turned her back to the window.

Rachel shook her head about the two of them. "You were fifteen when you had sex with Fabian. Who actually wanted you." She snorted. "And he'd still go with you, if you were okay with that."

Disconcerted, Samantha returned to her book, but then she leaned over to Rachel. "I'm sorry. You know I wanted this for you and him."

"You let him go," Rachel acknowledged, and her features softened. "I know. I guess I'm just disappointed with how it all turned out. You'd think 'your dreams coming true' would be more… dream like."

"Well, my first time definitely was not dream-like," Lucille announced in an attempt to lift spirits. "Just a quick bumbling in and out that left us both sore." She put a hand on Rachel's. "One day you'll find the one who loves you just as much as you do."

Rachel clearly didn't believe her, but she let it slide and pointed at the laptop instead. "I got one useful hit on Reddit. It's about people and their experiences with Nemesis, the relationship advice provider. Or it's supposed to be. Because it turns out that *no one* has any experiences. Either they don't get many clients, or they're not just experts in hiding the murder weapon but all traces of their cases. I'm going to leave a scam warning, just in case anyone else looks them up."

While Rachel did her thing, Lucille grabbed another book that would tell her all about Nemesis' role in the Greek and Roman pantheons. But Samantha shut her books. "This is useless. I'm going to check whether there's some kind of magical trace in the rivers."

Lucille pushed down the small sting of envy about the fact she didn't have access to the magical rivers like Samantha and kept reading. At least this book was a little more forthcoming. "What if it's not Nemesis herself, but the Erinyes, also called Furies? Sam?"

Her friend was sitting upright, staring weirdly at Lucille's desk. She also seemed to have stopped breathing until Lucille's voice called her back. "Uhm... and what do they do?"

Lucille scanned the text. "Okay, it says here that the Erinyes are attracted to the desire of vengeance. In ancient times, that meant prayers and sacrifices. I guess, nowadays, a phone call does the job. As soon as they bond with the person seeking vengeance, they are tied to them until vengeance has been served. As they need to stay in the proximity of the caller, it could take some time though." She put the book down. "I guess what they mean is that unless the vengeance seeker and their victim are in the same room, they can't do much to them. Thus, if they bonded with Saskia, nothing happened until Markus came home."

"How can we defeat them?" Rachel asked cautiously, while Samantha continued to stare at the same spot.

"We can't. They're divine beings. Once vengeance has been served, they move on, I guess."

Rachel shrugged. "In that case, there's not much we can do. Markus is dead, so Saskia's vengeance has been served. Poor girl. And poor Markus, I guess. But the Erinyes moved on, right?" Samantha shook her head, her eyes still fixed. "They haven't?"

"There's three of them," Samantha whispered. "One bonded to each of us."

Fabian

Fabian thought working on special effects for a group poem presentation was a tough task, but the poem was the least of his worries. As soon as he, Jan, Samantha, and Rachel had formed their group—Matt and Lucille were excused for drama rehearsal—Samantha and Rachel informed them about the Erinyes, creepy vengeance *goddesses* who had reinvented themselves by starting a relationship advice company. And killing people while they were at it.

"So, the three of them are bonded to you two and Lucille?" he asked, rubbing his back. His body hurt after an entire night of creepy nightmares that coincidentally had featured red-glowing women hunting him.

"Yep." Samantha looked less than enthused. "The question is what's going to happen now? We need to find out who... well, who we want them to take vengeance on."

Leaning back in his chair, Jan snorted. "Isn't it obvious? I mean, for you at least. Or is there any other person you want to see dead more than Matt?"

"I don't want to see him dead," Samantha hissed, then quickly looked around to see if anyone had overheard them. Mr Zobel was busy helping another group, and everyone else was playing with the sound effects. "But I suppose you're right. He'd be my target."

"Jan's right. Yours is easy," Rachel said softly. "But I have no idea who my target would be. My mother and I get along alright, since she started listening to me. Obviously, there's still a lot to make up for, but—"

Fabian couldn't hear it anymore. The pain in his back spoke his own language. "I'm your target."

To her credit, Rachel looked taken aback. "I don't hate you."

"That may be. I mean, I think it's ridiculous, quite frankly." Fabian rubbed his back again. "*You* broke up with me, but apparently, that doesn't matter to your new friend." Perhaps he was being unfairly cranky, but having a divine target on your back did that to you, he figured.

"I don't follow. Do you think breaking up with you is revenge for your sex dreams?"

Fabian pressed his lips together. The break-up wouldn't annoy him half as much if Rachel had given him a chance to explain. But just as she always did, she thought it through on her own, made her decision, and he either had to swallow or choke on it. "You need evidence? How about yesterday, when you made me splash myself and Samantha?" When she started rolling her eyes, he hissed, "And last night, I had the worst nightmares since that drude took up residence in my room."

"Meanwhile, *my* night was like a dream." Jan leaned back, crossing his arms behind his head and grinning from ear to ear.

"Shut it," Samantha muttered tiredly.

"Guys, I'm serious." Fabian saw Mr Zobel moving around and waited until he had settled with another group. Then he leaned in. "You know those running dreams? Where something chases you, and you keep running and running, up the mountain, through the forest, surreal moonscapes, but it never catches you. Or you wake up when it does. Not last night. Those red women chased me between them, and every time they killed me, I just woke up in a new space."

Rachel had the decency to look around uncomfortably, but then she shook her head. "I wasn't in your dream. I learned my lesson."

"Oh, did you now?" She hadn't shown him that courtesy when they'd been a couple.

"And I can't build dreams like that," Rachel said more urgently.

Fabian didn't believe her. Sure, it sounded a bit too powerful for her, but the connection was clear. "Are you sure? Because last night really was a shit show."

"For you," Jan said, still with that blissful smile on his lips. "My night, however—"

"Jan, I don't want to hear it," Samantha interrupted him. "She's my little sister, remember?"

Disgruntled, Jan rectified his chair and lowered his arms. "Sorry. But just so we're clear. I didn't pressure her into this, okay?"

"I know," Samantha said commendably calm. "I just really don't need the details. Not from you." The matter settled, she regarded both Fabian and Rachel. "Fabian might have a point, you know."

Rachel didn't take it lightly. "Of course, you'd be on his side."

"Because she doesn't want to see me hurt?" Fabian asked a little too loudly.

"Fabian!" Samantha suddenly called out.

His chair gave way underneath him and he crashed to the ground. His butt took the biggest hit, but his elbow hit the floor, and pain shot up to his shoulder. Laughter erupted around him as people assumed he'd been balancing on his chair and fallen. Mr Zobel looked less than impressed.

His face burning, Fabian got up and carefully took place on his chair again. When their classmates returned to their task, he whisper-hissed at Rachel, "Do you believe me now?"

Her face had turned ashen, and she nodded breathlessly.

Fabian held his grudge until the long break, when they came together in a sunny corner in the atrium.

"I didn't do this on purpose," Rachel pleaded, but she was clearly annoyed she even had to justify herself.

While Jan and Samantha tried their best to pretend they weren't listening, Fabian shook his head. "I didn't know I'd be hurting you so much when I agreed to give it a try." Apparently, it warranted bonding to a revenge goddess.

"The road to Hell is paved with good intentions," Rachel muttered.

"So, now I put you through hell?" Maybe it was the tiredness, but Fabian felt like he was caught in a hyper-realistic nightmare. *Everyone* had pushed him towards Rachel. Sure, it was disappointing that he'd never developed that ardent love for her he'd held for Samantha, but at least he was willing to try. Whereas Rachel had continuously shut him out and made him doubt her intentions. "You weren't invested in this relationship either."

Rachel gasped, but before she could answer they were distracted by Matt storming towards Samantha. Behind him, Lucille tried to keep pace, without success.

"You put the Erinyes on my case?" Matt accused Samantha. "Are you crazy?"

"I didn't do anything!" Samantha shot back.

Jan came to her defence with his limited understanding of the situation. "The Erinyes came to her."

"Of course, they would!" Matt was still glowering. He crossed his arms now and sneered. "So, you hate me that much?"

"Is that a trick question?" Samantha asked, her voice starting to sound brittle. "Yes, Matt. Yes, I hate you. Happy?"

Instead of answering, Matt almost doubled over, gasping for pain. "Enough to kill me? Or get me killed?"

"You're hardly one to talk," Samantha retorted, tears in her eyes. "But no, I do not want to kill you."

Despite her words, Matt winced, pressing his hands on his stomach. When he peeked through his fingers, blood was staining his light-grey shirt, and Samantha paled.

Huffing, Matt continued. "Well, if you didn't want that—"

His next words came out mumbled as Lucille had pressed her hand on his mouth. "Sam, you need to go. Remember, distance helps."

Samantha only stared at her. "I..." Abruptly, she turned around and walked away.

Fabian wanted to follow her, but Rachel was faster. Sighing, he remained seated, watching Lucille lower her hand and give Matt a baleful look.

"Seriously, Matt," she said. "Sometimes I think you enjoy being tortured. The Erinyes are bonded to us. Picking a fight with Samantha is like a death wish right now."

Though he tried to give the impression he was completely unfazed, Matt seemed shaken. Naturally, he didn't acknowledge it. "Oh, come on. As if there's any chance Samantha will consider her vengeance served before I'm dead."

Fabian felt his body grow cold. Rachel's vengeance had so far only been embarrassing—if he ignored the intense dreams. What if the only way to make the Erinyes leave was over his dead body? He knew Rachel wouldn't want that, but was there anything she could do to prevent it? Could Samantha?

"Hey, Lu." Jan gave her a nod. "I was wondering. Who's your target?"

To Fabian's surprise, Lucille smiled. "Oh, I don't hate anyone so much that I would want to kill them. But let's just say Cheryl is finding out how cruel her little games are."

Rachel

Now that they were away from the Erinyes, a solution had to be found. Rachel, Lucille, and Samantha had claimed the Magic Circle to continue their research. Matt had wisely bowed out. As had Fabian, which had prompted Jan to announce *he* wouldn't take part either. Rachel was fine with it. The three of them had started this whole thing. It was only right that they found a way to stop it again.

She and Samantha had already begun when Lucille came in—delayed by her rehearsal—looking white as a bedsheet.

"What happened?" Samantha asked alarmed.

"Cheryl," Lucille whispered. Rachel pulled a chair out for her, and Lucille just fell on it like a stone. "I thought it'd be like karma. A few pranks, making her taste her own medicine. But..."

She fell silent. Her eyes were looking inward, and she started hyperventilating.

Samantha hurried around the table and crouched next to her. With one arm around Lucille and the other holding her hand, she helped her calm down. "Just tell us. Is she alright?"

"No." It came out as a tortured little sound. "We... we had a fight when she tumbled off the stage." Now that the shock was wearing off, her words came out faster and faster. "I didn't push her, though of course it looked that way, and Cheryl claimed it, but... Guys, she broke her arm. Badly. She won't be able to play Hero." A few days back, Lucille would've been exalted about that, but now she sounded scared. "I don't like her. None of us do. But I don't want to be responsible for her death. What am I supposed to do?"

"The Erinyes will leave when vengeance has been served," Samantha whispered.

"Cheryl broke out in pimples, her costume was ruined, and she broke her arm," Lucille cried. "Isn't that enough?"

Samantha grimaced, but she shook her head. "Not for the Erinyes."

"Go away!" Lucille shouted, turning her head wildly in all directions. "I'm done. I'm satisfied." She caught herself again and buried her face in her hands. "I bet Saskia didn't want to kill her fiancé, either."

Swallowing, Rachel voiced what was on all their minds. "It seems to me the Erinyes only know one kind of vengeance." A terrible, permanent retribution. Tears shot to her eyes. "I don't want to hurt Fabian." She was angry with him, disappointed, but she would never want to hurt him.

"Speak of the devil," Samantha muttered as she looked over her shoulder through the door towards the shop in the front. A moment later, Fabian and Jan came in. "What are you doing here? It's dangerous."

Fabian ignored her. His intense stare made her guilty conscience flare to new heights. When he walked around the table, he suddenly slipped and fell. His head hit the floor, and Rachel jumped up, shrieking.

Groaning, Fabian pulled himself up again. In the meantime, Jan called out to the front, "It's all good, Caro."

"No, it's not," Fabian muttered, a little whiny, the intensity broken. He rubbed the back of his head before cautiously looking up at Rachel. "I came to apologise."

"No, no, no, you need to go. It's not helping," Rachel blabbered. She didn't want to accidentally kill him.

But Fabian wouldn't be persuaded. He pulled himself up onto a chair, then took her hands in his. "Rachel, I'm so sorry. I've talked this through with Jan. I didn't mean to hurt you." He carefully rubbed her hands while Rachel tried her hardest to keep her panic at bay. "Pretty much everyone told me how utterly in love you were with me. And I like you. I like you a lot. I really thought that something could grow between us if I just gave it a chance. But... I guess I didn't really give it much of a chance. I just took you and your love for granted, never proving myself worthy of it. You deserved better." He lowered his gaze. "And I feel like an ass now."

"You're not an ass." He'd been anything but. In fact, he'd been very sweet. "I put you on a pedestal. I had this version of you in my head, a dream, and I wilfully ignored your real needs." If she was honest with herself, *she* was the one that hadn't given them an honest try.

Fabian's smile looked a bit broken. "Can you give me a second chance? I promise I'll give you all my attention. Anything you want or need."

There he was. That sweet, sensitive boy who never hurt anyone willingly. Especially not her. They could try again with open communication instead of hidden signals, and realistic expectations instead of daydreams.

"I don't think I want that, Fabian." Rachel almost surprised herself. All her life, she'd wanted Fabian. Now he was right before her, ready to lay the world at her feet, but it turned out she didn't want it anymore. "You don't love me, and while that hurts a little, it can't be changed. Truth is... I'm not sure I actually love you like I thought I did either." Speaking her truth was like peeling away an iron casing she'd never realised was there. "I believe I fell in love not with you, but with how much you loved Samantha. How much you adored her. She was everything for you, the perfect girl. Maybe still is in some regards. I wanted that too, but I realise that's not something that can be forced. Or even replicated. You'll fall in love again, but it will be different. And it won't be with me."

"Rachel—"

"No." She shook her head and smiled at him. "I'll always love you, but we're better off as friends. You're obviously a very sexual person." She laughed nervously. "And I'm just not. I can never give you what you need. And you can't give me what I want. Partly because I don't actually *know* what I really want. I've been chasing a dream, but life... life doesn't happen in dreams. It happens here." Finally, she understood what Nico had meant. As painful as this was, it was so much more important. Real.

Fabian's face softened, and there were tears in his eyes. "Can I give you a hug?"

Rachel giggled. "Of course! Come here."

The hug was so much better than any kiss they'd ever shared. It told her how important she was to him, that he cared, and that she mattered to him. She could still have Fabian without forcing something that didn't exist. "Thanks."

"Do you think I still have to die?" Fabian asked as he sat back down. Hastily, he added, "Not that I apologised because of that, but... well..."

With her emotions rising high, Rachel had completely forgotten about the Erinyes.

"No, you don't," Samantha informed him, to her surprise.

"Do you have a plan?" Lucille asked, full of desperate hope.

Everyone in the room looked at Samantha with the same fervour. Samantha shook her head, but she still smiled. "No, but when Rachel forgave Fabian, her Erinye bond dissolved. She left you."

Samantha had barely finished speaking when Rachel found herself back in Fabian's embrace. "Oh, thank you, thank you, thank you," he blubbered into her shoulder.

His relief echoed her own, and she let out a deep, shuddering breath. "Thank you."

"I forgive Cheryl," Lucille called out loud. "She can have the role. I'm even making her a new costume. Is that good enough?"

Samantha grimaced. "No. Either you don't mean it seriously, or the Erinyes prefer deeds over words."

Lucille visibly deflated. "I need to apologise, right?"

"Uh-oh, that'll be cringe," Jan commented, in his usual less-than-helpful way.

"Yes, thank you, Jan." Lucille sighed, but then her face fell and she turned back to Samantha. "Oh no, does this mean..."

Rachel had had the same thought. "...Sam needs to forgive Matt? Looks like it."

Samantha had paled. Her breathing was so flat, she looked like she was going to pass out any second.

"That's impossible!" Fabian cried out. "Sam can't just decide to forgive him all of a sudden. He killed her boyfriend."

While Samantha whimpered, Rachel stuck to the cold, hard facts. "Well, if she doesn't, Matt's going to die."

Lucille

Lucille wanted to throw up. A part of her was still in denial that she was at fault for anything that had happened to Cheryl. She'd neither called the Erinyes nor had she asked for vengeance. It was not exactly fair that just because she had toyed with the idea of paying Cheryl back for her underhanded move; she had to grovel now. But the bigger part of her felt sick at the thought of Cheryl actually getting hurt—or potentially killed—because of a fleeting disgruntlement.

That didn't make apologising any easier. Cheryl wasn't exactly what Lucille would call a gracious person. No matter how willing she showed herself, Cheryl and she wouldn't just hug it out and make up. Cheryl had never forgiven her for shunting her offer to join her clique early in the year, only to hang out with her favourite target. But Lucille was too self-secure to be shaken by the same intimidation tactics Cheryl had used on Samantha, and that clearly grated on the other girl.

They could've been the best of friends, but because of Lucille's choice, they were bitter rivals.

With Samantha and the others on standby, Lucille waited in the corridor leading to the stage to intercept Cheryl. Soon enough, the queen bee, her king, and her lackey came around the corner. Cheryl had her arm in an unflattering cast that gave Lucille a deep-seated pang. *She* had done this to her.

The three of them frowned when they saw Lucille step into their way. "You stay away from me," Cheryl screeched, "or you're going to be served."

Lucille managed to keep her face free of any grimace. "I'm here to apologise." She glanced at Alan, her only potential ally in this.

He got the hint and announced, "Jen and I'll be waiting for you inside. Call out if you need help."

Jennifer whispered something in Cheryl's ear, and the queen bee put on a big show of being brave in the face of her tormentor. The evil glare Jennifer had for Lucille said it all.

As soon as the two had left, Cheryl's face became the stone-cold mask that made all of Lucille's hairs stand on edge. "What do you want?"

"As I said, I'm here to apologise." Going to great pains to keep her voice level, Lucille continued, "You were right. I was angry that you took the role from me, but I never intended to push you off the stage."

"But you did," Cheryl said unapologetically.

This was so much harder than Lucille thought it would be. A part of her wanted to rebel and throw a tantrum, to tell Cheryl she deserved every bit that was coming for her if she acted like that. Lucille pushed those childish emotions down before they could do damage. It didn't matter what Cheryl deserved; she was better than this.

"I know," she admitted, though she'd never raised a hand to do so. "And I'm really sorry about that. It's just... I was looking forward to showing my parents what I could do. Instead, I've only nabbed some minor pity role." To her surprise, Cheryl's icy stare lost a bit of its intensity. "I was disappointed when you got the role, but that doesn't justify sabotaging you. Again, I'm sorry." And she actually was. The vengeance had clearly crossed a line.

Cheryl seemed disinterested. "Well, now you've got the role."

Lucille knew an apology would never suffice. As Samantha had said, the Erinyes preferred deeds over words. She shook her head. "No, I don't. I've talked to Mrs Wertstein and told her that you're the better actress, with or without the use of your arm. So, if you don't mind going on stage with a cast, the role is yours." There was still a small part of her that hoped Cheryl would be too vain to take her up on the offer.

Instead, Cheryl was genuinely surprised. But then she narrowed her eyes. "Is this a trick?"

Once again, Lucille shook her head. "Not a trick. I mean it."

"Well in that case, okay." Cheryl raised her chin, quickly assuming her superiority. "I'll take it, and I accept your lousy apology. Now get out of the way. I've got a gruesome rehearsal ahead of me."

Lucille forced herself to smile as Cheryl walked by. As soon as the door closed behind her though, she allowed herself to relax. A few seconds later, Samantha, Fabian, and Rachel joined her. "Did it work?"

To her great relief, Samantha nodded. "Yes. As soon as you gave the role to her, the Erinye let go of you. Well done. I would've rather bitten my tongue off than apologise to Cheryl."

"Yeah, it wasn't easy. But my conscience will be much lighter if I don't have to worry about potentially murdering her." Lucille levelly looked at Samantha. "Speaking of biting your tongue off, have you decided whether you're going to forgive Matt?"

Samantha grimaced as if she was in period pain. "I'm going to try. After school."

Lucille knew how much it would cost Samantha. Her apology to Cheryl wasn't even a fissure compared to the canyon Samantha had to overcome. To give her a little of her strength, she put her hand onto Samantha's shoulders. "You can do it. Remember that it wasn't truly him at New Year. You know what he's really like."

That elicited a tired huff. "I know what he pretended to be like. To be honest, I can't see that much of him in his recent behaviour."

"That's because he's putting on a farce," Lucille told her while looking deep into her eyes. "Especially in front of you. But take it from me: he's suffering."

"And though he doesn't adequately show it, you mean a lot to him. Far more than he's ready to admit," Rachel chimed in.

Lucille wondered where she'd got that from, but the words rang true. She only had to remind herself of how he'd reacted to Cian when he'd admitted he had a crush on Samantha. Matt still had feelings. He simply had no idea what to do with them.

"If you say so," Samantha whimpered softly.

"Let me!" Fabian said surprisingly harshly as he took Lucille's hands from Samantha's shoulders. He then pulled her into a hug. "Don't mind them. Just focus on one thing. No matter what he did to you, you don't want to be responsible for his death."

That seemed to make it easier for Samantha to breathe. She nodded vaguely before squaring her shoulders. "That's right. Alright, I have to go to Chemistry. I'll talk to Matt after school. He's got soccer this afternoon, right?"

Lucille nodded and watched her go. Samantha had barely exited the building when Fabian whirled around. "You two are impossible."

"Care to explain?" Lucille shared a look with Rachel, who simply shrugged.

"You're making out as if the whole thing's her fault!"

"No!" Lucille shook her head, horrified. "That's not what I meant."

Fabian bulldozed over her protest. "Matt murdered Daniel, and he did it in front of her eyes. It doesn't matter how much he allegedly suffers or likes her. So far, he hasn't even managed a simple apology. No, instead he's making himself out to be a victim of our oh-so-complicated human emotions. And now Samantha's forced to do all the emotional labour and forgive him, without him budging even an inch. Forgive and forget. Who cares about a few dead people?"

Lucille couldn't hold his gaze. Every word was right. In her eagerness to sort the whole Nemesis chaos out, she had completely forgotten what it must be like for Samantha. Shocked, she realised that after all these months she'd completely forgiven Matt. She'd accepted his demon side and appreciated him as a friend. She'd even been annoyed at the prolonged fighting between him and Samantha. She wanted them to be friends again—or even more—but she understood now the ball was in Matt's corner. It had been for a long while.

"But if she won't forgive him, Matt will die," Rachel said, almost mercilessly. "He doesn't deserve that, does he?"

"You know, his victims would probably think he does." Fabian crossed his arms.

"Fabian!" Lucille was aghast. Yes, Matt was the problem, but he didn't deserve to die for his sins. Enough blood had been shed already.

Fabian shrugged and lowered his arms again, deflating a little. "What? It's true. Look, I like Matt as well, as strange as he is. I realise that the Blood Night made him do things he might've thought about but would've never gone through with if he'd been sane. Just like you with the whole Nemesis thing. But for Samantha, it must feel like a slap in the face. She's forced to forgive him without even so much as an apology, and you're putting all that pressure on her."

"I'm sorry," Lucille whispered. She felt even worse than when she'd started the day. "I just... I don't want him to die."

Next to her, Rachel nodded sharply. "We've had enough loss to deal with already. After the Erinyes are gone, we can sit down and figure this out—maybe lock the two of them in a room until they've talked it out—but for now, Samantha has to be the bigger person."

"A bloody big person," Fabian muttered, but he no longer protested.

Samantha

The wind was cold and unforgiving as Samantha sat on the stands and watched the soccer team finish up their practice. In a few weeks, they were attending the regional tournament, and by the looks of it, they seemed well prepared. Alan and Cian were a well-rehearsed team in the front, and with Matt's supernatural reflexes, not a single ball made it past him in the goal. It wasn't entirely fair, but Samantha didn't care nearly enough about soccer to interfere.

The boys rolled the goals to the side and secured them, then vanished to the changing rooms. Cian noticed her and gave her a quick smile, which she answered with a short wave.

Jan and Matt were the last ones. They both looked up to her. Then Jan clapped Matt's shoulder and said something before ducking down the tunnel to the changing room.

Matt held her gaze as he strolled up the stands. Two rows under her seat, he stopped. "Lucille said you've got something to say to me?"

Samantha took a shuddering breath. She wanted to scream and shout, anything to tear this blasé mask into pieces, but that would defeat the purpose of her visit. "You're not going to make this easy for me." And why would he? He didn't care about how his actions affected her, only his own perceived innocence.

"Might be because there's an Erinye on my case who's going to kill me."

"Which I'm trying to avoid," Samantha pointed out.

He crossed his arms, taking a tense breath. "So?"

Despite opening her mouth several times, no words formed on her tongue.

Relaxing again, he shrugged. "Look, I get it. It would be no different in Hell. You've been handed the chance to take your revenge on me. You hate me, so... a demon would do exactly the same."

"I'm not a demon," Samantha whispered. The wind had suddenly become colder, and despite him standing below her, she felt intimidated by his presence.

"I know," Matt said calmly, as if they were discussing homework and not his impending death. "Otherwise you would've done it earlier."

His nonchalant cockiness nearly took her breath away. "Humans don't kill each other every time they have a problem with each other." At least, most humans didn't.

"That must be why you recruited the Erinyes instead."

It was too much. Samantha huffed in indignation, and something tore Matt's feet out from under him, causing him to tumble down the stairs in a sickening motion. In horror, she watched him cartwheel twice before he saved himself with a space jump. When he reappeared on the bench next to her, she'd sunk to the floor, whimpering.

"I assume that means you won't forgive me," he said callously, while rubbing his shoulder.

Promptly, something hit him in the face.

Samantha pressed her hands to her ears as if she could somehow shut him out that way. "Please stop this!" Didn't he see how everything he said would get him attacked by the Erinyes?

"You want *me* to stop?" Matt asked, incredulous. "*You're* the one who can't stop hating me."

A flash of red moved in front of Samantha and stabbed Matt in the side. He gasped as blood ran through his fingers.

Samantha had seen enough. In a blind panic, she shot to her feet and started running down the stairs, nearly taking herself out in the process.

"You can't leave me alone like this!" Matt called after her.

"I have to!" Samantha cried out in her desperation. "The only way to keep you alive is for me to keep my distance from you."

She had to get away as fast as possible, but Matt grabbed her arm, having jumped after her. "So, how's that going to work? We go to the same school and—...Do you want me to give up all of this and go back to Hell?"

It was exactly what she wanted. It would make everything so much easier. "I can't forgive you. I can't. I just can't."

And from behind, the red woman stabbed him again. Matt's hand fell away as he sank to his feet, blood blooming on his soccer shirt.

Samantha stumbled backwards, almost falling down the stairs. She caught herself, turned around, and ran down them as fast as she dared. As soon as her feet hit the ground, she sprinted away.

Tears were running down her face, turned icy by the cold, sharp wind. It took her at least a minute to realise that Matt thankfully hadn't followed her this time. He finally must've got it into his proud head that staying close to her would only see him get hurt.

She wiped the wetness from her face, unable to control her breathing. Her pulse was still racing, as were her thoughts. She wished she could've simply given him his forgiveness. But they would only be words. In her heart, she was unable to forgive him. Not yet; maybe never.

At long last, she'd calmed herself enough to check on the red bond, expecting the Erinye to stand behind her. There was no sight of her.

Confused, she concentrated harder. The Erinye was gone, but a red band wrapped tightly around what looked to be her heart. The bond wasn't broken, but it was stretched thin, as the supernatural being had decided to stay behind. With Matt.

For a moment, Samantha contemplated continuing her flight. At one point, the bond had to snap. Either that or pull the Erinye to her. But what if it didn't? What if the Erinye stayed with Matt until vengeance was served?

She couldn't risk it. As much as she detested him, she didn't want to see him dead. Samantha took a deep breath, then turned and sprinted back to the stands.

The stands were empty. Not a sight of Matt.

Could he have jumped away in a desperate attempt to shake the Erinye? Samantha investigated the bond once more and noticed it led to the soccer field. What she saw there almost froze the blood in her veins.

Matt was kneeling on the grass, his arms locked in by the two other Erinyes who must've joined their sister. Blood covered his face and had soaked through his soccer shirt. Samantha ran.

The Erinye had a spear in her hand, an old Greek weapon that she raised high above her head and pointed at his chest. Just before she brought it down, Samantha slid through the bloody mud between the two and spread her arms.

The spear hit her in the chest. Unlike with Matt, the weapon didn't penetrate her skin, but it pushed her backwards into Matt. His eyes were wide open with shock, the white stark against the blood on his face. Meanwhile, the Erinye looked confused.

"Please," Samantha pleaded. Her chest hurt, but she pulled herself onto her knees, manoeuvring her body between Matt and the divine being. "Please don't kill him." She wet her lips. "I don't want to take revenge."

To her surprise, the Erinye nodded. There was still confusion in her features, but she took a step back. Her sisters let go of Matt's arm. The three of them flowed together, twisted, and vanished both from her visual and magical sight.

Shuddering with relief, Samantha sunk into herself. A sob tore itself from her chest and more tears flowed.

Matt didn't say a word this time. He gave her all the time she needed to pull herself back together and clean up her face. When Samantha was sure she wasn't going to start crying again, she turned around, half-expecting him to be gone now that his life was saved.

As it was, he still sat there, stunned into silence. Curtly, she informed him of what had happened. "You've got nothing to fear. The Erinye bond is broken."

In front of her, Matt's bloody lips curled into a smile. "You care for me."

Samantha stared at him, unable to do as much as blink. She'd just saved his life, almost sacrificing herself in the process, and all he could think to do was mock her?

"No, Matt. This doesn't change anything. I still hate you." But the words didn't come off quite as effortlessly as they used to.

Matt must've been delirious with pain. It was the only explanation why he would grin while his entire face was sticky with blood. "If you truly hated me, you wouldn't have forfeited your vengeance. A demon wouldn't do that. And I'm pretty sure humans don't jump in front of just anyone, either. You like me."

She couldn't believe it. This entire time, she'd been terrified. Even now, her knees were like jelly and her chest ached with every breath. But not the half-demon in front of her. He'd already shaken off the danger to his life and was solely focused on his perverted pleasure.

Clenching her fists, Samantha drew herself up to her feet. Anger flooded her, strengthening her legs and washing away the remnants of shock. "I don't care for you, much less like you. I'm just not willing to become a murderer for you. For all I care, you can drop dead."

He didn't refute her this time, just kept grinning. Samantha turned on her heels and stalked off.

What a conceited idiot, she thought. No apologies, no thanks. Next time he lay dying, she'd look the other way.

But in her heart, Samantha knew she could never do that.

Matt

Matt hadn't thought he'd be alive for the premiere. After finding out that the girls had managed to attract the Erinyes, he'd assumed his life was over. Samantha would finally get her wish, and he'd pay for what he'd done during the Blood Night. A part of him had even welcomed the release. There was something comforting about a certain, unavoidable death.

But Samantha had spared him. Not just spared him but risked her *own* life to save him. *He'd* been ready to die, but when she'd jumped in front of the Erinye's spear, Matt could've sworn his heart stopped. Fortunately, the Erinyes could only harm those they'd sworn to bring justice to. Samantha hadn't known that, though.

In the moments after, Matt hadn't been thinking clearly. The only thought that had stuck out was she couldn't possibly hate him enough if she'd risk her life to save him. Now that he'd had a day to process yesterday's events and what had been said, he was even more impressed. The alleged reason for Samantha's intervention couldn't simply be explained by undeniable fondness. He hadn't deserved that.

Instead, it'd been a show of her character strength, her convictions. Murdering people was wrong. What was a daily occurrence in Hescaryn was an abominable crime in Ashuan. However, humans were weak and far less social than they claimed to be. The sins had a strong grasp on Ashuan. Most humans just lied to themselves while they indulged in the same basic urges.

But Samantha believed it. Samantha truly believed putting anybody's life in danger for her own gains, her own emotions, was wrong. She would fight for her life, defend the city from monsters and demons, but she wouldn't kill him. And Matt was suddenly convinced that even in a Blood Night, Samantha would've stopped herself. She would've driven herself mad, but she wouldn't have killed anyone. Not even if they'd somehow deserved it.

Matt would be lying to claim it didn't shake him to the bone. All this time, he'd held up the Blood Night as a shield. Even when he let himself be convinced his own jealousy and strong dislike of Daniel had contributed to his death, he hadn't assumed full responsibility. It'd still been the Blood Night that had pushed him over the edge. But now he wondered if he simply hadn't been strong enough. Because deep down, he knew he was every bit as bad as Samantha said he was. He still couldn't bring himself to care about Daniel's death.

It was a disconcerting thought that didn't leave him, even while he was on stage. His acting was much better tonight, but he missed a couple of his cues. Only now, in the final scene, did he manage to pay attention to the play. Jennifer stood in front of him, but it wasn't her he saw. Taking a page out of Lucille's playbook, he imagined Samantha in her place.

"Do you not love me?" he asked and was reminded of how he'd told her that she liked him.

Jennifer shook her head, just as much in denial as Samantha. "Why would I? No more than reason."

"Hmm, then your uncle and the prince and Claudio have been deceived. They swore you did."

"Do you not love me?" she inquired now.

Love was such a curious thing. What did it truly mean to love another person? Even this play, which was all about love, didn't hold the answer for him. "God, no. No more than reason."

Jennifer looked amused. "Why then my cousin, Margaret, and Ursula are much deceived. For they swore you did."

"They swore you were almost sick for me."

"They swore that you were almost dead for me."

Matt allowed himself a grin as he shook his head. "It's not the truth. So, then, you do not love me?"

Still in denial, Jennifer answered, "No, truly, just as a friend."

Chris stepped up to them in his old man's make-up. "Come, cousin, I'm sure you love the gentleman."

Behind him, Alan and Cheryl joined them, their hands intertwined while they each held a letter. "I could've sworn he loves her," Alan claimed loudly. "For here's a paper written in his hand, a halting sonnet of his own pure brain, fashioned to Beatrice."

"And here's another," Cheryl replied, the piece of paper stuck between her fingers. "Written in my cousin's hand, stolen from her pocket, containing her affection for Benedict."

If only there were some simple letters that could take over the talking for him and Samantha. Matt gave Jennifer a cheeky shrug. "A miracle! Here are our own hands against our hearts." He put his arm around her and pulled her close. "Come, I will have you, but by this light, I'm only taking you out of pity."

"I would not deny you," Jennifer said likewise. "But by this good day, I yield only under great persuasion, and partly to save your life, for I was told you'd die without me."

"Peace! I will stop your mouth." Matt took a step forward and kissed Jennifer. In some rehearsals, he'd actually kissed her, because he'd had no idea how to only pretend to do so. Jennifer had never minded despite having a boyfriend, but this time, he couldn't bring himself to do more than press his lips onto hers. All these people he'd kissed—and had sex with—had never fulfilled his need. Not since last year. And after what had happened the other night, he felt as if they'd been nothing more than this play. A grand act without substance to distract himself from what he really wanted. And couldn't have.

The others performed the shortened finishing monologue. Then applause filled the hall. For a few minutes, they took their bows, blinded by the spotlight. Matt had paid little attention to the audience throughout the play, but he knew exactly where Samantha was sitting with their friends. She jumped to her feet now, clapping wildly. But she didn't look at him, only Lucille, who curtsied happily despite her parents passing on the play.

One by one, the actors filtered down into the hall, where their families greeted them. Some people sauntered over to the cafeteria that was beckoning with special—more expensive—premiere prices, but most stayed standing and chatting.

René managed to grab him and pull him into a hug. "That was awesome. Can't wait to see it again on Monday. Next time, I'll bring the camera."

"The camera?"

"It's a dad thing," René said off-handedly, but his big smile gave him away. "Keepsake memories."

Matt returned his embrace a tiny bit and then separated himself to find his friends.

Jan hollered when he saw him coming. "The man of the hour! That was impressive work. Seems like all those rehearsals paid off."

As he clasped Jan's hand, Matt checked with Samantha. As usual, she kept her head down or looked away. But without her, he could've never pulled off such convincing arguments. Or—as he admitted quietly to himself—the romantic resolution. "Thanks." It was one thing he'd forgotten to say out loud yesterday. "I'm lucky to be alive for the premiere."

"About that," Lucille said, giving Samantha the opportunity to ignore him. "I'm really sorry about how much pressure I put on you. I'm glad you found it in your heart to forgive him, but I shouldn't have forced you to do it."

"I haven't forgiven him," Samantha announced, and the other four exchanged worried glances. "We found a different solution."

This time she met his eyes, and a silent communication passed between them that neither would divulge the exact nature of their solution. Or rather, her solution. Matt had been entirely useless.

"But the Erinyes are gone, aren't they?" Rachel asked concerned.

Samantha broke the eye contact and nodded happily. "Yes, their vengeance has been served. No more magic bonds. You know there's just one thing I don't understand. Why they bonded to us in the first place. I mean, Saskia called them, but I'm sure neither of us was thinking of... well, our revenge targets when we visited her. Not like that."

The last addition made Matt frown. Did that mean he *had* been on her mind when she visited the alleged boyfriend-murderer? Now that he thought of it, it made perfect sense. Of course she had.

"The thing is, they'd served Saskia's vengeance, so why were they still hanging around?" Samantha asked.

"What if it wasn't served completely?" Rachel suggested.

Lucille's eyes widened. "Why would you say that?"

Rachel shrugged. "She was cheated on. Usually, it takes two to cheat. What was the name of her friend? Ina?"

"Inga," Samantha breathed.

"I hate to be the bearer of bad news," Jan muttered, his eyes fixed on his cell phone. "The police released Saskia this morning because there wasn't enough definite proof. Five hours later she was arrested for a second murder. Said she just wanted to talk."

The news settled on the group like a lead blanket. Matt reflected on how close he'd come to sharing Inga's and Markus' fate.

Fabian was the first to break the silence. "I feel terribly sorry for her. She's going to jail for a crime she hasn't done."

"Not necessarily. As suspicious as it looks, there shouldn't be any evidence, and since we don't rely on jury verdicts, Mr Petersen should be able to resolve it. It just became a lot harder," Lucille explained.

"Okay." Fabian nodded thoughtfully. "Let's hope for that, then. But either way, it means the Erinyes are gone now, right?"

Samantha took a deep breath. "I suppose so. Yeah."

"Alright." Jan clapped his hands loudly. "I need a drink. Who else?"

Lucille smiled gratefully. "I'm happy to shout a round here or we can go somewhere else."

"I vote somewhere else." Fabian gave the cafeteria a dirty look. "You're rich, but not rich enough for our school cafeteria."

"You know how messed up that sounds?" Samantha asked and laughed while the group got moving.

"I'm only saying the truth. That guy will ruin us all with his business acumen."

Matt trailed behind the others, lost in his own thoughts. It was as if he only now realised how close he'd come to dying. Two people were dead because they'd cheated on a third person, while he was still alive. It made him feel something complicated. Complicated and ugly. He hoped a drink would wash it away.

By the time he got home, the ugly feeling had only intensified. No amount of alcohol had helped, and his usual method of pushing away the things that bothered him hadn't worked since the whole disaster with Cheryl. Sex had become meaningless. Or perhaps it'd been meaningless all this time, but he'd experienced something meaningful in between, and failing to recognise it, he'd lost it again.

Matt sighed, leaning his head against the door instead of opening it. When had life become so complicated?

When he'd fallen in love with Samantha.

He shook his head. That couldn't be. Love was one of humanity's lies. He saw it all around him. People craved love, chased and embraced it, to where it blinded their true needs. That healthy relationship between Fabian and Rachel? Nothing but two people lying to themselves. Jan and Meg? Ridiculous. Samantha and Daniel?

Now that had been something, hadn't it? But if he were honest, it had been too short to tell. "And whose fault is that?" he asked, then hit his forehead against the door.

In a moment of clarity, he got over himself and opened the door to let himself in. The familiar pitter-patter of Crumbs' paws greeted him. The dog had grown so much, but he was still a baby and happy to see him.

Matt took his time to play with him before progressing into the living room. There, his father was waiting with a bottle of champagne.

"I was wondering when you'd be home. Should we celebrate your acting premiere?" René asked.

"It's not going to happen again." After this year, he would quit drama.

René smiled benevolently. "All the more reason to celebrate."

Matt watched him fill the glasses and sat down. And then, without a warning to his father or himself, he said, "I almost died yesterday."

Champagne dripped on the table. René caught himself remarkably well. He set the bottle down and grabbed a cloth to wipe the table clean. "I'm assuming it differed from... well, you get in danger a lot."

"True." Matt snorted. In Hescaryn, almost dying was how you got through life. The key was to never *actually* die. "But this was different."

He told his father about the Erinyes and how Samantha had saved him from his gruesome fate. René listened attentively without interrupting him.

"And I've been pondering it a lot, you know?" So far, Matt had managed to hold it together. "How her utter conviction that killing me would be wrong is what saved me. That she fought for my right to live, while I... well, I didn't exactly fight the blood thirst."

René shook his head. "That's not true. You *did* fight it. If not, you would've ditched your birthday party or attacked all of us. There were powers bigger than you at play. You fought valiantly, but you didn't stand a chance. Remember, not even Chay got around his Blood Night."

His had been even worse, though Matt knew no details. "You're my father. You have to say this."

"Learned that much, haven't you?" René raised an eyebrow at him, but then he put a hand on his. "Matt, you need to start moving on from this."

"I've tried."

"No, you've tried to ignore it. To pretend it didn't happen. Or that it happened but didn't matter. You've never acknowledged it or tried to make amends."

Matt pulled his hand back. "I tried once." Back in the early days. He'd intended to talk to Samantha, but she'd attacked him. And ever since, she'd lashed out at him whenever he'd come near.

René gave him a flat stare. "You can do better than once."

Groaning, Matt leaned back in his chair. It was such a René thing to say. Or maybe a father thing. "These human things are complicated" Far too complicated. And they left him with the strangest of conclusions. "Can I tell you something scary?"

Intrigued, René leaned in. "Scary to you?"

"Now that I think of it," Matt took a deep breath, "when the Erinye was set on me, I was almost relieved. Samantha would get her vengeance, and the whole affair would've been settled. You know, like would be the case in Hescaryn." Bitterness filled his mouth, and he had to swallow. "I was convinced I deserve to die. After all, I took a life—several. I'm not a good person. Human or demon."

That was the most shocking thing. In Hescaryn, he'd never asked himself whether he was doing good or bad. He just took action. And he was strong enough to survive. But now that luxury had been torn away from him. Seeing Samantha sacrifice herself because she wouldn't let him come to harm on her account had forced Matt to re-evaluate himself. He wasn't as far outside of human morality as he'd thought. He'd just chosen to ignore it. Because confronting it would've forced him to face the ugly truth: "I don't deserve to be alive after what I did."

"Matt." René swallowed. He rubbed his chin, clearly fighting the truth himself. His father knew he was right, but he'd never admit it. Not like this. "Listen. What happened on New Year's was a disaster. No contest there. You did some horrible things, but that doesn't mean you deserve to die. You weren't fully accountable and even if... it doesn't bring people back to life," slowly, he was gaining steam, "the truth is: we all make mistakes in our lives. Some worse than others. But being human isn't about passing judgement, or balancing dues, or requiting one wrong against another. It's not our mistakes that define us but what we learn from them."

"And what did I learn from it?" Matt asked, slightly overwhelmed.

René smiled warmly at him. "I think you know. Now's the time to apply that knowledge."

Matt made a face. If only it was that easy.

Part 4

Games & Fire

Fabian

The sun was burning down on the field. Even in the shadow of the stands, the heat was nigh unbearable. Fabian had no idea how the players on the field managed it.

The entirety of Year 12 and Year 13 had been given time off during the Greenvalley game. Their team had had a marvellous run so far and was the only one in the tournament that hadn't had a single goal scored against them. Since that was almost solely due to Matt's efforts, the goalie had gained a huge popularity. His good looks ensured his fan club even extended to the other teams' supporters.

The rest of the team wasn't bad either, though in Fabian's opinion they relied too much on Matt single-handedly fending off their opponent's attacks. Nevertheless, watching their team win game after game was fun. Fabian only watched soccer occasionally—usually to spend time with his father—but the atmosphere in the stands was so much better.

Not everyone seemed to think so. While Lucille was happy to cheer for their team, Samantha was reading an occult book, and Rachel was completing her Maths homework. "Guys, we're gonna reach the semifinal," he said, annoyed.

There was no response from the two distracted girls, but Lucille grinned at him. "They can't take this away from us."

"It's not really fair, though, is it?" Samantha muttered, her eyes still glued on some demon-summoning spell. "With his demon reflexes, Matt's unbeatable in goal."

Lucille shrugged. "Sure, but if you apply that kind of logic, it wouldn't be fair to mix club players with regular students. As far as I'm aware, Alan and Cian have been playing for a club since early childhood."

Samantha harrumphed and focused her attention back on her creepy reading material.

Fabian looked up and saw the cafeteria owner coming up the stairs. The man had seized the opportunity to make more money, selling refreshments from a hawker's tray. Naturally, his prices turned off even the thirstiest student. Fabian pushed his water bottle under the seat. Bringing your own drinks was strictly forbidden for some mysterious reason.

"Come on, blow the whistle." Lucille was bopping in her seat. For the last few minutes, the opponent's team had pressed forward, putting Matt under near-constant pressure.

Fabian shot from his seat when there was a bit of a scuffle, dreading to see the ball enter the net. A few seconds later, Matt had both hands on the ball and kept it safe. The players dispersed again, and Matt shot the ball almost over the middle line. Jan caught it and dribbled it further, but before he could pass it to the strikers, the whistle sounded.

The game was over. They were in the semifinal.

Overall, the applause was rather lacklustre, owing to the nature of a school tournament. Only Matt's fan club cheered loudly and started gathering at the field's edge. Most of the other students packed up their things and started filtering out.

The four of them also got up, though Rachel protested that she hadn't quite finished yet; she needed the game to go into overtime.

"We won!" Lucille laughed.

On the aisle they ran into the cafeteria owner, who glared at the non-buying students. When Fabian passed him, he held out his hand. "You're not allowed to bring your own drinks."

"Okay." Fabian plopped the near-empty bottle into his hand and continued on.

To their surprise, they found Menuha at the bottom of the stairs. Lucille greeted her like an old friend. "Hey, girl. Did you come to see Matt play?"

The demon smiled. Her low-cut green dress was almost sheer in the summer breeze. "René told me he'd be here. I have no idea what he's doing, but it looked good."

She waved at Matt as he walked towards the stands with the other players. The moment he raised his hand in response, a group of girls whirled around and shot daggers at Menuha.

"Uh-oh. I think you've angered his fan club," Samantha muttered.

"Fan club?" Menuha looked genuinely confused.

Lucille hooked her arm into hers and drew her closer to the barrier that separated the stands from the field. "Because of the tournament, a lot of girls have come to Greenvalley who aren't yet used to Matt. Naturally, they spotted him. Good looks and a flawless performance on the field—including a bit of showmanship—and he won them over. But what made his popularity really soar is a persistent rumour. Allegedly, he turned down a girl on day one, citing that he needed to concentrate on the tournament and can't let himself be distracted." She giggled. "Now they all think he's the second coming of Ronaldo or something."

"Matt turned her down?" Menuha asked, surprised.

Samantha shut her down instantly. "It's just a rumour." Then she sidestepped the team so Matt wouldn't arrive next to her.

Fabian clapped loudly, then clasped hands with Jan. "Great game."

"Hey Menu," Matt greeted his sister.

"Congratulations for making the semi-final," Lucille said to him and grinned. "I would give you a hug, but you're a bit sweaty, and your fan club is watching."

Matt grabbed his shirt to wipe his face, accidentally exposing his abs. The fan club went crazy, which prompted Samantha to roll her eyes and create even more distance between them.

Coincidentally, that brought her in front of Cian. To Fabian's surprise, Samantha smiled at the Elite Clique guy. "Hey. I saw your goal. Happened to look up at the right time." She laughed while Cian grinned. "It looked good as far as I could tell, though I have to warn you, if soccer was a class, it'd be the one I was failing." For some reason, she just kept on talking. "But the ball was inside of the goal, so I'm going out on a limb and saying you scored."

Cian burst out laughing, and Fabian instinctively braced himself for a nasty retort. Somehow, Mr Popular only had eyes for Samantha, though. "If I'd known you'd be here, I would've scored another one. I'm glad you're here." It sounded surprisingly honest.

"Typical!" There was the nasty undertone Fabian had expected, but even Alan put little effort into it. "Everyone becomes a soccer super-fan when there's a tournament, but never for the seasons."

Samantha frowned at him. "It's just a school tournament, not the championship. I spent most of my time reading."

Alan rolled his eyes. "Of course you would." He clapped Cian's shoulder. "Have fun with your nerd crush."

Crush? Cian was crushing on Samantha? When had that happened?

As soon as his friend had vanished into the changing rooms, Cian gave Samantha a shy smile. "Don't listen to him. He's just jealous there's nobody waiting for him."

Samantha returned his smile, equally shy. "Waiting is a bit over the top." She gave him a lopsided grin. "Let's say I was nearby."

"Were you?" There was a definite flirty undertone now as Cian raised an eyebrow. "I wonder what might've brought you here, then."

Fabian wasn't the only one who'd been completely captivated by the unexpected interaction, apparently. Matt was suddenly growling. He took a step closer, but Menuha grabbed his arm. "I need to talk to you. It's about Malcolm." She practically had to pull him along with her to make him go.

Lucille gave Fabian a confused look. "Malcolm? I hoped he'd lost interest in Greenvalley."

"That would've been too easy, wouldn't it?" Fabian sighed. Then he pointed at Samantha and Cian who were still pretty much flirting. "What's happening there?"

Lucille's guilty face gave her away. Apparently, the whole interaction wasn't news to her. "Uhm... as far as I know Cian has a crush on Samantha. A real one. No magic." She raised her hands to steer clear of it. "No idea how she feels about it."

It sounded like there was a story there. One that Lucille *and* Jan both knew, because the latter was suddenly very interested in the grass at his feet. "Right, changing room. Are we gonna meet for food afterwards?"

They all nodded and started to drift away. Reluctantly, Fabian was planning to leave Samantha behind, but they'd barely reached the end of the stands before she came running after them. "You're not waiting for me?"

He shrugged helplessly. "You seemed busy." Fabian wasn't sure how to broach the topic that she'd been flirting with one of Cheryl's closest friends. One who'd burnt her before.

"What? That?" Samantha looked over her shoulder to see Cian heading into the changing rooms. "I just congratulated him. It was a good goal, right?"

"Sure, but he missed a few others that could've made the game a little less nerve-wracking."

Samantha nudged his side. "Oh, stop being a sourpuss. Cian and Alan do a good job in the front, even if you don't like them."

"Just like Matt is doing a good job in the goal?"

Her answer was a significant eye roll.

"So, since when are you and Cian... *friends?*"

"Since the beginning of the year?" Samantha took a deep breath. "Well, not right at the start, but he's my preferred partner in Chem. We have lots of fun."

"Fun with an Elite Idiot?" Fabian raised an eyebrow.

Samantha jabbed her elbow into his side again. "Don't call him that. He's pretty much over Cheryl, by the sounds of it. He only cares about Alan and Shayna, or otherwise, he would've ditched the clique months ago."

Fabian had never told anyone about his conversation with Shayna, but he had to grudgingly admit she wasn't half-bad, either. Not his type of girl, but not irredeemable like Cheryl, either. Alan however... "I don't know. Anyone who's best friends with Alan carries a red flag for me."

"They actually grew up very similar to us. Their houses neighbour each other, and because Cian's mum had to work—you know, being a single mum and all—he spent a lot of time with the Asters instead."

"Woah," Fabian interrupted her. "You know a lot about him." He'd only learned of their friendship today, but Samantha seemed to be deeply entrenched already.

"We talk."

"That's all?" It was as close as he dared to venture to the subject of flirting.

Samantha gave him a long look. "Yes, that's all."

"Okay." Fabian gave in quickly. If Samantha wanted to talk to him, she would. Until then, he'd take her word for it. Swiftly, he changed the subject. "Did you hear about Malcolm?"

She shook her head, looking instantly worried. "What about him? Did he make a move? Is there a new monster?"

"Not that I know of. But Menuha came to talk to Matt. It's not going to be..." Uncomfortably, he shuffled his feet. "You know... about the prophecy?"

Samantha's brow creased, not an expression that instilled much confidence in him. "Let's hope not."

If the power of hope his feather symbolised ever planned to make a show, Fabian thought, now would be a good time.

Matt

Menuha didn't even give him a chance to shower before dragging him to the delivery entry behind the stadium. A few pallets of energy drinks were sitting outside the entrance. Not seeing anyone claiming them, Matt helped himself to one of the cans. After a game in the sun, his throat was parched. He also needed to wash out the bitter taste in his mouth from seeing Cian putting his moves on Samantha.

"So, what about Uncle Malcolm?" Matt asked, feeling grumpy. It had been almost half a year since the archdemon had bothered them. Not that it was a long time for demons, but after setting werewolves and hellhounds free, drugging teenagers with magic, beating the life out of him, and trying to steal their magic via nightmares, Matt imagined Malcolm would've kept going. "We haven't heard from him in months. Did he give up?"

Instead of answering his question right away, Menuha frowned. "Then you know what he's planning?"

"Not really. I assumed he hated me, but after Mum told him to back off, he didn't really seem invested anymore." As much as he liked Menuha, he wasn't going to tell her about the prophecy that pointed to Malcolm being their ultimate enemy.

"And he kept his promise to her?" Menuha asked surprised.

Matt shrugged. "Why wouldn't he? Mum can be quite frightening if she chooses to be." He definitely didn't want to get on her bad side.

But Menuha shook her head. "He's the Archdemon of Greed. If he wants something, nothing and no one can stop him." It sounded as if it was more than a euphemism.

"So, what do *you* think he's up to?" The energy drink tasted okay, but it somehow left him thirstier than before.

"I'm supposed to find out."

He connected the dots. "Melaney sent you here. Why?" As much as he'd wanted to believe his sister was only here for her own human-loving reasons, she happened to be one of his mother's confidantes. Nobody paid attention to sweet Menuha. Not when her twin brother made such a ruckus.

"Malcolm is acting erratic. He's missed half the council meetings and refuses to engage. He's planning something. Something big."

Matt shuddered, thinking of what that could mean for Hescaryn, and—since Malcolm was singularly invested in Ashuan—what it would mean for Greenvalley. "He doesn't do things by halves, that's for sure. It's all or nothing."

Menuha's eyes widened. She even raised a hand to her mouth to stifle a gasp. "The Black Throne. That's what he wants."

The Black Throne was the abandoned chair of the Lord of Chaos, Hescaryn's true leader. Once upon a time, it had been Lucifer, and then some unassuming girl who got herself killed within five minutes of sitting on the throne. Since then, the Council of Seven, once just advisers to the Lord, ruled Hescaryn. Most demons Matt knew had never lived in Hell with a single ruler, someone strong enough to keep the seven deadly sins in check. Just the thought of it was frightening. But it fit Malcolm's ambition.

"But what does he want with Greenvalley? Last time I checked, the Black Throne was still in Hescaryn." Not that Matt had ever seen the throne. It stood in the Council of Seven, and he'd rather hack off his sword hand before facing the seven archdemons. Their disagreements were legendary, and they never ended well for the poor supplicant in front of them.

Menuha seemed just as worried. If Malcolm's power move was successful, everything would change for Hescaryn. "I need to find out. Will you help me?"

"I'll keep my eyes open," Matt promised. "But this week, I'm busy trying to win this tournament." It might have been insignificant, but if Hescaryn was about to be overthrown, he wanted to enjoy the last peaceful moments.

"Good luck with that." She was about to turn away when she thought of something else. "Try not to mix them up, though. You know, the tournament and Samantha. It didn't go that well for you last time." And with that, she jumped away.

Dumbfounded, Matt stared at the empty spot. What was that even supposed to mean? Of course, he was trying to win the tournament. Samantha had nothing to do with it. Unbidden, the memories of her talking and laughing with Cian came back, and he crushed the energy drink can. "I don't care," he whispered to himself, but the tension in his body spoke a different language. A dangerous language.

"Are you going to pay for this, or do I need to report your theft to the police?"

Matt whirled around and came face to face with the cafeteria owner. The man glowered at him, but then again, he glowered at everybody. Matt stuck his hand in the pocket of his game shorts but came up empty. His wallet was back in the changing rooms. "I don't have any money with me right now, but I'll pay you back. I promise." He *had* drunk from it after all.

The cafeteria owner narrowed his eyes. "With interest."

Barely able to keep his eyes from rolling, Matt nodded. "Sure. How much are they, anyway?"

"Four fifty. Five for you."

"Five!" Matt almost choked on the number. Not that it was a huge amount of money, but it was almost double other energy drinks. "Of course. I'll give you your five euros tomorrow."

He walked away before the cafeteria owner could increase the price.

After he'd showered and changed clothes, Matt scoped out the competition with Jan. To keep his stupid fan club away, Matt had donned a baseball cap and sunglasses. It wasn't perfect, but at least he wasn't instantly recognisable.

Few watched the game, which was a shame, because the team from Liehnheim was world class. At least, compared to the other school teams. They played circles around the other team, already leading by more than five goals. If they didn't take pity on their opponents, they'd end up in the double digits.

Nope, no pity, Matt thought, as the ball slammed into the opposing goal again.

"Damn," Jan hissed. "They're good."

"Better than us," Matt muttered. While he was pretty confident he could hold most balls, he wasn't so confident about the constant pressure the Liehnheim strikers put on the goal. And the rest of the team was just as good. The ball rarely even crossed over the middle line.

Jan grimaced, unconvinced. "Let's not get ahead of ourselves. They'll have to get to the final first."

"As do we." Matt had no doubt anyone could stop Liehnheim before them. Their own team though... As good as his defence was, Alan and Cian weren't even close to this level.

"You think Fallerthal will beat us?" Jan asked incredulous. They'd be playing Fallerthal in the semis. "If they hadn't gotten that penalty in the last minute, they would've gone home."

Matt didn't share his conviction. "It's soccer. Doesn't matter how the goal happens."

"Yeah, but goals don't happen on our side," Jan said with a grin. "We're still the only team with a clean slate. Not even that awesome Liehnheim team can claim that. Are you planning to let a ball through tomorrow?"

Amused, Matt shook his head. "Of course not."

"Then I'm not worried. We've got this." Content with himself, Jan turned back to the game. After a quick check, he got out a cigarette and lit it.

The smoke must've bothered Robert sitting in front of them, because he turned around. "Didn't you hear the rumours? Not a single game of Liehnheim's has actually finished. Too many injured players, or the opponent doesn't show... disqualification. They've never actually won a game, but never lost one, either."

Matt narrowed his eyes at such an erratic turn of events. "So, they got lucky?"

Robert shook his head. "Perhaps. The more popular explanation is that they're cursed."

"Oh, shut up." Jan snorted. "If anything, their opponents are cursed. And besides, Liehnheim's winning now."

"Or not." There was something weird happening. A foul had been called, but that wasn't what had caught Matt's attention. He took off his sunglasses to make sure he wasn't just seeing things. "There's smoke on the grass."

Below them, the opposing team was arguing with the referee about the foul. The Liehnheimers were just as agitated, and none of them had noticed the smoke developing in the grass around the player who was still performing some dying swan routine. Matt was about to go down and tell someone about the smoke when the player on the ground burst into flames.

Shocked, Matt stopped, causing Jan to run into his back. Jan opened his mouth to complain when the second player caught fire. "What the hell?"

Matt was equally horrified. He'd never seen anything like it. The screams alone were enough to curdle his blood. "Robert might be right about a curse."

Lucille

The burning field even made regional news. The games had been paused while the cause was being investigated. Eventually, they'd come to the conclusion the sun must've set the grass on fire, or something equally plausible. Meanwhile, Lucille and her friends were doing their own investigation. And as usual, it involved a lot of books.

"Please tell me you've found something useful," Lucille begged as she noticed Samantha writing a huge list. It looked more promising than her own results.

Samantha winced. "Oh, I found a lot. Too much, to be honest. There should be a book. *'A hundred ways of spontaneous self-combustion.'*"

Lucille couldn't help but giggle. Even Fabian grinned. "That bad?"

"There's all kinds of stuff. Curses, potions, poisons, parasites, spells... You could even summon a demon that will let everybody burst into flames. I've learned about summoning, just in case anybody is ever that stupid." Samantha shook her head as if the thought made her shudder. "And of course, there's elemental magic."

Fabian was suddenly all ears. "Are you saying the Liehnheim team is full of fire mages or am I also running in danger of self-combustion?"

"You'd more likely get yourself soaked. You know, like when..." Samantha side-eyed Rachel, who raised her hands to show she was over it. "Fire mages are less fortunate when their magic goes havoc."

Lucille closed the book in front of her and propped herself up on her elbows. "So, is that it? Is it a bunch of elemental mages who don't have a grasp on their magic yet?"

"How likely is that?" Rachel asked. "Fabian's the only elemental mage we know. What are the chances there's a whole team of them?"

"There have been several burn-related injuries surrounding the Liehnheim team. They might not be elemental mages, but they're at the centre of this," Samantha pointed out.

"Alright." Lucille pushed her chair back and got to her feet. "I think it's time we did some field research. I'm going up to the youth hostel to find out more. I'm sure I can get one of those sweaty players talking." A little flirt and most boys her age would tell her all sorts of things.

To her surprise, Rachel got up as well. "I'll join you. Safety in numbers and so on."

Lucille wasn't really convinced that the Liehnheim team was behind the fires, but she didn't mind the company. "Great. You two continue the research. We'll keep you updated."

As they walked out of the Magic Circle, she heard Fabian say, "If they're truly elemental mages struggling with their fire, I wouldn't want to be in their shoes."

Lucille shared the sentiment, remembering her own loss of control of her magic. The affected players must've been terrified.

Greenvalley's youth hostel was located a little above town, on the flanks of the highest peak called the Witch's Hump, for its lumpy appearance. It was always well-visited, but these days, it was practically bursting at the seams with teenagers. Most of them spent their time outside, playing table tennis or soccer in the meadow next to the youth hostel.

The latter looked like a promising start for their research. Lucille nudged Rachel. "Let's try these guys."

"Okay."

Together, they walked towards to the meadow and watched them play for some time. It didn't take long for a guy to spot them and jog over. He had a wide grin, a face full of freckles, and jug ears. "Hey, beautiful. What can I do for you?" He completely ignored Rachel and only leaned into Lucille.

Behind him, a few others also drew closer, though they let this one have his shot first. Lucille had little interest in entertaining him beyond what was necessary. "Are you the team from Liehnheim?"

Instantly, his entire posture changed, and he clicked his tongue angrily. "Of course you'd be another of their fan girls. But you know what? They might look cool, but *we* actually won our games honest and true. Tomorrow we're beating Greenvalley, and if those Liehnheimers dare show their faces at the final, we'll kick their pompous asses from one end of the field to the other."

Lucille took a deep breath, feeling quite overwhelmed by the giant chip on his shoulder. "I'm not a fangirl. We're... we're from the student mag and noticed every single game they played got cancelled. Weird, huh?"

The guy mellowed again and gave her a flirty grin. "Why don't you write a story about us? We're more interesting than a pile of disqualifications."

"Sure. And you are...?"

He promptly took a superman stance. "Friedrich Halber of—"

"Fallerthal." Rachel stole his thunder in her usual uncompromising tone. "Greenvalley is facing Fallerthal tomorrow."

"Are you going to cheer for us?" one of the other guys asked, his smile a lot more honest. "I'm Milad."

Lucille smiled at him. "What position do you play, Milad?"

"Midfield."

"I'm a striker," Friedrich announced, positioning himself in such a way he blocked her view of Milad. "I'm the one who's going to destroy Greenvalley's clean slate."

She doubted that very much. "I've heard Greenvalley's goalie is quite something."

"You're into that kind of smoothy? I bet he's more interested in how he looks on social media than actual gameplay." Friedrich turned for a high five, but no one was that interested in giving it to him. Milad rolled his eyes emphatically instead.

"Me?" Lucille shook her head, amusing herself by knowing that Matt didn't even understand the point of social media. He would certainly crush it if he did but, then again, the world wasn't ready for demon content. "I would never."

"Well, you did once," Rachel traitorously muttered. It had been so long ago, Lucille rarely thought of it these days. They were friends, and she couldn't imagine wanting anything else.

Unfortunately, Friedrich picked up Rachel's words. "What's that supposed to mean?" he asked aggressively. "Did he rebuff you, so now you're trying to get it on with another player? Look, girl, I really don't like leftovers."

Lucille screwed up her face. What was wrong with this boy? His friend must've been thinking the same, because he tried to step in. "Easy, man."

But Lucille didn't need saving from a man. She pushed her hands into her hips and gave Friedrich a piece of her mind. "Don't call me 'girl'. I'm not here to *get it on* with anybody, player or not. As for you, you wouldn't even be my second choice." She took a deep breath. "We just want to learn more about the different teams."

Friedrich lunged at her and grabbed her arm. "So, you two are spies. You're from Greenvalley, aren't you?"

"Let me—" Sudden pain made her scream. Her arm was burning up under Friedrich's grip.

His friend jumped in and pulled Friedrich away. "Man, what's wrong with you?"

"Stay away from us!" Friedrich hollered as his friends dragged him away.

"What a bunch of jerks," Rachel muttered. "Everyone's looking."

Self-consciously, Lucille noticed they'd accrued a little audience. Now that the drama seemed over, they dispersed again. But there was no question people would be wary around them. Not that they needed to ask around anymore.

As they hurried away, Lucille showed Rachel her arm. "Look at this. His touch burnt me."

A fiery red handprint wrapped around her arm and had even formed two blisters.

"Holy—" Rachel caught herself, and they both threw a glance over their shoulders to study the players. "Maybe it's not Liehnheim at all."

Samantha

"Here. This is a burn potion but let me try something else first." Samantha put down the tube of burn salve on the table next to Lucille. Then she carefully took the flowers out of her bag. Purple blossoms would provide healing. She'd already tried to change the magic configurations linked to colour at home, but it still took some time.

Time enough for Jan to butt in and take Lucille's arm. "Ouch, that must hu—... It still hurts!"

He wanted to draw his hand away, but Samantha clamped her fingers around his wrist. "Wait."

Jan stared at her in confusion, then bit down on his tongue, still in pain. But Samantha barely registered his face. Her eyes were fixed on where Jan's fingers touched Lucille's skin. A golden shimmer was covering the burn mark. As it sank into the skin, the redness eased.

"You can heal like Nico?" Lucille asked what Samantha was suggesting.

"No, not like Nico." Rachel stepped closer. She looked at the arm, and her face twitched as if she was about to cry. "It was always you, wasn't it?"

Samantha let go of Jan when he gave her another tug. Confused, he shook his hand. "What are you guys on about?"

"Nico didn't have healing powers," Rachel whispered. "Not until he got bitten. He just thought he did." She shook her shoulders and took a deep breath before facing Jan. "But he was with you. And when he had convinced himself he had healing powers, he searched for trouble. With you."

All eyes were on Jan, who looked around nervously. He huffed, then made a face. "What are you saying? That it's my fault?"

Rachel shook her head. "Of course not."

"You healed me," Lucille said gently.

"Vesta was a healer," Samantha added. She was one of the two souls Jan carried. "There you go. That's your magic."

"That's ridiculous." He looked shocked to the bone. "I can heal?"

Now Matt also chimed in. "You were in pain, weren't you? When you took Lucille's away, you felt what she felt. That's healing. It's one of the reasons Caspar hates doing it." He shrugged. "And you know, the whole helping other people thing."

"Yeah, I don't think I'm the right person for this either." Jan shook his head, almost convincing himself.

Fabian snorted. "Because I'm the right person for water magic? Healing sounds really useful to me. Even if it comes with a little pain."

"All the pain," Matt corrected him. "A healer feels all the pain of the injury, including what's covered by the patient's adrenaline. That's why none of them try to heal a deadly wound. Oh, and keep your hands away from diseases. You can heal symptoms but not the cause, and the chance for infection is incredibly high."

"Does anybody want to be a healer?" Jan asked, incredulous.

Samantha put a hand on his shoulder. "A demon wouldn't, clearly. But your mum's a nurse. You know what she would do with those powers."

"Yeah, bloody kill herself," Jan muttered, but his shoulders relaxed. He looked up at Rachel with a surprising amount of compassion. "If I'd known, I would've tried to save him."

"I just said—" Matt started, but Samantha hushed him.

Rachel held Jan's gaze and nodded. "I know. It's not your fault."

"Well, it's high time that we get some healing powers," Lucille announced. "Especially with those highly inflammable tempers around. I assume we found our elemental mage?"

"Fallerthal wasn't around when those two people caught fire," Samantha replied. "It's something else. I'm leaning towards a curse on the soccer players."

Matt chuckled. "That's not it."

Samantha regarded him quite unimpressed. "Let's hear your idea, then."

"Malcolm. My sister thinks he's in town, planning something."

"And the Archdemon of Greed is a soccer fan?" Samantha retorted without really considering the idea.

"More like a soccer hater, if he's trying to set us on fire," Jan mumbled.

Matt sat back down in his chair and started playing with a pencil. "I've got no idea why he would limit his activities to the tournament, but he must be behind this."

"That's ridiculous." Samantha shook her head. When Matt opened his mouth to protest, she quickly added, "I'm not saying he's not in town, but what does he stand to gain from lighting up some high school soccer players?"

Matt started pouting. "What if he bet money on Liehnheim's victory and is helping the team along? That would fit, wouldn't it?"

Samantha still thought it was highly unlikely, but she'd already written down three dozen other causes. So, what would another matter if it kept Matt out of her hair?

"We should still keep an eye on Liehnheim," Lucille suggested. "Right now, they're the only ones profiting from these firebugs."

"You know, somehow, I don't want to be set on fire," Jan murmured in his typical blasé manner. "Especially with healing powers that only work on others."

Rachel pointed at Fabian. "It would be best if you hang around the team while we get to the bottom of this."

"What? Me?" Startled, Fabian glanced about. "Why?"

Samantha understood exactly what Rachel had meant. "Because you can stop any spontaneous self-combustion."

Jan nodded sagely. "We'll put our lives into your moist hands."

Half the room made a face and groaned. Fabian looked less than impressed, but he gave in. "Sure, I'll do it."

Grinning, Jan boxed his arms. "You'll be our team mascot."

Even with Fabian guarding the team, they still had to find out what was causing all these fire-related incidents. Sighing, Samantha returned to her research.

The next day, Samantha and the others arrived a little early at the stadium. The stands weren't filled yet, and the Greenvalley and Fallerthal teams were still warming up. She was about to sit down when Cian spotted her.

"Samantha!" His arm shot up to wave at her.

Humouring him, she descended the stairs and walked over to the barrier. Cian leaned on it and grinned wildly. "Hey."

"Do I get a kiss for good luck?" he asked, turning his cheek to her.

Samantha laughed. Teasing, she leaned forward but didn't touch his skin. "Perhaps after you win."

"I'll keep you to that!" Cian said good-naturedly and ran back on the field to practice passes with Alan.

She didn't know why she encouraged him like this. She was pretty sure she wasn't in love with him, but it was fun. Cian brought out a side in her that had been buried ever since that fateful winter night. He didn't pressure her, just was always there with a smile and a joke. But she would've had to be blind not to see he was angling for a little more. Problem was, Samantha didn't quite know how to feel about that.

Especially not with Matt watching her like that. Despite her continuous pushback, he seemed to be obsessed with her, lately. She didn't know whether it was some kind of sick game of his, but when he looked at Cian with such a dark face, she could only worry. And that brought up all the pain of Daniel's death.

Subdued, Samantha returned to her friends and ignored the curious look Lucille gave her. Fortunately, Rachel and Fabian were sitting between them, so she didn't have to talk to her. There was nothing Lucille loved more than boy gossip.

That plan worked well for the first half an hour. The game, which was still nil-nil at this point, didn't hold Lucille's attention enough, though. And since she hadn't brought books like Samantha and Rachel, she decided to squeeze in between Samantha and Fabian. "Care to tell me what that was earlier?"

"No," Samantha mouthed, not even pretending she had no idea what Lucille was talking about. "It was a joke."

"So, Cian likes to joke around with you?" Lucille asked, once more way too excited.

It used to be fun to discuss boys with Lucille, but her friend had either forgotten about Daniel or she thought she was helping by pushing Samantha into another relationship. "Sure."

Lucille leaned in, still delighted. "I think he's interested in more."

"He isn't." He absolutely was.

"Trust me. Cian publicly declared he had a crush on you in Marseille. He even asked Matt for permission first."

Samantha's book fell to the ground. "He *what*? Why would he do that? Does Matt own me now, or something? Why does he have to give his *permission*?"

Lucille finally dropped the cheerful curiosity. She licked her lip, then explained, "Apparently, there's a rumour going around that you and Matt are... something."

A rumour? "And did anybody care to actually look at us? Did *you* put that rumour out?" Samantha wouldn't put it past Lucille. She'd wanted her and Matt to get along again after what had happened.

But her friend looked taken aback. "It's not me, I promise. Maybe Cheryl put it out there. Or people saw how he saved you at my party. There were a lot of people there."

Samantha found herself shivering, though the temperature had climbed to thirty degrees already. Stupid Matt had jumped through space to prevent her from crashing into the buffet table. Since nobody had talked about the fact he'd suddenly appeared behind her, she'd assumed nobody had registered it. "I'm definitely not interested in Matt. And..." she sighed, "not in Cian either."

"Then perhaps you should tell him that. Instead of, you know, encouraging him."

"I'm not." It made Samantha weary to think of all the complications a flirt with Cian would entail. Sure, they had fun in Chemistry, and his flirty lines always prompted her to reply likewise, but a full-blown relationship was out of the question. For one, no deep feelings were involved, but there was also Cheryl to consider. And apparently, Matt.

"After the game two days ago, it certainly looked like encouragement. If Menuha hadn't pulled Matt away, he would've barged in," Lucille said, as if that was something to be excited about.

Dread filled Samantha. "Why can't he leave me alone?" She remembered how he blabbered on about her liking him just because she wouldn't let him die on her accord. He'd been so stupidly happy—and delusional. "So, what? He's going to kill everyone who's nice to me?" *That* was exactly why she couldn't even consider a relationship. The threat that Matt might destroy that as well hung over her.

"Well..." Lucille shook her head. "He wouldn't do that."

So, he might not *kill* people, but he obviously wasn't going to let them get close to her, either. Frustrated, Samantha threw a glance at the goal.

Matt's focus was on the game. Right now, there was an attack from the opposing strikers.

"That's the guy who burned me," Lucille muttered. "Friedrich."

Curiously, Samantha watched the striker take his shot. It was aimed straight at Matt. Matt caught what must've been quite a powerful shot. Expecting the players to disperse again, Matt drew his arm back, ready to throw the ball, making himself completely open to the Fallerthal player who barrelled into him.

"What?" Samantha shot to her feet.

Matt went down instantly. He held onto the ball at first, which made it possible for Friedrich to kick him.

The Fallerthal player had gone completely mad. Matt seemed to hold back, to hide his demon powers, but he also got quite the beating from what-was-supposed-to-be a normal human player. The referee was blowing her whistle angrily and pulling the red card, but that didn't stop the guy.

It wasn't until Jan stepped in, and with that action encouraged other players to grab a hold of Friedrich, that he stopped. Matt had curled up on the field, and Samantha believed she saw blood. Next to her, Lucille was starting to push through the people. Without thinking, Samantha followed her.

They were both running down the stairs when Friedrich tore loose from his teammates. He charged at Matt again, and to everyone's horror, he burst into flames as he did so.

Almost instantly, water splashed down from the sky in a single powerful column. Fabian. People turned their heads up, wondering about the weird weather, but the water seemed to have stopped Friedrich in his tracks. His teammates took the opportunity to drag him off the field, while the first aiders attended to Matt.

Samantha almost choked on the sigh of relief that broke through her lips when she saw him walking, or rather, hobbling off. Blood was all over his face, and he was holding his arm. Jan was at his side, but Samantha saw Matt glare at him, so she supposed no healing was going to happen. Or at least not more than he'd already done.

Lucille pushed through the barrier and joined the coach at the player bench where they'd brought Matt. Panicking, she was all over him. Samantha, however, had finally realised where her instincts had brought her, and kept a healthy distance. The sight still made her swallow.

"Never seen anything like it," Cian said worriedly, as he and Alan returned from the other side of the field. "What happened there?" he asked Samantha.

She could only shrug. "I have no idea. But be careful, okay?"

Whatever was happening to the soccer players was getting worse.

Jan

Matt had been right about the effects of healing. Jan had only needed to put a hand on his arm to realise it would be a bad idea to attempt to heal him. And while his healing powers pretty much seemed to run on autopilot, he'd been absolutely certain he would've had to do more to fix that splintered fracture. The fact he'd instinctively known it was a complex fracture had put Jan off the whole healing deal.

Still, he couldn't help but think about Nico. The moment Nico had discovered "his" healing powers, they'd been sitting on the docks. Jan had seen the golden shimmer, not realising he was the one behind it. Every time Nico had supposedly healed, it'd been immediately. But only because Jan had been right at his side when it happened, like at Alan's party. His wounds from whatever creepy monster the others had faced at the zoo had remained until they met. It should've been obvious.

But if it'd been obvious, then Nico wouldn't have felt invincible. He wouldn't have gone after the werewolf. Jan shook his head. There was no sense in entertaining that train of thought. Things had happened as they did. As usual, it'd been Jan's fault. *He* was the troublemaker. *He* was the one who dragged everybody down. *He* was the one who'd never amount to anything.

The healing powers wouldn't change that. If anything, they seemed to mock him. *He* of all people should have a useful, beneficial, or even self-sacrificial power?

Jan shook his head and grabbed another beer. The entire soccer team plus supporters were celebrating at Alan's house. After what had happened with Matt, the game had reluctantly continued. Perhaps the other Fallerthal players had been scared, but they'd never got close to the goal after that, while the Greenvalley team had been extremely motivated to fight for their fallen goalie. Everyone had played superbly, and Alan and Cian had battered the opposing goal into oblivion. Now they were in the final.

"You want one too?" Jan asked and handed Fabian another can of beer. While not a soccer player, Fabian stuck to the team like glue. And good on him, or Matt would have been incinerated on top of being beaten up.

Just then, people started cheering. Jan looked up and saw Matt had entered. With his left arm in a sling, he waved his right hand graciously. Jan let him have his fame and glory, then grabbed an energy drink for him. No alcohol with pain meds. If he was going to be some kind of doctor now, he might as well start to think like one.

"Here you go, hero." He opened the can and handed it to Matt. "How's the arm?"

Matt took the energy drink gratefully. "I don't think anything's still broken, but it's tender. I'll be fine by tomorrow, though."

"How are you gonna explain that to our coach? The first aider was sure your arm was broken."

"He made a mistake." Matt shrugged and drunk. "My father managed to get to the hospital around the same time, and stopped them from getting me an X-ray. Apparently, we're very fancy and have our own specialist. Either way, that was good enough for them. We were allowed to go, and by the time we came home, most of it'd grown together again."

"Does it hurt?" Fabian asked.

Again, Matt shrugged. "It's alright. Getting it broken hurt more."

Jan assumed that Matt was quite embarrassed he'd had his arm broken by a human, but he was glad the half-demon hadn't retaliated. "Any idea why that idiot suddenly went off on you? You'd already caught the ball."

"That might have been his problem," Matt said testily.

"My guess is he *was* an elemental mage, a very crazy, aggressive elemental mage." Both Jan and Matt looked at Fabian, confused. "Lucille said it was the same guy who burnt her."

That made sense. He must've been in the stands as well the other day when the two players burst into flames.

"What happened to him?" Matt asked.

"Nothing. His school is dealing with him, and the whole team are driving home tonight." Jan was still miffed. There should've been repercussions for such violent behaviour. He always got into trouble for every transgression.

Matt took the news with much less interest. "So, if he's the one, then the danger is over. At least for Greenvalley and the tournament."

"Let's hope so. Anyone want another drink?"

Matt raised his can, indicating there was still enough in there, but Fabian shrugged. "Yeah, why not? It's going to be a long night."

Two hours later, the party had definitely picked up. Most of the people were drunk, including Fabian, who hadn't had nearly the tolerance for alcohol he must've thought he had. Amused, Jan watched him bumble around and underline each sentence with a big gesture.

"And now he's crushing on Sammy," Fabian slurred. "What is he thinking? That Sam's into assholes?" He was complaining about Cian's interest in their common friend.

Jan had never had a problem with Cian and said so. "I wouldn't really call him an asshole." From his experience, Cian was a pretty decent guy who liked soccer, gaming, and a good party. He and Jan weren't friends, but they didn't have a problem with each other, either.

"Oh yeah?" Judging by Fabian's indignant tone, the same couldn't be said for him. "In seventh grade, he and Alan used to draw dicks in my comics before I handed it in. Can't say the teacher was impressed."

Despite trying his best, Jan couldn't keep the chuckle in. "Are you for real? That's, like, five years ago."

"He's friends with Cheryl."

Jan didn't really care for Cheryl, either. She was far too complicated for him to handle, annoying, and frightfully superficial. But again, she'd never bothered him beyond the screeching of her voice. "Unless he *is* Cheryl, I don't see the problem."

Fabian snorted and helped himself to another beer.

"Don't you think you should slow down?" Not that Jan was in the business of denying his friends a drink, but Fabian was on duty.

"Why? Do you honestly think something's going to happen tonight?" All of a sudden, Fabian raised his arms and crowed, "We won!"

Several people joined his cheer while Jan laughed. He'd never experienced Fabian really drunk, as he usually stayed home with Samantha on Saturday nights.

"You're right." Jan went to grab another beer for himself, when he caught sight of Robert having a go at Chris.

That didn't seem right. Robert was an annoyingly mellow guy who wanted to be friends with everybody but never seemed to stick with anyone. *That* was not the guy who was attacking Chris right now. "Why do they even put you on the field? You're not doing anything."

Chris was clearly annoyed. "Just leave me alone, Robert!"

"No, really, you're so slow." Robert kept encroaching on Chris' personal space. "If you'd been in defence, as you were supposed to be, it never would've got this far. But you rely too much on Matt. You secretly want to be a striker, right? Score some goals. But you aren't good enough."

The words had their desired effect. Chris clenched his fists and took a step towards Robert. "Listen well, you armchair expert. For someone who wouldn't even make the team as a mascot, you—"

"Woah, woah, stop it, you two." Jan stepped between them and pushed them apart. "Let him be, Chris. He's just talking nonsense, as usual." Then he turned to Robert. "And you, my friend, you've had enough to drink for tonight."

He wanted to take the beer from Robert's hand, but the can he held was only an energy drink.

Robert didn't appreciate him interfering and shouted, "You're not any better. How many times did they steal the ball from you?" He got louder and louder. "Every one of you plays so lousy, you don't deserve to be in the final. You only got here because the others were a player down and—"

Jan grabbed his arm and dragged Robert into another room before the entire team could turn on him. He found Robert annoying at the best of times, but he was harmless and didn't deserve what was coming for him if he continued on this path.

Inside the room, he pressed Robert against the wall. "Have you lost your mind? Since when were you such a soccer expert, anyway?"

"I'm on the team," Robert replied promptly.

"You are?"

Robert snarled. "For an entire year, yes! Do you think I enjoy being your gofer? The coach says I don't have the talent, but when I look at that pile of losers over there, that can't be right."

He was spouting such nonsense Jan put his hand against Robert's forehead to feel his temperature. He'd barely touched it when Robert lunged at him.

Jan's martial arts instincts kicked in and he caught the arm easily, only to watch it catch fire. Robert continued pressing him, forcing Jan to defend himself.

It didn't take much to subdue Robert and pin him to the ground. Even that little exertion left the boy breathless, but it took some of the aggression out of him. And he started to notice his own arm burning.

Robert started screaming, and Jan ran for the door. "Fabian!"

He looked around wildly until he found him. Fabian was hugging a pot plant, emptying his stomach's contents into it.

Groaning, Jan ran back to Robert. He grabbed a blanket and threw it over Robert's arm until the fire was extinguished. Tears were running down Robert's cheeks, and Jan knew he was in pain. He could feel it at the edge of his consciousness.

Cautiously, he searched for that edge, opening himself to it. The pain hit him like a freight train. Robert must've got away with third-degree burns, perhaps even worse. Even though the blanket covered it, Jan saw the damaged skin. And he saw what he needed to repair.

The magic slid from his fingers into Robert's skin, reconnected nerves, and encouraged new cell growth. The skin came together, but the pain was almost unbearable. At last, Jan tore his hand away. He couldn't do this. He simply wasn't good enough. Or selfless enough.

Robert carefully raised the blanket, clearly preparing himself for the worst. What he uncovered was red skin, like a bad sunburn not too dissimilar to the one on his neck. But there were no blisters, no charred skin, no deeper tissue damage.

Jan let out a huge sigh of relief. Maybe he *was* cut out for this. Not that he had the slightest interest in doing any more of it any time soon.

Something metallic caught his eye. Jan reached for it and picked up the energy drink Robert must've dropped at some point. The liquid had left a red stain on the carpet. But that wasn't what Jan had noticed.

Five big letters proclaimed the name of the drink and beneath it, the company's tagline: *FLAME—Awaken the Fire in You!*

"Damn it!"

Matt

Matt had been at the party for less than an hour when Cian slid into the seat next to him. "Hey."

"What do you want?" He'd had his arm broken and two ribs he'd never told anyone about. And on top of that, it had happened in front of hundreds of eyes. The last thing he needed was the Elite Idiot who'd proclaimed he wanted to get into Samantha's pants.

"Check on you," Cian said a little impatient. "Samantha said I didn't have to worry, but it looked absolutely horrifying. Are you able to play in the final?"

Trust the Elite Idiots to care more about their stupid game than their teammates. But what really grated on Matt was the casual mention of Samantha. He knew why Samantha had told Cian not to worry. She knew Matt would heal. And yet Matt couldn't ignore the sting her apparent disinterest caused. And to discuss it with Cian of all people.

Heat raced through his veins, fuelling a deep-seated anger that should have cautioned him, but Matt ignored it. Abruptly, he rose. "Come, I'll show you how my arm is."

Cian looked at him, confused, but he followed Matt out into the street like the idiot he was. Together, they walked down to the park at the corner. A nice dark place. By then, Matt had emptied his drink. He crumpled the can in his bare hand and threw it aside, feeling slightly better at having done so.

"Is there a reason we needed to walk this far? My house is just on the other side of the fence if you wanted to talk in private," Cian complained.

His whiny tone was more than Matt could bear. He whirled around and planted his right fist in Cian's face.

The impact threw Cian to the ground. Perplexed, he looked up at Matt. "What the hell, Matt?"

Matt languidly rolled his head from one side to the other. Rage was cursing through his veins, but he took more satisfaction from taking things slowly. "I told you to keep your hands off Sam."

"That's what this is about?" Cian got up to his feet and patted his backside. "You also said she can't stand you and there's absolutely nothing going on between the two of you."

"All true." Matt hit him again.

This time, Cian danced away from him, so Matt's fist barely connected with his chin. "You're not making any sense. Unless..." His eyes widened. "She hates you, but you love her?"

While Cian was distracted by his pseudo-revelation, Matt grabbed his shirt and pulled up his knee, burying it in the pit of Cian's stomach. All air went out of Cian as he folded. Far too soon, however, he straightened again and pushed Matt away from him. "I'm not fighting a cripple."

"You think I'm a cripple?" So far, Matt had only used his right hand and other body parts. His left arm was still healing, but that didn't stop him from hooking a leg behind Cian and sweeping him off his feet.

Cian went down with a huff. Before he could raise himself up, Matt had sat down on him, pinning the boy's arms to his sides. Then he raised his right hand and brought it down, again and again. With each hit, the fiery rage in him burned hotter. His blood seemed close to boiling point, the fire consuming him slowly.

Something hit his broken arm. The sudden pain shot through the fire and smoke, extinguishing the flame. Cian had got his arms free and was battering Matt's arm with the ferocity of desperation.

Each hit unset the healing until Matt was howling in pain. He rolled off Cian, tears stinging in his eyes.

"I'm sorry, Matt. I really am." Cian hastened back on his feet and took several steps back. Blood was flowing from his nose, and swellings formed around his left eye and chin. "You didn't leave me any choice." And with that said, he ran away like a coward.

Matt wanted to charge after him, but the pain in his arm still took his breath away. And there was something else, a moment of clarity. He wasn't allowed to beat up Cian. It wasn't how things were done in Ashuan. It had got him in deep trouble before, but there was a fire burning in his veins, and it begged to be let out.

Just as his breath eased, someone kicked him in the face. Hot blood spurted down his face as pain erupted in his brain once more. A hand grabbed him by the neck and pulled him up and away.

Matt knew they were jumping through space when the cold, slimy sensation grabbed hold of him. Whoever was attacking him was a demon.

They came out in what looked like a warehouse. Crates and crates of *FLAME* energy drinks were piled up around them.

The demon didn't give Matt a chance to get his bearings. He pushed Matt into a crate, then shot energy at him for good measure. Matt felt his body tearing apart at the hip just as he crashed to the floor among the energy drinks.

"You're going to pay for those," a familiar voice said.

"You?" Matt tried to pull himself up on his knees and threw a glance over his shoulder. There in front of him stood the cafeteria owner in all his disgusting glory.

While he was watching, the owner's features began to melt. Like a wax figure near a flame, the face dripped away until his true form was revealed. Malcolm.

Matt shot energy at him, but the archdemon just wiped it away as if it was nothing. "Pathetic."

Another attack picked Matt off the ground and threw him into the wooden wall. His arm was absolutely shattered, and the tear around his hip had widened. Blood was seeping into his pants, while the pain threatened to take his consciousness away.

Still struggling to remain conscious, Matt could do nothing to defend himself when Malcolm grabbed his arms and bent them behind his back. He only screamed as the shattered bone pieces cut through the muscles around them. Something was wrapped around his hands and arms. As soon as it was tied, a wave of breath-taking nausea hit him.

Something was wrong, terribly wrong.

His instincts told him to change to his demon form and fight for his life, but no matter how much he tried, he stayed human. Even worse, there was no tingling in his limbs to tell him his body was trying to restore itself.

Panicked, Matt tore at his arms, even though his left was screaming in pain.

"Hmm." Malcolm sounded slightly disappointed. "You never really burst into flame. I guess you're just not emotional enough."

Matt was insanely glad that he hadn't burst into flame, but he had the bone-chilling feeling it wouldn't matter either way.

Malcolm picked up one of the cans that had been scattered on the ground, opened it, and poured the content on the ground in front of Matt. "You still owe me for the can you drank. The first one."

"What?" Matt was still struggling to accept that the slimy cafeteria owner and suave archdemon were the same person. It fit, of course. The cafeteria was infamous for its exorbitant prices.

"In fact, you owe me a lot." Malcolm opened another can. "And as you know, I'm quite particular about repayment."

Somehow, Matt doubted he'd be able to repay Malcolm with anything but blood. His instincts kicked in, and he tried to jump away. Nothing.

"You're a bit slow, aren't you?" Malcolm abandoned his cans and came closer. "I bound you with an anti-magic rope. It blocks your magic. You're just a human now. No space jump, no energy shots, and no healing powers."

He followed his words with a kick between Matt's ribs. There was too much pain. Matt couldn't handle it, not when the rope around his arms sucked all the warmth out of him.

Malcolm crouched in front of him and grabbed his hair. From his swollen eyes, Matt's vision was too blurry to make out his features. "But since you happen to be part demon—however pathetic that part may be—that rope will kill you. It'll drain your magic until nothing's left. You can't be half a human when you're wounded like that."

Malcolm let go of him and put his hand into Matt's back pocket, retrieving the wallet he carried. In front of him, he sifted through the bills and counted them. Once he had what he wanted, Malcolm threw the empty wallet aside. Then he smiled. "I'll waive the rest you owe me."

That would've been a relief if the words weren't immediately followed by Malcolm tearing the cans apart with his energy. Red bubbling liquid splashed on the floor, soaking into the wood. He clicked his fingers, and the liquid caught fire. Within seconds, flames shot up to the roof.

Malcolm was gone.

But Matt was stuck. He couldn't jump through space. He couldn't even roll onto his knees and try to get out of there. The rope in his back made it impossible for him to heal, and it sucked away all that made him demon. Malcolm's words had been true: Matt would not survive on his human half alone.

"Menuha," he croaked. Demons could be summoned quite easily once you knew their names. Especially if you were familiar with them. But the call required magic, and all magic was blocked. "Chay!"

Neither of them heard his call. His magic was blocked, and no one knew where he was. There would be no help.

Rachel

While the boys were attending their party, the girls kept researching. Rachel had no issue with the way it had played out. Fabian had occasionally asked her to go to a party with him, but the one time she'd given in, it had turned into an exercise in boredom. She usually made it an hour in before asking Fabian if they could leave. The rowdier and sillier a party became, the more Rachel hated to be there. After all, there had been more than enough loud and drunken parties in her own home.

Researching firebugs wasn't that exciting either, though. Usually, they struggled to find any reliable information. In this case, there was simply too much information.

"We can probably ignore curses," Lucille suggested. "They are extremely complicated, *and* you need a lot of disgusting things: diverse body fluids, dead roosters, innards... It's a lot of work for the few times it's happened."

"You're right, it's highly unlikely." Samantha struck out the curses on her still-way-too-long list.

None of the other entries were viable enough to zone in on. "What about fire goddesses? Is there one like Nemesis?" Rachel asked. That would explain why only a few soccer players seemed to erupt into flames, while the rest were fine.

"When that Friedrich guy was led off the field, I checked his magic signature," Samantha explained. "There was nothing. No ties, no spell web. Not a single residue."

Before either of them could come up with another idea, Lucille's phone rang. "It's Jan."

The tension in the room rose. Jan would never call from a party if things were going well.

Lucille licked her lips before taking the call and putting it on speaker. "Is everything alright?"

"Far from it," Jan answered. "Robert went mad and then did the whole firebug routine. Fabian is utterly useless, *but* I found out what's causing it."

"*You* did?" Lucille's emphasis was more on the first word than the second.

Rachel didn't blame her. The idea that Jan was the first one to crack the code was hard to swallow.

"It's this new energy drink you can buy everywhere right now. *FLAME!* Should've been a clear giveaway," Jan explained.

The three girls frowned at each other. An energy drink wasn't on their list. Though several potions were.

Samantha leaned forward to ask, "So, what gives you that idea? Apart from the name, I mean."

"Luck. Everyone here is drinking beer, apart from Robert that loser. And who caught fire?" Jan hesitated, then cursed colourfully. "Shit! I gave the drink to Matt."

"And did *he* burst into flames?" Lucille asked, still doubtful.

"Not yet." Jan paused again, likely looking around. "But I can't see him anywhere."

The tension turned into apprehension. Lucille's doubts seemed to have evaporated when she asked, "Can you look for him?"

"Sure thing. This party is boring anyway. But one of you should pick up Fabian before he fertilises all the plants around here."

Samantha groaned, clearly volunteering by doing so. It wasn't like Rachel detested Fabian now that they'd broken up, but drunk people always made her uncomfortable. She realised most people loved to drink *and* get drunk, but to her, there was no greater evil than alcohol. It had already stolen too much from her.

"We're coming," Lucille promised Jan. "And I'm calling Matt now." She ended the call with Jan and called Matt instead.

While Matt's phone rang, Rachel watched Samantha closely. Her friend had her eyes trained on the list in front of her, as if she couldn't care less, but her body was entirely still, poised to jump into action.

Matt's voicemail sounded through the room, and Samantha threw her head back and took a shuddering breath.

Lucille ended the call with a shaky hand. "He's not picking up."

That much was obvious.

Rachel got up first. "Let's go and find him, then. Lucille, you track Matt's phone. Sam, you pick up Fabian. We're going to need him." Hopefully, he was still able to summon his water.

Contrary to her, Samantha took Fabian's intoxicated status with humour and grace. She patted Fabian's back as he threw up over the toilet bowl and quipped, "The one time I send you to a party."

"Shut up," Fabian mumbled just before he had to heave again.

Once he was done, he sank to the floor, but Samantha grabbed his arm and pulled him up to his feet. "Come on, you don't want to spend the night in Alan's toilet."

Rachel took a step to the side, holding her breath as the two stumbled past her to the living room. Soon after, Lucille came from upstairs, shaking her head. "I couldn't find him."

"Who are we looking for?" Fabian asked.

"Matt," Samantha replied.

"Did you search the beds yet?" Fabian started laughing, though no one else cracked so much as a smile.

"Let's get you out of here." This time, Rachel stepped in to help.

While Lucille picked up a can of the energy drink and stuffed it into her handbag, Rachel and Samantha steered Fabian outside. Just as they stumbled out of the door, Jan came around the corner.

He stuffed his hands in his pockets and shrugged. "Nothing. Honestly, I think he's found something else to amuse himself."

"He's not answering his phone," Lucille pointed out.

"Neither would I if I was busy with something else."

Fabian stared at Jan dumbfounded. "With what?"

Rachel nearly groaned. "Sex."

She noticed how Samantha pressed her jaw together, swallowing whatever biting comment had sprung onto her lips. Meanwhile, Lucille sighed. "You're probably right."

"Of course I am." Jan shrugged again. "Don't worry. I'm sure Matt will turn up again."

"I know where he is."

Surprised, they turned around. There, holding onto a streetlamp, stood Cian, his face green and blue and swollen. "We had a little argument..." He took a shuddering breath. "Fine. We had a fight."

"And you're still standing?" Jan asked, with all the sensitivity of a bull fighter.

A spark of anger rejuvenated Cian, and he pushed off the streetlamp. "Imagine that: I won. What do you think? I can't hold myself against someone with a broken arm?"

The four of them exchanged a concerned glance—Fabian stared on the ground. They still would've bet on Matt in a fight.

"I can show you to him," Cian offered. "But to be clear, he started it."

Samantha let go of Fabian and joined Cian instead. "Of course he did. I'm just glad you're fine. I mean, you're not *fine* fine, but..." She took a shuddering breath and forced a smile. They all knew what she was really worried about. "Never mind. Let's go."

Cian led them to the park further down the street and pointed ahead. "That's where he attacked me."

The ground looked as if a herd of boars had been digging for acorns.

"Were you ploughing the soil or what happened here?" Jan asked. He'd taken over supporting Fabian, for which Rachel was eternally grateful.

The sight seemed to confuse Cian as well. "It didn't look this way when I left."

Samantha was already on the ground, holding her hands over the disturbed soil with her eyes closed.

Before anyone of them could stop him, Cian knelt next to her. "What are you doing?"

Rachel exchanged a quick glance with Lucille. Samantha was clearly checking the area for magical disturbances, but Cian wasn't supposed to find out about that. He was Cheryl's friend, and if Cheryl got wind of Samantha "pretending" to be a witch, things would get very nasty.

"I'm looking..." Samantha caught herself, glancing around nervously. "Nothing. I hoped to find a footprint or something like that."

Cian wasn't having it. "In this mess?"

Someone had to do something. And that someone was going to be Rachel tonight. "Oh, I forgot!" she exclaimed, instantly drawing everybody's attention. "I know where Matt is. Thanks, Cian, but we can find him on our own now."

While she spoke, Samantha got up and hurried away from the park with Lucille, already whispering.

"Fine, I'm coming." Cian got up and wiped a dirty hand on his pants.

"No!" Rachel said a little too forcefully. When Cian raised an eyebrow, she quickly amended, "I mean, we'll take care of him. You've done enough."

But Cian was like a dog with a bone. Only, he looked suspiciously guilty. "I'm worried. His arm... I didn't know what else to do but hit him there. He would've killed me otherwise or sent me to the hospital."

"That's because of that damned energy drink," Jan said, then winced when he realised he'd given away some of what Rachel was trying to conceal. He shuffled his feet. "Uhm, I mean... Nobody's supposed to know, but Matt has a sugar problem."

"He's a diabetic?" Cian asked promptly, looking even less convinced than before.

"Yes. No... I don't know, just that his... impulse control! Yes, his impulse control is severely compromised when he gets too much sugar. Boy, you should've seen him when he had that slice of cake." Jan was starting to get really into it.

Rachel had no patience for that. Lucille and Samantha were getting further away, and she was not going to spend her night with Cian. "No offence, Cian, but we don't need your help. You, however, look like you need some medical attention. So, go back to Alan's and make sure you're fit for tomorrow."

"You know you *can* help," Jan claimed. Rachel was about to think of all the ways she'd haunt him in his dreams when Jan handed Fabian to Cian. "Take care of Fabi for us. He's a little drunk."

"A little—"

As if he'd planned it, Fabian swallowed, then threw up all over Cian's shirt.

Jan and Rachel shared a glance and quickly set off after the others. Cian shouted after them. But with his arms—and shirt—full, there was nothing he could do.

"Nice work there," Jan commented with a grin.

Rachel just rolled her eyes, but she was pretty pleased with herself.

It didn't take long for them to catch up with Samantha and Lucille, as Samantha was still busy following some invisible trace. "I'm telling you, if we just end up finding Matt in some bed, I'm going to scream."

"I don't think that's going to happen." Lucille shook her head. "Cian said he was hurt. His healing powers are good, but they're not *that* good."

"So," Samantha began slowly, "what do we think about him beating up Cian?"

"He drank that *FLAME* stuff," Jan replied instantly. "If *Robert* suddenly starts attacking people, I don't think we can blame Matt."

Samantha took a deep breath, which sounded quite frustrated. "Funny how it's always something."

Not wanting to poke that particular bear Rachel looked ahead. "Is that a fire?"

A few blocks in front of them, a flickering red shimmer brightened up the night sky. Thick black smoke was rising from a burning warehouse.

Instantly, the four of them started sprinting. Jan reached the house first, letting out a bunch of colourful expletives until the rest of them arrived. "This is *not* where the trace leads, right?"

Samantha was paling, her breath catching in her throat. "He's in there."

"Damn it!" Jan kicked the asphalt. "I shouldn't have given Fabian away."

"He's too drunk." Rachel shook her head. "He'd never be able to extinguish this. I'm calling the fire in."

"There's something else," Samantha said, as if she hadn't heard a word Rachel had said. "An emptiness. Lack of magic. Like a vacuum. We need to get in there."

Rachel stared at her, dumbfounded, but Lucille nodded. "I know a spell. It'll make us resistant to fire. If it works."

"Guys, Rachel's right. We need the fire service. The house is burning," Jan pointed out, as if none of them could see it.

Lucille and Samantha ignored him as well. Instead, Lucille spoke her incantation first over herself and then Samantha. Before either Jan or Rachel could stop them, the two of them ran into the burning building. The spell must've worked somehow because they didn't even hesitate to launch themselves into the flames. Or they'd actually lost their mind.

"I'm calling emergency services." Rachel took out her phone and began to call.

Just when she heard someone pick up the call, a terrible noise thundered through the night. The frame of the door had burst, and the front of the warehouse was starting to come down.

Rachel could barely whisper, "Help, please."

Lucille

The roof had caved behind them. The flames were burning high, and thick black smoke made it impossible to see.

Lucille had her hands on Samantha's shoulders, partially for comfort, and partially because her friend was the only one who could lead them with her magical sight. Her own spell was working well against the heat, but it didn't stop the smoke. They tried to keep their heads low, but the smoke found its way into their lungs.

"You know where we're going?" Lucille asked, while trying to keep her mouth as closed as possible.

Samantha groaned. "Yes, and everything inside me doesn't want to go there." She coughed and faltered for a moment. "And for once, it's not Matt."

Lucille sensed it too. Though she couldn't see the magic rivers around them, she sensed the black, empty spot ahead of them. It seemed tiny, but it was absolutely revolting.

Just then, something appeared in the smoke. "There!"

Matt was lying on his side, unmoving. His skin was ashen, where it wasn't heavily bruised. A sticky pool of blood surrounded his lifeless body.

Without further hesitation, Lucille ran to his side. "Resistar fiero!"

The spell should have encased him with the same fire resistance as them. But while she could sense the magic flowing from her lips, Matt's body seemed to repulse it. Her stomach lurched.

"It's the rope!" Samantha dug her fingers into a black-threaded rope that was wound tightly around Matt's arms. "It's blocking all magic. Yours, mine. And most importantly, his."

No magic. Suddenly, Lucille felt entirely helpless. She'd run into a burning building with magic in her hand, but without... "We can't carry him." Even between the two of them, they'd never manage to drag Matt out. Not without hurting him even more. There wasn't even a path back, she remembered. "We're stuck."

"He's still got a pulse." Samantha ignored her protests, still trying to loosen the knots. "Lu!"

The harsh tone of her voice snapped Lucille out of her panic. "What?" She regarded Matt and the rope around his hands. They didn't have magic, and Samantha couldn't untie the knots. "Scissors. We need..." Instead of talking about it, Lucille rummaged through her handbag.

She always carried a little manicure set. Armed with small nail scissors, she started attacking the rope.

Samantha let go of Matt and began weaving a spell. The smoke eased a little and fresh air swirled around them.

Grateful, Lucille took a deep breath. The spell wasn't perfect, hindered by the black hole between them, but it made working a little easier. Unfortunately, touching the rope also meant her fire resistance was failing. With sweat running down her face, Lucille sawed and sawed, until at last, the rope snapped.

Hastily, she pulled it away from Matt. When she spoke her spell this time, it covered Matt seamlessly. "What now?"

"Give me your scissors."

Lucille handed them over, then watched in horror as Samantha cut into her finger. "What are you doing?"

Though she grimaced with pain, Samantha cut deep enough for blood to flow freely. "There's a curse. Demons are cursed." She started painting a pentagram on the floor with her blood. "I read it in a book. They need to appear when summoned." Shivering, she withdrew her finger. "Menuha!"

Within a second, the pentagram lit up and Menuha appeared between them. Shocked, she ducked from the burning roof tiles. She was just about to jump away again when she noticed them. "Lucille? Samantha?" Her eyes widened. "Matt!"

"Can you carry him out of here?" Samantha begged. "Demons can transport others, right?"

"I can carry all of you. Hold on to me!"

Lucille immediately grabbed her shoulder. Menuha put an arm around Matt's chest, strong enough to heave him onto his feet, while Samantha ducked and picked up the cut rope. As soon as Samantha wrapped a hand around Menuha's wrist, Lucille felt a pull in her stomach. The flames blurred until there was nothing but perfect blackness.

She had just enough time to wonder why it was so cold when they stumbled onto a meadow not too far from the burning house. Wonderful clean air filled her lungs. "Wow. That was... incredible."

"Thanks, Menuha." Samantha looked at Matt. "Will he live?"

Menuha checked his vitals. "He's healing. But how did he get so bad?"

"We found him bound with this." Samantha pulled out the black rope.

Menuha stretched out her hands, but before she touched it, she jerked away. "That's vile. Even unbound."

Meanwhile, Lucille got to her feet. Two fire trucks had arrived at the warehouse, doing their best to extinguish the flames. Jan and Rachel were discussing with a fire fighter, constantly pointing at the house. "I'll be back in a moment."

She made sure an illusion covered all the soot that was staining her clothes and face before she approached the group.

"You need to get them out!" Jan begged.

"I'm sorry. It's too dangerous at the moment. We'll go in as soon as it's safe for us to do so," the firefighter explained patiently.

"Jan? Rachel?" Lucille asked, making sure she sounded confused. "What are you doing here?"

The two whirled around, their eyes wide with fears. Jan stumbled back. "Lu. Are the others...?"

"The others are back at the party," Lucille claimed. "I came looking for you."

Rachel glanced from her to the burning house. "We thought..."

The firefighter stepped in. "Is she one of the ones you thought was inside the warehouse?"

"We never went in there." But that wouldn't explain why Rachel and Jan would've thought so. "We wanted to meet here, but our plans changed. Didn't you get the message?"

Thankfully, Rachel was quick to react. "I didn't check my phone." She turned to the firefighter. "I'm sorry, there was a misunderstanding."

Tired, the firefighter nodded. "That's good. I'm glad to hear there's no one left inside." He walked away, conveying the message through his radio.

Lucille beckoned Jan and Rachel to follow her back to the others. They were hardly out of earshot before Jan hissed, "How did you get out of *that?*"

"Demon taxi. Samantha summoned Menuha, and she carried us out," Lucille explained.

"Did you find Matt?" Rachel asked.

Nodding, Lucille pointed ahead. "We did. And it was totally worth running into a burning building for."

Especially when she saw Matt had regained consciousness. He still seemed to be in a lot of pain, grimacing and gasping without pause, but as his eyes cleared and he saw the five of them standing around them, he managed to speak.

"We need to talk about Malcolm."

Samantha

They regrouped in Samantha's room—minus Fabian, who was either still with Cian or had made his way home. Samantha's parents and Meg were already sleeping, so they kept their voices to a minimum while Matt explained what he'd learned about his uncle.

"You're telling us Malcolm's spending his days selling overpriced pretzels?" It made an absurd kind of sense. Malcolm was the Archdemon of Greed. And while it was ridiculous to assume he'd found his calling in a school cafeteria, he would definitely have come up with such an insane price policy. "That means he came to Greenvalley the day you turned up." Belatedly, Samantha added, "And Lucille."

"Yeah, it's definitely Matt," Jan decided.

Since Samantha couldn't see any connection between Lucille and Malcolm, he was right for a change. She tried not to glance too much at Matt, but he still looked terrible, his face swollen, his eyes blood-shot. His left arm hung uselessly to his side while he pressed a pack of bandages to his hip with his right.

"I told you, I never met him before I came here," Matt said through gritted teeth.

His sister put an arm around his side. "But he knew about you. You're kind of Melaney's favourite. That plus the fact you're only half-demon has made its rounds. And so has your move to Ashuan." Menuha sighed heavily. "Most demons don't think much about it. They say it's where you belong—like Caspar—but others wonder if it isn't all part of some big plan. Balthasar was suddenly interested."

"What plan?" To his credit, Matt sounded honestly confused.

Menuha shrugged. "That Melaney sent you here for a reason. Perhaps to keep you out of harm's way until you matured enough, or to send you to obtain something for her."

"The spring of magic," Samantha inferred. "Your mother might not have sent you here, but when Malcolm investigated, he found our spring of magic."

"And he's been trying to harvest it ever since," Matt continued, nodding darkly.

"Okay, okay," Jan interrupted, "But what does this all have to do with the *FLAME* drink? Why is he lighting soccer players on fire?"

Samantha hadn't figured out that part yet. Again and again, her attention was drawn to the black rope on the table. Now that it wasn't tied, the magic flow was interrupted. Or rather, the anti-magic flow. But the spell was still there, waiting to be reconnected.

"I'm tired," Lucille admitted. It was rather late. "Even if we don't understand his reasons, is there a way to stop the self-combustions? Perhaps if we promoted a recall campaign? Fortunately, Malcolm set most of his stock on fire."

"Recall campaign sounds good." Samantha took the rope between her fingers. "I wonder if I can do something with this." The longer she stared at it, the clearer the pattern became to her. It was like an inverted shield with backwards weaving.

Jan snatched it from her hands. "What is this thing?"

"An abstract piece of anti-material magic weaving."

He stared at her blankly. "Translation please?"

Samantha massaged her temples. She was tired, too. Her body screamed for sleep. But there would be little of it tonight if she wanted to prevent an inferno tomorrow. "It's weird. It's like a lot of magic in a very tight space that pulls in even more magic, while bending the rivers of magic into negative infinity. Like a black hole. But it only works when the loop is closed."

Everybody was still staring.

"It blocks magic."

"Why couldn't you just say that?" Jan shot back.

Samantha waved him off, concentrating on Menuha. "It's like Caspar's runes. Did you ever get a replacement?"

Menuha nodded and took out the brittle twig binding. "There you go."

Too tired to deal with everybody's confusion surrounding their little interaction, Samantha placed the rune next to the rope and started comparing how they affected the magic around them.

She liked Menuha. It was silly. She was even more demon than Matt and had likely killed more people in her life than Samantha could stomach, but she didn't actually *know* that. And so her friendly and helpful demeanour had quietly won Samantha over. Menuha had saved her life just now, after all.

While she did her thing, Lucille yawned, and Jan's eyes occasionally drooped closed. Matt shifted on his chair, moaning softly. It was distracting.

"You know you can all go to sleep. I'll take it from here."

Promptly, Jan pushed back his chair. "Our coach will kill us if we fall asleep on the field tomorrow." He gave Matt a long glance. "And you look like you should go back to the hospital."

"And have to answer their questions while I'm healing in front of their eyes?" Matt shook his head. "I'll be fine tomorrow." He didn't quite sound like it, though.

"Yeah, but it's still easier to catch a ball when your eyes aren't closed." Jan offered Matt a hand. "Don't worry, I'm not into pain."

Matt took the hand, seemingly glad no additional healing was happening. Samantha noticed him looking at her and hesitating, but whatever it was, he changed his mind and vanished.

Jan scoffed. "Guess I'm walking."

"I can take you with me when my ride arrives," Lucille said. Then she turned to Samantha apologetically. "I need sleep, but I will get up early to start the recall campaign. We'll get the word out there."

When the two of them had left, Samantha turned back to her magic conundrum. How could she weave a spell with magic that repelled magic?

"Can I help?" Rachel asked quietly. She and Menuha were the only ones left.

"You could tell me how to weave a black hole," Samantha joked flatly.

Rachel only shrugged and took out her astronomy notes from her school bag. "I can check out the physics at least."

"And I know a little bit of binding runes," Menuha offered.

Samantha looked from one to the other, then she smiled. "Alright, let's see what we can come with up."

They'd spent most of the night coming up with a pattern for her to weave. Now it was bright daylight and the entire school seemed to have gathered in the stadium, waiting for the final. Samantha met Lucille on the outside. Everywhere she looked, posters recalling *FLAME* were hung. Lucille had been busy.

"You look tired," Lucille greeted her. "Did you figure it out?"

"I think so. Good job on the posters."

Lucille nodded. "Thanks. You know, it's funny, but after all of this, the Liehnheimer team had nothing to do with it."

"Correlation isn't necessarily causation," Samantha repeated what she'd heard again and again in science classes. "They only got lucky, after all." She regarded the giant stadium. "Let's make sure they stay lucky."

"Not too lucky, though," Lucille cautioned, before leaving Samantha to her work.

In her bag, Samantha had a complex sketch of the spell she was about to attempt and a piece of the black rope. It was the most complicated web she'd ever woven, but she'd tried it at home, and it had worked. In fact, it had worked almost too well, as she'd almost been unable to unravel the spell again after the test was concluded.

Now she took another look and got started. While the rope was a fine piece of art, compressing the spell into an impossibly small space, her web over the stadium was far more wide-meshed. It wouldn't be quite as absolute, which would allow Matt to enter under the spell without dropping dead an hour later, but he would have to face Liehnheim with his human reflexes. It also meant she had to anchor the web at twelve different locations. Rachel had marked them all out on a map, so Samantha started at the entrance and worked her way clockwise around the stadium.

The work was tedious, but after the first few stops her fingers were flowing on their own, and the further she got along, the more the web itself seemed to yearn for closure. Still, she consulted her cheat sheet every single time to make sure her spell followed Rachel's calculations and Menuha's experience exactly with her sleep-addled mind.

She had just tied off the tenth anchor when she almost ran into someone. At first, Samantha started mumbling an apology, but then she recognised him.

It was the cafeteria owner. Malcolm.

He took a step towards her, and Samantha stumbled into the wall behind her. When he raised his hand, she quickly squeezed her eyes shut. This was it. After all her work to stop him, he would simply kill her.

But Malcolm reached past her and ripped one of Lucille's posters from the wall. "Was this you?" Samantha swallowed, incapable of answering him. "Is there a reason you're trying to ruin my business?"

Samantha allowed herself a shallow breath. This wasn't a wrath demon who would've torn her apart and then asked questions. Malcolm was all about greed. "There were side effects."

He regarded her with narrow eyes, and Samantha felt as if she should cower in front of him. There was no doubt in her mind he *would* kill her once his business was concluded.

But instead, he snatched her sketch from her hand. "Where did you get that?"

When she didn't answer, Malcolm studied the sketch. Intrigued, he stepped past her into the mostly complete web.

Samantha watched in horror as his form melted, turning the grimy cafeteria owner into the dangerous demon she knew. Shapeshifting. It shouldn't have come as a surprise after he'd posed as a drug dealer late last year.

Malcolm drew one breath of magic-repelling air and took a step back. "Impressive."

Unsure what it meant to impress an archdemon, Samantha took a careful step towards the magic barrier. It was the wrong decision.

Malcolm moved lightning fast. He grabbed her wrist and brutally jerked her back. Samantha hit the wall with enough force to send a shock wave through her body. Malcolm's second hand was suddenly wrapped around her throat, the lingering strength in his fingers promising a swift death. If he let her go that easily.

"Now," he said in a menacing drawl, "let's talk about where you got my rope from."

Samantha whimpered, but her struggling only led Malcolm to squeeze tighter. In his yellowish eyes, she saw something that made her deeply afraid in a way his actions alone didn't. This was a human-killing predator.

And she was his prey.

Matt

Entering the stadium almost made Matt throw up in his mouth. After experiencing the effects of a magic-blocking web last night, he wasn't particularly keen for a repeat, but he had to agree it was the only way to keep the players and viewers safe while there were still too many energy drinks around.

His wounds had healed, though his body was still a little tender. Last night, he'd come incredibly close to dying. Help had come from the most unlikely source—and Lucille. It was the second time Samantha had risked her life to save him, and it confused him enormously. If she really hated him as much as she claimed, why run into a burning building? Because she was the only one that could find him? Because she was such a good person she'd do it for anyone? No, somehow he doubted Samantha made running into burning buildings a hobby. Lucille was the one with no sense of self-preservation. Samantha was usually more sensible.

The teams were warming up, but there was still a little time before the game. Matt glanced up at the stands. He found the others, but not Samantha. As the nauseous feeling around him was strengthening, he assumed she was still working on the web.

"I forgot something in the changing room," he told his coach, and headed away before the man could stop him.

He hadn't thanked Samantha yet for saving him. Last time, he'd forgotten, and that had been a mistake. This time, he'd get it right.

Matt walked down the corridor of the changing rooms to the outer perimeter when he heard a familiar voice.

"Where is that bastard?" Malcolm hissed somewhere around the corner.

The answering gurgle made Matt speed up. He couldn't jump through space under the spell, but his feet carried him to the corner well enough. His worst nightmare awaited him.

Malcolm had got hold of Samantha and was squeezing her throat, throttling an answer out of her. An answer she wouldn't give him.

Fortunately, Matt knew which bastard Malcolm was looking for. "Do you mean me?" he asked, almost sounding relaxed. He was still under the spell, but he would take on the archdemon if he had to. "Let her go!"

Amused, Malcolm loosened his grip on Samantha, but he still held her immobilised while he turned to Matt. "Are you trying to threaten me?" He gave Matt the once-over, and his lips twisted cruelly. "I don't think you're in the position to challenge me."

"Try me."

"Look at that. So much emotion. Where was all that last night when you could've burst into flames?" Then, to Matt's surprise, he flung Samantha into Matt's arms.

Matt caught her moments before a shot of energy hit the barrier only centimetres in front of his face. The blinding brightness frayed and dissolved along the seams until the energy had fully dissipated. Matt swallowed, while in his arms, Samantha shook like a leaf.

In front of them, Malcolm took out a vial of liquid fire. He snorted, seeming only mildly displeased. "Just stop getting in my way. That goes for you and the human witch." He snarled at them, then vanished.

Silence filled the space between them. Samantha was still shaking, softly gasping for air, sounding a little as if she was holding back tears.

"Sam?" Matt asked softly.

She didn't respond at first. Gently, he cupped her head with his hand and slowly ran his fingers through her thick, black curls. "He's gone," he whispered. "He can't hurt us in here."

At last, she swallowed and raised her head. Their eyes met. He saw expectation in them, but seeing it made Matt's throat tighten. There were words he had to speak. Words that might heal what he'd broken between them. She wanted to hear them, but his mind was empty. And he was scared, scared that if he said the wrong words now, he'd lose her forever.

"Matt?"

He had to speak, had to say something. "I..." Matt couldn't risk it, not unprepared like this. "I need to get back. The game's starting soon."

Those certainly weren't the right words. Samantha found strength in them, nonetheless. She straightened and pushed herself away from him. His fingers felt empty when she was gone.

Brushing off her clothes, she said matter-of-factly, "I still need to put down two anchors. Try not to die because of it."

"In your dreams." The retort left his mouth instantly. Matt almost bit his tongue when he realised what he'd said. Why was he fighting with her when he'd come to thank her?

Samantha glowered at him. Then she turned on her heels and stalked away, risking Malcolm's reappearance over staying with him.

Matt headed back to the field, anger broiling in his stomach. Why was this so hard for him? Why couldn't he simply say what his heart was already screaming? For once, she'd been willing to listen, and he'd had nothing to say to her.

Just before he reached the stands, Matt buried his fist in the wall. "Idiot."

The game was hard won, but not by Greenvalley. The Liehnheimers were every bit as good as Matt had known they'd be. His own team put up a hell of a fight, and he pushed himself as far as he could, but his body was sluggish, and by the second half, he was in pain. A particular sharp shot set his arm on fire. Not literally, though. There were no self-combustions today.

Then in the seventy-second minute, his defence failed him. His fingertips touched the ball, but it wasn't enough to stop it from scoring.

Matt had to give it to his team that they wouldn't let that stop them, but no matter how hard they fought and how much pressure Cian and Alan put on the opposing defence, Greenvalley never managed to pull even. When the final whistle blew, they were left exhausted and disappointed.

The frustration over his failure to hold the ball was eased by the thought of getting out from under the spell, though. By the time Matt and the team came together for the victory ceremony in the school hall, he was already feeling a little better.

Coincidence had placed him next to Cian, who still bore the traces of his beating from the night before. Not surprisingly, he gave Matt the cold shoulder. But for some reason, Matt managed to find the words that eluded him when he was around Samantha. "Hey, I'm sorry about what happened last night. I wasn't in my right mind."

Cian was far too nice. He glanced at him, then sighed. "Your sugar problem, I know."

Matt frowned. His *sugar* problem?

"It's alright. I'm sorry too. I'm glad I didn't break your arm." Cian looked away again to where Samantha and Adrian helped the principal hand out certificates to the third-place winners.

Cian most definitely had re-broken his arm again, but it wasn't as bad as what Malcolm had done afterwards. "You did what you had to do."

"So, we're good?"

Matt didn't want to be good with him, but he couldn't exactly hold a grudge after his own failings. "Yes."

Unfortunately, things weren't settled with that. Cian kept glancing at him, then apparently gathered some courage to ask, "So, what's the truth, then? Do you have feelings for Samantha?"

That was the money question. Instinctively, Matt denied it. "Nonsense, she—" His gaze found Samantha who had now reached their team with the second-place certificates. "Maybe."

Cian snorted. "You'll better get in quick, then. Otherwise, I'm going to steal her from you."

Matt admired his confidence. He snidely said, "I told you Samantha is taboo for you."

This time, Cian grimaced. "Do you really think she's into this macho thing? We're talking about Samantha, after all. She makes her own decisions."

That and the fact the little procession had reached them shut Matt up for good. Didn't he know firsthand how much Samantha hated it when he assumed to know her feelings? As much as Matt despised it, Cian was right, and if he wanted to win Samantha's heart, he had to earn her forgiveness first.

"Well done, Mr Funke. That was an incredible tournament." The principal shook his hand before moving on to Matt to repeat her gesture. "Mr Traidous, we were all very blessed with you in the goal."

Matt winced, remembering the one ball he'd let through. "Thanks."

Adrian came next with a silver medal. While he put it around Matt's head, Samantha handed Cian his certificate. "I still owe you something for the semi-final win," she said in a voice that made Matt's hairs stand up.

Cian frowned, which didn't stop Samantha from leaning forward and breathing a quick kiss on his cheek.

Matt's insides churned. His jaw hurt from biting down so hard to avoid grimacing at them. Meanwhile, Cian's whole face lit up, and the triumphant look he gave Matt over Samantha's head made Matt want to smack him down here and now. But Samantha was right in front of him, and so Matt kept still.

"Congratulations," she said coldly while handing him his certificate.

"What? I don't get a kiss?" Again with the snappy retorts.

Samantha narrowed her eyes. "In your dreams." She hurried away to catch up with the principal and Adrian, who were on the way to the team from Liehnheim.

Still grinning like an idiot, Cian put a hand on Matt's shoulder. "Well, looks like my prospects are a little brighter than yours."

This time, there was no flying rage. The words hit his ear, then dropped to the floor without being fully heard. Matt's gaze followed Samantha as she congratulated the winners.

How had he messed this up so hard? And why was he so incapable of fixing it?

The only thing he knew was that he yearned for her. That with every fibre of his being he wanted her. Not in his bed or anything like that, but in a different way. A more profound way. He wanted those lips on his cheek, those flirty words directed at him. But, most importantly, he wanted her to smile at him without the pain in her eyes.

Part 5

Blood & Greed

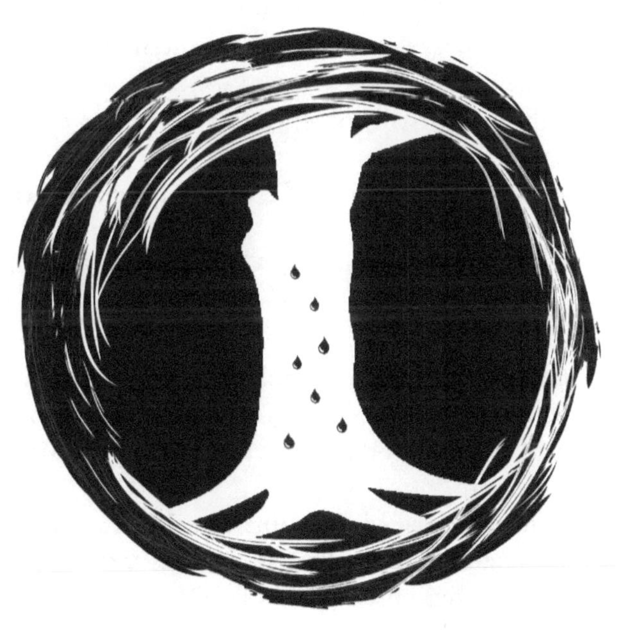

Lucille

Since the soccer tournament last week, the cafeteria had remained closed. Lucille was partially glad about it. It would've been too weird seeing Malcolm continuing his business here at school. She didn't think she could've concentrated on anything else in the student hall. As it was, she still couldn't concentrate, and neither could any of the others.

"Do you think he's still there?" Matt asked, his eyes almost burning holes into the shutters.

Jan raised his eyebrow at him. "You mean hiding in the dark cafeteria?"

"What if he hides his treasure there?" Fabian suggested, his hand as usual around a water bottle. Since the big revelation, Lucille hadn't seen him without one.

"Like a dragon?" Rachel asked doubtfully.

Lucille snorted. The image in her mind was quite something. "I'd much rather fight a dragon than face your uncle again, Matt."

"You and me both."

The only one who seemed to be unaffected by the closed-down cafeteria was Samantha. She had her study cards spread out around herself and never even raised her eyes. "Do you think Malcolm would let me go if I helped him get rid of you?" she asked Matt, while jotting down some notes.

Lucille glanced at Matt. She'd hoped things had improved a little between the two since the Erinyes, but Samantha's barbs were only becoming sharper each day.

And Matt didn't back down. "Even he wouldn't want to work with a scratching cat like you."

"You're so charming to each other," Lucille muttered, in the hopes of disrupting them before they got truly heated.

Jan was a lot less diplomatic. "You know your constant bickering is *so* getting on my nerves. I want to—"

"Mind your own business," Matt and Samantha said almost simultaneously.

Lucille exchanged a glance with Fabian, while Jan raised his hands in defeat, looking slightly weirded out.

"I don't think he's at school," Rachel said, not deigning the fight worth her attention. "It would be too risky for him now we know his secret."

"Because he's shivering in his boots, sure," Matt mumbled.

"Well, he should." Jan crossed his arms and leaned back sullenly. "We are the six chosen ones, aren't we? The descendants of the Twelve."

Samantha pushed her cards together and sorted them. "Theoretically. We also never stood a chance against him. Prophecy or no prophecy."

"But isn't that the point?" Jan leaned forward abruptly and hit the table with his flat hand. "We've got all six Emblems of Power now. We've been chosen to fight and defeat him."

"Technically, the prophecy is a little undecided," Rachel explained. "We either defeat him or die."

"Are we sure he's the Greedy One?" Fabian's voice was a little too high.

Everyone gave him a blank stare, and he sighed. Lucille shook her head. "There's nothing we can do right now. We don't know what he's planning, so we have no idea how to stop him. Like it or not, we have to wait for his next move." Inspired by Samantha's flash cards, she added, "And until then, we've got enough to keep us busy, like the last round of exams this year."

Jan noisily drew up spit and thankfully swallowed it again. "Don't remind me."

"Should I not? Aren't you the one who told us you'd have to repeat the year if you didn't get a passing grade in the upcoming exams?"

Annoyed, Jan stuck his hand into his bag and pulled out his Politics and Geography books. "Better?"

"If you're going to open them next, we're almost there," Lucille said in a mocking voice. They couldn't possibly lose Jan, which made her determined to help him with his exams. She just didn't know whether she had the patience for it.

For a few minutes, they managed to concentrate on exam preparation. Then a younger girl with a big, colourful bag approached them. "Excuse me," she said in a squeaky voice. "I'm Janina from the gardening club. We're collecting donations for our new school garden. We recently received a few plants that need special care. So..." She got out a handful of paper bags. "We had a fun idea. Collectibles. If you gather a whole set, you'll be in the draw for a surprise gift."

"How much are they?" Fabian asked.

Janina smiled brightly. "Only one euro. We put a lot of work into them."

Lucille couldn't help but find her adorable. "Do you happen to accept credit cards? I don't have any cash, sorry."

Janina's face fell again. "Oh, tomorrow then?"

"I'll take two," Samantha offered.

Grateful, Janina handed her two bags and collected the two-euro piece. Then she went to the next table, while Samantha put them unopened into her backpack.

"You support everything, don't you?" Matt asked, sounding slightly irritated.

Samantha gave him a long, cold stare. "Yes, I like to support people. It just makes me feel better than cutting them into pieces would."

Matt groaned. "Oh please, will you give it a rest? It was one time, and I wasn't sane. How many times do I have to tell you?"

"Yes, please!" Jan interrupted them loudly, drawing quite some attention from the surrounding tables. "How many times do we have to listen to the two of you bickering about it? Get a room or keep your distance."

Lucille admired his courage because both started berating him together, though contrary to Jan, they kept their voices down. Samantha sarcastically apologised for not being able to get over her boyfriend being murdered, while Matt claimed she wouldn't let it go, and how he'd never want to be in a room alone with her.

Jan had it right. It was annoying. Especially when the prophecy needed them to work together to stand a chance against Malcolm. Their fighting had to end, and since they both seemed incapable of ending it by themselves, Lucille would have to help. But not alone.

She pulled on Fabian's arm. "Can I speak to you?"

Confused, he nodded before following her to the stage, where they were out of earshot. "What's the matter?"

"What's the matter?" Was he deaf? "They won't shut up anymore."

"Who?"

Lucille groaned. "Fabian, please. Matt and Samantha, of course. Jan is annoyed. I am annoyed. Even Rachel is rolling her eyes. Don't tell me you don't mind."

With a sigh, he leant against the stage. "It's not my business."

"We are a *team*. Jan's right, we're the six chosen ones."

"I don't know..." Fabian studied the floor, then glanced at the table where Matt and Samantha had moved on to fighting with each other while Jan was packing up his books. "Just because our names are written in some old book—"

Lucille interrupted him promptly, "An old book written by Chay. Someone who can see the future."

"And someone who's a half-demon." Fabian looked at her, but when she gave him a hard stare, he sighed again. "I'm just saying. Do we know he isn't lying? What if we're all part of some sick plan which'll see us dead in the end? Probably."

Annoyed, Lucille shook her head and took a few steps. They had to concentrate on one problem before they could tackle the bigger one. "We need to do something about the fighting. Some kind of intervention. How do you feel about luring them into a room and locking them in until they've come up with some kind of truce?"

"How's that supposed to work? Matt would simply jump out of the room. And even if he stayed, they'd both kill each other and we're down two people."

"Is everyone always dying in your prognoses?" Lucille asked sarcastically.

Fabian chuckled. "In most scenarios. Look, the Archdemon of Greed worked at our school cafeteria for a whole year. He probably poisoned us months ago."

"Really?" Lucille was starting to run out of steam. "Come on, Fabian. I need your help." He was Samantha's best friend, after all. She'd listen to him if he only tried a little harder.

"I told you, it's not my business."

"Afraid they're gonna kill you first?" She regretted the harsh tone when Fabian made a face. "They just need a little shove."

He pulled up his shoulder, looking absolutely miserable. "And you think that's going to help? A shove?"

"If we all work together. Are you in?"

Fabian took time to consider it. At last, he nodded. "We can give it a try. It's not like it can get much worse. Unless they actually start killing each other."

Lucille slapped his shoulder and swallowed a chuckle. "They won't." She took another look at the table. Jan was gone. Matt and Samantha were both concentrating a little too hard on their books, while Rachel had put earphones in to block them out. "Alright. I think I've got a plan."

Samantha

Outside the window, birds were singing, but inside the chemistry lab, everyone was deep in concentration. As usual, Samantha was working with Cian and Robert on an experiment that required a complex build-up of several flasks, cylinders, a Liebig condenser, a separating funnel, and a heating element.

"I talked to Matt recently," Cian whispered while they were taking some notes.

"Was that before or after you two got into a fight?" The whole affair was still heavy on Samantha's mind. Matt could've killed Cian, and it would've been her fault again. No, not her fault, but she couldn't deny that she was the reason.

Cian winced slightly. "Both, actually. Do you want to know what we talked about?"

Samantha didn't really want to know the details. She had a feeling it would only complicate an already tense situation. "Something stupid, I suppose."

"You," Cian answered instead. Quickly, he lowered his voice again and gave her an apologetic look. "Apparently, we both have feelings for you."

Only through great self-composure, Samantha managed not to close her eyes and sigh. "Matt's crazy. Feelings." It was much easier to concentrate on her anger than on dealing with anything else. "He doesn't even know what feelings are."

"You think?" Cian didn't sound convinced.

The anger gave Samantha a safe direction, where she neither had to react to Cian's veiled proposal nor Matt's apparent feelings. "You know him, right? He sleeps with everyone who gives him half a smile."

"True." Cian leaned back, but then he smiled. "Does that mean you're not interested in him?"

"Oh, no! I'm very interested in him. Interested to see the earth swallow him up, so I never have to deal with him again."

Cian laughed but caught himself quickly when Mrs Richter raised her eyebrows at him. "Sorry." While Samantha adjusted the experiment, he leaned forward and whispered once more. "Would you go on a date with me?"

"What?" Samantha turned to him, leaving the experiment in Robert's incapable hands. This time there was no skirting around the case, no subtlety she could ignore.

"You and me," Cian continued, amused. "On a date. You can say—"

A sudden boom shook the room as hot glass splintered next to them. Cian let out a yelp as a thin shard buried itself in his arm. Meanwhile, Samantha jumped up and hid behind the splash guard. Robert was staring at the blubbering mess on the heating element. Dark soot covered both his and Cian's face, and by the feel of it, her own as well.

Cian pulled the splinter from his arm, drawing a few drops of blood. "Have you lost your mind?"

"You can't turn up the heat like that," Samantha said, noticing how high the element had been set.

By now, the teacher had reached their bench. "What happened here?"

Robert was cowering next to the experiment, quickly turning down the dial. "I just..." He mumbled something that was half an explanation and half an apology, something Mrs Richter had no patience for.

"Cian, get this washed up, and then we'll put a Band-Aid on the wound. If any chemicals hit you, please wash yourself carefully." She urged Samantha and Cian to get up, stopping Robert from following them. "You seem fine to me. You can start cleaning up. Since the three of you can't finish the experiment, I want you to write a report about how it was *supposed* to be and why it had such an intense exothermic reaction instead. Now, go, go."

Samantha and Cian hurried over to the washing basins and started washing their arms and faces with soap and water.

"I swear he's going to kill us one day," Cian muttered angrily.

"Pact," Samantha said, while holding out her pinkie to him. "Next year, we won't let him get close to the actual chemicals."

Cian glanced down at her finger, then wrapped his around it. He grinned. "Pact."

Writing the report about how the experiment was supposed to have happened at home was rather easy. Explaining how Robert had so quickly managed to cause an exothermic reaction took a bit more effort. Samantha came up with a few potential reaction equations, but none seemed quite right.

While still pondering the equations, she called her grandmother. Her mother had told her she'd called earlier, so she made sure there hadn't been a specific reason. "Hey, Granny. Mum said you called?"

"Hello, my love. How are you?"

Samantha gave her a super quick run-down of what happened at school. "So, apart from Robert almost getting us killed today, I'm good. And you?"

Her grandmother sounded tense when she answered, "I'm alright, but could you come by on the weekend? There's something I need your opinion on."

"Sure, I can do that. What is it?" Samantha asked, her curiosity piqued.

Behind her, the door opened, and Meg came in. Though her sister tried to be quiet, Samantha noticed her sneaking up to her backpack, which was lying on the bed. Irritated, Samantha stared at her and only half-heard what her grandmother was telling her.

"...wrong with the spring. It's as if the rivers are flowing backwards, which is impossible..."

"What are you doing there?" Samantha asked when Meg opened her backpack and stuck her hand in. "Sorry, Granny. Meg's in my room, acting weird."

"I'm not acting weird!" Meg held up the two bags Samantha had bought from the garden club earlier. "Do you need these?"

Samantha had only bought them to support the school garden, so she shook her head. Meg apparently took that as an invitation to grab them. She was out of Samantha's room before Samantha could stop her. "Hey, Meg!" Then she remembered her grandmother on her phone. "I'm sorry. What were we talking about? Got it. I'll come by at the weekend."

"I've got a bad feeling about this."

Confused, Samantha frowned. Bad feeling about what? Right, there had been something her grandmother wanted to show her. "Sure, I'll have a look at it."

"Thanks, love. Be careful."

"Bye." Samantha put the phone down, already distracted by Meg's impossible behaviour.

She left her room and walked into Meg's, where she found her sister sorting two little action figures into a glass box that held at least a dozen of them. "What was that about?"

Meg looked up sullenly. "What's the problem? You didn't want them."

"Sure, but maybe asking would've been an idea. Or a thank you?"

"Thank you," drawled Meg, with an acid undertone. "You can go now."

Samantha was tempted to give her a piece of her mind, but decided it wasn't worth her breath. She returned to her room to find two texts on her phone. The first was from Jan.

Jan: Hey! Do you have time? I could use some help with exams. My place?

Jan wanted *her* to help him study? He never asked, only tried to copy her homework when he found an opportunity. Samantha pulled up the second message.

Cian: Do you want to work on the report together? You could come over, or I could come to you.

Samantha groaned. She wasn't in the mood to deal with that at the moment. It wasn't that she didn't want to spend time with him—she would probably even enjoy a date—but thinking about it made her stomach hurt. Fortunately, she had an excuse ready.

Samantha: I have to tutor someone.

Then, after thinking it sounded rather cold, she added a second message.

Samantha: Let's compare notes before school tomorrow.

It wasn't much better, but it was as much as she was able to give him at the moment. And now, she had to spend the rest of the afternoon at Jan's, so he *might* be able to pass Friday's exam.

Jan greeted her surprisingly excited. "There you are. Great!"

"Ready to study?" Samantha asked rather doubtfully.

"Sure!" Again with the fake enthusiasm. He led her into the living room where they'd held a séance last year. "Listen, this wasn't my idea..."

Samantha frowned. Something was definitely off. It all became clear when they walked around an inner wall to the dining table in the corner. She wasn't the only one called in to help Jan study.

Matt saw her and immediately got up, while Samantha froze on the spot. Jan stepped in between them, grimacing. "You can't help me with Geography, so I thought... well, Lucille thought." He sighed. "Guys, I could really use your help."

Through the window in the wall that connected the dining area with the kitchen, Jan's mother smiled at her. "Oh, hey Samantha. It's so nice of you to help Jan out a little. Would you like something to drink?"

It was a complete trap. In front of Mrs Kerscher, Matt couldn't simply vanish, and she couldn't fight with him and accidentally mention that he was really a demon. She gave Jan's mother a tortured smile and said, "Just some water, please."

In the meantime, Jan had rounded the table and pushed Matt down in his chair again. He offered Samantha the chair next to Matt, put down her drink that his mother gave him through the window, and took a place as far away as possible from the two of them. "Awesome. I'm sure this is going to work splendidly."

Samantha had never heard him say the word splendidly. She got up again. "Just call me once he's gone."

"Sam, please."

"It's not like you can learn two things at the same time, so..." She swallowed. Just sitting next to Matt while he watched her with a guarded stance made it impossible to concentrate. "This is ridiculous."

For once, Matt took her side. "She's right. We're almost done with Geography, anyway."

"Almost done?" Jan asked irritated. "You told me which pages I'm supposed to read. I can read on my own."

"Wonderful. Then my work is done."

Samantha ignored Matt, hoping he wouldn't just talk about going but actually go. "Do you want to start with German or Politics?" They were the only subjects they had together.

"You're staying!" Jan told Matt, before he said to Samantha, "German. Politics is a lost cause."

"For what?" Matt asked argumentatively. "So I can explain terms to you, which are defined in the book?"

He'd obviously never had to tutor anyone. Samantha took out her stuff. "Don't give up on Politics yet. I've got test exams for you."

Jan stared from her to Matt, clearly agitated. He rubbed his face with both hands and shook his head. "Why do all the exams have to be in one or two weeks? How's anyone going to remember all of that?"

"It's not that bad," Samantha said, before admitting, "When you start early."

Apparently, Matt knew how to play this ignoring game as well as she did. "Tomorrow, we have Geography, so I suggest Sam put her exams away while we focus on that."

"Shall I go?" she asked, unable to keep up the pretence.

"Obviously," Matt hissed back.

Jan clapped his hands. "Guys! Can't you concentrate on me for once? Just for two hours."

"Sorry, Jan, but you're not that interesting," Matt drawled.

Jan gave him a flat stare. "Are you saying you're more interested in fighting with..." He stopped, for some reason, looking at Samantha now. "Oh." His tone shifted. "Oh." He shook his head in confusion. "I didn't know you were the type for BDSM. Though I shouldn't be surprised, I guess."

"What are you talking about?" Samantha asked, incapable of understanding the weird ways Jan's brain worked.

"BD-what?" Matt asked next to him.

Quietly, Jan said, "You demons probably have a different name for it, but—"

He was interrupted by his mother raising her voice. "Are you out of your mind?"

All three of them looked through the window into the kitchen. Anne had joined her mother there. Usually, she was a sweet girl, but today, she looked more like Meg when the latter had one of her teenage tantrums.

"I ask *once* for money up-front and you say no? Do I have to just take it from your secret spot like Jan does?" Anne asked, sounding outraged.

Jan started sputtering. "W-w-what?"

"You're stealing money from your mother?" Samantha whispered.

"One time," he said defensively. "When I was younger."

She rolled her eyes at him, seriously doubting that statement. It wasn't her problem, though.

"No, Anne," Jan's mother shouted. "I said no. I will not give you your pocket money early for some stupid collectibles. If you need more money, get a job."

"They're not stupid!" Anne screamed. "Thanks for nothing." She stormed out of the kitchen and, judging by the door slamming, went straight into her room.

Confused, Samantha checked with Jan, but he looked just as irritated. His mother leaned over the kitchen window and asked, "Do you know why these collectibles are suddenly so important?"

"No idea," Jan claimed.

His mum sighed. Then she gave him a warning glance. "We're gonna talk later."

"What did I do now?" Jan exclaimed full of indignation.

His mother only shook her head and left the kitchen to have another chat with Anne.

Matt leaned forward. "What collectibles?"

Samantha remembered how Meg had stolen her two bags in front of her eyes. She'd never even managed to open them and have a look. "The ones from the garden club, I assume."

"They can't be that great," Jan muttered. Sullenly, he threw his folders open. "Hit me with German."

Samantha glanced at Matt and sighed. It was only for two hours. Surely, they were able to make it through one afternoon.

Fabian

The collectible craze had taken the school by storm. While Fabian was eating his lunch with Rachel, Lucille, and Samantha, people around them traded and sold the little figurines with a passion they hadn't even shown for the soccer championship. It was disturbing to watch.

He was halfway through his lunch when Lucille bumped his elbow with a pointed stare. Fabian very nearly sighed. Instead, he swallowed and asked lightly. "How was the study group last night? Jan said he felt really good about the exams." He absolutely hadn't. Though, right now he was sitting the Geography exam and hadn't given up yet.

"Matt was there," Samantha said flatly.

Fabian knew this, of course. "Oh really? Did you help Jan together?"

"It's not like we had a choice in it."

He had no idea what else to say, but Lucille kept kicking his shin. "But it went well, yeah? You didn't... argue?"

Samantha frowned, but then she shook her head and continued eating. "We decided to take turns and ignore each other otherwise."

That didn't exactly sound like a roaring success, but for Lucille's benefit, Fabian said, "Sounds like progress."

"If you say so." Samantha's voice was starting to sound strained, usually a sign for him to drop it.

Lucille urged him on nevertheless, so Fabian tried a more direct angle. "Have you ever thought about approaching him?"

Annoyed, Samantha lowered her lunchbox. "Fabian, what do you want? Don't tell me Lucille got to you, too." She grimaced at Lucille, who was caught between being outraged and trying to seem innocent. "Sorry, but it's true."

Instead of rising to the challenge, Lucille jerked her head to the side, indicating she wanted to talk to him alone. Already exhausted, Fabian followed her to the other side of the atrium. He envied Rachel, who no one tried to convince to take part in ridiculous schemes. Then again, it was his own fault for agreeing to it.

"What are you doing there?" Lucille accosted him as soon as they were out of earshot. "That was painful to watch."

"Why didn't you say something, then?" Fabian huffed and walked a few steps. It had *been* painful to keep that conversation alive. "I told you this won't work. You can't repair a rift like that as if you're trying to set them up with each other. They *hate* each other, not secretly love each other."

Lucille crossed her arms and glowered at him. "In my opinion, hate and love lie often close to each other. Personally, I think the only reason Samantha hates him so much is because she used to... like him very much."

"Really? The only reason?"

"Fine." Lucille rolled her eyes. "What I actually meant was that her strong feelings of hate are exacerbated by how much he disappointed her. If Daniel hadn't been around, the two of them *would've* been an item and working through his half-demon issues together." She shrugged, as if to dare him to tell her she was wrong.

Fortunately, Fabian had no problems with doing so. "If Daniel hadn't been around, Matt would've broken her heart and moved on to other fancies. Stop kidding yourself, Lucille. They don't need to fall in love with each other, they need to find a compromise that allows them to exist alongside each other. And for that, Matt needs to apologise."

"How, if she doesn't give him a chance?"

Fabian bit his lip so he wouldn't start screaming. "Samantha is not the one who has to give him a chance."

"But she's the human in this relationship." Lucille unfolded her arms and put her hands on Fabian's elbow. "Look. I will work on Matt. I'll get him to apologise, try to explain why it is so important, but he's grown up among demons. This is all new to him."

"Because Samantha's so experienced with losing her boyfriend and making amends with his killer."

Lucille let her hands fall and stared at him flatly. "Could you please give it another try?"

"Sure," Fabian said only to stop her from pestering. He didn't feel like trying, though. In his opinion, the ball was so far in Matt's court, he didn't think he'd ever see it again. They might as well try to make friends with Cheryl.

He strode back to where Samantha and Rachel had finished their lunch. Samantha looked up wearily, clearly dreading his newest attempt. Well, he wouldn't hurt her anymore. "Lucille would like you to give Matt another chance. Is that something you want to do?" he asked directly.

"No?"

"That's settled, then."

Behind him, Lucille groaned. "Thanks, Fabian." She grabbed her bag and stalked off.

Much more softly, Samantha told him, "Thank you."

He sat back down next to her and took his abandoned lunch. "I'll get her to stop, okay?"

Samantha shrugged dejectedly. "I'm getting on your nerves, and I get it, but with Matt being... Matt, I don't see how I could ever forgive him for what he's done. Blood Night or no Blood Night, he's not interested in anybody's feelings but his own. And they're a mess." She sighed. "Perhaps it's better if we stopped pretending things will magically improve one day. We'd fare better apart."

"While Malcolm is preparing to take over the world?" Rachel asked bluntly.

Samantha took a deep breath. "Let's deal with Malcolm first. But after we've sent him back to Hell, I'm done with Matt."

"Sounds fair to me," Fabian muttered, and Rachel nodded sharply. For a moment, everything was crystal clear, but soon the doubts crept back in. "You really think we stand a chance against Malcolm?"

Rachel snorted. "If not, we'll all be done with each other, I suppose."

Despite the sombre statement, Samantha started chuckling. When Rachel also cracked a smile, even Fabian couldn't help himself and laughed. "True. I guess there's always a silver lining."

By the next day, the collectible craze had reached new frightening heights. Wanted posters plastered every open surface. People haggled over prices. Others chose to steal, then became aggressive when they were caught. But the worst behaviour was exhibited by the Elite Clique. Cheryl, Ani, Jennifer, and Boyd were intimidating younger students into handing over their figurines. A little girl cried when forced to give up her entire collection to Cheryl. A boy tried to run, but Boyd went after him, got a hold of him, and crashed him into a wall. Even then, the boy fought for his figurines, but a fist in the stomach made his grip loosen. In the time it took Boyd to bring the collectibles to the others, Cheryl and Ani were fighting over who got what.

Fabian and his friends managed to get a table far away from the madness around them. Still, they looked around, irritated, shaking their heads over their classmates.

At last, Lucille forced herself to look away from them. "What's so great about these collectibles?"

Jan shrugged. "No idea, but Anne and Meg are obsessed with them. You can't talk with them about anything else at the moment."

"We all know who's behind this, right?" Matt asked.

While Samantha nodded, Fabian was confused. "Who?"

"Malcolm, of course. This whole thing stinks of greed."

Jan groaned. "Tell him to come back next week. I have exams to study for."

"Never thought I'd hear that from your mouth," Lucille quipped. Then she leaned forward and whispered, "Do you think he chose another form?

"I'm sure of it," Rachel replied.

Fabian glanced at the closed cafeteria. "What does he even want from the school? If he needs money, there are way better customers than students with limited pocket money."

"It's not about the job. Or the money," Matt tried to explain. "I mean all the money he makes here is worthless in Hell. With greed, it's more about wanting to have... everything. Or he needs to have it all." He shook himself. "Chay can explain it better."

"Evidently." Samantha leaned forward, blocking out Matt. "It doesn't really matter what he wants or doesn't want. The important thing is that we stop him. And judging by everybody's behaviour, we need to do so soon. Otherwise, a war will break out by tomorrow."

A war in the school corridors was the last thing Fabian needed. It reminded him too much of when everyone had fallen under the spell of the bogeyman. They were more experienced now than then, but if it meant they'd have to fight their friends and family, he wanted no part of it. "So, how do we recognise him now? Do we have to wait until he tries to get rid of Matt?"

"That would be nice," Samantha said promptly, ignoring Matt's glower. "I think we should start with the girl from the garden club. She sold those bags. Is *still* selling these bags."

"You're going to tell me the Archdemon of Greed is a little girl now?" Jan asked, both eyebrows raised.

Rachel shrugged. "Why not? If I were him, I would definitely choose something inconspicuous."

Fabian got up first. "Let's go find her, then. School garden first?"

Everyone seemed surprised that he was the one to take action, but the behaviour of his classmates freaked him out. The sooner the madness stopped, the better for all of them.

The school garden was close by, behind the cafeteria, which boded well for Samantha's theory. It was a small area bordered by a knee-high fence. On one side, herbs and fruit bushes grew, while the other side was reserved for native plants and flowers. Fabian had always liked the little pond best, especially when they used to study the tadpole cycle for Biology.

Fortunately for them, they found Janina in a corner, digging in the ground. At first, it looked as if she was planting a seed, but then Fabian noticed she was pulling something from the ground. The collectibles.

Janina wasn't alone. A second girl stood next to her, chewing her nails nervously. "Janina, please stop this. This can't be right. Figurines like this don't just grow in the ground."

Matt stretched out his arms to stop their advance before the girls noticed them.

"These do," Janina declared. A few days ago, she'd sounded nice and a little shy, but now confidence oozed from all her pores.

"We should tell a teacher," her friend insisted.

"Already ahead of you. Now stop fretting, Lana, and hand me the bags. What we're doing here will keep the garden club alive."

Lana held the bags open for her, while Janina deposited her harvest into them. "Don't we have more than enough? With all the money we've made, we could replant half the school."

"It's never enough!" Janina said, so sharply her friend winced.

Fabian had heard more than he was able to stomach. That girl was definitely the embodiment of greed. He was just about to walk in when Samantha shook her head and beckoned for him to retreat.

Confused, Fabian followed her. "I thought we were going to question her?"

Samantha glanced over her shoulder. "She's not Malcolm."

"How so?" Matt asked impatiently, as if he couldn't wait to run Janina through with his sword.

Annoyed, Samantha clicked her tongue. "If Malcolm were to pose as a schoolgirl, he'd be a loner. This girl has a friend who's known her long enough to notice the changes. She's not him, unless Malcolm killed her and took her place, but that sounds a little over-the-top, even for a demon."

Next to her, Lucille nodded. "I think you're right. If Janina really existed and he took over her life, he'd have to keep up the pretence twenty-four-seven. I doubt he'd bother placating her parents by going home each day. So, if he did take over, Janina would be missing, and her parents would have already stormed the school."

"Unless they're dead too," Fabian muttered before catching himself. "I know, too morose. But if she's not Malcolm, what's wrong with her? She definitely acts greedy."

"What a coincidence," Matt said sarcastically, obviously still thinking that Janina was his uncle. "Where do you think she got that from?"

"We don't know," snapped Samantha. "We only know she's not him, so we can't just barge in there, hold her at knife point, and force her to tell us her secret. I know *you* wouldn't mind, but—"

"Oh, shut up," Matt muttered.

Jan was massaging the bridge of his nose while Rachel checked the time on her phone a bit too intensely. Lucille, however, smiled at Matt and Samantha. "I've got an idea. Why don't you two question her together? If all six of us go, it would be far too intimidating. It's better if it's just you two."

"Speaking from experience, anyone who has to spend time alone with these two would be even more intimidated than before," Jan chimed in, earning himself an elbow jab.

"Why us?" Matt asked. Contrary to Samantha, he didn't seem to have noticed how much Lucille was pushing them together. "Do I look like I love gardening?"

Samantha snorted, her arms crossed. "He's right. One earthworm and he's out of there. Not really the man for the job."

"School bell's ringing in a few seconds," Rachel said all of a sudden.

In his head, Fabian checked his schedule and came to the conclusion that they had Physics next. "Shit, aren't we taking a test?" He'd completely forgotten to look at his notes in the break thanks to the collectible mania around him. "Sam, we need to go."

She drew up her shoulders and took a deep breath. "I have time after sixth period," she told Matt.

He narrowed his eyes and gave her a curt nod. "Fine with me."

Lucille clapped her hands excitedly. Fabian could only roll his eyes at another ill-fated attempt to push their friends towards an apology. He had to give her one thing, though. She didn't give up. Perhaps he should start taking a page out of her book, his emblem being all about hope and everything.

Matt

They were supposed to watch a movie in French, but almost everyone was comparing and trading their collectibles. If Matt interpreted the teacher's intense stare correctly, she wasn't irritated about people not being quiet, but devising a plan on how to confiscate all the figurines for herself. The movie itself didn't hold Matt's attention, since he barely understood a single word, so he was almost grateful when Lucille leaned over to talk.

Until he heard what she had to say.

"So, Matt, when you and Sam do your thing this afternoon, you could insert a little apology, don't you think?"

"To that greedy girl?" He'd probably let Samantha do the talking, anyway.

Lucille stared at him intensely. "Stop being so wilfully obtuse. To Samantha."

Matt's eyelids fluttered, and he leaned back with a sigh. "Lucille, drop it." Perhaps, if he pretended to sleep, she'd leave him alone.

But Lucille only poked his arm to regain his attention. "No, I won't drop it. Things can't go on like this. You two need to make up."

Annoyed, Matt opened his eyes again. "That's not up to me. Unless you know a trick to stop Samantha hating on me, there's nothing I can do."

"I know a trick. It's called an apology." She crossed her arms and gave him a pointed stare.

Matt didn't deign her with an answer. Everyone was bugging him to apologise, but in his opinion it wouldn't change anything. What was he even supposed to say? *Oops. Sorry, I killed your boyfriend. Are we good again?*

"If you're struggling with the words, I could work with you on that," Lucille offered.

He couldn't imagine anything worse right now. To make her stop, he said, "I've got nothing to apologise for. It was an accident. You know that, I know that, and she knows it as well. She's just too stubborn to accept it." A memory flashed in front of him. Samantha in his arms, looking up expectantly. "It doesn't change anything. Just like a half-hearted apology wouldn't." He'd turned away from her.

Lucille huffed indignantly. "How about an honest apology?"

Keeping up his act, Matt shrugged. "I've got none." There were, in fact, a million things he wanted to say to Samantha, but every time she stood in front of him, his tongue was tied. Then she'd lash out at him, and he'd lash right back. "Sorry, Lucille, but Samantha will forgive me when she decides to, not a minute earlier." Hell would freeze over before that happened.

"You two are so incredibly stubborn. It's—"

There was a loud crash on the other side of the room. Cheryl had pushed Shayna from her chair. "Give them to me!" the queen bee snarled.

Shayna held her figurines close to the chest and glared. "You can't make me."

"Oh, yeah. Let's see about that."

But before the two got into fisticuffs, Mrs Lindenberger had walked over. "I've had enough of this. You two will hand over all your collectibles. That goes for everyone!"

"Never," Shayna and Cheryl barked as if from one mouth while the room erupted in protest.

Mrs Lindenberger grabbed one of the schoolbooks and slammed it on the table, screeching, "Give me your collectibles. I want all of them!"

"Is it just me, or is everyone losing their mind?" Lucille asked softly, having shrunk into her seat.

Matt grabbed her hand and his backpack. "Let's get out of here before it gets to blows."

He should've never mentioned it. Before Lucille could even get out of her chair, Mrs Lindenberger had grabbed a fistful of Cheryl's hair and pulled her over the table. The blond girl screeched in pain, then she pushed the table between them into the teacher, while Shayna used her chance to snatch some of Cheryl's considerable hoard, only to find herself attacked by the boy on their other side.

Without further ado, Matt and Lucille fled the room.

They reconvened in an empty classroom with the other four. There were only a few students who hadn't been infected with greed yet. Anarchy had broken out in the school corridors.

"Meg's officially lost her mind," Samantha told them, seeming quite unsettled. "She pushed me off my chair and stole my purse."

Next to her, Jan nodded ferociously. "Never seen anything like this before. She asked to borrow my money first, then went full-blown fury on Sam. Oh, and she claimed me."

Matt found it hard to follow them. "What does that mean?"

"You know why she pushed Samantha out of her chair? Because I was studying for German with her. Apparently, Meg has put a claim on me." Jan shook his head, flustered. "I don't do this kind of possessiveness. When girls get jealous, it always gets icky. Maybe I should just break up with her."

"She's not in her right mind," Samantha said. Despite never having been a big fan of her sister and Jan dating, she apparently didn't like the potential of a break-up either. "You can't hold her accountable for what she does while she's under Malcolm's spell."

Matt crossed his arms and leaned back. "How interesting."

Samantha shot him an evil glare. "This is different."

"How?" As far as Matt remembered, he hadn't been in his right mind either on New Year. He hadn't even noticed how many times he'd slipped out to kill.

"That doesn't matter now," Rachel said sharply, disrupting their discussion. "What do we do about the school?"

"Go home?" Jan asked.

Lucille jabbed her elbow into his side. "We need to stop Malcolm. Samantha, you summoned Menuha. What if we summoned Malcolm? I realise it's a bit risky, but I'd rather face him head on than potentially hurt our classmates trying to get to him."

Before Samantha could even open her mouth, Matt said, "Won't work. To summon an archdemon is much more complex than invoking his name. They also have to *want* to come, which Malcolm won't. And lastly, worst-case scenario, calling upon Greed might bring us a minor demon of his house." They probably didn't know about the houses so he added, "House of Greed. Every demon belongs to one or more houses, whether they're related to them or by choice. Anyway, we don't want to fight another demon while Malcolm does his thing."

"So, we need to talk to Janina now," Samantha decided. "She might not be Malcolm, but she could tell us where he is."

Someone ran into the door outside, and they heard voices. "Nobody touches the rares! They're mine!"

"Rares?" Fabian echoed confused.

Jan got up and opened the door, causing a boy to fall into the room. A second boy stood in front of him, no older than fourteen and at least one-and-a-half heads shorter.

"What rares?" Jan bellowed.

While the one on the ground bolted, the other boy looked up defiantly. Jan's size seemed to intimidate him, though. "They'll show the rares in five minutes down in the student hall. But don't think about getting them. They're mine." And with that, he ran off.

"Well..." Matt pushed himself out of his chair. "I guess we found out where Janina will be in five minutes. Let's go talk to her."

They made their way down to the student hall, which was completely packed. People were even standing on the chairs and tables to get a better look at the stage. The curtain had been pulled back, revealing Janina and her worried friend. A presentation screen was pulled out, showing nothing but the school logo at the moment.

The six managed to find a place at the door in the back of the room without getting squashed, when Janina rang a little bell and grinned widely into the room. "Oh, this is marvellous. You're just as excited as I am to unveil the rares. Though, let me warn you. These are not so easy to get. Can I have a volunteer?"

A sea of hands surged into the air. Janina picked someone, but Cheryl pushed the girl away to climb the stage herself. "I volunteer."

Janina didn't seem to mind. She asked her friend something and received a gnarly root from her. "To get the rares, you need to bring them to me. I will turn them into the collectibles you love so much. Like this."

The tip of the root touched Cheryl. There was a little pop, and she was gone, as if she'd suddenly discovered her demon heritage and jumped away.

Matt gave up his leisurely pose, leaning on the door, and stretched his neck. Janina was bending down to pick up something small from the floor. Then she held it into the air, and Matt's blood turned to icy slush.

It was a figurine of Cheryl.

Next to him, Lucille gasped, while Fabian's eyes widened in horror. "She can't be serious," he muttered.

The people in front of them weren't scared, though. An excited buzz rose, and everyone's eyes were glued to the front.

Janina smiled. "Awesome. Let's unveil our rares, shall we?"

When everyone had shouted a resounding "yes", she clicked the presentation forward. On the screen, six portrait photos appeared, taken straight from their student IDs.

Matt cursed the moment he recognised himself and his friends.

Jan

Jan dumbly stared at his own picture. His brain refused to make the connection between what his eyes saw and what Janina had just explained about rares. It made no sense. They weren't figurines to collect.

Not yet.

It didn't take long for the room to turn against them. The people next to them had recognised them and were pointing already. Someone tried to grab Jan's hand. He slapped it away.

To his side, Lucille shrieked when Fabian grabbed her arm and pulled her away. The others broke away a second later. Jan followed, and behind him, students squeezed through the door, shoving and screaming. It slowed down the bulk of them, but more than enough students managed to get out and pursue them.

Jan saw Matt and Samantha going for the stairs, while Rachel ran down the corridor. He had no idea where Fabian and Lucille had turned to and could only hope they hadn't been caught yet. He couldn't say the same for himself. Due to his late start, the mob was hot on his heels. He slammed through one door, letting it swing back into their faces, and bought himself a few more seconds. But then people appeared on the other end of the corridor, and he found himself caught between two groups.

He tried a couple of classrooms until he found one with a wide-open window, ducked in and jumped out of it without second-guessing. Jan landed on a patch of gravel, and instinctively rolled himself, like he'd learned at self-defence. The gravel bit into his shoulder and his knees, but he was back on his feet in no time and running away from the main building.

His lucky escape and speed made it possible for Jan to lose his pursuers. He ran behind the gym at the other end of the school and didn't slow until he'd ducked between the garbage containers. Despite wheezing from the effort, he pulled out his pack of cigarettes and lit himself one.

The smoke helped him calm down, though he had to take his inhaler between two puffs to counter the asthma. His hands kept shaking, while his brain finally caught up with what was happening: people were hunting him and his friends down to turn them into little action figures. How insane was that?

Just then, he heard steps and a triumphant squeal. "I told you he'd be hiding here."

Jan cursed. Why had he ever brought Meg to this place? It wasn't even romantic, just particularly secluded. He stomped his cigarette out and stood up. "Hey, girls." Naturally, his sister and Meg had stuck together. He didn't like the way their eyes lit up, though.

"You're mine!" Meg declared.

"No, he isn't," Anne argued. "Jan is *my* brother. He's belonged to me for sixteen years."

Meg pushed her. "Oh, please, you don't even like him."

Jan slowly edged away in an attempt to loop around the two and go for the school fence. Let them fight about him while he snuck off.

Unfortunately, their greed was stronger. Each girl grabbed an arm of his and hung on for dear life.

"You're not going anywhere," his sweet girlfriend hissed.

Anne smirked at him. "We're going to figure out who gets the Jan collectible once you are one."

Jan jerked his arms free. "You're out of your mind! Do you even hear yourselves? I'm definitely not going to go with either of you so you can put me onto some shelf."

"Nobody's asking you," Meg informed him coldly.

"But I promise to dust you regularly," Anne said, blinking rapidly in a show of innocence.

Not to be outdone, Meg yelled, "I'll take you to sleep with me."

Normally he'd appreciate the sentiment, but not when it involved him getting turned into a toy. "You're going to let me through, or I'm going to be forced to hurt you. I'd hate to hurt you, but I'm not a collectible. And I don't belong to anyone."

The girls shared an ominous glance before throwing themselves at Jan. He couldn't hurt them, not really, but their ferocity didn't leave him much of a choice. He hooked one leg around Anne and threw her on her back. When he lunged at Meg, she dove under his arm and wrapped herself around his body like a starfish. Jan grabbed her hands and used them to tear her arms from his body. Though she tried to hold on with her legs, gravity took care of it, and she landed on her bum. He tried to make one step, only to have Anne use the same technique around one of his legs. Annoyed, he dragged her with him, but she was too heavy for him to carry far.

In the meantime, Meg had got up. She grabbed a wooden plank from the containers and swiped at Jan's head, nearly decapitating him if he hadn't ducked in time. Her burning eyes told him she wouldn't stop at anything to make him hers. Even if it meant bringing him to Janina dead.

Jan didn't have a choice. He needed to fight them in earnest. If they stopped at nothing, he'd have to give it his all, too.

He caught the plank when it came for him again and gave it a tug, causing Meg to stumble forward. With a well-practised hit, using the hard edge of his hand on her neck, he sent her sprawling on the ground. Then he swung his leg around to get rid of Anne. His sister held on with everything she had, even biting him.

"Get off me!" Jan shouted as he used his hands to pry her arms open. With the next shake of his leg, she flew free, yelping in terror as she did so.

Jan caught her around her waist and slammed her into the nearest container. Anne cried out in pain as her legs folded under her.

"I'm sorry. I'm really sorry," Jan muttered, feeling like the worst person in the world.

"You're mine," Meg slurred.

Anne could barely keep herself upright, but her eyes flashed as she snapped at Meg, "No, mine."

Jan turned away from them and ran.

Rachel

Hiding under a desk was the worst idea Rachel had had in a long time. Now she was stuck under here with no open escape route. Worse, someone had seen her enter the classroom.

"Rachel?" Ani's sickly sweet voice called into the room. "Call out if you're here."

She certainly wasn't *that* stupid.

Someone else—or perhaps it was Ani herself—was toppling all the tables and chairs behind her. With every crash, Rachel moaned softly. She needed to get out of here.

Carefully, she lowered herself to the ground and peeked at the door. The path was clear. She only had to jump over a chair or two, and she'd be out.

"Found you."

Rachel bumped her head against the desk and let out a scream. Ani was lying on top of the desk, grinning down at her. Then Bjorn grabbed her from behind, his hand like a bench press around her arm, and pulled her out of her hiding spot.

"Aren't you worried about Cheryl?" Rachel asked, trying to distract them.

Ani jumped off the table and patted her handbag. "Oh, I've got Cheryl right here. She might not be a rare, but she's a pretty doll."

"And I'll be taking this doll," Bjorn growled while he dragged Rachel out of the door.

Ani followed them. "We're handing her in together."

"There's only one Rachel. That's why she's a rare."

"But Rachel likes me more than you," Ani argued.

Irritated, Rachel looked from one to the other. "Uhm, no, I don't like either of you." Just because she'd helped Ani out once didn't mean she bore the elite girl any sympathy. And it certainly didn't mean she wanted to join her collection.

"Oh, hey! You found one." A younger girl took a stance right in front of Bjorn. It took Rachel a moment to recognise her as Janina's friend, Lana. "I'll take her to Janina for you."

Repulsed, Rachel threw herself backwards, but Bjorn's grip was relentless. "She's ours."

"Of course she is," Lana promised quickly. "But she needs to be changed first. I'll take her to Janina, then you can pick her up later. What were your names?"

Ani pushed past Bjorn and poked a finger into the younger girl's face. "Don't try anything funny or I'll rip your throat out. Understood?"

With Ani busy reprimanding Lana, Bjorn had clamped a hand over Rachel's face and quietly dragged her away. His fingers partially squeezed her nose shut as well, which made it almost impossible to breathe. Rachel dug her fingers into his hand to no avail. He was stronger than her, and the greed gave him additional strength.

Just as she was about to pass out, she heard a screechy battle cry. Ani slammed into Bjorn's back, causing him to loosen his grip on Rachel.

She desperately gasped for breath, then broke the rest of his grip and dashed the other way—straight into the arms of Janina's friend. Four bleeding scratches crossed her face. To Rachel's surprise, Lana gesticulated wildly to the outside doors. "Leave the school. Quick!"

Rachel didn't question it. She'd overheard how unhappy Lana had been with Janina's recent collectible venture.

Bursting through the doors, Rachel took a couple of sweet breaths of fresh air. Ahead of her, she saw Fabian and Lucille running from a mob of angry students. Rachel joined them, glad to be no longer alone.

"You're still here," Fabian gasped, then shouted at Lucille. "Can't you make us disappear?"

Lucille must've lost her shoes at some point. Her usually immaculately coiffed hair was in disarray, and the heat and exertion had turned her face red. She shook her head wildly. "Their greed won't allow them to believe their eyes. But the fire-breathing dragon is making them think twice."

"We must have a lot of brave dragon fighters then," Rachel mumbled. The crowd behind them barely even slowed.

"Hey, guys!" Jan called. He was followed by another mob led by Anne and Meg.

The four of them ran harder, but Rachel could already feel her sides burning. She'd never been particularly athletic, and it was starting to show.

Just then, the entrance door of the administration building opened, and Mr Zobel waved at them with a serious face. "Get in quick."

They followed without hesitation. Mr Zobel shut the door behind them and locked all three locks on it. Seconds later, the students slammed into it. Mr Zobel shook his head. "This is outrageous. I've never seen anything like this. Come on. You can rest upstairs in the teachers' lounge while we get on top of this situation."

Relieved, Rachel and the others followed him up the stairs. Glass splintered behind them, and they quickened their steps.

The teachers' lounge was a large room with a long table, many chairs, and a little kitchen. Several teachers were present, among them Mr Herbert and a pair of PE teachers.

"The entire school has gone mad," Jan exclaimed and fell onto a chair as if he owned the place.

Mr Zobel nodded. "I know. The students may think they can turn you into rares, but they're deluded."

"Hear, hear." Lucille followed Jan's suite when none of the teachers complained and took a deep breath. "Can I have something to drink, please?"

"It's obvious that the rares are for us teachers," one of the PE teachers said.

Rachel backed into the door. "Oh no."

Mr Herbert put a hand on Fabian's shoulder and squeezed. "I can't think of anyone I'd much rather have in a display cabinet than you, my friend. Can't wait to see your father's face when I give him the tour."

"Let's tie them up before they get any strange ideas," Mr Zobel suggested.

Rachel spun around and grabbed the door handle. It wouldn't open.

Mr Zobel must have locked it and taken the key. Before she could even process the thought, someone slammed into the door from outside. A choir of voices began demanding their return.

A teacher grabbed her from behind and forced her into a chair. Someone had produced a set of jumping ropes from somewhere and was using them to tie them to the chair. Fabian had tears in his eyes and grimaced, while his arms strained against the awfully tight bond Mr Herbert was putting him in. Rachel felt her own bonds tighten while the back of the chair dug into her shoulder blades.

"There, that's better." Mr Zobel patted her head before joining the other teachers, who had gathered to discuss their next step.

"Matt and Samantha are still free, hopefully," Lucille muttered. She was panting, trying to keep the tears at bay.

Jan kicked the table leg in front of him in frustration, almost causing himself to topple over. "Yeah, I feel so much better now I know our fate depends on those two working together."

"We're so screwed." Fabian winced at the continued pain in his arms.

"It might unite them," Lucille said hopefully.

Rachel snorted at her. "Keep dreaming."

"I don't want to end up in Herby's display cabinet." Fabian swallowed down an enormous gulp.

"At least you won't get torn into two pieces." Jan kicked the table leg again and grunted.

Meanwhile, Lucille raised her chin defiantly. "I believe in those two. They're going to save us."

If this had been the dreamworld, Rachel would've granted her that dream. But as usual, reality sucked.

Samantha

Bad life choices saw Samantha following Matt's lead when running from an angry school mob. It wasn't the first time the entire school seemed to have turned against her, but it was certainly the first time they'd started an actual witch hunt.

Stairs. Matt chose stairs. When in doubt go to the place, you can only escape by jumping to your death, Samantha thought bitterly. The first thought triggered another. There was a silver lining to being stuck with a half-demon. He could actually jump away from anywhere.

"Matt, stop!" She tugged on his hand. Not that she was holding his. His hand just had her wrist in an unbreakable grip.

Annoyed, he paused. "What? You've got an idea?"

"Yes. Actually I—"

A door slammed open three stories below them and hasty steps sounded on the stairs. Three girls leaned into the gap between the stairs to look up. They squealed excitedly when they found the two of them.

"I so want a Matt!" one of them shouted.

"No, he's mine. He's the best of the rares by far," another answered.

Samantha gave Matt a sideways look. "Isn't it great to be popular?"

He glowered at the girls downstairs. "Shut up."

"I want them all," the third one announced, and destroyed Samantha's short-lived amusement.

Matt turned around and dragged her along so fast she stumbled on the steps. Samantha was just about to hit her knees on the stairs when the stairs vanished in front of her to be replaced by Matt. She crashed into him two stories higher than before, the weird cold, slimy feeling of a space-jump on her skin.

"Actually..." She remembered her half-formed plan.

Before she could say anything more, Matt pulled her into the corridor. He tried several doors until he found one that sufficed his needs. Looking over the shoulder, he pushed her into a cleaning closet.

Samantha steadied herself between the walls of the narrow room. "What—?"

"Stay here. I'll lure them away from here."

He slammed the door shut in front of her nose. His steps receded slowly. Samantha was just about to open the door again and ask him what the hell he was thinking when she heard the doors to the staircase being thrown open. A screaming mass of girls ran into the corridor.

"There he is!"

"He's mine!"

"No, mine!"

The steps closer to her sprinted the other way, followed by the eager crowd. Instinctively, Samantha put her hand on the door handle and pulled. Most people ran past the cleaning closet, but a few times someone jerked the door. Biting down hard on her bottom lip, Samantha held the door steady to give off the impression it was locked.

At long last, silence returned to the corridor, and Samantha let out a shuddering breath and sank to the ground next to a broom collection. For a few minutes, she did nothing but breathe.

If there had ever been any doubt Malcolm was behind the collectibles, it had been blown away when the rares had been revealed. He was after them. They were no longer a nuisance who had accidentally crossed his plans. They were stumbling blocks that had to be removed. Today.

Slowly, Samantha's eyes adjusted to the darkness in the room. There was no window, but the slit under the door let in a little bit of light. The room was a tight space between two classrooms filled with cleaning supplies and schoolbooks. What was she doing in here?

Outside, her friends were running for their lives, and she was supposed to hide until it was over? It wasn't going to be over if they didn't find Malcolm. A plan was forming in her mind as she examined the events of the day. Janina and Malcolm were connected somehow.

Right now, everyone was running around trying to get their hands on her and her friends. The last place anyone would search for them, and the one place they needed to go, was the school garden, to Janina herself. Now that Matt had lured his fangirls and boys away, she might be able to reach the garden. It grated on her that he'd sacrificed himself for her, but she wouldn't let it be for nothing.

She drew herself up and carefully opened the door. The corridor on the right was clear. She just had to get down the stairs, out the back of the building, and then walk around to the school garden.

"Samantha?"

Startled, Samantha jumped back into the room and pulled the door shut. Her heart was beating in her throat as she gripped the door handle. The voice had belonged to Cian, but she couldn't trust him. Couldn't trust anyone.

Steps in front of her door. "You don't need to be afraid of me."

"Is that so?" Her voiced broke even on the one word.

"I'm not collecting."

"And I'm supposed to believe you?"

His voice was soft, almost tired. "I'd never lie to you."

"It wouldn't be on purpose," Samantha explained. She didn't know why she even bothered to talk with him. As soon as she let loose a little, he would yank the door open and drag her to Janina. "Everyone is just... addicted."

A moment of silence, then: "You're the only one I'm addicted to."

"Not helpful." Samantha whimpered before biting down on her lip again. A metallic taste told her that she'd cut too deep.

"I don't want you as a figurine," Cian elaborated, a bit more agitated. "I want to go on a date with you. Talk and joke. I want to hold your hand." His voice grew softer again. "Kiss you."

Samantha's arms grew slack. He didn't sound like a man possessed by greed. "Cian..."

"I'm sorry. You'd think I'd notice when a girl isn't interested in me."

She closed her eyes, grimacing. So, he *had* picked up on her reservations. To keep things light, she teased him. "You've probably never had to deal with that." He was Alan's best friend, after all, one of the most popular guys at school.

"Oh, I have." Cian laughed at himself, a warm sound behind the wood. "But I think I've never had such a big crush on anybody. I really like you, Samantha."

"I like you, too." And she did. She just wasn't sure if there would ever be more.

Neither of them said anything for a while. Samantha appreciated that not once did he try to open the door. If this was a trick, it was a good one. And she was willing to give him the benefit of a doubt.

Her heart racing, she pushed down on the handle and opened the door. In front of it, Cian took a step back and smiled, but then his eyes focused on something behind her, and he screwed up his face. "What the hell?"

Confused, Samantha looked over her shoulder. There, in the back of the cleaning closet, Matt raised a hand. "Hey."

He must've jumped in just before she'd opened the door. Now, if this wasn't awkward, she didn't know what was.

Samantha opened the door wider. "Come on in." Whatever was going to go down would take a little while. She'd rather do it in the relative safety of the cleaning closet than out in the corridor.

Cian only hesitated for a moment before he squeezed in. With three people in the little room, it was starting to get cosy.

"Is he..." Matt nodded at Cian.

"He's clean, yes." Samantha closed the door behind her and pushed a broomstick under the handle to keep it closed.

Cian fumbled out his smartphone for light while he explained to Matt, "I'm not interested in action figures, especially not human ones. Did you see what Janina did to Cheryl? She turned her into one of them."

Matt and Samantha exchanged an uneasy glance. They hadn't even had a chance to figure out how to explain the weird events to their classmates.

"What do you mean 'turned her into one of them'?" Samantha asked, deliberately obtuse.

"We were in the back," Matt chimed in.

Cian looked from one to the other and frowned, clearly displeased. "Come on, everybody saw that. You know what's going on here, right? You always do. What kind of sick game is this?"

One thing she appreciated about Cian was that he was smart. Unfortunately, that was proving to be a problem right now.

"Fine!" Matt announced suddenly. "You want to know what's going on?"

"Matt."

He shook his head at her, irritated. "We don't have time to be mindful of him."

Cian's eyes narrowed. "What were you two doing in this broom closet, anyway?"

While Samantha blushed, Matt answered, "We were hiding, obviously." He pushed past Cian, forcing him to switch positions. "Lucille and the others have been caught by the teachers. I have no idea when or whether they'll hand them over to the students, but before that happens, we need to stop Janina. Right now, pretty much every student is storming admin, so the coast is clear."

Samantha nodded, but before she could say anything, Cian chimed in, "What are you planning to do with that girl?"

Matt stared him down, then regarded Samantha, for once giving her the choice for how to proceed. She knew he didn't mind telling the truth that much and only kept it hidden because it was simpler. When she wet her lips, unsure of how much they were able to trust Cian, he told the boy, "Why don't you wait outside until Samantha and I are done?"

"I'm staying here. I want to help."

Samantha moaned. This was going to be like Daniel. He'd also wanted to help, and the next week he'd been dead. "Alright." She could do this. "Let me think. I assume Malcolm got... into her head somehow."

"Who's Malcolm?"

Matt rolled his eyes. "My... the cafeteria owner."

"That disgusting old guy?" Cian asked.

Samantha ignored him this time. "It might be a curse or a possession spell. Unless..." She thought hard to find a description of the archdemon that would make sense to Matt, but not to Cian. "His status gives him certain privileges that make it easier to bind people to him. You know this stuff better than I do."

Fortunately, Matt got her. "Well, what I *do* know is that anyone my mother regales with a kiss will declare their undying love for her. At least, it seems that way."

She'd thought so. There was more to the deadly sins than the archdemons' own behaviour.

"Looks like you got that from her," Cian commented. "Everyone seems to be in love with you."

"Well, not me," Samantha snapped, then bit her tongue. There was no time for fighting. "Alright, so let's assume Malcolm has a similar gift. Not with a kiss, but... a coin. A part of his hoard. Like these figurines."

Matt nodded eagerly. "And once you've got a piece, you never let go of it. You want more."

"Guys, what are you talking about?"

Samantha's mind was racing ahead. "Janina must own the first collectible. She dug it up in the school garden right behind the cafeteria."

"Question is whether we just need to take hers away or gather all the collectibles."

"We start with her and hope for the best," Samantha suggested.

Matt grimaced. "Two potential problems. First, she won't give it to us on her own volition. And second, we probably have to destroy it to end this thing."

Annoyed of being left out, Cian asked sourly, "Do you even need me for something?"

"Not really," Matt said promptly.

But Samantha was of a different opinion. "We do. Matt, if one of us gets close to Janina, she'll attack us with that root. One touch, and we're done for. Cian could lure her to us."

"That could actually work." Matt sounded impressed. "Where do you want to lure her?"

"Assuming she's still waiting in the student hall, into the school garden. I'll make sure she can't flee, while you free the others." With his space-jumping ability, it shouldn't be too hard for him.

Of course, Cian didn't know that. "Alone?"

Matt didn't bother with a reply. "Will do. So, I'll see you in...?"

Samantha did a quick estimate on how much time she would need to get everything, including the trapping web, into place. "Fifteen minutes?"

"In fifteen minutes in the school garden." He took the broomstick from the door and squeezed out of the room.

Samantha turned to Cian. "It's very important that you wait until fifteen minutes have passed before you bring Janina to the school garden. Can you do that?"

He looked confused. "Yeah, that doesn't sound too hard."

"Thank you." She truly appreciated his help.

When she went to open the door, Cian got a hold of the handle and her hand. "What's the meaning of this? I know you've been talking circles around me, but I'm not stupid. Students who get turned into action figures, curses, and spells. What does Janina want from you? Or that Malcolm guy?"

Samantha regarded him carefully. A soft inner voice told her that he could handle it. That he was smart enough to figure it out himself if she didn't tell him. But there was this huge part of her that screamed at her to keep it a secret. For his benefit and hers. All she could tell him was, "I'll explain it to you. But not now. Later."

He nodded slowly and let go of her hand. "I'll keep you to that."

Grimacing, Samantha opened the door and hurried down the empty corridor. Cian was a problem for later. Now she had to face an archdemon.

Fabian

Fabian's hands were going numb, while his shoulders burnt from the strain on them. He twisted in his chair, trying to somehow ease the pain, but it didn't help.

Outside the teacher's room, students were banging against the door, demanding their handover. The wood shuddered in its frame, and a minute ago, the part next to one of the hinges had split, the tear growing with each impact. Sooner or later, the students would break through.

Not that Fabian and his friends were any safer inside. While the headmistress was shouting at the students to stand down, threatening to suspend everyone if they didn't return to their classrooms, she only did so, because the students were blocking their way to the school garden. The teachers wanted to hand them in themselves.

Fabian didn't dare to meet Mr Herbert's gaze. The Physics teacher carried a mad glint in his eyes, and he was the happiest he'd ever been around Fabian. Sadly, that gave him only more reason to worry. Even dying would be preferable to becoming a little figurine doomed to live its life out in a display cabinet at Mr Herbert's house.

"Shh."

Startled, Fabian sat up straight. There was a hand on his arm. Matt. He was trying to loosen the knots while avoiding detection from the teachers.

Fabian didn't even dare breathe, nor glance at the others. Matt gave up quickly enough and simply grabbed his arm. With a jerk, Fabian tumbled into nothingness.

When his eyes cleared again, he was outside in the last place he wanted to be right now. The school garden.

Next to him, Matt stumbled forward, his momentum causing Fabian and his chair to fall. His shoulder almost burst when he hit the ground, the pain so blinding he only saw stars for a minute.

"What's wrong?" Samantha was waiting for them. Instead of hurrying to Fabian's side, she regarded only Matt.

The half-demon was crouching on all fours, panting. "Something's not right with the abstract space. Jumping felt... wrong."

"Wrong how?" It was only when she spoke that Fabian noticed Matt had brought him and Lucille out of the room. Fortunately for her, her chair had remained standing.

Matt got to his feet and took a deep breath. His form flickered, then he was gone. A second later, he reappeared one metre to his side. "Damn it." He found Samantha's gaze. "Rachel and Jan will have to wait." Instead of trying to space-jump again, Matt walked over to Fabian and pulled him back to his feet.

"I can't feel my hands," Fabian whimpered as new pain shot through his arms.

This time, Matt got through his bounds quickly, and suddenly, Fabian could feel his hands with such ferocity, he almost started screaming. Chopping them off would've been nicer than this.

"I think it's this place," Samantha said, completely distracted by something else. "It's weird. Twisted."

"What's the plan?" Lucille asked the moment she was free.

"In about five minutes, Janina will come here. I've woven a spell that will prevent her from fleeing." Samantha pointed to the soil in front of her feet.

Fabian carefully massaged his hands, breathing through the pain. "We're back to Janina?"

Matt walked over to Samantha, apparently surveying the placement of the trap and from which direction Janina would come. "We believe she owns the first figurine, which started this craze."

"The first that got dug up," Samantha added.

"And we need to take it off her and destroy it," Matt finished.

Meanwhile, Lucille had crept closer to Fabian and whispered, "Aren't they working together beautifully?"

Fabian only snorted. "So, she walks in here and we... we do what?"

Pointing at a row of bushes to their side, Samantha said, "First, you need to hide. Lucille, use an illusion, so I'm the only one Janina can see. One person won't scare her away. As soon as she's caught, Matt will take the root off her. Once she's harmless, we'll talk. Or find the figurine ourselves." She checked her phone. "They're coming. Quick."

With no time for further questions, Fabian decided to simply follow along. He and Lucille hid behind the bushes, while Matt jumped away only to slam into the ground. Apparently, he'd been trying to land on the roof of the cafeteria, but instead, he'd missed it by a meter. Samantha shot him an irritated look, and he shrugged. Something was seriously wrong with his magic.

The perfect time for Janina to arrive. To Fabian's surprise she was led by Cian, while her friend was running after them.

"Don't do this," her friend begged. "It's not right."

"If someone's stealing from my garden, they'll have to pay the price," Janina declared with bone-chilling determination.

Samantha knelt down in the flowerbeds, pretending to dig, while Matt limped over to her. Fabian saw Cian's eyes widen when he saw them. "Uhm, they want to steal your collectibles. Get them straight from the source."

Fabian assumed Janina was either too far gone or not very clever, because to him, Cian was clearly a terrible fibber. No wonder he'd chosen art over drama.

"They belong to me!" Janina shouted. "They're mine alone."

"No!" Lana had noticed Matt and Samantha. "Run away! Quick!"

Unsure of how secure Lucille's illusion was, Fabian took great care not to make a sound as he brought his still itching fingers together in front of him. He'd noticed the water in the pond and in the pump they used for irrigation. There was also water in the building behind them.

Janina smiled and took out her magic root. "Now you're also mine."

Her friend found a bucket of courage and ran in front of her to block her way. She spread her arms out wide and bravely said, "I won't let you."

Definitely too far gone. Janina simply reached out and touched Lana with the root. Then she stomped the new collectible into the ground and continued her path.

Samantha whispered something to Matt when Janina stepped forward, gleefully raising her root. "You can't run from me."

"Shall we try?" Matt asked Samantha rather lacklustrely.

"Not necessary. At this point, we could crawl away backwards if needed."

The spell seemed to have worked. Janina was unable to lift a foot. Anger flashed on her face as she tore and jerked on her limbs. In her frustration, she even threw the root at Matt.

He easily evaded the object and commented drily, "Well, that makes my job easy." He raised an arm and shot blinding energy at the root, pulverising it. "That still works."

Fabian let his arms sink while he and Lucille came out of hiding. Without the root, Janina seemed to be no more than a furious girl who hadn't got what she wanted. "That was mine!" she screamed.

Somewhere in the distance, the noise of hundreds of people drew nearer. "They're coming. Whatever we're doing, can we do it quickly?" Just the sound of the rousing voices made Fabian's arms crawl.

"Give us the figurine you dug out first," Samantha demanded.

Janina stopped to struggle, an amused grin on her face. "You expect me to remember which one was the first and whom I gave it to?"

Matt shot Samantha a concerned look. "Did you talk to the cafeteria owner lately?"

"Yes," Janina admitted surprisingly. "And he gave me this."

Behind them, the students and teachers appeared, pushing Jan and Rachel in front of them as if they were pigs going to market. Fabian saw the terror in Rachel's eyes. Even Jan had turned ash-grey. A fresh bruise shone on his temple.

Janina pulled out a huge coin and let it dance on her fingers. "I'm afraid I can't give it to you, though. It's mine." She dropped it on the ground. "They're here. Grow!"

Matt dived for the coin, but before he could grab it, it sank into the soil. Despite digging his fingers in, he couldn't retrieve it. Meanwhile, Janina was sinking too. She stretched out her arms and raised her face to the sky as if welcoming salvation.

Fabian jumped forward to grab her under the arms. Though slow, Janina's sinking was impossible to stop. "Janina, he's a demon. You can't believe him. There's no reward or..." He didn't know what else to say to convince her.

In front of him, Matt shook his head. "She's sold her soul to him."

"Help me!" Fabian shouted instead.

Matt humoured him, but even together they couldn't slow Janina's descent. Soon, the girl had sunk too low for them to hold on. Her face was the last thing they saw of her, still full of creepy bliss.

Fabian stared at the ground between them. "So, did we win?" It was a horrible thing to say after what they'd just witnessed.

The mob had reached them, shoving Rachel and Jan forward, but they seemed unsure of what to do with them now. Matt swallowed. Not a good sign.

"Something's grow—" Samantha started.

An explosion cut her off. Next to them, the retaining wall of the cafeteria was blown to rubble. Thigh-thick roots and vines burst from the ruin, striking into the crowd that had surrounded them. Some people were hit and fell to the ground as collectibles. The rest seemed to wake up. Screaming, they ran away.

The six of them stared into the ruin at a flower growing in the remains of an oven, an empty vial next to it. It had meaty, red-pulsing blossoms as big as baking trays, and it emanated heat as if they were standing in front of a blazing fire.

"Did the school just blow up?" Jan asked.

"You wish," Lucille muttered as she hugged herself.

The plant was like nothing Fabian had ever seen. It reminded him of that stinking one from the Indonesian rainforest. But this was even bigger. "Sam, you know magical plants, right?"

"Not this one." Her voice was shaking.

"Looks straight out of Hell to me," Matt replied instead.

"How do we get rid of it?" The question wasn't asked by any of them, but Cian, the only one apart from them who'd stayed behind.

Samantha turned to him, surprised. "You're still here."

"So are you," he replied, then nodded at the plant. "So, what does this thing do?"

Behind him, a root broke out of the ground, almost as if it was sneaking up on him.

"Careful!" Samantha sprinted towards him, but it was too late. The root hit Cian in the back and he turned into a figurine, falling into Samantha's outstretched hands.

Samantha stumbled and fell to the ground. While she missed the root, a couple of vines came to life, quickly wrapping themselves around her body and neck. The root was lowering itself to her face.

Matt's sword cut through the wood. He hacked at the vines until Samantha could free herself.

Unfortunately, his aggression woke up the entire plant. All around them, vines and roots swung around like bewitched snakes. Jan grabbed a vine and pulled while kicking away another. Lucille threw fire at them, but her spells didn't burn. Instead, the plant grew. Meanwhile, Rachel picked up a spade and stomped towards the flower.

She walked five metres closer before she cowered and jerked away from it. "It's too hot!"

The air around the flower was flickering like a desert hallucination, but heat Fabian could deal with. He concentrated on all the water around him and pointed his delta at the blossom. Water shot out in a concentrated stream. A second later, four vines wrapped around his arms and brutally tore them to the side until he thought his shoulders would rip apart again.

"Matt!" Fabian shouted, then grunted in pain.

But the saving cut of Matt's sword never came. Looking over his shoulder, Fabian saw Matt defending himself and Samantha from various vines.

"It doesn't like water," Samantha shouted at him.

Fabian had found out that much. And because of it, the plant didn't seem to like him either.

Samantha gave Matt a push. "Go cut off the plant. I'll be fine."

Matt paused for a second. "And how am I supposed to do that? Throw my sword into that oven?" Instead, he shot energy at the flower.

The blossoms pulsed, burning red, and then it grew.

"Damn!" Matt cursed. "Definitely from Hell! Careful!"

He leaned over Samantha to cut off a root tip. As he did so, a vine wrapped around both of them. Samantha tried to stop it, but two more attacked them and tied her firmly to Matt, who wisely let go of his sword before he sliced Samantha open.

"Awesome," Samantha huffed sarcastically.

Matt looked distressed. "It wasn't my fault."

Fabian strained his head, jerking at the vines that held him. He wanted to help. Already, a fresh root had broken from the soil. "Sam!"

"I know." Unable to move, Samantha squeezed her eyes shut. The root touched first her, then Matt. Entwined as they were, the two fell into the soil as one piece.

"Damn it!" Fabian's voice shook. He gave his vines another jerk, but they were pulled so taut he was barely able to twitch.

Lucille had been running towards Samantha and Matt and was now quickly backing away as the root came for her.

Fabian's left arm shook suddenly, causing him to grunt. He looked around and saw Rachel hacking at the vines with her spade. Yellow juice was flying in droplets from countless little wounds, but the vines wouldn't budge.

Behind her, Jan was trying to keep seven vines at bay, sweat flooding his face. "Hey!" he shouted, breathless. "Does anyone have a plan?"

Water. The plant hated water, which meant they needed water to defeat it. Fabian couldn't bring his hands together, but they were in the school garden. "Water spout, left."

"I see it." Lucille called. She dashed through the bushes where the rusty valve poked from the ground. A water hose was attached to the spout.

Grimacing, Lucille managed to open the valve, then quickly picked up the water hose and pointed it at the flower. The red became a little less intense, and Fabian believed it was shrinking.

Lucille shrieked suddenly, and he quickly turned his head to watch her getting soaked by water. The hose had burst behind her when a root had twisted it shut. Now the root moved forward and hit Lucille over the head. She turned into a figurine and fell into the developing swamp at her feet. The water from the broken hose drained into the soil uselessly.

"Could. Use. Help." Jan kicked away one vine, ducked under another, and jumped over a root.

Then a vine got hold of his foot and pulled his leg out from under him. Before Jan crashed to the ground, the root touched and turned him.

The tension on Fabian's left arm was suddenly reduced as one of the vines snapped under Rachel's spade attack. Several vines had already wrapped around his body, immobilising him further, but his left arm was finally free. Unfortunately, the cut-off vine wrapped itself around Rachel's waist.

Leaning forward, he was only able to hold on to Rachel's hand when the plant ripped her off her feet. "Don't leave me!"

Rachel shrieked, then her hand slipped from his and she was dragged into the greenery.

Fabian huffed. Another vine had already caught his arm and returned it to its previous position. Ahead of him, three roots broke from the ground.

This was it. He'd always known they'd die one day. One by one, Malcolm's pet plant had taken them out, and though its weakness was Fabian's strength, there was nothing he could do with his arms apart like that. Stupid water. It was never available when he needed it and burst from him when he couldn't control it.

Startled, he jerked his chin. He'd never formed a delta with his fingers when his water bottles burst or when the pipes had broked in the Physics room. "Forget the delta," Fabian told himself, and instead concentrated on all his emotions. There was despair at seeing his friends fall, and there was anger. Terrible, burning anger at Malcolm, who thought he could come here and ruin his life.

Water burst from every crook and cranny. It shot up from the pond and out of the hose, quickly drowning the entire school garden. The roots—one of which was centimetres from his face—shook and wrinkled. Instead of lashing out, they withdrew into the ground as if that could save them from Fabian's wrath.

The vines around his body loosened, and he fell onto his knees into the mud. For a moment, his body shook uncontrollably as the tension left it, but then Fabian raised his eyes at the flower. It alone was still safe from the water, protected by the walls of the oven and the heat.

With a grunt, Fabian brought his arms forward, forcing the water around him to come together in one powerful jet stream. It hit the flower straight in the burning pistils. Steam rose, covering the cafeteria from his sight, but Fabian continued until all his anger was spent, and the water no longer followed his call.

Vines and roots had sunk into the mud. When the steam eased, soggy white blossoms hung listlessly from the burst oven door. Water glistened on every surface. And all around him, the figurines turned back into humans.

Under a row of bushes, Rachel rubbed the mud out of her face. Jan stumbled around, throwing another punch, only to realise his opponents were gone. Lucille groaned as she pushed herself up from the swamp she'd accidentally created. On the other side, Matt had his arm slung around Samantha, but she was holding hands with Cian, who looked confused.

"What happened?" Cian asked.

Matt glanced around. "The plant is gone."

"Could you let go of me, then?" Samantha asked tersely. She'd already released Cian. As soon as Matt followed her suggestion, she came running to Fabian. "Are you alright?"

Fabian was still too weak to hoist himself up, so he took her help gladly. "You're all back."

Her eyes widened. "Does that mean *you* defeated the plant?"

He gave her a lop-sided grin. "I thought it needed a bit of water." The grin grew wider. "The plant didn't think so."

Samantha burst out laughing and threw her arms around him. The tension of the fight was easing. Even Lucille had given up on trying to save her ruined outfit and proudly raised her mud-crusted chin.

"We did it," Fabian breathed.

Samantha grinned at him. "You did it."

Matt

School seemed to be out after the plant disaster. The six and Cian were the only ones left at school. They'd washed off the mud in the bathrooms, and Lucille had changed into her PE outfit before they gathered in the student hall with their bags. Samantha and Cian had been first there, locked into what looked like a tense conversation.

"Are you going to explain what's going on now?" Cian asked.

Samantha was looking down on her cell phone and frowning. Then she glanced at him apologetically. "Not today, okay? It's... it's a long story and I'm too exhausted right now." When Cian made a face, she added, "But I will. I still owe you a date, right?"

That made his face light up instantly. "Yes!"

"Get home safely."

"You, too." Cian nodded at Matt and the others and made his way out of the hall.

Samantha grabbed her bag and joined them. Before she could attach herself to Fabian or Lucille as usual, Matt walked up beside her.

"Do you like him?" he asked, proud of how even he'd held his voice. The sight of her and Cian together did something funny to his stomach. He never thought there was much of the House of Envy in him, but it seemed to be the opposite way when it regarded Samantha.

"No," Samantha said promptly, then sighed. "If I did, you'd only take him away from me, wouldn't you?"

Dumbfounded, Matt's feet stopped working. He stood there and watched her walk away, joining arms with Fabian, clearly putting on a mask as she laughed at him. For months, she'd accused him, confronted him again and again about what he couldn't undo. Reconciling had seemed pointless, because it wouldn't have changed anything.

But this... Was Samantha truly afraid he'd do it again? That he was out to ruin her life, to take everything from her, never letting her be happy? The old part in him, the one raised in Hescaryn, wanted to say that it wasn't his responsibility. That it was her problem if she couldn't understand it'd been a one-time thing, a fluke, an accident. Things had changed, though. *He* had changed.

Seeing her with Cian, kissing him... it scared Matt. The realisation hit him like Caspar's fist. All this time he'd convinced himself he didn't care, he'd been lying to everyone, including himself. Her barbs had annoyed him on the surface, but secretly he'd enjoyed her fire, enjoyed that she wouldn't simply back down, not even when her opponent could easily kill her—and had been proven to do such a thing before. He liked Samantha, even when she hated him, and as long as she was fighting with him, she was still his. In a way, at least. So, seeing her potentially move on with someone else scared him. He was losing her. No, he'd already lost her.

If I did, you'd only take him away from me, wouldn't you?

No, he wouldn't hurt Cian. If he did, everything he'd said about New Year's being a one-off would've been a lie. Another pretence.

Slowly, things began to shift in his mind, and Matt began to see what he'd truly done to Samantha. An apology wouldn't change what happened to Daniel. That would always stand between them. But this fear that he would continue to mess up her life because he couldn't let go of her—that didn't need to continue. An honest apology would help. Not him, but her. And it was high time he made this about her.

No demon would care, but that was only another lie he'd wrapped himself in. Matt wasn't a demon. He'd never had been.

"Are you coming, Matt?" Lucille called from further down the path.

Pulled out of his frightening thoughts, Matt jumped after the group and almost landed in a tree, feeling disoriented for a moment. "What the—" Why were his space-jumps suddenly all over the place? And why did they feel so unreliable? As if there wasn't any space to cross?

"Everybody, look!" Rachel shouted.

Rachel *shouted.* That girl never raised her voice in blind panic. She held all her feelings inside, curled up as tight as a ball.

"What is that?" Fabian asked, sounding similarly shocked.

Matt fought himself free of poking branches and thorny bushes and joined the group on the pathway. From where he stood, all he saw was one of the pavement stones tilted upwards, creating a bit of a hazard, but nothing more. It wasn't until he stood next to Fabian and stared straight down the stone that he felt his blood drain from his veins.

Where the stone tilted into the ground, a hole had appeared. It was only as big as his palm, but it gave view to a sight Matt had never thought he'd see in Ashuan: red glowing caves and endless darkness.

"Is that...?" Lucille started.

"Hell," Matt said glumly. They were looking down into Hescaryn. In the middle of the school. In an entirely different world. Nothing was making sense anymore.

"Uhm, guys." Samantha was taking a step back, looking at her cell phone. "So, I probably should have said that... five minutes earlier." They'd only had time to check their phones a couple of minutes ago. "My grandmother's called several times. She's messaged that we need to come to her as fast as possible."

They all exchanged gloomy glances. Even Matt began to worry. The sight of Hescaryn had unsettled him. And Elda was one competent witch. If she was reaching out like this, something serious was happening. And it most likely had to do with Malcolm.

"Well, let's check it out then," Jan said and started walking towards the exit.

"And here I thought I deserve a nice comfy pizza night after that plant madness," Fabian muttered.

Matt chuckled softly. "I'll shout you a pizza after whatever this is." After all, without Fabian he'd still be some tiny figurine. And likely would've been for the rest of his existence.

Jan reached the gate first, took one step out of school, and stopped, unmoving. Annoyed he was blocking the exit, Matt pushed him forward and squeezed through. He very nearly paused as well.

Greenvalley was not looking like it had this morning. Suddenly, the weakness of the abstract space made sense to Matt. No wonder he couldn't jump between worlds if the two worlds were practically sticking to each other.

Large patches of pavement had become endless pits. Buildings were tilting as if Ashuan's surface was sinking while still tethered to some shred of reality on one side. The streets themselves were deserted. People had either fled or fallen into Hell.

"Well…" Matt cleared his voice. "I guess we'd better get to Elda as fast as possible."

Rachel

Rachel swallowed heavily as she gathered with the others in front of the school. What she saw in front of her looked like a nightmare landscape. It was as if she'd stepped into the dreamworld, yet somehow taken everyone with her. Even the sky above was a sickly purple-grey colour that had no business existing in reality.

"I suppose the plant was a distraction," she said slowly, almost pausing after every word, as if she had to wrap her mind around it to fall from her lips.

Next to her, Samantha swallowed. "While we were running for our lives, Malcolm did this here."

Jan broke free from his stance, rubbing his face with two hands while he paced around. "What is this? What is happening here? And how the hell do we stop it from happening?"

"By stopping Malcolm," Matt said calmly, though he shrugged immediately after. "At least I hope that suffices."

"Not helpful, man." Fabian shook his head, but he seemed a lot less flustered than usual. "So, how do we find him?"

"At the spring of magic," Rachel said before Samantha could. "He wants its magic."

Samantha nodded. "I don't know how this is helping him, but it might just be a side effect of whatever he is planning. We know he's not exactly mindful."

"What he really wants isn't magic, though," Matt explained. "He wants the Black Throne."

"The Black Throne?" Lucille asked.

"Whoever sits in it rules Hescaryn. It's been empty for over a millennium."

Rachel snorted. If there was one thing Malcolm was lacking, it certainly wasn't ambition. "I think it's safe to say the day of the prophecy is today, then. We need our Emblems of Power to stop him."

"I need to see my family," Jan declared instead, about to stride off. He took his cell phone and walked a few steps to make a call. Almost immediately, he put the phone away again. "No signal."

Rachel ignored him. "My dreamweb is at home. I'll need to get it." This was what she'd been waiting for.

"Same with the feather," Fabian said, and Samantha added, "My flowers are also at home."

"I also need to go home," Jan declared.

"Guys, stop!" Matt shook his head. "We have no idea what's out there. We need to stick together."

Lucille put a hand on his arm. "We can't. If we have to go to Rachel's, Fabian's, and Samantha's, it'll take too long." As Jan was about to open his mouth, she gave him a hard glance. "Jan, you're wearing your bracelet." She touched her necklace to make sure it was truly there.

"This is a different one," Jan shot back, then kicked the ground. "I just want to check whether Anne got home alright."

"But your place is the furthest from here and the forest," Lucille pressed, not unkindly.

Matt stepped towards Jan, reaching out a hand. "Lucille's right. We don't have time for check-ins."

Jan batted his arm away. "Demons might not care for their family, but I do. I actually do." He'd never given the impression that he did, but the distraught expression on his face said otherwise. "Aren't you worried about your parents? About Meg?"

"Of course we are," Samantha said gently. "But the only way we can help them is by reaching Malcolm as fast as possible and stopping him. We don't know how long it'll take for all of Greenvalley to sink into Hell."

Beaten, Jan lowered his head.

"Okay," Rachel said after a little pause. "We split into teams of two. This way, no one is alone, but we save time. We meet at the Magic Circle..." She swallowed again. "If it still stands."

Rachel was going with Matt, which would've been the jackpot if he could reliably space-jump. As it was, they had to do it a couple of times to get across large patches of Hell that had swallowed parts of her neighbourhood. With every jump, though, Matt appeared more and more exhausted.

"Are you okay?" she asked when he had to catch his breath after a particularly bad jump.

Matt shook his head. "It's getting worse. The whole space is twisted."

"You don't say."

They walked down the street, past what had been a thriving corner shop this morning. Now there was only a huge hole in the ground, while the neighbouring houses were tipping down. It was as if gravity had given up on itself and abandoned all physical laws. The thought was deeply unsettling. As comfortable as Rachel was with the dreamworld doing such things, she preferred her real world stable and well-defined.

"Can I ask you something?" Matt said softly. He had his hands in his pocket while his gaze roamed their surroundings continuously.

Rachel shrugged.

"Samantha said... Well, she indicated that I would kill everyone who gets too close to her."

"Is it true?" Rachel was of the opinion it certainly wasn't too far off from the truth. Ever since his nightmare, she knew how much Samantha meant to him, but he seemed to be incapable of showing that love in a healthy way. She just found it hard to blame him for it when she reminded herself he'd grown up in the world that was shimmering through the cracks in the pavement.

There was no sun in Hell and no sky. It was a world that completely defied earthly physics. A place of magic, but also darkness. Even as they walked past the rim of it, Rachel only dared a few quick glances. She saw pitch-black corridors and glowing red. Once, she noticed a field strewn with bones and hurried on. She couldn't even imagine how one could spend their life in such a place and retain a shred of humanity. When life was all about survival, death had a different meaning. It wasn't something the survivors were used to caring about.

"Of course I wouldn't." Matt scrunched up his nose. "It *was* a one-off thing." Then he sighed. "I mean... I know it's wrong. What I did was wrong." That was new. "If I were a true demon, I wouldn't care. I-I would've walked away from her, but I keep coming back. And Cian... gosh, he's so obnoxious." Slowly, Matt's confession was turning into a rant. "He thinks we're friends or something, and keeps asking me if I'm okay with him going for Samantha. Like, dude, if you want to make out with her, just do it. Stop rubbing my nose in it."

"So, you're okay with them?" Rachel knew he wasn't, but Matt was so stubborn about pesky feelings that he generally refused to acknowledge his own.

He shrugged and said, "Yeah, sure..." His shoulders deflated again. "No, not really. I mean she's not into him, right?"

Rachel didn't have an answer to that. Samantha had never spoken about Cian. She certainly hadn't gushed about him like she had about Daniel. Rachel was aware they had Chemistry together and it was a small class, but beyond that, she had no idea.

"Fine," Matt continued, without waiting for her response. "I'm not okay with it. Absolutely not. I don't like him, but I'm not going to hurt him. I've learnt my lesson."

Rachel stopped, staring at him in surprise. "You did?"

Matt looked down, more self-conscious than she'd ever seen him, and rubbed his neck. "I'm starting to see it... the human way."

There was still some resistance, then. Rachel thought about whether she should tell him what Samantha had said. That after they'd dealt with Malcolm, she'd be done with him. Lucille would do it, being her usual meddling self, but not Rachel. This was something Matt and Samantha had to figure out for themselves one way or the other, so all she said was, "Good."

She kept on walking, finally reaching her own street. Like most of Greenvalley, it was tilting, slowly sinking into Hell. "We need to hurry."

The street became steeper and steeper, forcing her to slow down. Still, Rachel skittered on the asphalt until she almost slammed into a lamppost. Matt caught up to her and extended his hand. "Your house is sinking."

Rachel looked ahead and gasped. It was true. Her house was already sinking into Hell. The entrance door was gone, which meant most of the first floor would be too. "What will happen to it?" Where was the other half of her house? Was it still salvageable, or would they all be homeless by the time they'd dealt with Malcolm? *If* they were even alive, to care.

"We can't worry about that now." Matt grabbed her and they space-jumped once more, straight into her room.

Seeing her dreamweb gave Rachel hope. Surely, with their Emblems of Power they could stop a power-hungry demon. They were legendary artefacts that once stopped the most powerful mage in all of history. As frightening as Malcolm was, he still felt only... demon to her. Just one person. And they were six, carrying the souls of legendary heroes. They could do this.

"Help!" her mother screeched from somewhere further down the corridor. "Is there someone? Please! Help!"

Rachel grabbed her dreamweb and hurried outside. She found her mother holding onto the bannister on the stairs. She was lying on the floor, her lower body trapped in black tar.

She saw Rachel and sniffled. "I fell. Rachel, please. Something's down there."

Matt strode past Rachel, grabbed her mother under the arms, and pulled. He almost had her out when something pulled from the other side. Annette screamed, and both she and Matt almost tumbled back down the stairs.

Reflexively, Rachel grabbed something off the shelf next to her—an ugly souvenir—and threw it in the hole. Two books and a flat bowl followed.

The hole hissed back. Apparently, she'd hit something, and Matt managed to pull Annette out of it. Her mother's legs were bleeding, looking as if a tiger had attacked her with its claws. She stumbled into Rachel's arms and sobbed.

What followed out of the hole almost made Rachel scream. It looked reptilian, like an over-grown elongated toad the size of a large pig, but it walked on six legs, each of them with curved claws.

"What is this?" Annette screeched.

Matt had drawn his sword. "Get her into your room!"

Rachel didn't hesitate. She took her mother's hand and dragged her along. The safety of her room was laughable. That monster toad could easily break down her door, and more importantly, the house was still sinking. Her room was about as high as they could go in the house.

"Rachel, what... what is going on here?" Her mother paced around, unable to sit despite her bleeding legs. "There... there's a monster. And the house..."

The door opened, and Matt entered. There was a scratch on his arm, but it was already healing. Splatters of green covered his already mud-stained clothes. "The house stopped sinking. Have you got everything?"

Rachel assured herself that the dreamweb was still in her hand. "Let's go."

"Rachel, where—?"

"Mum, we don't have time for explanations. Matt and I need to go. You... push the closet in front of the door." Hopefully, the house had truly stopped sinking. Rachel took Matt's hand.

"Rachel!"

Once more, they tumbled through the abstract space, landing outside of her home. The landing was bad enough to make them both stumble into the greenery. Matt winced and rubbed his chest, but then he looked up at the house. "Do you want me to get her out?"

"And bring her where?" Rachel's heart was beating like a drum roll. Had she just abandoned her mother to certain death? She hadn't even taken care of her wounds. But what else could she have done? The only thing to stop her world from falling apart was to find the one who had caused this madness.

"I'm not sure I've got another jump in me," Matt said, before finally getting himself back to his feet.

Rachel nodded. "You need to conserve your energy."

While she believed they'd stood no chance without the Emblems of Power, the same wasn't true for Matt. He was the only one who could match Malcolm's power. It would be his sword that would end the archdemon, just as it had been Kairos' sword that had ended Draken. As much as she wanted to avenge Nico, the way to do so was through Matt.

He was their only hope.

Fabian

Apart from a few roads on the mountainside, the township of Greenvalley was mostly flat. Fabian's neighbourhood was definitely flat. The street Fabian lived on had always been flat. Not so anymore. He and Jan were climbing up a fifty-degree incline, having to use the fences on the side to steady themselves against the pavement.

"Are you sure we're going the right way?" Jan asked in front of him. "I don't remember you guys living on a hill."

"I don't either." Fabian pointed at the house behind the fence. "But that's Keschecke's house, and they're just down the street from us."

They kept climbing a little further. There seemed to be a top to the incline, which made Fabian hope his house was in a normal state. But when Jan reached the top—or rather, was high enough to look over the edge—he cursed. "Looks to me like you're the ones living down the street."

He held out his hand. Fabian pulled himself up—and almost lost his footing as his mind jumped into full-alert mode for fear of falling. His fingers dug into the edge of the street. The *edge* of the street. While they'd been walking up a really steep incline, it was nothing compared to what the street looked like on the other side. They were facing a near-vertical drop for as far as they could see. Somehow, the houses, their fences, and gardens were still intact. At least everything attached to the ground was. Jan pulled a pen from his backpack and put it on the surface. It fell straight down.

"How is this even possible?" Fabian swallowed, looking down on his house and garden. "I don't see our chickens."

"Sorry, man." Jan took his backpack off and rubbed his hands. "Let's concentrate on reaching the feather. I'll hold your arms while you try to reach the streetlamp below us. From there, we can make it to your fence and use that as a ladder to climb further down."

Fabian stared at him as if he'd gone mad. "You want to go down there?"

"Do you want to kick Malcolm's ass or not?"

Once more, Fabian glanced down at his house. If Rachel was right with her prophecy, they needed all six emblems. Giving up was not an option. "Alright."

He started slowly by swinging one leg over the edge. Jan grabbed his wrists and looked him darkly in the eyes. "I've got you."

Fabian swallowed heavily while his fingers clenched around the edge. Then he pulled his second leg over. The angle was just enough for him to find a little purchase as he pressed his knees on the asphalt. His arm muscles, already over-exerted enough for one day, screamed when he forced them to hold his weight. He carefully stretched one leg down, searching with his foot for the lamppost.

"A little to the right," Jan said. "And lower."

Lower meant not being able to use his upper arm strength. Fabian wasn't the strongest. He could barely manage a pull-up. If he let loose, he'd never get himself back up again.

"Do it."

Straining as hard as he could, Fabian tried to lower himself millimetre by millimetre. He couldn't do it. It wasn't possible. And then his arms gave way, and the tension was lost. His body plummeted into the deep.

A jerk went through his shoulders, and he stopped falling. Hardly breathing, Fabian looked up. Jan held him, only his set jaw betraying his exertion. "Can you reach it now?"

Fabian felt the lamppost against his right shin. Adrenaline was coursing through his veins, his heart racing. He managed to raise his leg enough to put his foot on the lamppost. From there, he pushed himself up again to plant his second foot on it. Then he pressed his face against the asphalt and breathed.

Jan gave him a few seconds, his grip still strong around Fabian's wrists, before he asked, "Can you reach the fence?"

Slowly, Fabian turned his face to glance down on it. The fence line started around half a metre below the streetlamp, one-and-a-half metres to his right. He almost cried. "I'll have to lean that way."

"One arm. You stretch out your right, lean that way, and then you jump."

"I jump?"

"You jump."

Fabian's head felt impossibly light. He tried not to think about how deep the street was falling or where it landed, but it was impossible to ignore the looming darkness. On the other hand, there was no going back up, which seemed like a huge oversight, assuming they didn't only want to grab the feather, but make their way back. Panic was rising from his belly and tightened his airways. He was caught here, in a precarious balance on a lamppost with an endless drop to Hell below him.

"I've got you." Jan's voice was as strong as his grip.

Peeking up, Fabian saw the bracelet around his friend's wrist. It was supposed to give its bearer strength. He was pretty sure Jan didn't love him, as his emblem was the power of love, but he probably liked him enough not to let him fall.

He fixed the fence with his stare. It was doable. Not easy, but doable. Slowly, he lowered his right arm. Jan let go of it, instead holding on to his left with both hands. The sudden lack of a hold on his right arm caused Fabian's stomach to lurch, but he breathed through his nose and slowly the feeling passed.

With his now-free hand, he ran over the asphalt, looking for anything to hold on to. There was nothing. Jumping was his only option. Slowly, he turned his body towards the fence. He contemplated stretching one leg out and seeing how far it would get him. Not that he had ever tried lying on the street, straddling a fence and lamppost at the same time, but he was sure his legs were long enough to do so without having to do the splits. He couldn't jump on one leg, though, so instead, he bent his knees slightly. The lamppost beneath him appeared to shake, but he figured out quickly it was his legs instead.

"Jump!"

Jan's single word jolted his body into action. Without thinking, Fabian flew forwards, one arm outstretched, legs scraping on the asphalt. Jan gave his other arm an extra swing before letting go. Fabian fell.

One foot touched the edge of his fence, then slipped off. While his knee hit the fence, his body's momentum catapulted him flat against the fence line. Fabian slammed into the wooden slats and knocked his chin against them. Immediately, his fingers searched for the slats and clawed into them, holding on for dear life, though his body was lying flat on the side of the fence.

It took him several minutes to relax his grip and pull himself up to a sitting position. His entire body felt like pudding, but he found his breath.

Fabian looked up at Jan, who'd been watching him the whole time. "I hate you."

Jan cracked a smile. "Good. Get ready to catch me, then."

It was three metres down to the fence, and the slats weren't that stable. Fabian doubted they would hold Jan if he crashed straight into them. But Jan didn't jump on the fence. Instead, he lowered himself to the lamppost with admirable ease. His shorter length meant he had to hang with his whole body extended to reach the lamppost, but he barely paused before turning around and jumping into Fabian's arms.

Together, they stumbled across the fence line. One of the slats cracked, the sound making Fabian's heart stop. A few seconds, neither of them moved. The fence held.

Jan grinned. "Alright. Let's use the fence to climb down."

He went first, gripping the slats as if they were rungs of a ladder. It wasn't the most comfortable climb. The slats hurt to hold on to and the gaps were large enough to put a hand through, but not large enough to push their shoes in further than the tip. Still, they climbed until they'd reached the post box.

"Bushes," Jan said, pointing to the row of bushes lining the path to the door. "It's a little flatter here, so if we hold on to the bushes, we should make it to the door. If we fall, the lower row of bushes will catch us."

"Roses," Fabian muttered. "They're roses."

Jan gulped. "I suggest not falling, then."

Fabian gave him a mirthless laugh. His mother was very particular about her roses, and now they'd be using them like monkey bars. And if they were unlucky, their safety net was another layer of thorny rose bushes.

Since there was no point in going back, the rose bushes it was. At least Jan was right, and the terrain was a little flatter. Using the corner stones of the pavement as a ledge, the two boys balanced over to the house, ignoring the thorns tearing their palms open.

At last, there was the door. Fabian was thankful for the architecture, which allowed them to stand on the side of the doorway while he bent in half to put his key in the keyhole. He pushed the door open, wincing as it slammed into the opposite wall. Then he stepped inside and walked a few steps before his legs gave in and he sank onto the wall.

Jan lay down next to him, at last letting go of his controlled mask. He rubbed his eyes with the balls of his hand and moaned. "Why rosebushes? Why?" Like Fabian's, his hands were full of bloody scratches.

"At least they're sturdy wood."

"True. Okay, where's your feather?"

Fabian pointed to the side at the stairs. "Up in my room. I mean, to the side in my room."

Jan snickered and sat up to regard the lying staircase. "Interesting architecture choice. Let's go." He reached out his hand and pulled Fabian up. "This part should be easy."

They'd managed to retrieve the feather just fine, and Fabian even found little Merle curled up in the crook of his desk, frightened out of her mind. The cat was now snuggled up in an old backpack, mewling softly. In the attic, they'd found a ladder, which Jan had used to help them climb up the last part of the street from the fence line. They'd also found leftover fireworks from New Year's and taken those.

Safely back on a more reasonable geography, they hurried towards the Magic Circle, arriving there at the same time as Lucille and Samantha. The store was still standing, but it was being attacked by an ogre-like creature with a thorny club. Both Fabian's mum and Matt's dad were fighting against the monster, aided by Menuha.

Fabian had no idea what had brought these three together in this place. He pushed the frightened kitten into Jan's arms and joined the battle with a powerful stream of water that hit the ogre in the chest and caused it to tumble sideways. Next to him, Lucille put a spell on the creature, summoning a swarm of black moths that swept over the ogre's head and covered its eyes.

The monster swayed from side to side, then blindly whirled its bat around, nearly taking René's head out. Menuha shot energy at it, but it hardly made a scratch. The ogre roared, smashing its club into the witch puppet display outside of the shop. Little heads and broomsticks flew everywhere, showering the pavement.

Footsteps sounded behind them, then Matt jumped into battle, sword drawn. Meanwhile, Samantha took the flowers she had retrieved and turned them a pale pink. "Fabian, I need wind. You've got your feather, don't you?"

Confused, he nodded. Then he remembered that his feather could summon wind if flicked. He pulled it out of his pocket and took position. "Ready when you are."

"Go."

Fabian struck with his feather, causing a small gust to blow against the ogre. Samantha shook pollen from her flowers, and the wind took them straight into the ogre's face.

It made one step, swayed to the right, then pirouetted around its left, and crashed to the ground, snoring. Menuha jumped forward, opened its mouth, and shot energy into it. The snoring stopped.

"Not bad," Menuha said with a grin to Samantha and Fabian. "You usually have to wear them down for ages."

Matt nodded tightly. "Their thick skin—" He suddenly gasped and fell to his knees.

Next to him, Menuha did the same, her eyes widening with terror. Both of them were writhing on the ground in some deep, invisible pain.

"What's happening?" Fabian asked.

Samantha's eyes widened. "It's the rivers of magic. They're gone."

Matt

The lack of magic, fortunately, didn't last longer than a few minutes. Still, it left Matt weak and aching inside, just like he'd felt when Malcolm had blocked his magic and left him for dead.

This time, Caroline came through with a special tea that restored him sip by sip. She also had cookies, which were very welcomed by the group. Only Fabian refused to even acknowledge them. Instead, he sat cross-legged on the floor and watched a tiny fountain of water springing from his hand.

"We'll never defeat Malcolm," he said at last. "Unless he doesn't like to be splashed like that plant of his."

"We've got fireworks." Jan sounded almost upbeat. "Some of them are as good as magic."

Samantha had her hands wrapped around a cup of her own. "The rivers are flowing again, but they're weak and unstable. Nevertheless, they're still connected to the spring. If Malcolm is there, magic is too. Probably. He won't be able to do much if he's lying writhing on the ground."

Matt winced, remembering how he'd been writhing on the ground only ten minutes ago. "So, we just have to get to him."

"And in the meantime, monsters attack Greenvalley," Fabian claimed. "At least, the part that hasn't sunk into Hell yet." He looked at his mother, who was cradling their cat. "We lost all our chickens."

"Chickens can be replaced." Caroline sighed, though, and pressed the cat closer to her chest. "I'm glad you're still here."

"I wonder if they're true Hellchickens now," Rachel said almost wistfully.

Fabian shot her an outraged look, and then he started laughing. Little later, Samantha giggled as well. Confused, Matt checked with Lucille and Jan, but they didn't seem to have any more idea than him.

Resolving himself to the fact that he'd never understand those three, Matt turned to his father and sister instead. "How come you're here?"

"Chay said you'd be coming here on your way past. And your father wanted to come along," Menuha said.

Matt swallowed at Chay's mention. "Is Chay coming too?" They could use the seer.

Menuha shook her head. "He trusts you'll do the right thing."

Chay hadn't come to see him since the Blood Night. After everything that had happened since, he couldn't help but feel like the older half-demon had abandoned him. Had Matt disappointed him? Matt snorted and shook his head. Of course he had. Chay would've never done the things Matt had. Nor would he have wasted half a year running from the consequences.

Suddenly, his father put his hand on Matt's. "If Chay says he trusts you, it means something." He gave Matt a wry smile. "I have to admit it gives me hope that he thinks you can handle this."

"René convinced me you could," Caroline said, her arms crossed defensively. She fixed Fabian with a teary stare. "If I could ground you, I would."

"Please don't. Just getting into the house once was enough," Fabian quipped.

The corners of Caroline's mouth twitched. "Well, you'll never leave the house again if you get yourself killed. Understood?"

Instead of pointing out the fallacies of that logic, Fabian got up and pulled his mother in a big hug. "I love you," Matt could hear him whisper.

Matt glanced at his father. In his eyes, he'd found a similar emotion, but both of them felt too awkward to voice it out loud.

"I'm glad you're coming with us," Jan said to René, as if to clear the air. "That gun you have will be very useful against Malcolm."

René shook his head. "I'm not coming. Caroline and I will do our best to fight off the monsters who're crawling into this world." Then he reached into his jacket and held the gun out to Jan. "But you're right. You could use this."

Jan stared. "But... didn't you say I needed to get a license or something?"

René chuckled. "I think we can all agree that this is an exception. You're going to need every help you can get to face an archdemon." He handed Jan the gun, who took it as if he'd been handed a newborn baby. René turned back to Matt. "Can I speak to you?" He nodded his head.

Confused, Matt got up and followed him to the back of the store. "What's the matter?"

"I know you're going to try to kill Malcolm. Apparently, your mother wants you to, as well." He nodded at Menuha.

Suddenly wary, Matt tensed. "My mother wants me to?"

"I'm sure your sister will make her case on the way." His father took a deep breath. "I just want you to think about it. I know Malcolm poses a huge danger, he needs to be stopped, but as for killing. He's still your uncle."

"You know that family in Hescaryn doesn't work that way," Matt said uneasily.

René nodded. "Yes, but... you're not in Hescaryn anymore. Just... if it can be avoided, think about it."

Matt frowned heavily. In his opinion, there was no scenario in which Malcolm could be stopped without being killed. Not without leaving the door wide open for deadly retribution. But his father was human, and softer-hearted than him. And he'd always advocated for Matt's humanity. Still... "There might not be a choice." He couldn't promise such a thing.

"There's always a choice."

"The rivers are getting weaker. We need to go," Samantha announced.

Matt nodded at his father. "I'll see you on the other side."

René put his hand on his shoulder and squeezed. "It's not just Chay who believes in you. I do, too."

It turned out his father was right. Menuha had been sent by their mother, with Chay merely telling her where to find them in the half-sunken Greenvalley.

"Why does she want her own brother dead?" Matt asked as they walked through the forest.

Even here, Hell was taking shape. They often had to change their path to walk around large holes or hold on to trees to cross particularly steep sections of forest. He and Menuha were walking at the back, while Samantha led them with her uncanny magic-sensing ability.

"Because he's begging to be killed." Menuha shrugged. "You're obviously going to fight him to defend your town. She just wants me to make sure you're the one who strikes the killing blow."

Matt scowled. First, his father asked him not to kill Malcolm because he was family, and now his mother had sent someone to make sure he *would* kill his uncle. Annoyed at himself, he shook his head. Malcolm deserved to die. He'd tried to kill Matt less than a week ago, and he'd do it again without thinking twice. Why did he have to consider sparing Malcolm's life just because he was supposed to be half-human?

"He's going to die tonight." Matt wouldn't let Malcolm kill his friends, that was for sure. "It won't matter who's the one that deals him the last blow." Samantha's Thorak dagger would be a nice choice as well.

"Oh, but it does. It matters a lot," Menuha said mysteriously, leaving Matt with a headache.

Just then, the group in front of them stopped. "What's up?" Matt asked and made his way to the front.

He'd only made it a few metres before he saw it for himself. In front of them was a huge strip of Hell. The other side was more than a hundred metres away and there was no way around it. The strip was just big enough that they could see a clear image of the place Greenvalley was being sucked into. It was a jagged, drab area with few remarkable landscape features.

"So, this is Hell?" Lucille asked.

"Not exactly the prettiest part of it, but yes." At some point, Matt wanted to show them the world he'd grown up in. As dangerous as it was, it was far more beautiful than those slivers were making it out to be. "Do you recognise this place, Menu?"

She nodded darkly. "Those are the training grounds of the Black Guard. I've visited Caspar a couple of times there. It'll be full of minor demons and other... discomforts."

"And that's where he's relocating Greenvalley?" Fabian asked, before huffing. "Awesome."

"How is all this possible?" Lucille asked, shaking her head. "How can Hell be here? I thought it was another world."

"It is." Matt raised his head, tearing his eyes away from the grey landscape, and found Lucille looking at him expectantly. "Do you really want to hear about world theory *now*?"

Next to her, Samantha raised her eyebrows. "Do you know anything about it?"

It was one of the subjects Chay had taught him. "A little. It's quite simple, actually. Or it's supposed to be. All the worlds or universes move through the abstract space on parallel... lanes. Sometimes worlds collide, but that's very rare." He swallowed, only now realising that the theory he'd once learned was a reality. "I suppose whatever Malcolm is doing is causing Ashuan's lane and Hescaryn's lane to cross."

"Are you saying the entire world will become one with Hell?" Fabian asked, his eyes wide with terror.

"Either that or Greenvalley simply breaks off and Ashuan jumps back on its original path." Matt shrugged. Both scenarios sounded equally horrible.

Jan clicked his tongue and kicked a pinecone into Hescaryn. "Guys, if I'd wanted another geography lesson, I would've stayed at school. How do we get across?"

Matt turned to Menuha. "Jumping?" He wasn't confident that they'd make the landing. But with the two of them, they'd at least be able to take his friends in one go.

His sister shook her head, though. "The magic around here is too weak and the stretch too big."

Matt sighed. "In that case, we're no longer wondering how we're gonna get across, but how we're going to go through."

"You want us to go through Hell?" Fabian asked. "Literally," he added belatedly.

"I don't see another choice."

Samantha stepped up to the edge. "It looks like we can climb in here. It's only a hundred metres across and I can still sense the rivers."

The eager part of him that simply refused to die was delighted she was keen to step into his world. Matt hid his burgeoning smile by making a flourished bow. "After you, then."

Naturally, she rolled her eyes at him. A small intake of breath was all that betrayed her apprehension. Carefully, she sat down on the forest floor and swung her legs over the edge. Just as she was about to touch the ground, Matt jumped ahead of her, almost spearing himself on a protruding spike.

Confused about his sudden appearance, Samantha stared at him. "You okay?"

Matt's heart was pounding. "Don't touch the grass. Unless you're keen on a week-long bleeding rash."

She nodded slowly, carefully digesting the information. "Okay. Can I lead now?"

"Sure." He stepped out of the way, accidentally brushing the grass he'd just warned her to avoid. Annoyed at himself, he clicked his tongue. A lack of caution got you killed in Hescaryn. So why was he bumbling around like a fool?

The others climbed in after Samantha, and they slowly made their way across the stretch. Matt glanced around nervously, expecting minor demons who'd be drawn to the weakness in space. Instead, he spotted a green lichen.

"Stop." His hand shot out to grab Samantha's arm.

"What now?" Samantha asked, starting to sound a little irritated.

Matt didn't reply. Instead, he bent down to pick up a stone and throw it at the ground in front of Samantha. She jerked back when the ground started to hiss and steam. The stone dissolved within seconds.

"That's what I thought. You see the lichen on the ground?" He pointed at it, while Samantha squinted her eyes. "They grow on acid soil."

"Acid soil?" she asked weakly.

Behind them, Fabian moaned. "Are you saying every step in Hell could be our last?"

"That's a given, but here especially," Matt replied, slowly regaining his confidence. "Maybe I should lead the way."

"Maybe you should," Samantha said pointedly. Then she nodded ahead. "The exit should be over there."

Though they only had to cross a hundred metres, it seemed much longer in Hescaryn. They couldn't even see the part which was Greenvalley. And with every further step, they ran in danger of not just running into a minor demon but the elite soldiers of Caspar's army. Or even Caspar himself. Thus, when something suddenly moved in front of them, even Matt got a fright.

It was even more embarrassing when he realised it was only a leathersnout: a grey, hairless creature that camouflaged perfectly in this drab area. Its snout was short but looked as if it had been longer until someone punched it into its head, thick rolls of leather surrounding it.

"It eats the grass," Matt shouted before anyone could think of attacking it. While the leathersnouts weren't particularly aggressive, their thick skin was near impenetrable and their weight enough to squash intestines and bones.

Everyone side-eyed the creature, but when it hardly moved, they all hurried along. The leathersnout snivelled louder and louder while they walked past. Then, when Lucille passed, it suddenly drew its head back and sneezed forcefully, covering Lucille from head to toe with green snot.

She shrieked and jumped to the side and would've fallen to the acid soil if Menuha hadn't held onto her.

Ruefully, Matt rubbed his neck. "I forgot they're allergic to humans." He'd once failed to escape the snot rain himself, one of Caspar's more harmless jokes. "It comes off with spit easily enough."

Lucille huffed. "Does it?" She looked as if she was about to faint. "I'm so going to throw these clothes away when we get home."

"I found it," Samantha announced. She'd walked a little further, wisely staying clear of everything but the ground.

Matt caught up to her and peered down into a pit. Tall pines grew below them. For a moment, his head spun. "How is it down, if it was up before?" There was no doubt about it that they were looking down on Greenvalley's forest.

"I guess the abstract space is called abstract for a reason." She pointed to one of the trees. "Do you think we can reach this one and climb down?"

If he'd needed more proof things were serious, it was Samantha's complete lack of passive aggression. She was concentrating solely on reaching their destination, there was no time to fight him. It made Matt heady from thinking how they could've been if he hadn't screwed it up.

He cleared his throat and checked out the tree. "That should work, yeah. Just let me go first."

Even with the limited space-jumping the melding allowed him, he managed to land on a good branch. Holding onto the trunk, he reached out for Samantha.

She took his hand, leaned forward, and managed the jump just fine. Her eyes glanced over at him before she faced the tree itself, picking her best way down. Matt watched her vanish between the branches. When he was sure she had safely reached the ground, he helped the next friend over and down.

When he'd finally made his way to the forest floor, Hell was below them again. Irritated, he shook his head and looked at the Greenvalley side in front of them.

Lucille was trying to rub off the sticky tree sap their hands were covered with and failed. "Hey, Sam, can we go to your grandma first? I swear I'm not being extra, but I'd really appreciate a break—and an opportunity to scrub off my hands."

"It's probably a good idea." Samantha nodded ahead. "Her house is close, and she might be able to help us. At the very least, we can pick up the crossbow for Rachel."

"Yes, please," Rachel said immediately.

It was a reasonable course of action, and so it was agreed.

While they walked down the driveway to Elda's house, Matt took Menuha to the side. "Be careful. Sam's grandma can smell demons or something like that. And she strikes first and asks questions later. Don't drink her tea."

Menuha chuckled. "Sounds like you've had some experience."

"Some bad experience."

"No, no, no, no..." Ahead of him, Samantha had suddenly started running.

Elda's house had appeared around the corner, not a piece of Hell around. Instead, a window was shattered, and the door was hanging on one hinge. All of Matt's alert systems flashed bright red.

"Sam, wait!"

But she was already inside. Matt jumped after her, mentally preparing himself to draw his sword. He crashed into the doorframe instead of hitting the steps and groaned. When would he ever learn that space-jumping wasn't much of an advantage right now? Without wasting any more time, he followed Samantha inside.

It was soon obvious there had been a fight in the house. Frames were splintered, and the floor was littered with fallen objects. The trail ended in the library. So many times, they'd sat here and discussed how to defeat monsters, from hellhounds to gnomes. They'd shed tears and shared laughter here. And they'd discussed the meaning of the prophecy that was tying them together.

Now, many of the books were lying on the ground, the armchair was overthrown, and in the middle of the room, a big blood stain coloured the carpet red. Samantha was kneeling in front of it, her hand hovering above the blood.

"Elda?" Matt asked softly.

His voice broke the spell on her. Her hand shook, and a loud sob tore from her throat. Then she burst into tears.

Samantha

They didn't have time for this.

Her grandmother had been attacked.

Greenvalley needed them.

So much blood.

She needed to snap out of this.

How?

"Here, drink this." Rachel pushed a cup of hot cocoa into Samantha's shaking hands.

Vaguely, Samantha became aware of Fabian kneeling next to her chair and stroking her knees. "She's alright," he whispered.

No one was alright after losing so much blood.

But her friends refused to believe it. Lucille looked at her with a reassuring smile. "Elda will be fine. This could've been Malcolm's blood. And now she's kicking his ass out of here."

"I should've come when she called."

Her grandmother had asked her to come at the weekend. She'd sounded worried, but Samantha had been distracted. Just as Malcolm had planned.

"I should've been here."

Sternly, Lucille said, "You couldn't have been. Just because there's blood doesn't mean your grandmother is dead. She's not here. That means she's alive. She's out there somewhere, giving Malcolm something to fear. She *is* the Greenvalley Witch, isn't she?"

"She's also seventy-two."

For years, Granny had defended Greenvalley, but she'd given up that task to them only too gladly.

Fabian grasped her knee. "If he's harmed her, we're going to end him."

It only made Samantha burst into tears again. Of course he'd harmed her. And ending him wouldn't bring her grandmother back.

Suddenly, Matt stepped up to her. The last person she wanted to see right now.

For a moment, he looked as if he was going to reach out to her, but then he thought better of it and stared at her with a hard look in his eyes. "Do you remember how she poisoned me?"

The question was so far left-field, Samantha stopped crying for a moment.

"You were all distracted with figuring out the konnurar. She gave me some tea and less than a minute later, I was on the ground, choking. She made me promise..." He looked down and swallowed. "I would've been dead within ten minutes of entering this house."

"And you think Malcolm stayed for a cup of tea?"

Matt's mouth twisted, half-amused. "No. What I'm saying is your grandmother is an extremely skilled witch who knows her way around demons. She's tough, and she has a bag of tricks, or she never would've gotten this old. Trust her."

"Matt's right," Fabian said. "Elda's one tough nut. And more importantly, we're going to find her. Everything will be alright."

"The faster we're on our way, the higher the chances she'll make it out alive," Matt said.

That did the trick. The real world came back to Samantha in painful clarity. She couldn't waste her time here crying and shivering. Her grandmother needed her. "Let's go and kick his greedy ass."

Matt smirked. "Yeah, let's do that."

Nobody talked on the way to the spring. With the continuing shifting of the worlds, the forest grew darker by the minute. The forest floor became firmer until they walked on more stone than pine needles, though the trees were still standing as close as they ever had. Whatever part of Hell this bit was sinking into, it was more artificial, hewn instead of grown. Samantha's suspicions were confirmed when a wall with beautiful but disturbing frescoes appeared. The artwork was exquisite, but the scenes depicted were enough to make her stomach turn.

"Greed," Menuha whispered next to her. "These walls show what happens to people who think they can steal from the Archdemon of Greed. We're entering his residence."

"His residence?" Was that where he was planning to suck them into? "He literally wants the spring of magic." When Menuha frowned, Samantha explained, "Malcolm has been trying to steal our magic for a year now. All his attempts failed, so instead of stealing the magic, he's stealing the spring itself."

Menuha shuddered. "Greed knows no boundaries."

"Yeah, but his guards do," Matt said, suddenly drawing his sword.

Two demons appeared between the trees, looking slightly disoriented. They were probably wondering since when the residence had become a forest habitat. As soon as they noticed the group, though, they launched into an attack.

"Scutum protecto!" Lucille shouted. Her shield appeared just in time to catch the incoming shots of energy, but the power of the impact made it fizzle out immediately.

Matt and Menuha shared a look, then they both stormed forward and answered the attack with some energy of their own.

Samantha fingered her Thorak nervously. It was a weapon designed to kill demons, and here were demons that would show no mercy. They might have looked like humans, but they were deadly monsters through and through, sworn to greed. She didn't really have a choice but to defend herself. Her grandfather must've killed dozens of demons with the Thorak in her hands. It knew their blood.

Fortunately, with so much deadly energy being shot around, the scuffle didn't last long enough for her to make a decision. The two guards ended up dead, and her Thorak unused.

Menuha looked down on them, not a twinge of regret in her face. "Simple uniforms, functional but unadorned. Definitely Malcolm's lackeys."

"There's more," Matt said, his head already whipping around.

Sure enough, four more demons came running at them, drawn in by the fight. Two of them extended their wings and launched themselves into the air. Energy burst into the trees, causing it to rain branches and pinecones.

Thunder tore the air apart, startling all of them, even the demons. Lightning wrapped around the wings of one demon. Her eyes widened in pain as her back arched against the crackle of lightning. Bereaved of her momentum, the demon tumbled to the ground. Meanwhile, Jan's arm was almost ripped out of its socket by the recoil of his gun. He ducked when two energy bolts shot at him. The demon he'd hit, though, was writhing on the ground, clearly without the resilience of an archdemon.

Matt stepped in to end her suffering, and Samantha quickly turned away. She knew he was being practical and was saving their lives by ending the demon's, but seeing the glint of metal brought back memories. Memories that shouldn't matter. Not now, at least. Matt was on her side. He was fighting for her city, her grandmother. He only did what had to be done. Now Samantha had to do the same.

Energy, magic, water, and crossbow bolts were flying across the clearing, making it almost impossible to differentiate friend from foe. Smoke was rising, and a swarm of moths soared. The demons jumped around at will, frequently disappearing just before a spell hit, only to reappear behind in a different spot. But they were also affected by the unstable rivers, or they would've dealt with the intruders in an instant.

One of them used his teleporting skills to put himself behind Rachel, who was expertly loading and shooting her crossbow. He reached with both hands for her head, as if to break her neck, when a shot of energy from Matt's hand made him reconsider and stumble back. He escaped Matt's attack and ran straight into Samantha's dagger.

She couldn't even remember moving forward to plunge the weapon into the demon's back just below the ribs, but it clearly stuck there. Hissing steam rose from the wound as the flesh corroded around the dagger, turning an ugly purple. The demon grunted and reached around his back to grab her hand, already turning towards her.

Panicked, Samantha pulled the Thorak out and stabbed the demon again, first in the arm and then in the soft tissue of his stomach. The dagger slipped inside his flesh with sickening ease, causing another burning wound. Then his hand wrapped around hers at the hilt. For a moment, the grip was so strong, she felt her knuckles chafe against each other. But then the strength in his fingers faltered, and he staggered into her, gasping for air. Samantha tore the Thorak out as she stumbled to the side, and he crashed to the ground. There was almost no blood, but the steam brought with it a pungent, nose-biting smell. As if she'd burned the demon alive.

He looked even more human dead.

Samantha's hand shook, her knees were about to buckle. She forgot how to breathe in, her mind filled with the sensation of slicing into healthy skin. Just as she was about to fall, Matt caught her.

"Take a breath," he whispered. "And keep your senses sharp. The battle's not over yet."

His words were the only thing that made sense. Her body complied, drawing in a sharp gasp of forest air, while her eyes re-focused on the battlefield. Matt was right. She couldn't afford to fret about the demon when two of his mates were still alive and kicking. Her conscience had to wait.

The third demon—drenched from head to toe—had her neck broken by Menuha. Meanwhile, Fabian shot his water at the remaining one. Shortly after, she was also hit by Lucille's destructive arrow and Matt's energy. Another second later, a bullet from Jan's gun struck her chest, sending crackling lightning across her lifeless body.

"That one's dead," Rachel commented with a dryness that Samantha envied.

Menuha nudged the dead demon with the tip of her shoe. "More than dead."

"God, I love this gun!" Jan exclaimed.

Samantha felt queasy, but she kept breathing just like Matt had told her. She had killed a demon. Stabbed him three times with a dagger. If she hadn't, one of her friends might have died. As human as they looked, most demons were like the monsters of her nightmares. They knew no conscience, and certainly no mercy.

"You okay?" Matt asked softly, his chin nodding slightly at the weapon in her hand.

Her hand was still shaking, but she gave him a sharp nod. "I will be once I sink this into Malcolm's chest." She knew it was a bold claim, but it called to the rage broiling inside of her. She'd need the rage to stay alive.

Matt smiled at her appreciatively, and she almost rolled her eyes at him. "I might have to beat you to it."

The part of her that was scared to the bones was glad to hear it. Let the demons fight it out, while she made sure to protect what she loved. "It's not far now."

Once more, she led the way. Though the forest was getting even darker, combining with the Residence of Greed, she could sense the spring ahead. Slowly, Samantha began to see the twisted rivers around her. Many of them were mere trickles of magic, a testament to whatever sinister thing Malcolm was doing to the spring. And then she saw him.

The clearing was near unrecognisable, the mossy ground almost completely replaced by stone. But the trees stood around the clearing like sentinels, silent witnesses to the perversion of the spring. Malcolm stood in the middle, his back half-turned to them. He had built an altar on top of the spring. A blue-black shimmering stone, the size and shape of an ostrich egg, was lying in the middle, hungrily accepting the stream of blood Malcolm poured from a silver pitcher. Each drop of blood sizzled on the stone until it was absorbed. When the last drop had fallen, the earth shifted underneath them. Another stone wall rose, while three trees gave way.

"Those stones cost a fortune," Menuha breathed, clearly in awe.

Lucille tugged her arm, also lowering her voice. "Is that stone responsible for Greenvalley sliding into Hell?"

Menuha nodded. "They destabilise the fabric of reality. They're dangerous and forbidden, but—"

"...everything that's forbidden can be bought for the right price," Matt ended darkly.

Meanwhile, Malcolm lowered his pitcher and walked towards the trees opposite them. Samantha leaned forward to get a better view of what he was doing and would have screamed if Matt hadn't clamped his hand around her mouth just then.

Ahead of them, Malcolm put the pitcher to the feet of a gnarly tree that was half stuck in Hell and half growing in Greenvalley. On that tree, he'd hung her grandmother. Metal pegs had been driven through her wrists, holding her upright, while several wounds leaked blood. The blood poured in a slow controlled manner into the silver jug. Elda had already lost consciousness.

Samantha threw herself against Matt, who'd wrapped his other arm around her chest and pulled her away from the clearing, drawing her away from the horrible sight. And any chance to help her grandmother.

"Hold still!" Matt hissed into her ear when she kicked his shins repeatedly. He brutally jerked her head around so he could stare into her eyes. The look in them was so intense Samantha whimpered into his fingers. "I swear to you, we'll save her. She won't die there."

It wasn't what she'd expected to hear, and thus, Samantha finally calmed. The irrationality of her behaviour became clear to her. If she'd run out there, Malcolm would've shot her. They needed a plan.

"Good. You've got it." Matt nodded and let go of her mouth.

Samantha breathed in heavily, filling her lungs with air. Tears shot into her eyes, but she fought them back. She needed to calm down if she wanted to have any chance of saving her grandmother. And fast, because Elda's time was running out.

Lucille

"Can't we just shoot him from behind?" Jan asked after they'd withdrawn enough to talk freely. They kept their voices low, but agitation coloured them, nonetheless. "I've got the gun. Lucille has her arrow. You two have energy. We go all in while his back is turned to us, and the whole affair is done before he even notices us."

It wasn't the worst of plans, Lucille thought. Surely, a quadruple attack from behind should do the trick. Add in Fabian's water, a well-measured crossbow bolt, and one of the potions Samantha had picked up from her secret stash at home, and it could just work.

But Menuha shook her head. "He's not like the demons before. He's over a thousand years old and extremely powerful. He will have protective wards that either alert him the moment we step into the clearing or fend off attacks."

"We need to save Elda first. That's the highest priority," Matt said.

Lucille stared at him. Matt had shown a commendable amount of empathy to Samantha ever since they'd found out about Elda's abduction. And she seemed to respond to him like no other.

"How do we do that?" Fabian asked softly. He seemed shaken as well, but he hadn't whined once since the battle at school.

Samantha took a deep, shuddering breath. "We would need to go around the clearing, but that will only work if a few of us distract Malcolm." She made it sound as if those few were doomed to death if they did.

"I'll distract him," Matt offered without missing a beat. "He hates my guts, so we might as well use that. We'll deal with him once Elda is safe."

"Don't be ridiculous, Matt," his sister chided him. "You don't stand a chance against him alone."

Now Jan stepped forward, patting his gun. "Who says he's going to be alone? I'll stand with him." He gave Samantha an apologetic glance. "I know. What about my healing? But... I don't think there's anything I can do for her without—"

"Killing yourself," Matt ended for him. "That's right." He faced his sister. "That's why I need you to go with Samantha. As soon as you get Elda free, you need to take her to a human hospital."

Lucille thought it wasn't the only reason why Matt would want his very capable sister to stay with Samantha. Menuha seemed to understand as well. She nodded. "Of course. If that's where you need me to be."

"I'll go with Samantha as well," Rachel announced. "I won't be much help with my crossbow, but I might be able to protect our backs." She looked at Fabian. "I assume you're coming, too?"

Fabian swallowed slightly, then he shook his head to everyone's surprise. "You know it makes me queasy just thinking about attacking an archdemon. The rescue group sounds a lot nicer, sure, but my powers are needed where they're most useful. So, I'm with Matt. I'm not going to let that greedy ass take our city."

Samantha fell around his neck, snivelling. She squeezed him tight, then looked him in the eye. "You can do this, Fabi. You've already thwarted him once today."

That left only Lucille. She'd known where she was going ever since there'd been mention of a distraction. "I will make sure you're covered by an illusion," she said to Samantha. "To do so, I need to keep an eye on Malcolm, so as dangerous as it is, that's where I'll be. He won't notice you."

"Good." Jan gave them all a sharp nod. "This is it, then. All or nothing."

His words made Lucille's chest tingle. She didn't feel ready to live up to the prophecy, but Malcolm hadn't given them a choice. It was now or never. "Take care everyone."

"We'll beat him," Matt said confidently, which made Fabian crack a smile.

"I sure *hope* so," Fabian quipped.

There were a few tired smiles, and Jan clapped him on the back. "Yeah, I'd *love* to kick his ass."

"Let's do that," Lucille said. She faced Samantha, Rachel, and Menuha and concentrated on weaving her illusion tightly around them. Since Malcolm didn't know any better, it should be easy to fool him. "You're good to go."

The three of them slunk away to the side, keeping their heads low despite the spell hiding them. Meanwhile, Matt squared his shoulders, then strode into the clearing as if he owned the place.

It didn't take long for Malcolm to notice him. Once again, he was pouring blood over the stone, but he cracked a lazy smile when he saw them coming. "Look at that. You finally made it here."

"The plant was charming," Matt said in an equally upbeat tone, "but not enough to stop us. What have you got next?"

Malcolm hardly seemed bothered by their presence. "I have to admit, I didn't expect very much of you."

"We know what you're planning to do." Matt nodded at the stone. "They're forbidden for a reason."

"The only reason they're forbidden is that others are scared. I'm not." Malcolm returned to his ritual, not minding them at all.

Jan raised the gun, but Lucille shook her head. The others weren't there yet. Instead, Matt let off a warning shot, purposefully missing Malcolm by a hair's width.

The archdemon raised an eyebrow and put down his jug. "I suppose I can spare five minutes to finally make an end of you."

Matt forced a grin. "What did you say to me once? Don't give a promise you can't keep."

"Six minutes, then?" Malcolm offered generously.

Once again, Jan's hand twitched towards his gun, and Fabian glanced at Lucille. The others still hadn't arrived, so she gave her head the slightest shake.

"Melaney knows what you're up to. She knows everything," Matt continued.

That made Malcolm laugh. "And what do you think your mother will do? Drag me into her bed? Been there, done that." Not only Matt made a face at that. "Even gave her a son. A true son. You might know him. Tall, powerful, intelligent. Got my eyes."

"Balthasar?" Matt almost choked on the name.

"The very same." Malcolm's face hardened again. "And the only reason your mother is lying in that bed. And if she wants to keep her comfortable sheets for a few more centuries, she'd do better to remember who took care that she reached adulthood."

Matt's fists were clenched, and his jaw shook under the tension of gritting his teeth.

"Aren't they siblings?" Fabian whispered behind them.

Jan shrugged. "Demons."

"I hope you don't expect Mummy to save you today. I'm sure she's busy spreading her legs for—"

"Sageat negru distrugere!" An arrow of black magic shot from Lucille's hands and only missed Malcolm, because he jerked his head aside at the last moment.

Invisible to the demon, Samantha, Menuha, and Rachel had finally reached Elda and were starting to free her from the tree.

Lucille stepped back to make space for Fabian, who immediately brought his fingers together. Water blasted at Malcolm as thunder roared from Jan's gun. Matt had drawn his sword, switched to his demon form, and jumped into the clearing. Slicing through the air, he aimed at Malcolm's head.

The demon shot energy at Matt, forcing him to abandon the attack. The energy hit the trees instead, bringing down a huge branch. His defence against Matt left Malcolm open for Fabian and Jan, though. The bullet hit his shoulder and paralysed him just long enough for the water to burst into his face. The force of the water stream almost broke his neck, but Malcolm managed to escape by jumping through space.

Fabian's water shot into the forest when the demon appeared to his side, arm raised.

"Scutum protecto!" Lucille shouted, willing the shield around Fabian.

Malcolm's fist slammed through the spell, barely slowed. Blood spurted as his fist connected with Fabian's bones, and the water mage crumpled to the ground, unmoving.

The demon turned to Lucille, his cruel eyes burning into her skin. Whatever she could throw at him would take too long and merely leave a scratch.

Just then, Matt barrelled into Malcolm, pulling him with him to the ground. The two rolled over the stone floor, hands and wings locked into each other. Matt pulled away first and drew his sword. This time he managed a blow to the leg before Malcolm grabbed him and threw him against a tree. Blood sprung from the thigh cut, but the demon-inherent magic was already healing him.

Or it would have if Jan didn't kick him in the exact same spot. The bracelet around his arm was shimmering slightly. It must've provided him with some extra strength because Malcolm staggered. Jan pressed his advantage and attacked with a flurry of kicks, forcing Malcolm into the defensive.

Meanwhile, Lucille whispered a spell she'd picked just for Malcolm. It was a binding spell, developed against the most powerful demons. "...hores avariccia al a dem—"

Suddenly, her mouth closed, and she was unable to speak another word. Irritated, she clawed at her face, only to find skin where her mouth should've been. Panic flooded her brain, and she forgot how to breathe through her nose. Tears shot into her eyes, and she dropped to her knees, where Fabian was writhing in pain.

Lucille tried to scream, but not even a whimper escaped. Her fingers dug into the leaves, finding stone. The pain of scraping her nails and knuckles on the stone cut through the fog of panic and allowed her to take a shuddering breath through her nose. Slowly, her heart rate calmed, and she stopped clawing at the stone.

She was alive. She'd figure her mouth out later. Though there was little she could do if she couldn't speak spells.

In front of her, the battle was continuing. Jan had landed another good hit, causing Malcolm's shoulder to spring from its socket. For a minute, his arm hung down loosely to his side, but then it began to right itself with a sickening crunch. Meanwhile, Matt was back on his feet, putting pressure on his uncle from the opposite side. Forced to defend against two opponents, Malcolm accepted Jan's blows to push against Matt, but his energy bounced off Matt's sword.

It didn't take him long to step through between the two and end their advantage. He raised both his arms and shot a different kind of energy at them. This one was less deadly, but came with more force, throwing both boys across the clearing.

Jan pushed down on his knee, shakily getting up to his feet. Blood was running down his face from a wound above his left ear.

Matt jumped up faster. He was about to storm back into battle when he stumbled and fell flat to the ground. Irritated, Lucille checked what had caused him to trip, only to notice the ground below him was giving way, as if he'd suddenly landed in a swamp. Matt managed to get to his knees before his upper body sank as well.

The ground gave way everywhere. Jan was holding on to a tree while his feet sank deeper and deeper. Lucille tried to get up, but her lower legs were already covered in grey slush. Next to her, Fabian coughed, his face turned to the ground. In a few seconds, his airways would be blocked.

Lucille leaned forward and grabbed his head with both hands, ignoring the pained whimper as she pulled him up on her lap. His legs had already sunk into whatever awaited them below.

Satisfied with his feat, Malcolm limped back to his altar and reached for the silver jug. It slipped from his fingers and fell onto the ground, spilling its blood. Malcolm sunk to his knees, choking on some invisible force.

The ground stopped moving. It was stone again, unyielding but no longer threatening to pull them under.

Malcolm was clearly struggling, though with what Lucille couldn't discern. His face contorted and his eyes blazed. He doubled over, fingers clawing at the stone, but then he whirled around towards Elda's tree and shot a blinding beam of energy at a fast-weaving Samantha.

Rachel

Trusting an invisible spell to cover them should've been easy for someone who was used to walking in dreams, but Rachel struggled with it. Every time Malcolm almost looked at them, she flinched. Samantha and Menuha seemed to be less concerned, though both kept their heads low and took a longer but safer route around the clearing.

As soon as they'd reached the other side, the battle started. Rachel forced herself to keep her attention ahead instead of worrying about her friends. They were four against one. Matt was a good fighter, Jan had his gun, and Lucille had her spells, while Fabian had already proven how strong his water skills were. They would protect each other and give Malcolm hell.

In front of them stood the tree Elda had been nailed to. The old woman looked worryingly pale and frail.

"Granny?" Samantha rushed to her side, forgetting all about eventual cover. "Oh, Granny, please."

Elda was still unconscious. When Menuha pulled out the metal pegs, she sank into Samantha's arms like a bag of potatoes.

Rachel helped Samantha carry her grandmother a little further away so they wouldn't be hit by any stray magic. She watched Samantha frantically looking for signs of life.

"Her pulse is so weak," Samantha sobbed. Her fingers were shaking as she pulled out her flowers and turned them yellow. The pollen fell onto Elda's wounds and covered them with a film of healing magic. It wasn't fast by any means, but it stopped the bleeding.

Carefully, Rachel took Elda's hand and looked for her pulse. "She's lost so much blood." Elda's white face reminded her of Nico's when he'd bled out in the forest.

"She can't die." Samantha shook her head.

"She won't." Menuha lowered herself and gently scooped up the frail frame of the old woman. "I'll bring her to a safe place. There'll be healers."

Samantha got up to her feet. "I'll come with you."

But Menuha shook her head. "You can't run from this fight. Chay has been very clear that all six will be needed."

Rachel swallowed heavily. "The prophecy." If they didn't stop Malcolm now, his actions would tear not only Earth and Hell apart, but all the worlds. She put a hand on Samantha's arm. "We need to stop him."

Her friend's arm shook under hers, her eyes never leaving her beloved grandmother. "Please save her."

"I will," Menuha promised, and then she was gone.

Samantha inhaled sharply. "Did I just entrust Granny to a demon?"

"Menuha is on our side, and there's nothing else you could've done," Rachel reminded her gently. She looked over the shoulder where the others were struggling to gain ground against Malcolm. "Our friends need us."

"I've got an idea," Samantha muttered. She took her flowers and turned them blood red. "This is the colour of death. The pollen won't fly without help, but if I can copy the pattern, I might be able to wrap Malcolm in it."

Rachel nodded appreciatively. "Try that." Sullenly, she stared at her dreamweb. The prophecy seemed to agree that the six Emblems of Power were needed in this battle, but she had no idea what to do with hers. It helped her in the dreamworld, but that was it, as far as she knew. In this fight, she was better off sticking to her crossbow. But since she was almost out of bolts, a flimsy web was all she had.

Samantha began her weaving. Rachel didn't fire her crossbow to keep Lucille's illusion intact as long as she could.

In front of them, the battle had turned. Lucille was on the ground, cradling Fabian's head, while her face looked as if her mouth had sewn shut. It certainly explained why she couldn't speak spells anymore. Jan was holding onto a tree, struggling to keep upright, and Matt was on his knees, as if stuck in the ground. They all were, Rachel realised with a shock.

Malcolm turned away from them, not even fearing Matt's energy bolts. He stepped towards the altar when his knees gave way under him. Samantha's web pulled tight. She stared at the demon intensely, while her fingers moved up a storm, building more and more layers around the demon.

He was on the ground, choking and writhing. Samantha was doing it. Her death web was working.

But then Malcolm whirled around and looked them straight in the eye. A second later, he shot a massive bolt of energy at them.

Rachel didn't know what to do. She couldn't jump away like a demon. Ducking wouldn't help her or Samantha. With a split-second left, she held the dreamweb in front of her like a shield.

The energy hit her with full force.

Rachel's arms shook from the impact, but her body was still upright. In fact, she was completely unharmed. And so was Samantha. The dreamweb had sucked in the energy without so much as a scratch.

She wasn't the only one surprised. Malcolm was also staring at her, disbelief on his face. His features contorted again, and he clawed at the altar. Samantha's web continued tightening.

This time, he didn't bother with another energy bolt. Instead, he jumped behind Samantha, grabbed her wrist, and broke her fingers in one swift motion before moving on to the second hand. Samantha screamed in pain, and the death web fell apart around Malcolm. He was instantly breathing more lightly.

There were a couple of energy bolts from Matt, who was yelling at Malcolm to let her go. But the demon wiped them away almost carelessly. "I'll get to you in a minute," he promised, before dragging a weeping Samantha to her feet. "I thought my plant would at least get rid of a few of you."

Though she was clearly in pain, Samantha answered sharply, "Sorry to disappoint."

Just then, Malcolm noticed the blood-stained tree and Elda's absence. "Where is she?"

"Safe," Samantha answered proudly.

Malcolm glanced at the tree and then at Samantha. All bravado left her, and her eyes widened as her face paled.

Rachel understood Malcolm's intention at the same time. When he started to drag her friend over to the tree, she launched himself at his back. The archdemon reached around, grabbed her arm and hurled her to the side with such force, Rachel flipped over twice and slammed into a tree.

Gasping for air, she watched Malcolm shove Samantha into the bloody tree. "You're also a witch. You'll do." He held her arms up above her head and thrust the metal pegs into both of her palms.

Samantha's scream tore through the clearing, causing a phantom pain in Rachel's own hands. But Malcolm wasn't done yet. He ignored the tears streaming down Samantha's face and raised a hand. In front of their eyes, his fingers turned into razor-sharp claws. With them, he opened Samantha's arms and chest.

Like before, the blood was pulled partially away from her body before it flowed down the tree. While Samantha writhed in pain, Malcolm stepped back and went to grab the silver jug. As soon as he put it to Samantha's feet, the blood dropped into it.

Rachel was waiting for him to attend to his stone again. As soon as his back was turned, she would run over to Samantha and try to free her. But before the jug was full, Malcolm turned to Rachel and gave his hand a little flick.

The ground beneath her gave way. Before she could properly react, her legs, hips, and elbows were locked in stone. All she could do was watch as Malcolm grabbed the jug and carried it back to his altar.

"Let her go!" Matt shouted at him.

Malcolm chuckled. "You're not really in a position to tell me what to do."

"You can take me," Matt said, undeterred. "Take me and let her go."

That made Malcolm pause. "What a fascinating offer, Melchior. But unless it's a well-kept secret, you're not a witch. And the stone only likes witch blood. But don't worry, I will fulfil your wish for more pain."

He took some time off from pouring blood on the stone and gave Matt a few well-placed kicks he couldn't defend himself against. When finally Matt was doubled over, spitting blood, Malcolm let go of him and returned to his ritual.

The clearing shifted the moment the last drop fell on the stone. It was even darker now, walls replacing most of the trees, but not the one Samantha was bound to.

"I'd say, one more portion, and we're good to go." Malcolm put the jug back under Samantha's feet.

She feebly tried to kick it over, but her feet wouldn't reach. Malcolm put a clawed hand on her face in an almost gentle gesture. "Don't worry, little witch. It won't take long." Then his claw drew down her jawbone, opening another wound.

"Melaney will hunt you down and kill you," Matt promised darkly. He was human again, which told Rachel there was even less magic in the clearing now.

Malcolm walked a few steps towards him. "You really think your mummy cares, bastard? I told you, you're too sentimental. Poor Chay, he's put all his hopes in you. But he's just a sentimental fool like you. Let's end this charade, shall we?" He raised his hand and drew energy again.

Just then, another bolt of energy hit him in the back. Menuha had returned.

"Oh, it's you." Malcolm barely acknowledged her with a nod. "See, bastard. Your mummy sends you her useless daughter." He glared at Menuha. "Does Melaney truly think you could kill me? Or was your brother not willing to risk his life for a half-human?"

"Neither. I want to kill you myself." Menuha launched into an attack.

Their fight was of a different calibre. Energy shot around wildly, and the impact caused both demons to flinch. Menuha slowly drew Malcolm out of the clearing, away from them.

"Rachel," Samantha whispered.

"What?"

Her cheeks were wet with tears, sweat, and blood, but her face was hardened. "I need you to get Lucille's attention. She's also a witch."

Frantically, Rachel looked around. She didn't dare call out for fear of drawing the wrong kind of attention. Instead, she found a bunch of pinecones around her. The stone didn't give her much movement, but she managed to flick her pinecones across the clearing.

Lucille and Fabian, who'd been enthralled by the fight between Malcolm and Menuha, looked over, confused. Since Lucille couldn't speak, Fabian asked, "What?" His face was a bloody mess, both of his eyes swollen.

Rachel gave a sharp nod towards Samantha.

"You need to weave a spell for me," Samantha told Lucille. "I'll tell you how. Close your eyes and concentrate on the magic."

Lucille stared at her a little desperately, but she closed her eyes and gave it a try. Samantha closed hers as well in an attempt to control her breathing.

"Raise your hands. Good. Try to reach for the magic. There's a thread just above Fabian's head."

Lucille tried for a little bit, but she soon opened her eyes and shook her head.

"She can't do it, Sam," Fabian translated. "She's not seeing the magic like you."

Samantha winced, but she kept her eyes close. "No, no, continue. The pattern is taking shape. You just need to hold the loops with your left, then guide the thread with your right hand..."

"That's not Lucille," Fabian said, after Lucille had shaken her head again. "That's you."

Surprised, Samantha opened her eyes. "But..."

Rachel stopped her before she lost the spell. "The hands are only a tactile aid. You can weave without them. Continue."

Samantha gave her a sharp nod, already quite pale and closed her eyes again. "This is anti-magic, like Malcolm's rope. Matt..."

Rachel looked over to Matt, who seemed confused at first, but then rose from the ground, no longer sunk into it. Despite drawing himself up, he was still aching.

The next spell to be loosened was Lucille's mouth. Lucille took a shuddering breath. "Thank you."

Meanwhile, Malcolm had gained the upper hand on Menuha. Rachel winced when she saw Menuha tossed through the air like a ragdoll. Matt's demon sister screamed loudly when a blast of energy hit her mid-air, then she fell to the ground in a boneless heap.

"Matt," Samantha said frantically. "I've put all the remaining magic in the clearing into you. There's not much left, so use it wisely."

The magic infusion was healing Matt, and he nodded before disappearing.

Malcolm was returning. He frowned when he didn't see Matt in the spot he'd left him.

In the meantime, Fabian had pulled out his feather and was drawing as he lay in Lucille's lap. Thick, fleshy vines, reminiscent of the plant this afternoon, wrapped themselves around Malcolm and tied his arms to his body. He was starting to rip them off when Lucille grabbed the vines and spoke a single word.

"Stranca!"

The spell turned the vines to stone, locking Malcolm in.

Rachel felt a surge of hope in her stomach. They weren't beaten yet.

Just then, Matt reappeared in front of Samantha and pulled the pegs out of her hands. She weakly sank into his arms. "I told you to use it wisely."

"You always find something to complain about, don't you?"

He gently lowered her to the ground and leaned her against the tree before glancing at Rachel. "Take care of her for me."

Rachel snorted. There wasn't much she could do in her position, other than to hold up her dreamweb for protection.

Matt drew his sword and walked towards Malcolm, squaring his shoulders.

The demon frowned. He stared at Matt's sword, then at Fabian's feather. His eyes continued to Lucille's necklace, the dreamweb in Rachel's hands, and the fallen flowers in front of the tree. At last, he glanced at Jan's wrist where the bracelet shone with a soft shimmer.

"And here I was wondering how six kids could be so damn tough to kill. That explains a lot," he hissed. Obviously, the archdemon was familiar with the prophecy of his potential death.

Matt's mouth twisted. "Too bad those kids are going to kill you now."

"You're sure of that?" Malcolm asked. He ran his eyes up and down Matt's body. "I'm your mother's brother, after all. Your... how do you say it? Your uncle."

It was an oddly sentimental notion. Rachel had no idea what he was playing at.

Matt didn't seem to know, either. "As if demons cared."

"But you're not a demon and won't ever be one. Half-human."

It only served to make Matt angry. He threw himself at Malcolm but had to duck when the archdemon freed his left arm. A shower of stone shards rained down on Matt, who rolled on the ground, brought himself behind Malcolm, and put the tip of his sword between his shoulder blades. Rage flashed in Matt's eyes, but for some reason he hesitated.

Malcolm didn't seem bothered in the slightest. He didn't even glance over his shoulder. "Come on, bastard. Prove to everyone that you're a real demon. Your father would love that, right? Fresh blood on your hand, and not just any blood, but your family's."

Rachel opened her mouth in soft wonder. Matt's hand was shaking. Now, when they needed his ruthlessness the most, he hesitated to kill.

"What are you waiting for? Show us what you're made of, you wannabe-demon," Malcolm teased.

"Shut him up, Matt!" Jan yelled.

But Matt lowered his sword. Malcolm smirked. "I knew you were too weak. *Bastard.*"

Rachel was speechless. She wanted to jump up, tear the sword out of Matt's hands, and cut off Malcolm's head herself. This man had killed her brother. He'd turned Nico into a monster and caused his painful and shameful death as he bled out in the grass. He'd taken the only person who'd loved her unconditionally from her. And he might even have caused her mother's death if the house had sunk any further, or more minor demons had clawed their way to the surface.

"What the hell?" Jan asked what they were all thinking. "Matt..."

"I can't," Matt said weakly. He stepped away from Malcolm and let his sword vanish. Instead, he reached for the blood stone. "But I can do this."

Malcolm's head whipped around. "You leave that—"

Matt took the stone and vanished.

"Matt!" Lucille cried.

But he was gone. He'd abandoned them, leaving them alone with an enraged archdemon.

Jan

Jan couldn't believe it. After everything they'd been through... After all their support when he'd failed them at New Year... In the middle of a prophesied battle... Matt had abandoned them.

"Serves you right to trust a half-demon," he muttered to himself.

The other demon, the one they now had to deal with while stuck to the ground, was highly amused. He rubbed his face with his free hand, unable to keep the grin in. Then he strained his muscles and blew the stone encasing him to pieces. Ragged shards flew all over the clearing. One nearly took out Jan's right eye, cutting into the temple instead. Another burrowed itself into his arm.

Free once more, Malcolm stepped out of the stony ruins and strolled over to Samantha who flinched away. "And to think you put all your hope into him. But don't worry, little witch. I'll make him pay for stealing from me. Right after you've paid your debt."

Jan spat. He hated how Malcolm was mocking them. As if they were nothing but a bunch of rodents that occasionally annoyed him. Or sacrificial lambs. He still couldn't get the image of Samantha hanging on the tree out of his mind. It looked like Malcolm intended to return her to that position, but not with Jan.

He raised his gun and carefully aimed it at Malcolm's head. Even the archdemon wouldn't simply shake off a shot to the head. Slowly, he let out a breath, keeping his arms as steady as he could. At last, he pulled the trigger.

The recoil hit him deep in his shoulder, but the bullet flew true. It hit Malcolm's head and threw him forward. Lightning crackled around his head, hopefully doing as much damage as possible, but of course the demon didn't fall.

"Do you think we're nothing but Matt's lackeys?" Jan called out, while he aimed again, hoping to hit Malcolm's ugly face this time. "He's only one of six, and we're not giving up just because he has."

He pulled the trigger again, but all he heard was an empty click. No more bullets left. Jan tasted bitterness on his tongue. Still, he wouldn't give up. If need be, he'd throw the gun at Malcolm's head. Whatever course of action was left to him, he'd take it.

"Jan's right," Fabian said with a rare confidence. Though his face was swollen and bloody with a broken nose and possibly more, he stretched out his arms. "This is our city you're stealing. Our families. Our friends."

"We're going to fight to the end!" Lu added loudly.

Jan had never been prouder of his friends. Who needed half-demons if he was one of five? They wouldn't stop until the battle was done. *Until all of them die or one fails twice*, the prophecy claimed. It was all or nothing.

Water shot at Malcolm, followed by a spell. Samantha must've picked up weaving again, because the demon shuddered, and a crossbow bolt buried itself in Malcolm's shoulder.

The glory lasted for all but thirty seconds. Then a pressure wave blasted all their spells back at them. Jan fell against the tree he'd been holding onto, knocking his head against the trunk.

Slightly stunned, Jan righted himself. He tried to blink the pain away, but when he looked up, he saw a storm broiling over the clearing. Wind roared above them, tugging on their clothes and pushing them off their feet. Jan landed on his butt when lightning flashed over the clearing. Thunder followed almost instantly.

Malcolm had his arms spread, making the storm dance to his tune. All prior amusement had been wiped away. They were not going to survive this.

"You are nothing!" Malcolm yelled. "Just because the Emblems of Power fell into your hands, you think you're some grand heroes? Do you truly think a bunch of teenagers will save the world one day?"

One day? Jan thought. They wouldn't even live to tomorrow.

"Don't be ridiculous. You'll die tonight," Malcolm promised. "And the Emblems of Power will find better bearers in the next cycle. Until then, they'll belong to me. Just like your town, your families, and your magic. It all belongs to ME!"

His speech was followed by more lightning and thunder as he roared into the storm. A particularly bright flash followed, blinding them all.

No thunder followed. Instead, the wind calmed as quickly as it had been called. The forest cleared again. Jan, who'd squeezed his eyes shut against the bright light, opened them carefully.

Malcolm was still standing in the clearing, but he'd gone completely silent. Instead of crafting a spell, he stared at the large hole in his chest. His gaze slowly turned to Rachel, who was still lying behind him, her dreamweb between her hands, and looked just as confused as Malcolm. The archdemon's eyes rolled in his head as his body accepted the inevitable truth, even though his mind hadn't yet.

He dropped to the ground, dead.

With Malcolm's death, his spells broke. The ground under Jan's feet firmed up again, letting go of his feet. He stretched them out with relief before pulling himself up. Curiously, he walked over and gave Malcolm a shove with the tip of his foot.

Definitely dead.

"Well, that one's done for," he said, unable to call upon the necessary gravitas.

"How did you do that?" Fabian asked Rachel, but she only shrugged helplessly.

Instead, Samantha answered, her voice a little shaky. "The Dreamweb of the Old Orenja gives back in multitude what it takes. It enhanced the blast of energy Malcolm had shot at us before."

"Killed by his own magic," Jan surmised. "I like it."

"I suppose nothing we could've thrown at him would have been strong enough." Lu turned to look around. "But we're still half in Hell. Shouldn't that spell dissolve with Malcolm's power?"

Samantha shook her head, breathing hard. "It's the stone."

Jan got it. The realities shifted because of the stone. And the stone... "Well, Matt took off with that one."

"I'm sure he had a good reason," Lu started, and stopped when they all glared at her.

"If Rachel's dreamweb hadn't have gone off, we'd all be dead now," Fabian complained. "I'd be very interested in his reason."

"The reason doesn't matter," Rachel said. "Not now. We need him to come back."

Samantha reached to her side, weakly swatting at the silver pitcher that had collected her blood. At first, Jan thought, she was trying to somehow put it back into her body, but instead she said, "Lucille, take the blood."

"The blood?" Lu's lips formed a perfect little 'o'. She nodded sharply. "I'm on it."

Jan watched as Lu got the pitcher. She made a face as she looked inside it before putting a finger inside. Like a child experimenting with finger paints, Lu drew a star on the ground. No, not a star, but a pentagram.

"Matt," she called, then shook her head. "Melchior."

Instantly, Matt appeared in his demon form inside the pentagram. Confused, he glanced around before letting out a sigh of relief. "It's you."

Rage boiled over in Jan. He pushed his fists into his hips and sneered at Matt. "Yes, *only* us. Your friends."

But before Matt could answer, his white-blond brother, Menuha's twin and the general of Hell's army, appeared at the edge of the clearing, his face twisted by wrath. "Don't think you'll get away this easily."

"I already told you, she's..." Matt checked the forest, "over there."

Jan had all but forgotten Menuha. Now that was a demon to be trusted. She had fought Malcolm to buy them time. And she'd paid for it dearly. Now Caspar was running towards her, quickly running his hands over her body, healing her. It reminded Jan that he was a healer too now, and one of his friends was in desperate need of healing.

While Matt sorted out his issues with his volatile brother, involving a bunch of energy bolts and yelling, Jan strode to Samantha's side. Her pulse was weak, and her eyelids fluttered. He put a hand on her forehead as if to measure fever and closed his eyes. There was too much wrong at the same time. The wounds weren't that bad on their own, though the holes in her hands were gruesome. It was the blood loss, which was her main problem.

He almost turned around to ask Caspar how to fix that, only to notice that Caspar and Menuha had left.

"Do you have the stone?" Samantha asked Matt weakly.

Matt eyed her cautiously before shooting a pleading glance at Jan, for once not reminding him how stupid healing such deep wounds were. Jan pretended to ignore him but did exactly what Matt wanted. After all, he wasn't enough of an asshole to make Samantha suffer for his grudge. Carefully, he put his hand on the wound that was bleeding the most and sank his magic into her body.

The pain struck him sharply. *Samantha is hurt much worse,* he told himself. *She's suffering much worse.*

"You can try to destroy it," Matt talked about the stone in the meantime. "But it is indestructible. Neither my magic nor my sword worked."

"Which means you abandoned us with your kill-crazy uncle for nothing," Fabian said sarcastically.

Jan grinned grimly. Good on Fabian for not letting Matt get away with this, just because he liked Samantha—who was thankfully strengthening a little under his healing.

Matt seemed to only notice Malcolm's corpse now. "You killed him?"

"Well, you certainly didn't," Jan shot back before he moved on to the cut on Samantha's right arm and bit his tongue as he melded flesh and skin together again.

"Rachel, my bag, please," Samantha said, using what little strength the healing was giving her to simply move on with whatever plan she had hatched.

Rachel glanced around and brought her the bag Samantha had carried when she'd returned from picking up her flowers. Jan had wondered what had been inside of it. He watched Samantha reach for the bag and wince, and promptly took it away from her. "Your fingers are broken. What do you need?"

"Whatever's still intact."

Jan opened the bag and found a collection of glass shards and leftover liquids in it. A swarm of butterflies rose into the air and glowing moss was growing in the bag. There was only one flask that wasn't broken. "That's the only one."

Samantha snorted. "Of course it is." Her eyelids fluttered again, and she sighed. "Did anyone carry something explosive with them?"

"No," Jan said immediately, but then he remembered. "Yes! Yes. We've got your dad's fireworks!" he told Fabian.

Fabian screwed up his face in irritation. "You think some fireworks will manage what Matt's magic didn't?"

Jan almost told him where he could put Matt's magic, but Samantha was faster. "Not alone, but with this one, maybe."

"And what is this?" Matt asked, having the audacity to sound doubtful.

"Robert's failed experiment. He almost blew up the chemistry lab. And it's not magical. Which is good—" she had to pause to breathe "—because the stone is full of magic and either repulses other magic or sucks it in."

"If we have to thank Robert for saving Greenvalley, I'm going to eat my shoe," Jan quipped, but he handed the potion to Lu and attended to Samantha's other arm.

Lu wanted to directly pour the potion on the stone, but Matt picked it up and carried it to the altar. Only then did he allow Lu to pour the contents of the flask into the basin. This time the stone didn't drink the liquid but sat in it like an ordinary rock.

"Fireworks?" Matt asked.

Fabian was still glaring at him with mutiny in his eyes, but he strode over and handed Matt the biggest firecracker in the bag. Matt carefully placed it next to the basin and returned to Jan and Samantha. "I need your lighter."

Annoyed that Matt actually *did* need that, Jan grabbed his lighter from his cigarette box and threw it at Matt.

Matt caught it and returned to the basin, where he proceeded to tell Lu and Fabian. "You better keep some distance."

"Oh, so now you want to be a hero," Fabian said with enough snark to light the fire himself.

Lu took his arm, turning away. "Let's go."

They returned to the rest of the group and turned to watch Matt carefully light the firecracker before quickly putting some distance in between himself and the stone. At first, it looked like the firecracker might've been a dud, but then it sparked. As it blew up, red and green sparks covered the clearing. Half a second later, a much bigger boom sounded. The entire altar exploded, and the earth shook, throwing them all to the ground.

Jan sprawled next to Samantha, desperately grabbing for something to hold on to. His fingers sunk into soft forest floor until they wrapped around some roots. Irritated at the sudden change of surface under him, he looked up.

The first stars were standing in the sky on the cusp of a summer evening. All around them, trees rose, while the ground below them was covered in moss, small plants, and pine needles. Not a slab of rock in sight.

"Greenvalley," he heard Fabian sigh in exhalation. "How I missed you."

Next to him, Lu sat up. "We did it. Malcolm is dead, we're alive, and Greenvalley is no longer sinking into Hell." She started laughing.

Jan got to his feet and dusted off his pants. "Yeah, *we* did." He clenched his fists and approached Matt. "And because of you, we almost died."

"Word." Fabian sat up as well. "What were you thinking?"

Even Lu didn't defend him this time. "I can't believe you'd betray us like that."

"Half-demon stays half-demon," Rachel added coldly.

For once, ashamed, Matt lowered his head.

"I get it." Surprised, they all turned to Samantha. She had pulled herself up, still terribly pale and leaned on the tree. "After all, he *was* your uncle." A weak smile crossed her face. "Seems like there is a sliver of conscience inside of you. Half-human."

Then her eyes rolled into her head, and she fell backwards. Jan jumped forward, but Matt was there first. He caught her just before she hit the ground. "Sam!"

Jan stood there, feeling more helpless than he had while fighting Malcolm without a weapon and stuck in the ground. "She needs to go to the hospital," he managed to say.

Before he'd blinked, Matt and Samantha were gone. All the joy over their victory drained out of him. The prophecy had never said they'd all survive if the Greedy One failed.

Lucille

Two weeks after the battle of Greenvalley, summer holidays started. Lucille was meeting Rachel and the boys in an ice cream parlour, looking down on the Reese River as it flowed through town. It was a sunny day and all Greenvalley seemed to be out and about. While she tried to enjoy the day, it was marred a little by the fact that Matt and Samantha were missing. Matt was still persona non grata, and Samantha had only been released from the hospital last night.

"Look at them," Jan said, shaking his head with an air of superiority. "There they all are, going on their way, knowing nothing."

Fabian chuckled. "My mum said the spell works on anyone who's not attuned to magic."

Lucille sighed, contemplating the massive spell the Harzer Witches had cast over Greenvalley to make the people forget their town had been sinking into another dimension while demons trawled the streets. Fortunately, there'd only been one death, two if they counted Janina, who'd fed herself to Malcolm's plant. "I wish I could've been there."

Jan grinned at her. "Well, you shouldn't have got yourself grounded, then."

While Lucille made a face, Rachel giggled. "Because of a ruined outfit."

"That was Linda's reason," Lucille clarified. "I assume my father knows what happened and only took it as an excuse to keep me safe." Inadvertently, she smiled. While she hadn't talked to her father about magic, it was nice to know that he actually cared for her. And remembering the disastrous chat she'd had with him under her spell, this non-talking but accepting stance was a much better outcome.

She turned to Jan, frowning slightly. "I'm surprised you didn't get grounded for quitting school."

Jan shrugged. "What are they supposed to do? I'm old enough to make my own decisions. And I suppose even they get how useless it would be to torture me for one or even two more years. It's not like I don't have a diploma."

It was true. They'd all achieved a basic diploma in tenth grade. Many of their peers had left school to pursue professional training instead. The diploma they were striving for now would grant them entry to tertiary education. Still, most parents preferred the academic path.

"Don't you think you could've managed one more year?" Fabian asked.

Jan shook his head. "No chance. Thanks to Malcolm, I completely tanked my last exams. As it turns out, the excuse 'I couldn't learn because a crazy demon tried to grab our city' didn't fly with Zobel. I guess that's one disadvantage of this spell. I'm sure exams would've been cancelled otherwise. Anyway, my parents are convinced I didn't apply myself enough. So, now I've got the absolute maximum of failing grades you're allowed to have on your report, and chances I'll make it through another year without failing a course are pretty low. So, no, no, you'll have to go to school without me."

"What are you going to do, then?" Rachel asked.

"Get a job, I suppose."

Lucille gave him a sideways glance. "You? A job?"

"You'll see. This will be a good thing." He folded his arms behind his head and grinned.

A message on her phone distracted Lucille for a moment. She glanced at it, then said into the round. "Matt wants to know if Samantha has been discharged yet."

"No comment," Fabian advised. "She's done with him. As are we."

Jan was equally gruff. "Yeah, he can stay in Hell or whatever bed he fancies today."

"I suppose with the prophecy fulfilled, we don't need him anymore," Rachel said.

"Really?" At first, Lucille had been angry with him as well. Now that everything was well and peaceful, she had a different opinion. "I think he's sorry."

Fabian shook his head. "*You* think. He doesn't. He's highly unreliable, doesn't have a smidgeon of morals, and no idea what loyalty or friendship means. Malcolm was right about one thing. He's shown us what he's made of."

Jan nodded eagerly, but Lucille still sighed. "If Samantha can forgive him for that, we should give him a chance at least."

"He had a chance," Jan claimed. "A damn big one."

"I'm still going to answer him," Lucille decided. Matt had a lot to answer for, but he did what he could under the circumstances. And what Samantha had said about his uncle had festered in her as well. She certainly wouldn't have been able to murder one of her relatives when they'd gone mad.

The boys rolled their eyes, but nobody stopped her from texting back.

When she put her phone away, Rachel leaned forward. "So, what's going to happen now? The big prophecy is fulfilled. We defeated the Greedy One."

"Now we get back to normal," Fabian declared.

"I'm going to miss the monster hunts." It was what had brought them all together in the first place. While Lucille would very much enjoy her holidays, it made her sad to think it was all over. "I suppose I'll use the downtime to practise my magic."

Jan snorted. "Don't wrap us all in a spell just because you're bored, okay?" Then he smiled. "I'm sure there'll be enough monsters to go around. I mean, we've got one living in the city."

This time, Lucille rolled her eyes and made a decision. The others could pout all they wanted. She was going to visit the monster.

Matt hadn't left town like the last time. He'd attended school with them, finished his exams, and received his end-of-year report yesterday. Lucille hoped he'd still be around today, though.

As she walked up the stairs, she worried he'd returned to Hell permanently now. Perhaps his exploration of their world was over. It wasn't like he'd had much left here. Perhaps he'd rather return to the drab and dangerous place he'd grown up in.

Through the door, she could hear Crumbs barking and smiled. Surely, he wouldn't abandon his puppy here. She pressed the doorbell.

The barking intensified and steps neared the door. Then Lucille heard his voice. "Get out of the way, Crumbs."

Matt opened the door, wearing nothing but a pair of boxer shorts—and he was waving a fly swat around. "Lucille."

She had to tear her eyes from his abs and shook her head. "I hope I wasn't interrupting anything?"

"Just trying to get rid of a particularly pesky fly. Do you want to have a go?" He offered her the fly swat.

Lucille tried to remember if she'd ever used one before. "No, I'm good."

Matt regarded her for a moment, then stepped aside, suddenly sombre. "Come on in."

She followed him into the living room, where a fly was buzzing around, never settling anywhere for longer than half a second. Crumbs was brushing past her legs, begging for attention. Lucille gave in as soon as she took a seat on the couch.

"So, what brings you here today?" Matt remained standing and crossed his arms. "I thought you guys didn't want me around anymore."

With a sigh, Lucille let go of Crumbs. "Matt. A lot of things have been said in the heat of the moment."

"And things have calmed now?" The doubt was evident in his voice.

Lucille shook her head. "Fabian and Jan are still mad about it. You abandoned us."

He let go of his tight stance. "I know that."

"You..." Lucille licked her lips. She'd very nearly asked for an apology. But she'd learned her lesson. Matt didn't really do apologies and pushing him only made him dig in his heels. "Personally, I'm okay with it now. It was a high-pressure situation, and all went well in the end. We all survived. I don't think Malcolm would've simply let you kill him, anyway. He was way too calm about the whole thing."

"He trusted I wasn't demon enough to do it," Matt admitted. He finally took a seat next to her. "You know I came here because Chay suggested I should experience my human side. But I'm not human. And it turns out, I'm not demon either."

"You're a half-demon," Lucille said gently. When she thought about it, it was an impossible predicament. Demons and humans were so fundamentally different in how they viewed the world. Life had a different meaning to them.

Humans depended on the social communities they built all through life, but those communities only worked so long as the majority of people within it adhered to the rules that kept everybody safe. Demons, on the other hand, lived in a constant battle of survival, and they held on to complete personal freedom.

Matt let his head hang. "Yeah, I am." Then he straightened again. "I thought I knew what that meant, but really, I only ever saw myself as a demon. A demon who ages faster and gets picked on by his older brother for having a human father."

"I'm not sure that's an inherently demon issue. Though I have no experience either way." No sibling had ever picked on her.

He gave her a half-smile. "Maybe not. But it means so much more. Chay... I've always admired him, but I feel like I finally *get* him. He doesn't just save all these worlds because he can, or because he's some badass, but because he cares. Chay cares."

Lucille slipped her hand into his. "And you care, too. Even if you're too stubborn to admit it most of the time."

Matt smiled weakly. Then he leaned into her, bedding his head on her shoulder. "You're probably right about that."

"I usually am." She laughed before leaning her head against his. So much for him being nothing but a monster. "You asked me something earlier." He tensed under her ever so slightly, awaiting her answer with bated breath. "She's been back home for a few days."

He didn't say anything at first, but then she caught a single word on his outgoing breath. "Thanks."

Samantha

"Oh my god!" Meg burst into Samantha's room, almost running over one of the many flower bouquets people had sent. "You'll never guess who's down there to see you."

Samantha took a stab in the dark. "Cian—"

"Cian Funke!" Meg held back suddenly and frowned. "Wait, you knew that?"

"I told him to come," she said with a smile.

Meg's eyes widened. "Oh. Well, he's here. Currently chatting to Dad. I'll send him up."

She was out of the door before Samantha could thank her. Samantha glanced down at her hands, which were still wrapped in gauze, with some of her fingers in a splint. It made for a very boring start to the holidays, worst of all, forbidding her to swim while the sun burnt down on Greenvalley.

Her father must have held Cian captive with talk of soccer, because it took him almost five minutes to come up to her room. "Hey," he said with a soft smile, and closed the door behind him.

The Harzer Witches had put a spell all over town to make everybody forget what had happened on the day Malcolm had attacked, but Cian had been suspicious long before that, and even if he'd forgotten her promise, she owed it to him. "Hey."

"How are your hands?" he asked, worried.

She carefully patted the bed next to her. "Much better than two weeks ago." She still had nightmares of hanging on the tree. Or her grandmother hanging there in her place. Fortunately, Elda had survived the torture as well. She was still in hospital but recovering nicely.

Cian sat down just as gently, his brow creased with worry. "What happened?"

"Well..." Samantha took a deep breath. "You know how Cheryl always calls me Witchy Sam?"

She told him everything. About her own powers and her friends, the prophecy and what had happened at the Walpurgis Night party, his soccer tournament, and the day he couldn't recall. Cian never interrupted her once, though on his face, a million emotions passed. When she was finally finished, he let out a long breath.

"Wow." He repeated himself quickly. "Wow. And all of that is true?"

A part of her tensed, remembering how Cheryl and her friends had always disparaged her. But Cian wasn't like them. Not anymore. "Every single word."

"You all have magic powers and Matt's a half-demon?" When she nodded patiently, he continued with an increasingly frightened pitch. "And he murdered your boyfriend at New Year? That's why you hate him so much."

She swallowed but nodded again.

"And his uncle tried to drag Greenvalley into Hell, but you guys stopped him?"

"Well, the others did. I was busy playing blood supply." She raised her hands for him, then showed him the faint scars on her arms.

Cian reached out his hand and gently ran a finger down her arm. "This is insane."

Samantha sighed. "Yes. Yes, it is. By the way, this is the point where you're allowed to run away screaming." She half expected him to.

What she didn't expect him to do was to thread his hand behind her neck and look her in the eyes. "I'm not going anywhere." He leaned in to kiss her.

His touch was so soft it almost made her cry. She'd missed featherlight kisses. She'd missed love and unconditional support. Even if things were insane. Samantha wrapped her arms around him and pulled him closer. It didn't matter that she wasn't head over heels in love with him. This was nice. And Cian was nice.

And she damn well deserved some nice things.

Cian had stayed half the night. They'd kissed some more and talked even more. About Daniel. And magic. And things that had nothing to do with either of them. When Samantha woke up in the morning, her heart felt a little lighter than it had in months. She had no idea what this thing with Cian was going to be, but she was going to enjoy it for as long as it lasted. And she'd keep it to herself, lest Matt try to take it away from her.

Unfortunately, Meg was already gone when she dragged herself to breakfast. Her parents were at work, so she had the whole house to herself. While she made herself a bread roll, she thought about what she'd do to pass the time. Visit her grandmother at the hospital was one idea. Or maybe just read a book in the garden. Her plans were interrupted when the doorbell rang.

Samantha got out of her chair and walked over, wincing as she opened the door with her injured fingers. The first thing she saw was a massive bouquet. Then she noticed the boy behind the flowers. Matt.

Her fingers tightened despite the pain, and she only managed not to slam the door into his face by pure determination. "What's this?"

"Lucille said flowers wouldn't be amiss," he said. "Though I'd have to be an idiot not to know that you love flowers."

Of course, she loved flowers, but she wouldn't do him the favour of accepting them from him. Especially if Lucille was behind this. "Lucille sent you?"

"No, she didn't. She's given up on making me apologise or making you forgive me when I don't deserve it." Matt lowered his flowers a little so she could see him. "I'm here on my own accord."

It was something, at least.

He took a deep breath. "I'm here to apologise."

Samantha's heart missed a beat. A snarky reply came to her lips, but she swallowed the words. She'd told everyone how it bothered her he'd never ever apologised. If she didn't want to be a hypocrite, she had to listen to him. "Go on."

Not surprisingly, he didn't go for the important bit. "I'm sorry I abandoned you at the spring. I didn't know what else to do. I wanted to kill Malcolm, but... I couldn't. The whole time I heard my father in my head, telling me how he was my uncle, while Menuha had said my mother *wanted* me to kill him. Malcolm deserved it, but... I just couldn't. So, I thought if I destroyed the bloodstone, everything would come alright. Only... I didn't manage that either."

"It's alright," Samantha said, hiding her disappointment by glancing at the ground. "I told you that I—"

"Get it," Matt finished for her. "You really do, don't you? You probably get it more than I do. Just like you got me the whole time. You understood my humanity before I did. You..." He lowered his eyes and stared at his feet for a moment. When he looked back up, his shoulders were squared. "Sam, I was an idiot, an ass... and I've murdered people, including Daniel."

She swallowed heavily, her body swaying backwards. If she shut the door now, she wouldn't have to listen to him justify his actions once again.

"There is nothing I can say to make that go away. And while every demon knows that they have no control over what they do in their Blood Night, I'm different. I'm not saying I was unaffected by the bloodlust or anything, but when it came to choosing my victims, I didn't do so at random. I chose Daniel."

"Why—?" Her voice broke before she could ask him why he would think she wanted to hear that. Emotions ragged her throat, and she swallowed a sob. In her mind, she saw Daniel's half-frozen corpse all over again.

"Because you were with him." Matt took a shuddering breath. "I hated him so much, and I was convinced that he'd come between us, that he'd stolen you from me, but the truth is, I didn't even understand what it was that the two of us shared before he came along. I hardly understand it now." He bit his lip. "I want to believe that without the Blood Night, I would've never harmed Daniel, but I can't be sure of that."

Samantha grimaced at him, unable to speak. This wasn't what she'd wanted to hear, far from it, and yet, she couldn't deny the raw honesty in his words. He was giving her the truth, not some sanitised lie that would've been easier to swallow.

"I still can't bring myself to fully regret what I did," Matt admitted, blind to her anguish. "Daniel never meant anything to me. Just like the others I killed never meant anything. Their lives were irrelevant to me. I guess that's why it was so easy for me to tell myself it was only the Blood Night. That it wasn't my fault, when clearly it was."

At least, he admitted to that now. A tear ran down Samantha's face as she stared at him blindly.

Matt took another deep breath. "But you. You mean something to me. I don't understand what or why you do, but it hurts me when you say you hate me. That you no longer believe in me. Or when you look at me as if I'm the most disgusting being you've ever come across. But what pains me the most is that I scare you. That you think I'm out to ruin your life. We had something special, something I don't even have a name for, and I ruined it. I tore it to pieces and stomped it into the ground."

More tears followed the first.

"And that's what I came to apologise for. I deeply regret betraying your trust. I might've wanted to kill Daniel in the heat of the moment, but I never wanted to hurt you." He swallowed heavily. "I wish I was a better man... human for you."

Samantha had nothing to give him. No words, neither mean nor forgiving. There was too much pain in her mind. All the pain of losing Daniel in such a gruesome way, and of losing Matt who'd become such a good friend before he'd shown his true colours. The worst thing was, she got him. To an extent, she understood where he was coming from, how little knowledge he had of her world and its ways. She could've even seen herself helping him navigate humanity. Despite everything he'd done to her—to Daniel—she got his reasons, his convoluted ways of thinking, his struggle to marry the two worlds he was forced to straddle.

It didn't make it hurt any less.

Matt handed her the flowers. "I'm not asking for your forgiveness. I know I don't deserve it, but I want you to know that I never meant to hurt you—and I don't plan to continue hurting you. My apology was overdue for the longest time."

Unable to say anything, she took the bouquet into her arms.

"I'm sorry," he repeated.

"Thanks," she mouthed, and closed the door into his face.

Her knees gave way, and she leaned against the door. Behind the wood, she heard him walk down the steps. When the crunch of his steps had ebbed, Samantha squeezed her eyes shut. Tears were running over her cheeks, and this time, she let them run freely. They loosened something deep inside of her.

Something that might finally be able to heal.

Matt

Despite the fact Samantha had only thanked him for his apology, not forgiven him, Matt was in a high mood. He'd planned his speech for the last two weeks, but when he'd opened the mouth, different words had come out. Not an elaborate apology, but honest words, his true feelings on just about everything. And it had felt good. As if he'd been finally truly honest with her—and himself.

Matt was well aware this didn't fix anything—it wasn't supposed to—yet he couldn't help smiling whenever he thought of her accepting his flowers. And maybe his apology.

He would have to do more if he wanted to get back into her good graces. He would also have to apologise to the others, something that filled him with far less dread than the apology he'd just given. There was no way around the fact he'd screwed up. When it'd truly mattered, he'd been unable to kill Malcolm.

It was ridiculous when he thought about it. He'd never had a relationship with the archdemon, hadn't even met him before coming to Greenvalley, and Malcolm had despised him and tried to kill him several times before. In the clearing, he'd been threatening everything Matt had cared about: Samantha, his friends, the magical little town he lived in. And yet, killing his own flesh and blood had felt wrong for a moment.

Because he was half-human.

Samantha got it. Though she despised him, she understood his motivation behind it. Matt would have to prove himself worthy of her faith. Not by getting rid of rivals or intimidating her, but by showing her that he was trying to be a better half-demon. Perhaps he never would be, but Matt promised himself he would at least try.

He arrived back home, as usual not bothering with the key. "I'm home!" he called from his room.

Since not even Crumbs came running at him, he assumed René and he were out for a walk. But when he opened the door, he found out he was far from alone. Chay awaited him in the living room.

Matt's feet stilled when he saw him. They hadn't seen each other since the older had left him at his most vulnerable. "You're back."

"You did it."

Matt frowned. "Did what?" Manage to apologise? Accepted what had gone down on New Year? Or fulfilled the prophecy?

"The six of you protected this city and stopped Malcolm." Chay smiled softly. "And you, Matt, didn't kill him."

"I thought the prophecy was all about me being the one who killed him." The other lines were quite clear that the five emblems of the others had to come together to give him the necessary strength to strike down the Greedy One. His friends had come together for him, but he'd never followed through.

"About that." Chay winced slightly. "Malcolm never had anything to do with the prophecy."

Matt was convinced he'd misheard. How could Malcolm not be part of the prophecy? "If he's not the Greedy One, then who is?"

"The same as before. Draken." Chay took a deep breath. "After breaking the world, Draken's soul was sealed in the Land of the Death. It never joined the cycle of rebirth. He's been there for aeons and hopefully will continue to stay there for a long time to come. But it won't be forever. He will be freed, and then he'll threaten all that lives. Humans, demons, every creature in every world. The prophecy has only just begun."

To be continued in Ashuan Lust.

Hell Hath no Fury

Hell hath no fury like a brother scorned

Last year was hell. And Matt grew up there. Just as he's begun to learn what it means to be human, his demon mother tempts him with a life-changing offer. Problem is, he's not the only one she's offered it to. As Matt returns to Greenvalley for another year of school, love, and monster hunts, his half-brothers are out for blood. One has a thousand years more experience than him, while the other hunts humans for sport.
With his friends caught in the crossfire, lying low is not an option. But to accept the challenge, he'll have to give up his hard-fought humanity, and with that, his life in Greenvalley, his friends, and the human girl he's somehow fallen in love with.

Hell Hath no Fury is the fourth book of the action-packed *Ashuan* series, kicking off the *Ashuan Lust* trilogy. If you like *Buffy's* wit and snarky one-liners, the magic of *Charmed,* and the supernatural drama of the *Vampire Diaries,* you'll love this monster-hunter urban fantasy series.

Buy *Hell Hath no Fury* now to discover what adventures are in store for the Greenvalley Crew as they enter their sophomore season.

JANNA RUTH

HELL HATH NO FURY

ASHUAN LUST BOOK 1

A Force of Nature

I've trusted nature spirits with my life, until the storm king decided I had to die.

Did you ever wonder what living on the streets of Berlin is like? My name is Rika and I've been homeless for eight years. It's not too bad, since I've got salamanders to warm me in winter and dryads to protect me from stragglers. People say I'm crazy, because to everyone else, those nature spirits are invisible. But they're real. Real and *dangerous*, as I learn when I accidentally cross the plans of the Erlking, an ancient and hate-filled spirit. Now he and his deadly storm are after me.
My only chance are the Spirit Seekers, an elite group of soldiers trained to battle nature's wrath. Since their precious commander is missing in action, they need me to be their eyes. Signing up with the Spirit Seekers is the opposite of run and hide, but they offer me protection and the tools to fight for my survival. All I have to do is betray my old spirit friends and try not to die.

Join Rika and the Spirit Seekers in this action-packed stormy urban fantasy adventure and start your supernatural trip to Europe today!

JANNA RUTH

A FORCE OF NATURE

SPIRIT SEEKER BOOK 1

Ghosts of the Catacombs

I'm a ghost whisperer, not a catacomb crawler. But when you live in Paris, sometimes you end up being both.

Hi, I'm Alix. During the day, I'm a history student at the time-honoured Sorbonne University. After class, I hang out with the ghosts of the revolution, the many undead misunderstood Parisian artists, and adventurous scientists that glow in the dark. None of them are alive, but they come to me to solve their problems with the living. When a recently deceased catacomb tour guide asks me to retrieve a mysterious personal item from the underground, things take a turn for the weird. Suddenly, I find myself in a city of ghosts, hunted by murderous cave crawlers, and stumbling across haunting secrets. If I'm not careful now, I might end up a ghost myself.

Urban Fantasy with a French twist. If you like cave-crawling adventures, hopeless romantics, and ghosts, you'll enjoy Ghosts of the Catacombs, the first book of the Parisian Ghosts series. Travel to Paris today to embark on your catacomb adventure.

JANNA RUTH

GHOSTS OF THE CATACOMBS

PARISIAN GHOSTS 1